Ultimum Judicium

The last Judgment

David Navarria

Ultimum Judicium
The Last Judgment

David Navarria

DISCLAIMER ───

Although the author and publisher have made every effort to ensure that the information in this book was correct at press time, the author and publisher do not assume and hereby disclaim any liability to any party for any loss, damage, or disruption caused by errors or omissions, whether such errors or omissions result from negligence, accident, or any other cause.

No generative artificial intelligence (AI) was used in the writing of this work. The author expressly prohibits any entity from using this publication for purposes of training AI technologies to generate text, including without limitation technologies that are capable of generating works in the same style or genre as this publication. The author reserves all rights to license use of this work for generative AI training and development of machine learning language models.

This book is a work of fiction. Any similarity to any persons alive, deceased, or things published or otherwise is purely coincidental. Any likeness to any businesses, institutions, places or things is also coincidental.

CCPC Organization Publication • DavidNavarria.com.

Author's Message

Throughout my life, I've watched the media evolve. I had the advantage of studying media formally during a time before the major changes that transformed it. From the Cowboy Westerns that started appearing on television in the late 1950s to the rise of the miniseries in the 1970s and 1980s, all of these developments significantly influenced our lifestyles. Our clothing, our speech—everything changed, including the architectural styles of our homes, all due to the impact of the entertainment media industry.

As we are currently experiencing the most severe effects from entertainment media ever, the news media has also undergone significant transformation during the same years I mentioned. When I was a child, Americans called the news media the fourth estate, a respected institution under God, the Church, and the clergy as higher estates. Back then, the news media reported the news—only that, using editorials to express personal opinions in a professional way, rather than the bad-mouthing we see today. Reporters now create division among people based on political and social differences. Arguments have turned into violence, and we are witnessing riots in the streets like never before, caused by disagreements that the news media is intentionally fueling for ratings that bring them capital. Influences of media are one-way—from them to you, much like hypnosis.

My novel isn't like typical post-apocalyptic stories that project our culture into the future. Instead, it offers a unique glimpse into a very distinct culture with customs and traditions that differ from our own. It takes place over two hundred years after civilization has fallen in a broken world caused by events happening today. Although it features many religious characters, it is not a religious book. It includes the brutality of violence and sexuality—even some perceived as erotica—set in a fallen world that could happen in the future.

For Grazia

Prologue

There were predictions and warnings—both spoken and written—but no one paid attention to them. As the ominous signs grew, still, no one obeyed. The unrighteous one kept everyone from seeing what was coming, even though it was obvious; he cast veils over their eyes. Not long after the final recorded year of 2040 AD, humanity faced a worldwide economic disaster of catastrophic proportions following years of street riots. Over time, human moral transgressions led to the collapse of societies worldwide. Countries turned against each other as the world became a wicked and ungodly place. More than two centuries after the last civilization fell, people lost the ability to speak—their capacity to verbalize had ended years earlier.

Guided by angels, a prophet chosen by God leads His remaining followers on an odyssey to a place of redemption. Anointed as Manhig, or leader, he and his armies of male and female warriors are the only hope of preserving some form of civilization, where everyone must obey the laws or be forever banished into the now-wild wastelands of the countryside, overrun with destructive intruders. Our future became our past—one marked by brutality and barbarism.

The manhig leads his warriors and people from one temporary stronghold to another for defense in an otherwise shattered world—a place now dominated by hordes of nonhuman beings: evil cannibalistic beasts, demons, and other mutations—created centuries earlier by the science of that long-ago era. Now living in a surreal culture, while following strange laws, customs, rituals, practices, and speaking a vernacular of the future, the manhig commands his warriors while battling these creatures alongside many evil humans: thieves, wicked gangs, slave traders, and other nefarious characters who roam the wilderness as the followers journey toward a confrontation between good and evil—Armageddon the final battle before God's last judgment.

Chapter One

Zipporah

Gray clouds of dust rose high in the distance, spreading as if a gloomy sky were descending upon the earth. It approached quickly, floating closer. A tall, sturdy man spotted it immediately and waved his arms, extending them upward as he jumped to alert the others. He grabbed the boy next to him by the arm and pulled him down to avoid detection by the incoming raiding party. They crouched together beneath a bank by the stream, hidden among the willows and dogwoods, waiting as they heard the clatter and commotion of the advancing hordes drawing near. The towering man squatted low and used his fingers to brush back his long, jet-black hair to peer through the dense blades of summer Indian grass that concealed him. He dared not use his field glasses; the mere glint of the sun beating on them would give away his position, and he waited with the boy as the spine-chilling sounds came closer.

They emerged as a parade of ghouls, marching to the dull and unharmonious beat of a deerskin drum and grunting like the demons they were—unable to verbalize. A horned, mutated ogre steered a large wagon, its wooden wheels flinging dirt and mud into the air from water-filled holes. The arms of four grotesque, hoofed male-beasts, two on each side, wrapped around the dual poles and pulled the heavy cart where the demon leader sat. A gold-toned statue of a horned beast accompanied them as a masked and painted naked female with cloven-like paws and hooved feet danced erotically around it—their stench putrid. Tortured, unclothed human prisoners—all tied in lines—followed behind, trotting and desperately trying to keep up with the wicked buckboard's pace, their blistered feet unprotected from the rough, stony, unpaved trail. Their screams echoed: the terrorized, high-pitched voices of women mixed with the deep, painful moans of men, some still bleeding from severe beatings and castrations, as the captured children cried. Those of them who could no longer walk lay prostrate and dragged behind, their bound, lifeless bodies bouncing on the bumps and rocks that tore at their flesh; some scraped so badly only tatters of tied bone and flesh trailed.

The striking, rugged-looking man calmed and comforted the frightened boy in his sturdy arms as the invaders swiftly passed by. The plumes of dark dust began to settle when he noticed what appeared to be a human teenage female tied up, collapsing at the end of the dwindling line of captives, her body succumbing to the rough, gritty surface of the stony road. He placed a forefinger to his lips to signal the boy to remain quiet and gradually released him. Taking his silent, handheld, heat-searing weapon from its holster on his belt, he carefully aimed at the rope binding the young woman, the last captive in the group. The soundless blast of intense heat from the solar weapon scorched the hemp, instantly breaking it apart and freeing the unconscious woman. In his haste to follow the beat of the drum, the eager demon guarding the end of the mob failed to notice the woman whose freed body continued to roll forward. The boy smiled and gestured to Mochè in acknowledgment of such an excellent shot, fully aware not to make noise until the demons passed.

Mochè, known to his people as 'Manhig,' the leader, was a man nearly 39 years old who looked much younger than his age. He had a tall, athletic, and muscular build, a result of years of hard manual labor, building and stabilizing many temporary settlements, and guiding his followers to escape the demons and other wicked hordes' captivity. He assessed the current situation and carefully searched for traps or possible stragglers from the horde that had just passed. Once he was sure everything was clear and safe, Mochè whispered loudly enough for the boy to hear, "Gershom, stay here until I call for you." He waited for the boy's acknowledgment, then jumped, his powerful legs propelling him from the riverbank to the road. Approaching the woman cautiously, he heard her moans. Realizing she was alive, Mochè rushed to her side, removed his small shoulder expedition pack, and took out bandages and medicines. "Gershom!" he called just loud enough for the boy to hear, "fill your waterskin and bring some fresh water here!" The boy's head bobbed above the Indian grass that had concealed him, nodded, and then disappeared as he ran toward the stream.

Mochè and Gershom, the boy, had separated from a division of Mochè's army during a hunting mission. The two went down to the stream to assess the water's toxicity and found it drinkable. They then searched for any living creatures, such as fish, frogs, turtles, or other edible items that could help sustain Mochè's seven divisions. Another division of his army had fanned out across nearby territories with a shared aim, but was hunting larger animals. Earlier, Mochè had instructed everyone to proceed to a pre-planned regrouping location in case of unforeseen circumstances, such as the one that had just occurred. They never engaged an enemy without prepared plans, as their leader valued each and every life of his soldiers. Joshua, Mochè's right-hand man, had stayed behind with several of his warriors to provide support if his leader needed it.

Coated in dirt and dust, revealing a layer of colored paint the demons must have applied to her face and naked body, Mochè comforted the teenager in his arms. Noticing his friend and second-in-command out of the corner of his eye, he called, "Joshua, please bring a blanket to cover this young woman so she can regain her dignity." He muttered to Joshua, "God only knows what happened to this poor child."

"At once, sir!" Joshua turned to one of his men and shouted, "Get a blanket from one of our wagons hidden in the brush right away!" He paused and added, "Find a woman's outfit; any kind will do!"

Mochè worked on the young woman for nearly fifteen minutes, trying to revive her while waiting for the doctor he had sent for. She regained consciousness in the arms of the man who had freed her; the eyes of the teenager finally opened wide to reveal their deep green color, the most stunning he had ever seen. Shivering from fear and poised to scream, she froze at Mochè's gentle touch on her forehead, realizing he was there to help and comfort her. The girl's mesmerizing gaze widened and engaged his, and unexpectedly, she could verbalize, "Are you a holy one, an angel?" Her soft words emerged hoarse as tears filled the young woman's eyes.

Most of the various age groups that Mochè encountered could no longer speak or verbalize, as they referred to it. They had lost that ability generations ago. Some older followers had learned to speak long ago or from their leader. Mochè established schooling for his followers at the beginning of their journey, which now seemed so long ago. Most of those he led could verbalize to some extent, with some performing much better than others. Mochè mandated that all his followers learn to read and write in order to comprehend God's written word.

The manhig smiled down at the young woman he was still holding and consoling, gently stroking her face, which was now a mask of dirt, hardened mud, and sludge. He saw those most beautiful eyes he had ever looked upon peeking out from behind it. "No, my child, I am not an angel, just a priest."

"There are still priests?" Her words were gentle and soothing to his ears, and the roughness in her voice had gradually dissipated. "What do you do?"

He smiled and told her, "I am a man ordained to serve God. My name is Mochè; I am the leader, or Manhig as my people refer to me."

Sitting up now, she felt a unique bond with this man—a feeling she had never experienced before. She replied, "My name is Zipporah of the family Celestine, and I follow Him too." Despite her bruises, cuts, and minor injuries, Zipporah felt at ease and rattled on; it was evident her nervousness stemmed from trauma. She wanted to share her story with Mochè, and he thought it best to keep the girl talking so she didn't slip deeper into the shock she was apparently in: "Oh, great Manhig, I–"

"Mochè is adequate, my child," his handsome, manly face broke into a smile.

"Yes, Master, I—"

Mochè swayed the forefinger of his right hand before the teenager in correction, quietly saying, "Mochè, not master." His finger then pointed toward the heavens as he declared, "Only He is Master."

The mask of mud and road residue folded into a smile, and her piercing, marvelous dark green eyes glowed with loveliness as the young woman explained, "I was born into a family of wonderful people, and I learned to speak at a very young age." Zipporah continued, "I remember moving often, like so many others, trying to escape from the wicked hordes and demons." Then her face went blank, and her expression shifted to terror; tears streamed from her large green eyes as she recalled that dreadful time. Zipporah was emerging from her shock too quickly and remembering the horrors of her past—exactly what Mochè had feared. "A vicious gang took my family and me hostage." Her eyes widened at the horror story she was telling. "I was a slave. They just recently traded me to the demons," she cried, recalling. Her beautiful eyes locked onto Mochè's once more before she said, "Those horrible people in that gang did terrible things to me," looking at him with shame. "They forced me to commit terrible acts of immorality." Zipporah trembled and sobbed, tears rolling down her dirty cheeks, clearing some of the grime that had accumulated there. "I'm not worthy to be among good people any longer."

"Shh," Mochè comforted the teen once more, fully aware of

how brutal gangs and demons tormented innocent young virgin women. "Shh, Zipporah," he whispered softly, with affection, "you're safe now, surrounded by those who care for you." He ran his fingers through her dirty, tangled, and unkempt hair. Zipporah had never known the gentle touch of any man besides her father, who had always embraced her tenderly, and that seemed so long ago to her.

Mochè stayed with Zipporah until his stronghold's head doctor arrived. "Gloria," he told the physician, "please take her to our fortress and provide her with the best care. The poor thing escaped from the demons. Before that, she was a slave to a wicked horde. If she doesn't require hospitalization, let her live in the small vacant house by the prairie."

"I understand, Father," the doctor replied sympathetically while tending to the young woman. "We'll take good care of her, and I'll keep you updated on her progress." Gloria was a striking young woman with dirty blonde hair, almost wheat-like in color, and captivating dark blue eyes, nearly gray. The multi-pocketed field vest and slacks couldn't disguise her curvaceous and proportionate figure.

"Thank you, doctor. Oh, and have someone arrange for a governess to care for her." He then called out to Joshua, "Come, my friend; we need to talk."

"Mochè?" the young woman called out. "When will I see you again?" Her question conveyed trepidation after experiencing tenderness from a man for the first time in a long while.

Turning away from Joshua momentarily, Mochè addressed the young woman fondly, "I will come to see you, young one."

Zipporah smiled through her mud-smeared face as Mochè turned back to Joshua.

"Yes, sir?" Joshua eagerly awaited instructions while standing beside his leader, his manhig.

Mochè observed his adjutant fondly. With a build and height similar to his own, Joshua possessed naturally sad eyes and a weathered face for a man of almost the same age. Although he lacked Mochè's youthful appearance, he was strong, an excellent warrior, and a natural leader. Always faithful to God, he followed his chosen leader's orders meticulously. "Joshua, first, have some of your soldiers gather those who scattered to the higher ground to avoid the demons. Most should already be at the designated location by now. Tell everyone to regroup with their division commanders. Then, send a scout immediately to find out where the demons took those prisoners."

"Will do, sir!" Joshua rose to leave Moshe's side.

"Oh, Joshua?"

"Yes, sir?"

"I recommend Leah," Mochè quietly told his subordinate. "She's tall, agile, and light on her feet," the manhig reflected, considering his decision to choose Leah, one of his female warriors. He added to justify his recommendation, "She understands the language of the beasts, and her naturally darker skin will help her blend into the night, allowing her to get close enough to hear anything important and conceal herself from demons or bandits on her way back to us." After a moment of thought, he continued, "Leah is an expert archer, and using such a weapon will keep things quiet if she encounters trouble. What do you think, Joshua?" Mochè softly asked, always prioritizing the protection of his people, especially when selecting capable individuals for raiding or surveillance missions.

"I considered her one of those to choose from. She'll do fine and return safely. I know that's what worries you, sir. It always does." Joshua smiled, knowing his leader well. He was also aware that Mochè knew that Leah's older sister, Naomi, like her, a beautiful and brilliant warrior, had gone missing a few years ago, probably captured or killed.

"Have her take no communication devices or any items that could fall into the hands of our enemies; God forbid someone captures her like they did her sister, Naomi."

"Yes, sir, of course."

"Joshua?"

"Yes, sir?"

"When will you stop calling me sir? We've been friends for

years," Mochè smiled.

Joshua smiled back and, while chuckling, said, "When He or one of his messengers tells me, sir."

"Oh, Joshua, one last thing."

"Yes, sir?"

"When Leah reports back with the demons' position and strength, have Isaac assess the likelihood of an attack. I want to try to free those prisoners they took before it's too late."

"Yes, sir!" Joshua's tone conveyed his approval and eagerness to rescue those poor souls. He admired and loved Mochè, his manhig, and always believed that he made wise decisions, thanks to his immense intelligence and Moshe's deep love for the people who followed him.

Then, turning to the boy, Mochè softly said, "Come, Gershom, let's go." The boy was mute but could hear well.

Chapter Two

The Rescue

David and Andrew, priests like Mochè and elders among his followers, always enjoyed chatting with their manhig by the fireside in the evenings. They set up a campfire in a small meadow near one of the high walls within the stronghold where everyone lived. David, an older man in his early seventies, moved his hands closer to the fire to warm them against the chilly evening of the wilderness. They were heading toward the far southwestern part of that region to a final stronghold that they would eventually fortify as their last place. An angel had guided Mochè from the very beginning. The holy one referred to that final spot as the place of redemption, but many other settlements like the one they were currently in were necessary along the way to gather more followers of God to them.

"Be careful your beard doesn't catch fire, David," Mochè chuckled, glancing at the boy who was now fast asleep. Knowing he was tired, Mochè always tried to put Gershom to bed, but without fail, the boy insisted on staying as close to his manhig as possible. Mochè believed the boy found comfort in being near him, which was true, but there also seemed to be a deeper reason. Gershom was born mute yet blessed with the gift of sight. A holy one had commanded Mochè to keep the boy close to him. Mochè had taught him some of their language, and Gershom communicated by writing in the soil or scribbling on the pad he carried. Thus, the boy always joined his leader by the fireside for evening discussions, usually falling asleep within minutes but waking promptly when they ended.

"So, Manhig, how do you fare this fine evening after rescuing a young maiden from that horde?" David smiled, his forefinger and thumb caressing his long gray beard in a habitual gesture. The entire army had heard about their manhig's valiant deed and was proud of him, as always. Mochè was a hands-on leader for his people and had consistently proven it in countless ways.

Before he could respond, Andrew, who was slightly older than David, asked eagerly, "Will you try to lead a rescue party for the others?"

"Well, my friends, perhaps the Lord should have anointed both of you as leaders since you know so much about my intentions," a smiling Mochè replied.

Andrew presented one of his performances. Kneeling, he pulled back his long, thinning gray hair as he uttered, "Oh, great and wise Manhig, I ask for forgiveness for this humble servant," with his hands placed on his chest.

"Rise, Andrew, or in a minute or so, your arthritis won't let you," Mochè replied to David's burst of laughter. "Now, throw out the dice so we can play while we talk. Remember, no gambling of possessions or garments; use only stones," their leader reminded them.

The tears of morning dew brought another uneasy day to Mochè. Joshua had taken Leah and Isaac directly to his manhig during his dice game the night before, wanting Mochè to hear her account word for word. He moved the trio away from the campfire but sat them close enough to see by the light of the flickering flames. David strained to hear the conversation; Andrew didn't bother, as he was already partially deaf in one ear.

Joshua started to speak, but his leader, or manhig, politely interrupted him, saying, "Let Leah speak for herself. Why else did you bring her here?"

Leah bowed and placed her fist over her heart, then extended her arm in the warrior's style of saluting a military general. She spoke softly, "Manhig, we have a great opportunity if we assemble our forces and attack before next nightfall." Leah's eyes lit up as she continued, "The demons brought the prisoners to a temporary location with minimal fortification. We can ram right through their defenses. In addition to the prisoners you saw them taking yesterday, there are many others." Leah bowed her head, slowly twisting it sideways as she reflected on the horrific sight of men and women tortured and raped, witnessing one they sacrificed to the demon's pagan god. "It was a terrible sight, Manhig," she explained it all and added, "They devour the children, sir." She sighed, "I moved in close and heard them grunting in the language of the beasts; they are only about 700 strong and need to recruit more. Their leader sent out a small raiding party for that purpose." Her eyes appeared desperate as she told Mochè, "There are around two hundred hostages. The demons plan to sacrifice all of them in a pagan ritual at today's sunset, as it is already past midnight."

Mochè's keen senses felt her pain, and he understood well what the young warrior had witnessed. It was too much for any civilized person to comprehend. "You did an exceptional job, Leah. You've saved many lives," Mochè said while saluting her in the warrior way, his fist pressed to his heart and extended forward.

"Thank you, Manhig," she said as she bowed again.

"I want you to get some rest. Later, you will ride alongside Isaac, Joshua, and me at the front of the army."

Leah was astonished by such an honor. She was speechless, her eyes widening as a tear rolled down her cheek while she attempted to thank her manhig, muttering, "Thank you—"

"Go now and rest, my great warrior—interrupting her— you've done your job meticulously, as always. We have much fighting to do later, and you should refresh yourself."

Isaac listened attentively, as always, worry evident in the lines on his face and the dark circles under his somber eyes. Shorter in stature and slightly hunched, he was wise, having received a great amount of education throughout his 61 years.

Mochè turned to Isaac, his chief military strategist, and commanded, "Isaac, gather all division generals and council members to discuss appropriate plans for an attack. We're going to rescue those captives from the hands of those savages."

On that same morning, which brought fresh tension to his demanding job of managing his people, the manhig strolled casually along one of the many streets of the seven divided towns inside the massive fortress he oversaw. Scrumptious scents of many breakfasts cooking filled the air, clashing with the pleasant aromas of budding flowers. The clattering of pots and pans, crying children, and soft morning conversations flowed from the homes as the towns came to life.

Moshè possessed beauty in body, mind, and spirit. His facial features and tall, muscular build were magnificent, reminiscent of a sculpted angel or Michelangelo's David brought to life. But it was his eyes that truly captivated the souls of all who beheld them. Large, dark blue, and innocent, they conveyed the tale of deep love and devotion within him. Still, those eyes also carried a sadness, almost as if they were tormented, from the years he spent guiding his followers of God through both good times and, more often, difficult ones.

Before finalizing his battle plans for the rescue, Mochè reflected on the teenager he had freed. The doctor had said she was doing well, but he wanted to see for himself. Dressed as always in the dark clothing typical of a priest, he wore solid black military utility pants and a matching long-sleeved shirt, rolled up past his forearms, both of which accentuated his well-built physique. Sporting his usual black cuffed leather pull-up boots, he made his way to Zipporah's quarters, recalling those incredibly beautiful eyes that had looked into his soul. Mochè never wore a hat except in extreme sunlight and usually carried some type of holstered solar sidearm and a sheathed dagger on his black suede belt, which also held a small pouch containing his scapular, rosary beads, holy water, and a vial of anointing oil. A beautifully crafted wooden crucifix hung from his neck as he strolled, his black cape draped over his shoulders to shield him from the soft, chilly morning breeze.

Glancing midway down a block and across the street, Mochè stopped in his tracks upon recognizing a young couple. It was Caleb, a young man in his mid-20s, whose morals he questioned, attempting to kiss a younger girl in her late teens. Caleb had been a problematic child, the manhig recalled well from Bible school—a bully and a hothead who had grown into a lost soul, wandering from one menial job to another with no drive or ambition. Mochè knew Caleb harassed teenage girls and young women, undoubtedly sexually assaulting some. His keen intuition sensed this strongly, but he couldn't prove it; all of his victims were far too frightened to come forward—afraid to be even a mere part of the ultimate sin of adultery.

The teen girl, Eliza, whom Caleb was manhandling, appeared frightened of the larger, muscular young man. Mochè remembered her mother, Elisabeth, as a dear woman who tried to raise her only daughter to be respectable. However, her father was a no-good and wicked man, he recalled.

When Caleb spotted the manhig, he abruptly released the teen girl and hurriedly walked in the opposite direction from where Mochè stood, hastening his footsteps as he did.

"Eliza?" called Mochè.

The startled girl turned toward her manhig and, with a trembling voice, answered, "Yes, Manhig?"

"Are you alright, dear?" Mochè was concerned, and his tone reflected that.

"Yes, Manhig, I'm fine."

Mochè didn't buy it; the young woman clearly appeared shaken. He began walking toward her. Standing before the girl, Mochè gently placed his arm over her shoulder and warmly said, "If you explain what happened, I can help you." Looking in the direction Caleb had gone, he added, "He shouldn't be allowed to get away with what he does."

"It's fine, Manhig." Her stunning hazel eyes drifted to where Mochè glanced as she responded. "Really, I'm okay, sir." A shiver ran up her spine, and she feared telling her manhig where Caleb had placed his hands on her body.

Mochè knew that many other young women feared the larger bully, yet he kept his anger in check, embodying the qualities of a Christian and a leader. He said only, "Please come to me, child, if you ever want to talk." He gazed at the girl, seeing her now as a young woman before him, her amber hair gently swaying in the breeze, the sun illuminating its golden tones and complementing her delightful hazel-colored eyes.

"I will, sir," her eyes widened while she spoke. "Thank you, Manhig."

A young man standing behind a pole observed the incident. The young cavalry lieutenant, Matthew, spotted Caleb attempting to molest the young woman he adored and ran to stop it before his manhig intervened. Though a formidable warrior, ready to clash with Caleb, whom he loathed for his despicable acts toward women, he was too bashful to approach Eliza for an introduction, despising himself for that single fear he would never admit.

As the tall, handsome figure of Mochè approached the simple, unadorned house—a vacant one among many nicely decorated ones within the stronghold of his encampment—a soldier opened the entrance for him. Mochè had stationed the guard and nodded as he climbed the two stairs and entered, squatting to fit his tall frame through the doorway. "Zipporah?" he called. From a small corridor outside the main room, a fully nude young blonde woman joyfully ran toward his voice. Not recognizing her at all, Mochè stood in shock as this beautiful goddess embraced him. Never before had he seen a lovelier woman, and he didn't initially notice another older woman's voice trailing after the young lady, finally catching up to her.

"Mochè!" shouted Zipporah as she embraced him, her body pressed against his while her fingers playfully explored the hardened muscles of his arms.

"I'm so sorry, Manhig, but I can't get her to keep clothes on her body. The poor thing has been without clothing for so long, living with those heathens and then the demons; she doesn't favor wearing them." The older woman, Maya, draped a sheer bathrobe over the girl as she spoke, then added, "It's all I can get her to wear—sometimes." Maya reminded Mochè of a bird with a thin, pointed nose and squinted eyes. Turning her attention to Zipporah, while separating the young woman's body from the leader, Maya corrected, "This is Manhig, and you will address him as such!" Even Mochè, caught off guard, felt a tad frightened by her bark.

Mochè waved his hand, signaling Maya to leave the young woman alone, and asked, "How are you feeling, Zipporah? I came here to see you, just as I promised," smiling at her, though his eyes drifted elsewhere as he could still see partial nudity through the sheer garment Zipporah now wore. The day before, he couldn't appreciate her beauty, as her face and body lay hidden beneath layers of mud and road residue; only her marvelous, large green eyes stood out. The young lady was not the teenager Mochè had thought; she appeared stunningly beautiful after bathing, cleaning up and styling her long blonde hair.

Noticing his awkwardness, Maya said, "Oh, where are my manners? Would you like to take a seat, Manhig?"

"Yes, please," he responded. Maya even walked almost bird-like: pigeon-toed, her gait swaying as she led him to a chair at the table, placing Zipporah beside him. The arrangement of the table and her position obscured nearly all of the young woman's nudity, easing Mochè's discomfort. He could smell the sweet fragrance of the recently cleaned home. Her radiant presence and the way she gazed at him clearly indicated that Zipporah had fallen in love with her rescuer—a common occurrence for a young woman in such a position that Mochè understood well from other encounters.

"She can't help her behavior, Manhig. The poor thing probably hasn't seen a civilized man in a long time," Maya said, raising her eyebrows as if perplexed. "She mentioned her father as the only kind man she has known, besides you." The older woman whispered in Mochè's ear before taking her seat, "I think she has a bit of a crush on you, Father."

After talking with Zipporah for a while and respectfully resisting her persistent urges to feel his strong arms and chest, Mochè knew she was safe and in good hands. As he announced his departure, with many things to accomplish that day, he noticed the minor cuts and scrapes on Zipporah's body caused by the demons dragging her. While Zipporah thought Mochè was admiring her body, she rushed up and hugged him, trying to kiss him. He understood that her behavior stemmed from probably weeks of living with vicious people who did unspeakable things to her. As he pried her away, he saw that the doctor had covered many of her wounds with lotion, and some had small bandages. Her feet, also bruised from marching, were as dainty and appealing as her hands. As he turned to leave, Mochè couldn't see the red glow in Zipporah's striking, wide green eyes.

After Mochè checked on the young woman he had saved, his next stop was to preside over his council of appointed officials, and generals, where he would clarify battle plans with Isaac and the others. As he walked, his mind wandered to the origins of the post-catastrophic, shattered planet where all surviving humans now lived.

Centuries before that day, brainwashing tactics impacted the majority of the last civilization, leading to political and corporate corruption that tainted the world. Yet, it was the media that pulled the strings of those in power, as it always had. Most humans now living never even knew of the various forms of what was once referred to as media. Nor did they realize it was the driving force behind much of the wickedness that led to the ruination. The news media misled the public with lies, while the corrupt entertainment media lured people into sinful behavior, including lewd acts. The influence of those many sources was so profound that what began as casual adultery evolved into the acceptance of widespread global immorality. As evil escalated, belief in Him and religious devotion waned. As the worship of God diminished, people began seeking fulfillment from the Dark Angel. Church and temple attendance had decreased years earlier, transforming those spaces into sanctuaries for believers seeking refuge from the wicked hordes that rejected God's followers.

Artificial intelligence had advanced rapidly during the pre-darkened days. Not long after its inception, humanity became increasingly dependent on AI and electronic components for nearly everything. Advanced AI techniques eventually gained the ability to implant neurological devices, or chips, into human brains, enabling the transmission of thoughts expressed on a network of devices. For the first time, as telepaths, human beings no longer needed to verbalize words and eventually lost their ability to speak. Dependency on AI-provided thought processes accelerated all forms of silent communication, simplifying interactions between people, businesses, and even nations. Over time, the media exerted control over all decisions in international leadership and the people within the environment they had helped spawn.

The old ways ended abruptly after AI was perfected, and the world relied entirely on technology, causing physical beings to fall prey to Satan, the Dark Angel. They became weak-minded and worshipped him for the bodily pleasures he promised, depending completely on technological assistance to attain them.

The masses, driven by the media, went too far in their pursuit of pleasure. What began as a means of artificial and genetic assistance for sexual pleasure evolved into something far worse—the enhancement of scientific experiments aimed at improving the human body's appearance started to alter the human species. Men and women yearned to be bigger, stronger, and more appealing, initially through various chemical injections. In laboratories, pharmaceutical companies sought ways for individuals to perform sexually better. They committed the gravest sin against God when they began cross-breeding humans with animal DNA in labs to create robust beings capable of superhuman performance. God intervened and destroyed those labs that had spawned human beasts. Those grotesque mutations evolved into demons with cloven hooves united to destroy the believers of God. Other forms of human mutations mated and gave rise to beastlike creatures that also preyed on God's faithful. Demons possessed the ability to seize souls through the inherent powers of Satan, acquired through the wicked experimentation he directed in modifying them.

Artificial intelligence later displaced workers, leading to corporate prosperity and growing dissent among people across all nations. As greed flourished, individuals became unemployed yet reliant on new technologies that offered immense pleasures. This dependency ignited widespread turmoil, violence, and rebellions that inadvertently dismantled AI systems everywhere.

AI technology had maliciously controlled people for years before its collapse. The only means of communication implanted in people disappeared, leaving them mute when AI fell. The global grids failed and ceased to function. Nuclear power, electricity, and all forms of transportation stopped operating. The failure of newly developed weapons forced people to seek out and use older, outdated weapons before those malfunctioned and their ammunition was depleted. The global order disintegrated with the downfall of once-great countries worldwide.

As Mochè continued walking through the streets of the compound, he greeted the people who approached him. His followers, always in awe of their manhig, constantly sought to engage with his charismatic personality. Asking him questions or simply greeting him gave them a sense of security during a time that was otherwise chaotic, without the stronghold and reassurances he provided.

Grasping the intensity of it all while he strolled, as illogical as it seemed, a living being among the ruins caused by his ancestors, Mochè reflected on the origins of his past. Sometimes, amid his many duties, including battling and nurturing the lambs of his God to restrain them from sin while clinging to the only remaining bland excuse for civilization, he had to recollect how he began.

Mochè was born Damien Ignatius, with a surname derived from the ancient Roman name Egnatius. Hiding and fighting to survive in one of the remnants of a city that had fallen centuries earlier, his father, Solomon was, knowledgeable in the old ways. A professor who nurtured Damien's brilliant, God-given mind from birth, he shared stories of the past with Damien and explained how people, generations before his own time, used to read and study, just as he taught his son. Damien discovered that when people stopped reading, they lost their independence. He learned about the times long before when bi-directional learning declined and uni-directional methods of what they called 'media' became dominant—one-sided means of indoctrination.

Solomon Ignatius learned from an angel that God had chosen his son for a divine purpose. Damien studied the effects of what Satan inflicted upon people through the media. He understood how individuals ceased to engage their minds and fell victim to all manifestations of that wicked, destructive, shrouded entity—the media. Damien grasped the now forbidden knowledge of what had deceived people out of greed and entertained them with sinful portrayals—those elements that marked the beginning of the end as foretold in the Bible. Solomon's son discovered how artificial intelligence, or AI as it became known, amplified the influence of the media and transformed humanity into vessels of Satan, contributing to the wave of violence that had flooded society. When the situation grew too dangerous, Solomon left his child with the last bishop.

A messenger from God appeared to that bishop of the enormous cathedral at the final stronghold in what was once known as the great city of the East. That angel delivered God's command, designating Damien as the leader, or 'Manhig,' when he was still a child. Raised for that purpose and already blessed with sacred intelligence and intuition, he began studying theology and various advanced subjects early on. His studies were far more advanced than what his father had taught him and included war tactics learned from former military strategists, one of whom was named Isaac. An elder priest instructed young Damien in the church's confidential ritual of exorcism, which was crucial for casting out demons during a time when many suffered from demonic possession. God endowed Damien with a large, muscular body capable of remarkable and powerful feats and purified his mind and spirit, thoroughly preparing him for the life he would one day face.

The last bishop of the East consecrated Damien into the priesthood at 18 years old before the city fell. Guided by a holy being, or angel, as many referred to those messengers of the Divine, God renamed Father Ignatius as Moshè after the one who led His people from slavery in ancient times. Angels, spiritual beings from an unknown realm to humans, communicated nonverbally; instead, they conveyed their blessed messages through a sense of perception—a feeling of ecstasy enveloped in a typically invisible brightness. They expressed their thoughts in a way that artificial intelligence, or AI, once attempted to replicate. This interference with the essence of His creations was one reason God allowed humanity to destroy all they had built, including AI, as many at that time turned to sin.

God ordained Moshè as the 'protector' of His faithful. The mighty arm of the Lord cast a great globe of light encircling the cathedral, shielding His followers from the satanic forces and demons who could not withstand the brightness. Those who chose to journey to the designated place of redemption with Moshè gathered in safety. Manhig led the first pilgrimage out of 'the city of the East' before it fell into the hands of the wicked. Supplied with all necessary sustenance and provisions from the Divine One, the encirclement of light followed the many faithful until they were well out of the city. Moshè glanced back and watched as the entire wicked city of the East erupted into a fiery ball while the demons, the evil followers of the Dark Angel, and other unbelievers of God burned alive in the flames of His righteousness.

In the post-catastrophic remnants of a shattered world, guided by an angel, Mochè led his people westward, crossing into unknown territory. Manhig consistently spread them out and employed military strategies he had learned for defense. Since leaving the wicked, devastated eastern city, they had gathered many other survivors from the malicious gangs and demons that had tormented them. A great number of them were in the early stages of demonic possession, and Mochè, being the only trained and ordained exorcist, performed numerous exorcisms. Over that time since their departure, Mochè oversaw the construction of several temporary fortifications, each designed to protect God's people from invasion.

Under the angel's guidance, Mochè remained on elevated ground, far west of the city of the East, in what became referred to as 'the Unknown Territory,' overlooking a large stream. Surrounded by natural hills and rock formations that provided geographical protection similar to that of ancient castles, he oversaw the construction of a massive stronghold. Mochè directed laborers in assembling factories and research facilities. Doctors developed natural medicines to fight infections from all known diseases. With the assistance of God's angels, engineers and scientists harnessed solar power to create weapons and vehicles for both transportation and combat.

His workers also felled trees for timber. A mill, built by a creek that was a tributary of the larger stream above, processed lumber for various construction needs. Small dwellings erected within the compound provided his people with secure, heated living spaces. Mochè participated in various types of physical labor while also utilizing his creativity to develop more advanced engineered items. He and Isaac consistently taught his division commanders military tactics as his army expanded. They used some of the wood to build many traveling carts and wagons of different sizes to transport large materials, the wounded, other disabled individuals, and animals for food and breeding, including both wild and domesticated poultry.

Knowing he would need cavalry for quick maneuverability, the manhig prioritized capturing various breeds of horses that were now breeding in the wild. Wranglers gathered hundreds of herds of wild broncos and broke them into trained riding mounts. They continually bred and trained the horses for cavalry service.

As beekeepers produced honey, carpenters constructed wooden barrels for beer. The same oak casks were used to produce both red and white wines from grapes that grew wild around the ruins of what were likely the homes of people who lived there centuries earlier. Later, they nurtured the tender grape plants and carefully transplanted them into specially cultivated soil. Those who managed the wine also knew how to create a syrupy, condensed substance and later convert it into wine in case of a shortage. Brewers made coffee from chicory plant roots mixed with seeds and spices. Skilled hunters cautiously ventured into the woods to capture animals such as deer and stray cows for milk and breeding as food sources. They were prepared to relocate on short notice, always maintaining an exit plan.

Factory workers wove cloth and created a variety of items, including clothing, furniture, and household goods. Stronger individuals excavated old mines and harvested minerals from God's earth. They produced gunpowder for explosives and older weapons in case they ever lost solar power. With angelic guidance, Mochè miraculously obtained the materials necessary to forge Wootz steel, a metal used by ancient civilizations. He taught skilled metalsmiths the lost art of honing the strongest and sharpest sword and dagger blades of that time, as well as other weapons and vehicles. He sent parties out to capture as many animals as possible, escorted by armed cavalry for protection. They returned with more horses, mules, oxen, steers, and cows, corralling them with others they had collected during their journey. Mochè created the only civilization his followers had ever known.

As Mochè's workers toiled, angels guided additional faithful to the gathering place. Alongside them, more people, including former military-trained personnel, doctors, scientists, and engineers, arrived.

Mochè also oversaw the construction of chariots for his division commanders to use in battle. For reasons unknown, these chariots instilled fear in the demons and wicked gangs, causing many to flee at their sight. The cavalry followed them in battle, with infantry and tanks maneuvering into designated positions.

The demons never developed advanced weapons; they only wielded spears and blunt swords. Their mutated hands could neither grasp nor create other weapons or construct vehicles like the faithful. They spent most of their time indulging in bodily pleasures, parading in obscene ways, and violating the innocent for sport and lewd satisfaction. They regarded their mutated women solely as carnal objects, painting their naked bodies and faces in bizarre colors, typically engaging in sexual acts with each other or various objects. Too lazy to hunt, fish, or raise livestock for food, the demons and many rampant gangs of mutations resorted to consuming the flesh of their captives. Only demon leaders and those commanding wicked hordes and armies could form basic words, grunting as they did in what the faithful called the language of beasts.

The demons exploited their master Satan's gift of possession, which served as their most potent weapon. They tormented innocent victims with evil spirits, compelling them to obey their wicked commands. Many succumbed to demonic possession, while only the more faithful had the blessed power to resist. The demons sacrificed those who fought against their powers in pagan rituals. The number of demons and ruthless raiding armies grew, far surpassing that of the faithful.

Mochè and his followers survived in that past stronghold within the Unknown Territory for ten years. During that time, families procreated and expanded, and Mochè's trained army grew under his personal supervision. Scouting reports revealed massive hordes planning to overrun them, and the manhig, along with his chief military advisor Isaac, believed this was likely to occur within a year. Mochè meticulously developed his exit strategy, ensuring that everything they produced was ready for transport. They established another temporary yet heavily fortified stronghold where they had resided for almost five years, situated in more western territory, beyond the half-way mark to the place of redemption. The manhig intended to keep his people there until heavenly beings instructed him otherwise. God had not yet revealed to Mochè the exact location of their final destination.

***

Mochè stood in his intricately carved wooden chariot, dressed entirely in black as always, even his armor. A black headband restrained his long, thick hair against the harsh winds that whipped around him as he awaited the return of his scouts to confirm the demons' numbers and the exact location of the prisoners. The demons always feared those swift, two-wheeled wraiths descending upon them, but they had yet to reveal themselves. Until the scouts returned, he would not move his forces; his primary concern was minimizing casualties and ensuring the safety of the hostages. Beside him in the war vehicle, a helmeted Gershom gripped a metal handle with both hands to brace himself against the inevitable bumps and jolts. The steel-rimmed, wooden-spoked wheels shifted forward and back as the four harnessed stallions restlessly recoiled. Isaac's chariot was close on one side of Mochè, within hearing distance, while Joshua's waited on his other side. They all wore helmets except for Mochè and Leah, whose tall figure proudly awaited in her chariot beside Joshua's. Her midnight hair, perfectly braided, accentuated her battle garb, highlighting her long, slender limbs and a striking face, unwavering as a true warrior.

Mochè led an army of seven divisions, composed of battle-hardened men and women, spread out across the vast field in front of the dilapidated ruins of a large building where the demons held their captives. Each division had approximately 700 warriors, with all commanders appointed by Mochè. Out of nearly 5,000 soldiers in the army, 1,000 stayed at the encampments as home guards to protect non-military personnel with various skills, such as medical care, research, and production, along with another 700 non-combatant loyal followers. Mochè's total number of followers was around 6,000, including men, women, and children, all journeying to the place of redemption. According to Leah's report, Mochè didn't need such a large force for the upcoming battle, so the division commanders kept many troops in reserve that day.

The sounds of two galloping horses approached from the rear; Mochè's scout party was returning. Both riders rendered a military salute, placing a fist to their chests before extending their arms toward their leader. "Manhig," one male scout called out respectfully in his baritone voice, "the demons have all the prisoners tied at the center of their compound. They are waiting atop a pyre of wood prepared for their evening sacrifice ritual. Counting all the men, women, and children, their numbers total around two hundred prisoners."

"It's the perfect time if we act quickly, Manhig," the young female scout with long flowing blonde hair said. "We need to use caution, as they may attempt to ignite a fire beneath the prisoners the moment they see our army advancing."

"The demons never post sentinels, so apparently they haven't spotted us," Mochè answered.

"No, Manhig, they're all caught up in a wild and savage pagan orgy," the man bowed his head, recalling the sinful sight. "Their lustful actions have entranced them."

"Commanders, listen up," Mochè shouted into the solar-powered radio microphone after flipping the switch on the unit mounted near his chest. He waited for each division leader to respond with their confirmations. Once all had acknowledged, Mochè calmly yet firmly issued his orders: General Jeremiah, secure the rear area. Use your infantry after the cavalry eliminates any demon stragglers. General Helen, have your division attack the left flank of their compound while General Luke engages the opposite side. General Sarah, send your tanks to break through immediately on all sides of the demon compound; you're the closest. Then, quickly deploy a company of crossbows and archers to take out anyone approaching the hostages in the center of the grounds. Use a squad of snipers to eliminate any of them near the captives. General Luke, provide support to General Sarah. General Joseph, secure the perimeter. General Mark, your division is responsible for guarding and protecting the prisoners. God be with you all!" Mochè shouted to his commanders. He turned to the charioteers beside him and shouted, "We attack the front! Ride now! Fast pace!"

The ground trembled beneath the thunderous sound of thousands of horses' hooves and supply and rescue wagons bouncing and jostling down the slope of the vast meadow. Sarah's tanks had already begun carving an opening for the division led by Mochè, Joshua, and Isaac. Other mechanized vehicles rushed into the gap, moving swiftly toward the compound. The tanks had loudspeakers mounted on top; their blasting sounds startled and distracted the demons, who were caught off guard as Mark's division entered and advanced toward the hostages. Mochè's army utilized the weapons of the civilized believers, most of which his craftsmen had produced at their last stronghold in the Unknown Territory. Each division's cavalry primarily wielded their exceptionally sharpened sabers, with some using solar-powered handguns. The infantry regiments had heat-searing rifles or automatic solar-powered weapons. Some had shoulder-supported sonic mortars and other explosive projectiles but refrained from using incendiary weapons in this battle, fearing harm to the captives.

Once inside, Mochè dismounted his chariot, Gershom running at his side. Mochè used his sword and attacked the demons, who finally realized what was happening. As the glowing red eyes of a demon bulged, his face contorting, Mochè swung his mighty arm and seamlessly decapitated the beast with one stroke of his saber's razor-sharp blade. His return swing blocked and broke the spear of another ogre, and Mochè's sword lodged into the gut of that surprised demon who still held his half-lance. The demon's red eyeballs nearly popped out of its socket from the powerful thrust before it perished, blood splattered and spurted in a straight line, smearing Mochè's face. He grabbed his dagger from its sheath on his belt and flung it at a huge, heavyset, monstrous demon who stood ready to spear a captive. It hit the demon at the center of his back, and Gershom quickly ran to retrieve the weapon and return it to his manhig. Mochè sheathed the long knife, took a spear from a fallen beast, and threw it at an ugly female hoofed demon who was trying to set fire to the pyre of wood beneath the frightened tied hostages. It flew hard and entered the back of the woman-beast, and she clutched the front of it as it pierced through her body. Screaming from pain, she continued toward the dried wood, the long lance still in her body. Another warrior saw her preparing to torch the wood and ran as fast as she could. Swinging her saber, she sliced off the head of the painted woman beast, watching the eyes of the dying beast bulge while its head rolled on the ground.

Mochè looked around him proudly as his faithful soldiers fought bravely to save the captives. The entire operation was swift, taking less than half an hour. The battle was over. His commanders converged in the demon compound, instructing their fighters to care for the hostages. Wagon after wagon filled with those poor souls whom the demons had interned rolled out, heading to a holding center within the followers' stronghold.

"Destroy any remaining demons," Mochè yelled to a young cavalry officer he recognized. "Major Benjamin, have your soldiers behead them all so they do not cast spirits."

"Yes, sir," the young major answered, raising his saber in recognition of his manhig.

As Mochè spotted General Sarah, he ran to her. "Sarah," he called. She turned and gave him a military salute as the manhig remarked, "Your face is bloody, Sarah; you must have fought well," he praised, smiling at her.

Sarah smiled back and replied, "Manhig, I think your face is bloodier than mine."

After a brief discussion about the battle, Mochè instructed his commander, "Sarah, remind the other division commanders to have their soldiers take all hostages to the designated holding center. We must carefully screen them for demonic possession, as this is a common consequence of captivity by demons."

"Yes, Manhig, I will remind all of them immediately."

Mochè's own words shocked him. "My God almighty, why didn't I realize it?" He grabbed the reins of the nearest horse and galloped out of the compound like a madman.

"Manhig?" General Sarah called after him. "Is everything okay?"

Mochè didn't answer Sarah. He rode hard and fast through the countryside, murmuring, "God forgive me; I never checked Zipporah."

As Mochè's sweating horse approached the small house where Zipporah was staying, he slowly dismounted, listening intently for sounds. Startled by footsteps rushing toward him, he drew his sidearm from its holster. A crying Maya shouted, "Manhig, don't go in there!" The older woman bowed her head while catching her breath, then said, "It's terrible. I can't believe my own eyes!"

He held the woman gently and said, "It's okay, Maya. Please calm down." Mochè spoke softly. "When you're ready, let me know what happened. Take your time."

Maya's piercing, birdlike eyes glanced up at Mochè's face as she spoke more slowly. "Manhig, the young woman wanted to live alone and asked me to leave right after you left earlier. I did, but I returned to check on her. It's awful; she has become a terrible creature. Manhig, please be careful if you must enter this house."

Mochè held her shoulders and firmly said, "Maya, you'll hear terrible sounds coming from this place after I enter. No matter what you hear, don't come in. If I'm not back outside by morning, call Joshua. Do you understand me, Maya?"

"Yes, Manhig." The frightened woman looked at him with wide-eyed concern, no longer squinting like a bird.

"Please bring me a large bucket of fresh water and as many clean old clothes or rags as possible. Leave them by the door. Remember, do not come in, regardless of what you hear."

"Yes, Manhig. I'll gather those things you need right now." The terrified woman hurried away, her body swaying from the brisk stride of her pigeon-toed feet.

Mochè waited for Maya to leave before stepping up the two stairs leading to the door, thinking the guard must have had to rejoin his regiment for battle. With so much on his mind, Mochè didn't even consider replacing him. He slowly opened the door and crouched to fit his towering frame through, inhaling the rancid odor inside, which was no longer the pleasant scent of a recently cleaned home. Hearing nothing, he called, "Zipporah?" The early spring sun was already setting. It would be dark soon, he thought.

"Hi, Mochè," the young woman's pleasant voice called out.

Mochè peered into the dark interior, which was devoid of light. As his eyes adjusted, he spotted a figure partially illuminated by the setting sun streaming through the open door. The young woman's nude body was pressed against the far wall, suspended off the floor, her hands and feet pierced with bloody nails, her head tilted to the side. Mochè lit a lantern on the table before closing the front door. As he moved closer to the figure, a sweet female voice asked, "Is this how you want me, my love?"

Moving a little closer, Mochè commanded firmly and loudly in his deep, masculine voice, "Come down, demon. I command you in the name of the one God, the Father, the Son, the Holy Spirit, and his heavenly archangels!"

"Piss off, priest!" a man's deep, raspy voice retorted, echoing loudly within the small dwelling that shook from the blaring sound. Then, Zipporah's voice returned, saying, "Take me, Mochè; I know you want to. I know everything you're thinking. You're admiring my voluptuous breasts. Make love to me, Mochè. You've never experienced a woman's body before. I can offer you pleasure beyond anything you've ever known."

Blushing from his impure thoughts and tempted beyond any way he had ever been, Mochè prayed to God for strength while resisting his manly desires. He looked toward the hut's side wall as a ray of light from a small crack in the wood descended upon him, and he said, "Thank you, my Lord." Taking his holy water from his belted pouch, Mochè sprinkled it upon the demon. Deep-throated howls came from the mouth of the beast as she jumped from the wall, her body smoking. Her face was monstrous, and the delicate body contorted in pain, twisting muscles spasmed horrifically, moving and bulging to outrageous shapes and making cracking sounds as it did. Afraid the demon would break Zipporah's spine by such unnatural distortion, he took his anointing oil from the same pouch and leaped upon the standing woman, knocking her over. His legs wrapped around her lower body, locking the evil being in place. Mochè, his fingers wet with the holy oil, smeared it on the possessed woman's forehead, making the sign of the cross with it. Her forehead was in flames as the mighty beast within the frail body used superhuman force and flung the muscular man's body into the air.

Stunned by the impact of hitting the hardened wood floor where the demon had hurled him, Mochè sat disoriented. Realizing that Zipporah was impregnated with a powerful beast, Mochè rose and used all his strength, smacking her on one side of her face and backhanding her again on the other side. While in a momentary daze, he put the demon in a headlock and poured more oil as he pronounced the sacred words of exorcism over her. Seeing that he was weakening the beast within her, he continued his prayers, adding, "Leave, demon of Satan, the fallen one! Leave, I command you in the name of Christ!" he roared.

Zipporah's sweet voice answered softly, "Oh, Mochè, you

saved me once again." Her deep green eyes gleamed with happiness.

Mochè sensed it was a ploy from the father of all liars and removed the crucifix from around his neck, placing it on the young woman's heart. It sizzled and smoked, searing into Zipporah's bare skin. He continued to bless her, proceeding with the rite of exorcism. A massive, dark entity bearing beastly horns sprouted from Zipporah's petite body and hovered above them. It growled in a deep, horrifying voice, "You're mine, priest!" The giant horned demon transformed into an enormous serpent, releasing a dreadful odor of smoke as it crept and slithered close, raising its head near the priest's face, its reptilian eyes fixed on Mochè's. It roared a monstrous shriek, snapping and trying to bite. Mochè stood firm, unafraid. That rattled the grotesque beast, and it bellowed in a thunderous howl, "I know you want the woman! By my power, you will succumb!" it screamed before gradually fading and vanishing into the darkness of the room.

Mochè continued the rite of exorcism over the motionless body of the lovely young woman until its completion. A jellied substance oozed from all the pores of her body, and she coughed up phlegm before discharging vomit and other vile-smelling, bloodied clots.

Though God blessed him with extraordinary intellect and the intuition of a clairvoyant, Mochè knew little of the seductive power of women; he was naïve in that regard. Yet he was a man, and like most, had a need for a woman. Understanding that one weakness, Satan tempted Mochè unyieldingly, knowing that if he could lead the manhig to fall to the ultimate sin of adultery, his ministry would unravel. Then, his followers would fall to him one by one. Satan planned for the day he would succeed.

Zipporah was asleep, and Mochè gently lifted her, carrying her to the bed in the next room. He then opened the front door to retrieve the bucket of fresh spring water Maya had left, along with a large bag of old clothes and rags. Mochè began washing away the excretions of pus, vomit, and bodily fluids that Zipporah had expelled during the exorcism of the powerful demon that had possessed her. After thoroughly washing her body with scented soap while fighting the temptation to admire the soft, fair skin of her nakedness, Mochè dressed Zipporah in clean clothes from one of her chest drawers. He scrubbed the floor with the remaining water and a cleaner he found in one of the cabinets.

He could not go to the fireside to meet David and Andrew that evening, as he felt it necessary to protect Zipporah in case of any further episodes of demonic possession. Although he felt confident he had cleansed her, demons sometimes lingered, and hers had been a strong one.

As the dawn light broke through the tiny cracks and spaces of the small house, Mochè awakened to find a smiling Zipporah standing over him. He had fallen asleep on the floor beside her bed.

"Mochè!" the happy young woman exclaimed upon speaking with him for the first time. He stood as she spoke. "I'm so happy you came, but I didn't hear you when you arrived. Maya must have gone out on an errand. I don't even remember dressing in the clothes I had on," she smiled enticingly at Mochè. "I changed into something more appealing—if I must wear clothes—knowing you had come." Zipporah had no memory of her exorcism and was in her glory as she pulled Mochè to sit at the table. "I waited for you to awaken. Now, I'll make the best breakfast you've ever had!" Standing close to Mochè, she rose to her tiptoes, fondling his crucifix. Admiring it, she asked, "Where did you get this? The craftsmanship is exquisite. I've never seen one lovelier."

"It was a gift from my father. He gave it to me many years ago." Mochè removed it from his neck and draped it around the lovely, slender neck of the young woman. "I want you to have it."

"Oh, Mochè, I couldn't take such a precious heirloom."

"I wish you to keep it always to guard you on our journey."

"Oh, thank you, Mochè. I'll treasure it always."

Chapter Three

The Trial

As his people gathered on a lush, green hilltop, Mochè preached to them through a loudspeaker, as he did every week during warmer weather. Armed guards protected the scattered crowds, all inhaling the fresh scents of Virginia bluebells and mountain laurels blooming around them. The crowd now numbered about 6,500 followers, with new arrivals joining him daily. As nesting cardinals and blue jays fluttered their wings and chirped among the trees, Mochè spoke to instill confidence, uphold morals, and strengthen their faith. His followers always appreciated their manhig's brilliant, powerful, and lively sermons. Zipporah always arrived early to sit closest to Mochè, just as she had that day.

A major and second-in-command of one of General Jeremiah's cavalry brigades sat off to the side. Benjamin, a highly admired and skillfully trained military officer from the family of Joyce, now relaxed among the shrubbery and grassy slopes, his large gray eyes gazing at someone nearby. The uniquely handsome young man did not possess the chiseled features that many considered conventionally attractive. Instead, his softer, statuesque facial characteristics and dignified expression, paired with a tall, well-proportioned body, made him striking and appealing to women.

The deep blue eyes of the young woman who glanced back at him widened. Her fair skin blushed, realizing she had been caught looking at him. She quickly turned to resume her focus on her manhig's lecture, her long blonde hair gently floating in the soft breeze. Pretending to fix her flowing hair, she discreetly peeked through the long strands, only to be exposed once more as the dashing young man maintained his gaze, his lips now gently cracking into a hint of a grin. To him, she was the most beautiful female he had ever seen in his entire life.

An excellent equestrian and dispatch rider, the young woman had crossed paths several times with the handsome officer while serving in the ranks, yet both were too shy to strike up a conversation. There they sat, always near each other, whether in the green pastures or inside one of the church buildings, always knowing which one the other would attend, making eye contact but never speaking.

The young lieutenant, Matthew, from the family of Tamstone, sat beside Major Benjamin, his friend and superior officer. The two had bonded two years earlier when Matthew became an officer. Ben, whose parents had both been generals, took him under his wing and showed him the ropes as he humorously referred to a new officer's training. The friends always maintained a first-name basis, even though Ben held a much higher rank.

On that day, Matthew had eyes only for Eliza, who didn't even know he existed. Matt watched the golden highlights of her amber hair sway gracefully with the rhythm of every breath of the morning breeze. Stiff-lipped about his feelings for the beautiful young woman, he had never shared his hidden emotions with Ben.

After talking for about half an hour in a fiery voice, Mochè exclaimed, "Ask, and it will be given to you; seek, and you will find; knock, and the door will be opened to you. For everyone who asks receives; the one who seeks finds; and to the one who knocks, the door will be opened." After quoting these sacred words from the Bible, Mochè stood silent for a moment, observing the crowd. Finally, he inquired, "What does that mean to us?" It was a rhetorical question, but Mochè noticed little six-year-old Jimmy sitting nearby, waving his hand anxiously. Smiling, he called to the boy, who had just begun Bible school, "Come, young James, stand beside me and share your answer," unaware of what to expect.

The little boy's heart raced, and his face flushed with fear at the thought of speaking to such a large and far-reaching crowd. Noticing the boy's stage fright, Mochè leaned over and whispered, "Don't be afraid, young James. It's very courageous of you to do this, and I'm so proud of you." Now making eye contact with the child, Mochè continued whispering, "I'll be right beside you, son."

Jimmy expanded his chest while drawing in his stomach. After taking a deep breath, he shouted into the microphone, "It means God is here for us and wants us to pray to Him!" Quickly glancing at his manhig, Jimmy whispered, "Did I do okay, Father?"

Mochè lifted the little boy and held him in his powerful arm, responding softly, "You did better than okay, James. You are a true warrior of God." Taking the microphone from the boy and turning back to the crowd, with Jimmy still in his arms, Mochè declared, "Psalm 8:2: Out of the mouth of babes and sucklings hast thou ordained strength!"

After putting the boy back on his feet and sending him to his parents, who were now smiling proudly, Mochè declared, "Jimmy is right. God is available to those who seek him through prayer. He is great, all-powerful, and filled with divine mercy, but we must seek him. We do that by praying. Now, my friends in Christ, please stand and recite the Lord's Prayer." Everyone stood and spoke those words together with their manhig. Afterward, Mochè cried out, "Now go in peace and give praise to God!"

As Major Benjamin rose to leave with his friend, he noticed the fair-skinned young blonde woman standing on her tiptoes, embracing the manhig, her head tilted and resting on his chest. Apparently, she knew the manhig well.

Mochè, along with David and Andrew, typically heard confessions weekly or upon personal request, continually granting absolution to the faithful. However, after preaching to his congregation that day, Mochè had to sit as a judge before the jury known as the council. David, Andrew, and Isaac were among the twelve who sat in judgment, with Mochè presiding. The case involved trying a young man and a teenage woman for adultery, a serious crime among the followers. Although it was no longer rampant, immorality represented the most significant offense that led to the downfall of the last wealthy nations known as the West and contributed to the degradation of the world. The revelations of the Holy Bible described how sexual immorality would bring about the end, yet nobody paid attention. Adultery was now the greatest offense among the followers, paralleling the crime of murder.

As the adulterers awaited their fate in a separate room, the crowd in the courtroom, unaware of their identities, listened as Mochè spoke before his council. He explained, "The holy blessed mother gazed into the flames of hell, where most cast there had committed sins of the flesh." He glanced back to observe those seated at the grand judgment table. "If the two accused indeed turned away from our Lord, they committed one of the greatest sins," Mochè continued. "If they seek penance, I will grant it to prevent them from eternal condemnation." The manhig bowed and addressed the council, saying, "I relinquish judgment to you, eleven men and women." Mochè lowered his head, admitting only to his inner self that he couldn't judge the young couple who had succumbed to the same temptation that now plagued him. Tormented by constant thoughts of Zipporah and his longing for her, his mind constantly distracted from his duties because of a woman, Mochè recused himself.

"Is it confirmed that penetration occurred?" asked General Sarah, a council member who initiated the discussion in a private chamber separate from the accused. According to the law, the complete act of sexual intercourse constituted a charge of adultery.

General Joseph affirmed, "The young woman admitted she was penetrated but stated that Caleb forced himself upon her."

"Most women charged with this crime state that," General Mark commented dryly.

The young General Helen quickly snapped back, "Not all women are prostitutes!" She glanced at Mark angrily. "As Mark here suggests!"

The discussions continued back and forth until all council members had presented their points without Mochè's involvement. The eleven cast their votes anonymously into a ballot box, which Isaac then read.

Isaac stood at the head of the courtroom and announced that the council had reached a decision, although it was not unanimous. The vote was six to five against the couple, excluding Mochè's vote. "Bring in the two accused of this hideous crime," he ordered, and two hefty guards had to drag Caleb in, who was furiously fighting back, while a passive Eliza sobbed and followed behind.

When Mochè raised his head to see the couple who had committed this grave offense, his eyes bulged in horror at the sight of Elizabeth's daughter standing barefoot, shivering with fright, while the bully Caleb struggled against the two guards restraining him.

Mochè quickly arose and ran to Isaac, who stood as the spokesperson for the council, even though his military advisor and council chairman had already begun pronouncing judgment before he noticed Mochè approaching him. Isaac stood erect, the stress of this verdict adding another wrinkle to his weathered face as he addressed the court, "It is with regret that we find the two accused guilty and have chosen banishment, the recognized punishment for committing adultery. May God watch over you both."

"Isaac," Mochè called, finally getting his attention. He

waved him over, "Come here!"

"Yes, Manhig?" Isaac was already beside his leader.

"Surely, there must be some mistake here. Eliza would never act in such a way," Mochè appeared intolerant of the decision for the first time ever. "Just yesterday, I saw Caleb making lewd advances toward Eliza, who fought to restrain him."

"Why did you relinquish the decision to the other eleven, Manhig? You could have ruled by your own words, yet you didn't even cast a vote." Isaac stood in awe. "If you had at least voted, it would have resulted in a draw, forcing you by law to decide."

"I didn't know it was Elizabeth's daughter," Mochè answered, growing angry, though his ire was directed inwardly at himself for his sinful distraction of contemplating the stunning Zipporah who had captured his heart. "The girl's innocent! I'll rule now!" he shouted, and some bystanders heard him.

"Manhig, please compose yourself," Isaac whispered. "You know, by law, you cannot rule after yielding your authority. If you do, it will be blasphemy."

Mochè believed that the gift of life was precious and valued it; therefore, he forbade capital punishment, allowing it only in cases of murder and only then, depending on the circumstances. Banishment was the usual penalty for any crime less severe than murder or taking a human life in any form. To protect against demons and roaming mutations, the followers provided the banished with ample food, supplies, and a horse for each person. Mochè always hoped that God would permit those banished to seek out other groups of exiled believers and collaborate positively, granting them a chance for redemption. He believed that, ultimately, the Lord's hands held that decision.

Now Mochè sat as a victim of his own laws; he could do nothing for Eliza. He could have ruled as a supreme leader, as God had given him that right from the beginning, but his studies warned him of the fates that befall such dictators, and he himself established the council to provide a voice for his followers. Even though he had the right to rule over any trial, he had legally forfeited that privilege. Ruling after a verdict was read would be deemed hypocritical and could cause dissension among his people. His hasty decision to yield his ruling capacity before knowing who was on trial stemmed solely from his secret desire for a woman, which made him harbor inner revulsion for himself, but it was now too late; his hands were tied.

Mochè calmly surrendered to the circumstances and reverently asked, "Caleb, do you wish to receive penance for your sins before you depart?"

Caleb's piercing, nearly black eyes conveyed an image of wickedness as he glared at the manhig, angrily declaring, "Never!" He sneered and continued, "I did what any man desires, what God gave me the ability to do!"

"He also blessed us with humanity and commandments to live by, son," Mochè stated, privately wishing to strike the young man but maintaining a cordial tone. Then he whispered to Caleb, "I know you forced yourself on that defenseless child, and the Lord will show you no mercy if you don't confess."

However, Caleb waved his hand, whispering at Mochè, "I've forced myself upon many of your female virgins. That's what real men do!" Then he turned away abruptly.

Mochè fought desperately to control his temper, knowing that if he didn't, he would seriously hurt Caleb for what he admitted doing to his young female followers and what he did to the teenager he held dearly. "Eliza, my child, please let me hear your confession so God may forgive you for any misdeeds you have committed."

Eliza fell into the arms of her manhig, crying. "I'm so sorry, Father."

"There, there," Mochè held her close, comforting the young amber-haired woman in her late teens. "Come. Let's sit together so God may hear your words of regret for any other transgressions you may have committed, for I am certain that you didn't willingly submit to Caleb regarding what you are charged."

"Do you believe me, Father?"

"I certainly do, but there's nothing I can do after the council has ruled." Mochè felt deep regret plaguing him. "I'm so sorry that I was distracted by a personal issue and didn't rule on this myself. I saw how Caleb treated you yesterday."

"I only care that you believe me, Father," her eyes welled with tears.

"But I failed you, my dear child," Mochè fought his tears.

"No, Manhig; you never did. You were always so wonderful to my mother and me. I can still remember how kind and generous you were to us both when I was just a little girl. I know you helped her financially before she died."

After Eliza finished her confession and the man of God blessed her with the sacrament of penance, they sat together and talked for nearly half an hour—the manhig purposely extending her time in the safety of the stronghold for as long as possible. Mochè's soul ached for this young woman, who was only eighteen, and he wanted to help her in any way he could. They embraced again before Eliza's glimmering hazel eyes met Mochè's in a way that nearly severed his heart as she whispered, "Thank you, Father," now smiling, her radiant eyes widening, "for everything. I feel better now."

"There's a cloistered nunnery not far from where a guard will escort you both. Tell them I sent you. I have many soldiers watching over that place. Have Caleb leave you there. Tell him they'll feed him so he'll take you, and then be rid of him. The nuns will feed and shelter you, child."

"I will, Father."

"Don't be afraid. God will be with you, my child," he answered. "I will take care of this matter another way. For now, stay with the nuns."

Mochè watched sorrowfully as a tear rolled down his cheek while the two rode away on horseback, laden with supplies. He had generously provided them with two mules to carry additional necessities. Mochè had granted forgiveness to the young woman as she repented for her minor transgressions. In his heart, he wished he could suspend her sentence, knowing he couldn't because the council had decreed it. He had approached Caleb once more before he left, but the young man again angrily rejected the Lord's forgiveness.

The assigned soldier, Ethen, was escorting Caleb and Eliza to a safe location, typically about ten miles from the stronghold. Mochè couldn't help but think of Zipporah and the comfort he now craved, which only a woman could provide for his humanity. He prayed to the Lord for strength. His eyes turned to the heavens as he whispered, "I am nothing more than a hypocrite, my Lord. I should have judged that poor soul myself and granted her sanctuary. She is innocent." Lowering his eyes, he asked, "Forgive me, Master."

As the day gradually turned to early afternoon, hours after that fateful judgment, Mochè heard shouting and commotion from a crowd gathering near the fortress entrance. Rushing toward the noise, he witnessed the unfolding events.

Spotting his manhig, Joshua rushed toward Mochè. After rendering a military salute, Joshua said, "Sir, the escort soldier, Ethen, who led the banished couple, collapsed and fell off his horse after entering the gate."

Mochè asked quickly, "Is he alive?"

"No, sir. I'm afraid not." Those words tormented Mochè. His people were the most important part of his life, and the loss of even one was a blow and unsettling for him.

"Did he say anything before he died?" His instinctive sensitivity searched for a reason or cause behind this tragic loss.

"Yes, sir. With his dying breath, Ethen told us that Caleb, the man we banished, deceived him. He rode up close as if he were about to ask a question, but then he jumped, taking Ethen down. After a struggle, the stronger young Caleb wrested Ethen's dagger from him and stabbed him with it several times. It was a miracle from God that he managed to make his way back to us. Ethen bled out in my arms, sir, after recounting what happened." Mochè could clearly see Joshua's distress over losing one of his subordinates.

"Why would he kill Ethen?"

"For his weapons, clothing, and body armor, sir. You can see Ethen is almost naked. Caleb now has a solar rifle, sidearm, and—"

"To kill someone over weapons and garments, Joshua? We provided both of them with sufficient defensive armaments and even additional garments and supplies."

"Sir, everything holds value on the open trade market among the bands of sinners who roam nearby. He was a wicked one, sir," Joshua sighed. "I neglected to mention that Ethen wanted you to know the young woman, Eliza, tried to help him by fighting back against Caleb and offering assistance in their struggle; she refused to participate in that treacherous act. Ethen made that clear, sir." Joshua bowed his head and said, "Caleb might have even traded Eliza into slavery, too, for all we know." Raising his face back to look at his manhig, he added, "Ethen also pleaded for your forgiveness for his incompetence."

Mochè gently placed his hand on Joshua's shoulder for comfort and said, "He was not incompetent; it could have happened to any of us." Then he asked, "Was Ethen your soldier's christened name, Joshua?"

"Yes, sir."

"Let me administer the last rites to this brave soldier, with the hope that his spirit still remains in his body," Mochè paused, reflecting on the courage of the young woman, Eliza. "In the meantime, gather a group of fifty of our finest warriors, Joshua. We will ride as soon as they are ready and assembled."

Mochè's warrior party galloped swiftly through the vibrant colors of the sweet-smelling countryside in the early afternoon, as the sun cast its intense golden rays upon the riders. Gershom rode alongside his manhig, matching his pace. Mochè focused solely on Eliza's well-being, believing he should never have permitted her punishment, regardless of the council's ruling. Logic didn't apply in his haste to find her now. He feared that roaming gangs would capture Eliza, and a man of Caleb's depravity would flee for himself and not fight for her safety—if he hadn't traded her yet. An attractive young human woman like Eliza would command a substantial price as a slave for wicked villains and thieves on the open market. Buyers prized pretty women as sexual slaves for trade or personal use, much more so than human males, who were sold mostly for heavy labor and breeding stock to spawn human females, a valuable commodity.

A dog led the way, sniffing out the path to where the two banished were. Joshua and the furious soldiers eagerly sought revenge for the death of one of their own. Their fallen comrade, Ethen, was a friend to most of those advancing toward the banished man. Riding ahead, Mochè shouted back to them, "Vengeance is mine, saith the Lord. I will repay," reminding them of their duty and cautioning them not to exceed it.

In the distance, Mochè's party spotted something; flying birds glided, encircling something that wasn't yet clear. As they urged their horses on, driving them faster, they saw what they later wished their eyes had never laid upon. The warriors dismounted before a grisly sight. Close to where they now stood, holding the reins of their horses, a massive oak tree loomed in a clearing, surrounded by smaller trees, bushes, and drab shrubs. Tied spreadeagled and naked to one side of the tree's thick trunk was the banished young man, still alive. A group of demon men and women had gutted Caleb from his throat to his loins and were now feasting on his innards and flesh, vultures flying down to join. The man's intestines lay strewn in a long trail as savage, naked, and painted beast-women devoured them, and large vultures fought to peck at whatever they could. Caleb's screams were horrific as he watched the monstrous, hooved-footed females consuming him alive as the birds nipped at his eyes.

"Stop them!" shouted Mochè. "Decapitate them all! Quickly!" The only way to ensure a demon's demise was to remove its head from its body. Evil spells cast on other mortal wounds could reanimate them—a lesson learned long ago. Mochè struggled to witness the horror unfolding before him. Some of his brave warriors, who had faced terrible things in battle, vomited at the sight. "Leave the man who betrayed his Lord and refused to repent. He's now dead in more ways than one. Take the weapons he stole along with Ethen's personal belongings so that we can bury him with them."

Mochè scanned the area for Eliza, dreading the worst. As he guided his stallion through the butterfly milkweeds and flowering dogwoods, he meticulously searched for the girl, his deep remorse escalating. It felt futile. The demons or other nonhumans had likely already taken her, or slave traders had captured her. He envisioned Elizabeth's only daughter—the young woman he had known since she was a little girl—enduring the life of a slave. This teenager, to whom he felt a bond, was now offering herself to pleasure any wicked, brutish slob who demanded her. And it was entirely his fault. Then, from the corner of his eye, he spotted a figure running toward him.

"Manhig! Manhig!" Eliza shouted, tears streaming down her face as she yelled. Mochè tied his horse to a small tree and rushed to the young woman.

Holding her in a tight embrace, he comforted the traumatized young woman, who seemed like a child to him. Mochè whispered, "It's over. You're safe now, dear."

"Manhig," Eliza huffed, struggling to catch her breath. "Manhig, I dismounted to help the soldier, Ethen." Her voice broke as she tried to breathe evenly.

"I know, dear. Ethen told us," Mochè smiled.

"He's alive? Thanks be to God!"

Mochè frowned and replied, "No, Eliza. I'm afraid he didn't live long after informing Joshua about what occurred."

Eliza's joyful expression conceded to one of sorrow, yet she said, "God has shone His grace on me today, Manhig. Because I dismounted to stop Caleb from harming Ethen, I saw the horde of demons before he did, which gave me time to run." She gazed into the distance, her eyes widening with concern, and added, "A kind warrior helped me, but I don't see him now. He slayed several demons who came upon me." Eliza kept looking and said, "My mules and the horses have wandered off. I need

50

to gather my supplies." She turned back to Mochè and said, "If you wait, I'll return Caleb's share to you."

Mochè smiled at Eliza's honesty, reflecting on how deeply he loved her in a fatherly way. She could have been his daughter if he had married at a younger age—if everything had been different. "I'll have one of my soldiers gather them, but you won't need them," he said, still smiling as he stroked the strands of her golden-toned amber hair.

Eliza looked at him, puzzled, and asked, "Manhig?"

Mochè hugged her once more and wept softly while holding her closely, "That same grace of God desires your return to us."

Eliza cried, and through her tears, she uttered, "Oh, thank you, Manhig!"

While gently stroking her hair, he told Eliza, "God has saved you, child. He knows you never submitted to adultery. It was my fault." Yet, he found comfort in the arms of the child he thought of as his own.

As she basked in her joy, Eliza spotted the warrior who had helped her, riding back with her horses and packed mules trailing behind him. "Oh! There he is, sir. That's the man who helped me."

Mochè smiled as he recognized the man Eliza referred to when he came closer, saying, "I should have thought it would have been you, Augustine, who else would appear from nowhere to do a noble deed?"

"It's good to see you again, Mochè. What's it been, almost two years?"

"About that, my friend," Mochè looked upon this man fondly, then spread his arms wide and asked, "Why don't you rejoin us, Augustine? You can re-take your commission as general and lead an army again as you were born to do."

"It's kind of you, but I still can't let go, Manhig."

"You still wrestle with your loss, I see." Mochè appeared deep in thought, filled with regret. "Pray to God for comfort, my friend. He will help you."

"But, it's He who took away my wife." Augustine bowed

his head as his memory of her overcame him. "Respectfully, Mochè, you're a priest and can't know the grief of loving someone so much that she almost became part of my soul, only to lose her."

That statement awakened Mochè to the realization of his love for Zipporah and its intensity, which pierced his heart. That struggle showed on his face. "I'm sorry, Augustine. I didn't mean to resurrect more pain than you've already suffered."

Seeing Mochè's expression, Augustine remarked, "It's I who am sorry, Manhig, for I seem to have delved to a place I shouldn't have. Please forgive me for that."

Mochè merely waved his hand as if it were nothing, but smiled and said, "So, you won't be my general, yet you save people in the remote countryside?"

Augustine chuckled, saying, "I ride with a few good men," and pointed to where he came from. "We battle demons and mutations to spare people. The wicked take many young women as slaves to use or sell them in the marketplaces of the gangs. We try to free them often."

"So be it then, my friend. You're young; my God, you never seem to age. When you make your peace with God, always know there is a place for you with me."

"Thank you, Mochè." He bowed and asked, "Will you bless me, Father?"

After Mochè blessed the young man, they embraced in a gesture of military camaraderie, each holding the other's arms. Augustine smiled at Eliza, and after she thanked him once more, he rode away on horseback.

"I couldn't help but overhear some of your conversation, Manhig. His story seems so distressing," Eliza became teary-eyed again.

"Yes, it is." A tear rolled down his cheek as Mochè spoke, recalling the young warrior's tragedy. "Augustine is a good and noble man." Mochè smiled at Eliza and asked, "Are you ready to go home, young lady?"

"Yes, sir, I am."

After the day's events, particularly after witnessing such a gruesome demonic ritual, Mochè made his way to visit Zipporah. Following her exorcism, he usually dined with her in the evenings. She had no recollection of that rite or the event itself. Drawn to her, he resisted temptations from a dark place, recalling his own words from his last sermon. Even so, he felt that simply being in her presence was enough to satisfy his longing for her, and it felt morally safe, especially after his conversation with Augustine.

He knocked on the young woman's door. It opened to reveal the striking, wide green eyes of Zipporah's smiling face, always a delight for him after a long day. "Hello, Zipporah," he said cheerfully, then asked, "How was your day?" Mochè loved entering Zipporah's house. It was immaculate and smelled as such. Those spotless fragrances of a clean house blended with the delicious foods she always prepared, creating an atmosphere that made him feel he was coming home.

"It's lovely now," she laughed, rushing up to hug him, her body close to his. Embracing her while smelling her perfume, Mochè felt a pleasure he had never known. However, he stopped her as her lips reached for his.

Smiling, Mochè stated, "I told you we can't do that."

Her beautiful green eyes glancing down made her appear like a disobedient child. Then, beaming with a wide grin, she told him, "Sit here, my love," completely ignoring his repeated insistence that they had to remain friends and nothing more. Never hungry, Gershom lay himself near the door.

Mochè sat in his regular place at the head of the table, with Zipporah seated close to him after serving his plate. The young woman now wore lovely dresses, sometimes choosing tight-fitting slacks, colorful blouses, and a touch of perfume, but always proudly showcasing the beautiful crucifix Mochè had given her, which became precious to her.

She also applied a touch of makeup that Rosetta, one of the other young ladies, had taught her. Zipporah looked stunning and caught the attention of many young men, but she only had eyes for Mochè. "I would like to teach," she began the evening conversation. "My parents, both being professors, taught me to speak properly at a young age, as I've already mentioned."

After Mochè finished thoroughly chewing and swallowing his first spoonful of food, he replied, "You never mentioned they were professors. My father was one, too. By the way, this is the best polenta I've ever tasted. Where did you learn this recipe?"

"My mother," Zipporah smiled. She loved her dinners with Mochè and their discussions during them.

"Getting back to that you were saying, what would you like to teach?"

My parents eventually taught blind students. They discovered that the metal plates used to create the raised dots on paper, known as Braille, far outlasted any remaining printed books, even those manufactured closer to the fall of civilization, which they called 'hard works,' and had become obsolete centuries ago. Together, using Braille, they were able to revive many educational subjects that they had taught to others and me.

Zipporah hadn't yet touched her dinner. She enjoyed watching Mochè eat in such a mannerly and gentlemanly way. It was so unlike everyone else who gulped down their food, reminding her of her father's wonderful table manners, even in the most barbaric conditions. "I learned the proper use of English grammar and writing. I noticed that many among us don't speak correctly, and numerous people don't know how to write," she said, carefully watching Mochè's astonished facial reactions to her skills. "I also learned some forms of mathematics. I think arithmetic would be best to teach first."

Mochè sat up straight in his chair, nearly speechless, but finally said, "Wow! I'm amazed. I never knew you were so educated. I think it's a wonderful idea for you to teach." Zipporah rested her elbows on the table, her hands cradling her smiling face as she proudly listened to her love's compliments. "Most people here haven't had the opportunity to gain your vast expertise. Those with some education don't have the time to teach others, as they apply their skills differently. I'll make plans for more school buildings. We only have the one that teaches verbalization, as people here have come to call it." Mochè smiled, "With your help, we can teach throughout the seven towns."

"Yes, and it's a wonderful way for me to contribute to the community and earn my keep without relying on you." She smiled at Mochè, her gorgeous, big green eyes shining, and said, "It was very kind of you to support me while I adjusted to this new place." Then she leaned her long, elegant neck forward, bringing her face closer to him, and added, "And it's something I can continue to do after we marry, even when we have children," she said with a charming smile.

Mochè coughed and nearly choked on her last words. Once he had regained his composure, he replied, "Zipporah, I told you I couldn't marry."

"I heard that many priests married before the end of civilization."

"I'm a chosen one, sweetheart." He inadvertently used the term as a subtle gesture of friendly affection, but Zipporah took it literally.

"See? You called me sweetheart."

"It was not intended to mean…" Mochè lost his train of thought. "It was a twist of the tongue, a mistake."

"There are no mistakes in psychology or with God," Zipporah said boldly, a smile crossing her face. Her dreamy green eyes locked onto those of the man she loved.

Mochè realized he had misjudged this woman's intelligence and said, "Even if I weren't a priest, I'm too old for you."

"Are not," she answered, still smiling as her ravishing eyes remained gazing into his.

"I'm nearly 39, and you're 24. That's too old."

"How ridiculous, Mochè! Sometimes, you amaze me; being such a brilliant man must blind you. You don't have a wrinkle on your beautiful face and are as strong as an ox. You look precisely my age. God has blessed you with youth; make the most of it!"

"But I can't!"

"I love you, Mochè. I felt it the moment I first saw you, and I know with certainty that you love me. I can sense it in every part of my being. I'm a woman, and you're a man. I know you desire me, Mochè. I realize how much you long to touch my body, but I won't tempt you, my love. If you won't take me in the sacrament of holy matrimony, I'll continue to live alone. We'll share dinners and conversations in the evenings as friends. I won't tempt you anymore, but I'll take no other man, Mochè," Zipporah declared, tears streaming from her marvelous yet now defeated heavenly green eyes. She gazed into his beautiful, deep blue eyes once more and whispered, "Until you come to your senses of your own accord."

David and Andrew waited longer than usual for Mochè to arrive at their fireside for their evening chat. When Mochè finally showed up, he sat beside his older priest friends and made himself comfortable. A smiling Andrew couldn't contain his feelings and remarked, "You've been arriving late, Manhig." His smile grew wider as he asked, "It wouldn't be that young woman you often dine with who kept you, would it?"

A blushing Mochè answered, "Have I no privacy in this compound?"

"No," David answered curtly but smiling. "You are the mighty manhig of your people, and they gossip and—"

"Gossip is a sin!" Mochè replied defensively, interrupting David's words.

"We mean no disrespect, Mochè, only concern," David softly said.

"I understand," Mochè said humbly, shaking his head in disgust at his discourtesy. "I apologize for being rude. I've had a lot on my mind." He raised his eyes to the moon, not yet full in the sky, and explained, "I usually have dinner with Zipporah before coming here, and sometimes, when I stop by to check on her, we end up having lunch together."

"There's no need to apologize, Mochè," Andrew calmly

added. He could see and sense the turmoil within his leader.

"Do you have feelings for the young woman?" David asked. "It's only natural if you do."

"I have a strong affection for Zipporah." He bowed his head, cradled it in his hands, and confessed, "There is a passion within me, a kind I have never before felt. A tenderness I have never before known."

"You're human, Mochè, and quite a fine-looking young man," David said as the short, stocky man stood. "Look at me," he stretched out his arms, posing. "I'm a short, ugly man with a long beard."

"I'm almost 39 years old," Mochè chuckled, unable to resist his friend's acting gig. "Sit back down; you'll scare the wild animals."

"That's young, Mochè," David chuckled as he sat down by the fire. "Have you expressed your affection physically?"

"That would be adultery, the ultimate sin. Besides, the boy is always at my side." Gershom lay sleeping by the fire.

"I meant in other bodily ways that are not adulterous," David clarified. "Like those young people who court and fondle one another as they explore the beauty of the opposite sex—much smaller offenses that I frequently hear in confession. God understands the drives of his human creations and is a forgiving God."

"He must also be a just Supreme Being to be God," Mochè added to the growing conversation. "In Matthew 5:27-28, Jesus clearly states, 'But I say to you that everyone who looks at a woman with lust for her has already committed adultery in his heart,' may I remind you," the manhig continued.

"There are many interpretations of that," David reflected. "Every ordinary person has done so, even those of the faithful who strive more diligently. We are all sinners and ultimately rely on God's Divine Mercy in the end."

"We've both lived a life of celibacy," Andrew said, referring to himself and David. "I have struggled with it many times." Andrew, taller and thinner than David, appeared to have been handsome in his youth. Slightly older than David, he still possessed the chiseled features of a striking face, now weathered with wrinkles from age and years of travel.

"But you never conceded to it, did you?" Mochè asked.

"Once, I almost did," Andrew sighed, gazing into the distance. "I was in love with a woman for years. Her name was Sarah; she was beautiful. She loved me, but we lived in very different times," Andrew admitted, his expression grave as he reflected on his past. "Even back then, many priests gave up their vows and married. I never did, but as I mentioned, everything was different then. We served our flocks in our own way. We were young priests in an era when some broken cities still held on shortly before they fell. We had to fulfill our priestly duties as only a few remained."

"I think you should consider marrying her," David professed. "In these days leading to the place of redemption, I think our Lord would understand. Pray on it, my friend."

"I agree," declared Andrew. "Within the sacrament of holy matrimony, it would not be adultery. It would be understandable, and your followers would support you. They always do with your decisions."

"This is different, my friends. God anointed me to be Manhig when I was still a boy. I cannot marry."

David intentionally changed the subject for a purpose: "Mochè, do you recall from our holy scriptures, Genesis 6:4 and Numbers 13:33, the Nephilim?"

Mochè thought quickly and replied, "Yes, from the Septuagint, the giants. The Book of Enoch describes them as the offspring of fallen angels, derived from the Hebrew root word 'naphal,' which means the fallen ones."

"Yes," David replied, stroking his long gray beard as usual, especially when deep in thought. "While there were various interpretations, we believe they were fallen angels who bore children with human women. Their offspring were the Nephilim or giants."

"It was a time of great wickedness, the reason God commanded Noah before the great flood," Andrew interjected.

Mochè, his bright, handsome face now clouded with sadness, stated, "You remind me of these things because they parallel what we currently face in a fallen world." He understood where his friends were headed with this: the manhig, like God awakening the patriarchs of the Hebrew faith and guiding His people during a time of great sin. "Our future became our past."

"How true," said David.

"Remember how you almost decided to change the language we speak to a new universal one?" asked Andrew. "We had so many people coming to us from these and nearby lands and other countries, unable to speak or communicate—some for centuries. Those few who could verbalize used languages, dialects, and accents from all over the world.

"Yes," answered Mochè, while deep in thought. "The English language—a more difficult one to learn—had been a global language for many of our ancestors. The manhig's eyes reflected on those early transformative days. "I was educated with older, actually restored antique books written in English, except for the Latin I studied to be a priest. So I decided to use that language as our common one. We speak and write in the style that the former Britannia Empire did in their marked year of nineteen hundred and sixty-five—or thereabouts." Mochè, still contemplating, added, "Our schools teach our students the same stylistic manner of the great scholars and authors of that era."

"It was a wise decision, Mochè," David affirmed.

"But in the end, humanity failed God," Mochè said softly and solemnly.

David smiled as he proclaimed, "Christ came to us to open the gates of heaven. He knows we are sinners; yet, he offers his loving divine mercy to all who believe in him. You bring hope and the prevailing civilization under God—the same as our biblical ancestors did."

"Yes," Andrew agreed. "You are the one guiding His people in times reminiscent of those long ago, facing much of the same wickedness as our ancient forefathers. We live in different times now, Mochè. You have fulfilled your priestly duties; consider marriage."

Chapter Four

Revenge

As Mochè finished his sermon for the week, he noticed Isaac eagerly waiting to convey something important, obvious from Isaac's anxious pacing that wore down the grass beneath his restless steps. Mochè's final words to the crowd gathered on the hills were, "So, my loyal and dedicated followers, I leave you with these thoughts to ponder until next time I speak: remember, God rules our minds, and Satan, the fallen angel, governs our physical desires. We must be strong, keep our bodies pure, and avoid temptation. Now, my friends in Christ, please stand and recite the Lord's Prayer." Everyone rose and recited those sacred words together with their manhig. Afterward, Mochè exclaimed, "Now go in peace and give praise to God!"

As the crowd dispersed in different directions, Major Benjamin and Gabriela exchanged a final glance simultaneously, their lips remaining sealed. The fair-skinned young blonde woman blushed, as she always did when caught in one of her gazes at the young man who tugged at her heart. It was the day Eliza caught her first glimpse of Matthew, but she quickly dismissed any impure thoughts after her recent redemption, freeing her from false accusations of adultery. The memory of that experience was still fresh in her mind. Eliza's only lingering memory of seeing Matthew was how handsome he was.

Isaac rushed up to Mochè and asked him, "May I sit with you, Manhig? I have something important to discuss with you."

"Of course, Isaac," Mochè replied apprehensively. His chief military advisor was always calm, even in the most critical battle situations, but now he appeared unsettled. He understood that Isaac internalized his anxiety; the wrinkles on his face and the dark circles under his tired eyes were telling. He sat on a patch of grass, extending his arm for Isaac to join him.

Isaac got right to the point: "The young woman, Zipporah, the one you saved, has been attacked, Manhig."

Upon hearing those words, Mochè instinctively began to stand up to go to her. "I need to see how—"

Isaac held Mochè's wrist, restraining him, knowing his manhig well and his temperament at times. He said, "Please, sir, sit beside me so I can explain everything." When he saw Mochè sit back down, Isaac continued, "She's fine. A drunken man named Amos tried to assault her, but passing soldiers heard Zipporah's cries and the struggle in her home. They subdued the man and arrested him. Amos is now in jail, awaiting trial. I wanted you to know first, Manhig."

Mochè, realizing his occasional impulsiveness, said, "Thank you, Isaac, for informing me so promptly." He pondered momentarily and continued, while suppressing his anger, asking, "Was the young woman hurt?"

"Not too bad, Manhig. She has a few slight bruises on her face and body, nothing serious. However, she was traumatized, sir."

"I would expect. I'll ride over to see her later."

"Sir, we must judge the man swiftly. People are already talking."

"They're condemning Amos without a trial?"

"They were initially, but surprisingly, some have changed their feelings and are now denouncing Zipporah." Isaac didn't want to explain why.

So Mochè asked what Isaac wouldn't elaborate on, "Why

on earth would they renounce the young woman?"

Isaac bowed and said, "They question her ways and wonder why she won't marry." He paused, reflecting on how to express what was being conveyed among the communities within the stronghold, finally adding, "They believe she deliberately entices men with her beauty and the way she dresses. Many have seen you visiting her home, Manhig, thinking she bewitches you too."

"Okay," Mochè said calmly. "We will first judge the man, Amos." He paused, then boldly added, "Then I will ride over to see the young woman—just as I would with any of my people who are harmed. Assemble the council!" he barked.

Mochè sat in his judge's chair behind the large oak desk at the head of the council and commanded, "Bring in the prisoner, Amos!" Guards quickly brought in a rugged-looking, unshaven, disheveled fat man before the council. To Mochè's surprise, Zipporah and Eliza sat beside the gathered council.

Isaac declared, "You are charged with assault, with notice to the court regarding a person who is significantly lighter in weight and weaker than you." He glanced with disgust at the huge, heavy but muscle-bound man who stood accused, then continued, "and attempted adultery. How do you plead?"

"I ain't guilty," Amos crudely and disrespectfully answered.

"We have witnesses," Isaac spoke first from the council.

"Ha!" Amos scoffed, "Friends of the great and mighty manhig."

Helen, a young army general and council member, firmly warned, "Curb your disrespect toward our manhig and this council."

"No! I won't!" argued the prisoner. "I ain't done nothing wrong. The woman's a whore and a temptress!" howled Amos. "I'd do it again and give her what she wants!"

Mochè pounded his hammer repeatedly, then, while keeping his composure, firmly said, "There will be no talk like that in my courtroom."

"Your courtroom! Your everything! Great and wise, Man-hig! You're one of the bitch-temptress's victims yourself; she even wears your crucifix around her pretty little neck. Ain't that sweet, you hypocritical bastard!"

"Restrain the prisoner!" cried out Helen.

Isaac, the council's chief spokesperson, shouted before a courtroom filled with stunned spectators, all of them murmuring and sharing their thoughts, "Take the prisoner back to jail so this council may reach a verdict."

Mochè sat in a daze, stunned by Amos's words. He shook off his stupor and gestured for Isaac to come closer. As the chief spokesperson stood before his manhig, Mochè said, "Isaac, considering the circumstances, I believe it's best for me to withdraw from this case."

"I disagree with you, Manhig." Isaac's loyalty to Mochè was firm in his eyes. "However, if you insist, I—"

"I do insist," Mochè calmly answered.

"So be it then," Isaac conceded.

The courtroom emptied as the council convened in judgment, leaving only Mochè with Zipporah and Eliza.

"I'll wait for you outside, Zipporah," Eliza said softly, concern in her voice. Since her return to the compound, Zipporah had been like an older sister to the teenage girl. Feeling sympathy for Eliza, whom many still regarded as an outcast, she helped her settle in and offered her a position as a teacher's assistant.

Zipporah smiled at the teen girl and said, "Alright, sweetheart."

People stepped outside into the fresh summer air, stretching and chatting about Amos's disrespectful comments. Others echoed their opinions about Zipporah, mainly envious wives and less attractive single women struggling to find husbands. One woman remarked, "Banish her, I say," as Eliza softly walked past her. "And that other little harlot she keeps company with!" She sneered as Eliza walked away from the group.

Zipporah approached Mochè and softly whispered, "I'm

sorry for your troubles, my love, but I haven't done anything wrong."

Afraid to make eye contact with Zipporah for fear he might succumb to her beauty in public, Mochè replied, "Of course you didn't. Amos is an animal. The army kicked him out for war crimes, and he has lived with anger ever since. He spreads the poison of hatred to feed the jealousy of single, mule-faced women who can't find husbands because they don't truly want to."

Zipporah asked, "Is it a crime that the Lord has given me beauty? He bestows different blessings upon us all. I have never flaunted myself as my accusers claim."

Mochè chuckled, "No, it isn't a crime to be beautiful. But many sinners among us seek no repentance. Satan always stays close to God's people. The Fallen Angel's followers always find ways to punish those of us who remain faithful to God." As he finished speaking, a guard announced over the loudspeaker that the council had reached a decision. All the scattered people returned to the courthouse and, once seated, awaited the verdict. Amos stood behind Isaac, who faced the anxious crowd.

Isaac stood before the followers and announced the council's decision: "We conclude that the prisoner, Amos, be sentenced to five years of hard labor for his crimes against the victim, Zipporah. As civilized followers of God, we abhor adultery or any attempt at it. And—"

Amos's large arm seized Isaac around the neck, squeezing tightly and stifling his words. He jumped like a heavy ape, landing on a chair and roaring, "Tramps, harlots! Hypocrites! Let all of you so-called believers in God rot in hell!" It took four husky guards to restrain the wild man. Amos broke free and leaped again as the guards fell to the floor. Agile for such a heavyset man, he balanced himself while walking along the high backs of the chairs occupied by the seated council members, ultimately landing beside Helen, the youngest general. Grabbing her long, golden hair in his fist, stretching her head, Amos came face-to-face with the young councilmember. Her vivid blue eyes widened in surprise as the brute spoke to her, "Ain't it nice how you lure me with passion," his open mouth exposing broken, blackened teeth as he blew his rancid breath onto her. "I've taken many of your women right under your noses!" he admitted in his fury. "But I'd love to bed a beautiful whore with authority—a general no less. That would feel so good." He forced his cracked, stiff lips to hers, irritating her cheek with his porcupine-like facial hairs. Helen spat out his kiss, wiping her lips, and tried to kick Amos in his groin to disable him, but she couldn't move because the enormous, fat man blocked her limbs. "I think I'll take you next." His laugh was wicked as he howled once again, flashing open his horrible mouth and licking Helen's cheek, the one chaffed by his rigid whiskers. The raging man now appeared insane.

Mochè swiftly sprang over his large oak desk. Grabbing Amos's mangy hair with his sturdy arm, he tossed the massive man around, kicked him in the groin, and punched him once in the forehead, causing the burly man to collapse onto the hard wooden floor. "Guards!" Mochè shouted. "Handcuff this man with his wrists behind him. Chain his legs!" He turned back to the council and calmly said, "Proceed with the case. General Helen, my apologies."

As soon as Amos awoke, now fully restrained, he continued to ramble with his profanities. Sarah, another general and council member, yelled, "Guards, gag the prisoner at once!" and the court soldiers quickly complied, avoiding bites coming from the drooling prisoner as they bound his mouth.

Mochè interrupted and shouted, "After his sentencing, put him in solitary confinement at the holding place. I want to examine Amos for demonic possession."

Amos, now completely restrained and controlled by four equally sized guards, faced the court as his sentencing continued. Isaac announced, "Furthermore, it is the decision of this council that, due to his disrespect toward this court, General Helen, and our manhig, that Amos shall serve an additional five years of hard labor in addition to the initial five years." Isaac paused, turning to the heavyset prisoner before continuing, "Prior to your sentence, you will be confined in jail on a diet of just one piece of bread and one glass of water each day during that three-day period."

Mumbles and murmurs from the crowd echoed throughout the courthouse, drowning out all words from the council. Mochè struck his hammer against the wooden block on the judge's high desk once more. "Silence in the court!" he commanded, and everyone ceased speaking at their manhig's order.

Isaac bowed sadly, his sullen eyes reflecting his remorse as he finally spoke, "It is also the order of this court that the unwed young lady, Zipporah, must marry within four months. So be it, the orders of this court." Sounds of approval, primarily from envious women, rang out. Eliza held Zipporah's hand tightly.

As General Helen passed the bound prisoner escorted from the courthouse, she whispered, "After that sentence, and that kick the manhig gave you," Helen smiled, "oh, that must have hurt!" Her smile widened as she continued, "You'll have the sexual strength of a eunuch if you ever try to pursue any other women." She smiled, her big eyes gleaming with glory. The large, ornery man, now passive, merely bowed his head as the guards led him away. Amos had said and done things he would later regret.

That evening, Mochè walked over to have dinner with Zipporah as always. He knocked on the door but heard nothing, so he knocked louder. Soft whimpers came from inside, and he waited, but Zipporah still didn't open the door. Finally, Mochè called to her, and he heard her footsteps approaching to open the door. She cracked it open slightly, revealing only her beautiful, wide green eyes shining through the shadows that concealed her face, and asked, "Why have you come here, Manhig?" Mochè could now see that her eyes were filled with tears.

"I've come to have dinner with you and share conversation, as usual."

"Haven't you heard that this is a place of sin, Manhig, and I am a tempestuous seductress?"

"Gossip from foolish women and men."

"Why aren't they held accountable for that sin, my Manhig? It's not just gossip; it's revenge they inflicted upon me, and vengeance is also an offense against God, isn't it?"

"Please open the door so we can talk, Zipporah." She complied and opened the door for Mochè to enter.

Zipporah turned and walked over to the table. Knowing Mochè well and that he would arrive, it was set as usual, with food steaming on her stove. "Please take a seat, Manhig. I follow your orders as I must."

Once settled in his regular seat, Mochè said, "I had no idea the court would rule as they did regarding you, Zipporah. I am truly sorry and will do everything I can to rescind that order forcing you to marry without love."

"Will you?" Zipporah looked surprised.

"It's unfair and came as a total shock to me. I'll do everything I can."

"My love, you can wave your powerful arm and declare anything, but I doubt you can or will take action regarding this."

"We'll see," Mochè said as a smiling Zipporah filled his plate.

Mochè sat at his fireside chat with Andrew and David after leaving Zipporah's home. His priest friends could see and sense his mood, but they didn't bring up Zipporah until Mochè said, "I'm thinking about rescinding the council's order for Zipporah to marry. How could they possibly force her to marry someone she doesn't love?"

"If you do that, you give more ammunition to those who demanded it in the first place," David answered. "Marry the young woman yourself, I say. How will you live with yourself knowing the one you love sleeps in the arms of another man?"

Andrew looked at Mochè with an expression that supported David's opinion. "It will torment you to no end, Mochè. Take it from one who knows, as I already told you, I once loved a woman." He sat glancing at the stars forming in the sky. "It was so long ago, but I still think of Sarah."

Mochè quickly changed the subject to history to avoid talking more about Zipporah with them. He said, "Did you know my father once told me that before the fall, corporations sold medicines that harmed and even killed people? Some actually went as far as to alter the chemical structure of humans. I've always wondered why they committed such sacrilegious acts when I first learned about them. That's what led to further experiments that mutilated humanity."

"It was greed, my son," David spoke in a fatherly manner. "Many great sins existed then, but all stemmed from what was once referred to as the media. Every form of it contributed to the indoctrination of the masses toward evil. They had done it before and after the sin of AI."

Andrew explained, "At first, AI seemed like a good thing for humanity. My grandfather told my father stories about how technology paved the way for the widespread implantation of AI devices into human brains, even in infancy. That occurred centuries before my grandfather was born, but it led to total control over the remaining population. AI ultimately dominated their thoughts and made them believe whatever it wanted."

"Of course," David added to the historical discussion, "look at what natural deoxyribonucleic acid changes have evolved to do." Many who wanted to be physically appealing to attract members of the opposite sex found ways to enhance their God-given DNA. Men and women injected themselves with so many chemicals that they destroyed their natural deoxyribonucleic acid structure, which affected their brains." David went on. "Then, they created, consumed, and injected chemicals from animal DNA. That gradually turned them into beings that found a way to mate with beasts for physical power."

"They weren't as bad as the ones we're fighting now," Andrew reasoned. "They've mutated into what we see and battle. Those demons and mutants—or transmutes, if you prefer—who we're now fighting and killing are no longer human."

"You both must realize that demonic possession was rampant long before all these things happened," Mochè informed his friends. "Satan positioned his demons skillfully among the leaders of that long-ago time, even within what you refer to as the media. Those 'influencers' of his made humanity accept the unthinkable."

Looking troubled, Andrew turned to Mochè and explained, "There are groups of wicked transmutes, followers of Satan, who have scientists just like we do and probably have created advanced weapons, just as we have. Although we've never encountered them, they exist out there. When I was a boy, my father told me that my great-grandfather explained how many of those mutated evil beings prepared for the end times in their own immoral way."

The conversations of the three priests led to a discussion about their traveling to another temporary stronghold before the winter, and David and Andrew questioned why and when.

Mochè told them, "My friends, this next temporary fortress will be the last before we construct the enormous final place that will house the many more arrivals we will have by then."

"I always wonder why there are so many more demons and bands of sinners than of the faithful?" asked Andrew.

Mochè replied, "The first angel told me it would be that way. Many faithful would become prey to the sins of this fallen world, particularly those of the flesh." He explained, "After they succumbed to the seven deadly sins described by Saint Thomas Aquinas, lust, the second sin, would manifest. It is written in the Bible, which is why God commands His angels to lead as many good people to us. That is why we wait in temporary strongholds. Some have come from the great fallen lands to the north, while others have arrived from the east, the west, and the southern places. Angels guide all His faithful of every color, race, creed, and ethnicity to us from lands near and far."

"I wonder what will happen at the place of redemption," David expressed, hoping that Mochè would finally address it, as he had previously requested.

"The Holy One who first guided me out of the city of the East and accompanied us from the very beginning later told me," Mochè looked up to the heavens, recalling that blessed time, and continued, "it will be the site of the last battle between good and evil. Afterward, we will all face judgment from our Lord," Mochè replied, visibly distraught.

"You've never mentioned that before," Andrew remarked as David, taken aback, stroked his gray beard more quickly than usual in response to his own question. "So we go to the place that is written."

"It is written, 'No one knows the day or hour of the Son of Man's return, not even the angels in heaven; only the Father knows.' We remain unaware of the Father's choice of that time, only that we are getting closer to the place." Mochè glanced at his friends and commanded, "Keep as silent about the sacred nature of what I just revealed to you as you do about your priestly knowledge of confessors when you administer penance."

Chapter Five

The Beasts

Though Mochè regarded the protected compound he and his followers lived in as a temporary stronghold, it was indeed massive. Naturally shielded on three sides, a tall, double-reinforced wooden wall, with all gaps filled with mud and moss, guarded the open area in front. It resembled the old forts of the American West. Flowing water from the nearby stream's tributary surrounded the compound and covered the rocks and boulders of the sides and back. Whenever a sentry lowered the large, lumber-slotted barrier gate over the flowing water of the gully, the opening became spacious and wide enough for transport wagons to roll, and the cavalry to ride completely over it. When raised, the gate closed and secured the compound at night and during potential attacks. The sentries lowered it again at sunrise, covering the surrounding trench to allow entry.

The vast interior of the fortress resembled seven separate towns, with each division commander residing in one to ensure the prompt assembly of their troops at a moment's notice. Houses, huts, and smaller dwellings served as homes for the followers, including the soldiers and their families. As more people arrived, they constructed second-floor apartments on top of the existing homes for the younger ones who could easily climb the stairs. The fortress contained a courthouse, new schools, hospitals, a solar power center, research facilities, stables for horses and mules, various-sized wagons, and production centers. Places of worship welcomed all believers in God within this predominantly Christian fortress. Numerous supply buildings stored every type of resource separately, including armaments, building supplies, tools, and canned and jarred goods. The complex included a slaughterhouse managed by butchers, along with coops for chickens, ducks, turkeys, and other poultry. There were also gated enclosures for steers, buffalo, deer, and other livestock. Wood supplies, cut from the Unknown Territory during their ten-year stay, were stored out of sight. Every necessity was available within the fortress. Taverns served food, wine, and beer in all seven towns. After they arrived from the Unknown Territory, laborers worked tirelessly, day and night, for nearly four months to reconstruct all buildings and other dwellings now in place. During the earlier part of that reconstruction period, people slept in temporary tents and lean-tos to protect themselves from the elements.

In the late afternoon, as sentries stood watch on all sides of the massive fortress, a lookout spotted four unidentified figures approaching from a distance and shouted his warning. "Strangers sighted!" he yelled while ringing the large alarm bell. A siren blared to alert everyone throughout the vast compound's streets and sidewalks; the loud bongs from the bell tower nearly deafened those nearby. Men and women called out for their children, grabbing them as soon as they spotted their wandering boys or girls.

Mochè dropped what he was doing and sprinted two blocks to the gate. As soon as another sentry spotted him, she shouted, "Manhig, four very large men wearing hoods with ropes binding their robes."

"Are they bearing arms?" he yelled back, skipping the steps to climb to the top of the wall.

"None visible, sir." The military salute was not customary

during emergencies, and Mochè now stood beside her.

"Can I borrow those for a moment?" he asked, reaching for her binoculars. As soon as he peered through them, the man-hig whispered to the guard, "They appear to be monks, giant ones at that," he said, hesitation in his voice. After handing back the field glasses, he spotted his division commander, Luke, and shouted, "General Luke, send out six fully armed riders to check them for weapons. Instruct them to look carefully under the robes they're wearing." Mochè quickly added his thoughts, saying, "Form a dozen cavalry riders for a scouting party to search the area for others."

After closely examining the four men, the leader of the six riders said to Mochè through his communication device, "Manhig, they are unarmed."

"Send them through the gate."

The four enormous monks knelt before the imposing figure of Mochè. "Master," one rose and walked close to him, saying, "We have heard of you and are mere, humble servants on a mission of the Lord to provide food and clothing to the poor and seek out those who cannot travel and bring them to places of sanctuary like yours."

"If you are a monk, you know it is blasphemy to call me master, as there is only one God," Mochè spoke softly to avoid embarrassing the monk who towered over him. The monk's manner of speaking puzzled Mochè. It was rough and jarring, more suited to a thug or hooligan than a holy man. His face was ape-like, covered with abundant facial hair, but enveloped within the large hood that concealed it. However, who was he to judge beauty?

"Forgive me, great Manhig. We have journeyed so long I have forgotten my brotherly—"

Mochè interrupted him and asked, "What is your request from us?"

"I am Brother Anthony, and I humbly ask only that we may enter and rest for a day and night under your protection."

"You and your brothers may enter and rest for as long as you wish." Mochè waved his hand gracefully, signaling for them to enter. "My general will personally escort you to comfortable quarters. You will dine with us this evening," he glanced up at the sun to check the time, "in about an hour." Mochè had a mechanical watch but preferred the reliability of God's nature for telling time.

"If it is your will, Manhig, may we have a tiny amount of bread now as we are fasting, then retire for the night since we are exhausted."

"As you wish. Please wait here while I inform my general of your wishes." Mochè placed his arm around Luke's shoulder and whispered, "Luke, take them to a holding area. Tell them it's our custom to check all visitors for demonic possession, and since they're so tired, I'll do it tomorrow." Mochè whispered even more quietly, "Have four of your best soldiers guard them closely. Something isn't right here," his mind racing as he searched his memory. "I've rarely encountered such colossal men who don't want food, and these monks are all enormous."

"As you wish, sir." Luke saluted and chose four of his best soldiers to escort the towering monks to a secure holding area. Mochè observed as Luke and his soldiers led the four brothers away. His sharp intuition sensed something was amiss, but he couldn't quite identify what.

Mochè had dinner with Zipporah as usual. She was polite and smiled sweetly, but didn't bring up or even acknowledge his comment from the previous evening about revoking the council's order for her forced marriage. Deep down, Zipporah believed that her love would never allow her to bed another man, and she prayed to God every night for His will to permit Mochè to marry her. "Did you have a good day, my love?" asked Zipporah.

"Four visitors showed up at the gate today," Mochè answered, rubbing his chin.

"You always do that whenever you're troubled," a smiling Zipporah said.

"Do what?"

"Rub your splendid chiseled chin like that," she giggled in a way that Mochè found innocently cute. "Are you worried about these new people? We always have those guided by angels coming to us."

Realizing his habit, Mochè stopped caressing his chin, sometimes believing this woman who captivated his heart was a sorceress. Then, realizing that type of intuition women only possessed, forced a smile on his face. "These four seem…" he still couldn't find the words.

Zipporah's stunning green eyes widened as if reading his mind, and it tortured his soul that he couldn't take her in his arms. "Perhaps it's only your imagination, my love. Here," she placed his plate of food before him, where he sat at his regular spot at the table.

"Thank you, Zipporah. For this meal, and allowing me to dine with you always."

Zipporah was now concerned as Mochè had never acted like this before; she had never seen him worried, always confident and assured of everything. "You're welcome, my love. I do it because I love you and always will, no matter what happens."

Her words pierced Mochè's heart, which was apparent in his eyes. "Zipporah," he whispered, reaching for her hand and holding it gently. "If you ever hear the emergency siren, lock your door and go into the root cellar I built for storing food beneath the floor near your cooking area. The wooden-slotted hatch blends in seamlessly with the floor, and you will remain hidden. Stay there until I return or send someone you trust."

"My love?" Zipporah didn't understand. "Do you suspect we are in danger?"

"Maybe," he looked at her in a way she had never seen before; it was a loving expression. "Please obey this one order I give you."

"I will, my love," her marvelous eyes beamed as she spoke.

"I always came to your house for dinner because before you, I never had someone to go home to. I don't know what I

would do if I lost you. I must leave at once. Come, Gershom."
The boy awakened immediately.

Zipporah sat stunned, realizing Mochè was worrying about her safety. "He truly loves me," she whispered after he closed the door behind him.

Mochè quickly mounted his horse and galloped away from the house, with Gershom trailing behind. He no longer trusted himself around Zipporah; the temptation to be with her had grown stronger than ever, forcing him to acknowledge his true love for her and the vulnerability he felt.

After calling his commanders for a short meeting and instructing them to fortify the compound's internal defenses, Mochè headed for his evening fireside chat with David and Andrew. His friends immediately sensed his anxious mood, which was out of character for him. Both of them noticed that their manhig was wearing his sword opposite his dagger. When he cut their conversations short, they understood that something important was troubling him that he apparently didn't wish to discuss.

As Mochè rose to leave, he told David and Andrew, "If you hear the bell ring or the siren, seek shelter immediately, my friends." That warning made the two wise men realize that something was indeed wrong.

As their manhig turned to leave, the emergency siren blasted, followed by the bell. "Seek shelter!" Mochè shouted back to David and Andrew; then he ran swiftly to the sound to help assemble his army, now sure that something had happened.

The thuds of arrows piercing each sentinel's chest were too soft for anyone near the walls to hear. Nor did anyone hear or notice the grappling hooks as they flew high and clung to the crest above the large gate near the fallen guards. Five armed males scaled the towering fortress and dropped inside. Two opened the gated passageway, allowing a horde of over four hundred giant, armed, and fierce-looking, unkempt raiders to run amok.

These bizarrely appearing males were extremely muscular, much bigger and brawnier than even the largest adult human males, wearing furs as clothing. At a closer look, one could see that they weren't men but hairy creatures. Around the ropes that bound their waists hung what appeared to be scalps of men and women. They were a gang of one of several forms of cannibal mutations that had evolved from the sins of humanity: beings that science had genetically mated with wild, beastly animals. Crouched over like gorillas, they roamed from place to place, satisfying only primal bodily needs of kidnapping people to devour as food, raping men, women and children, and pillaging. Like the wild animals they became, they harbored no morality or principles.

As they ran through the compound, five hastily-built wagons followed them, bouncing and jostling as their wheels jumped over potholes of the unpaved roads. The monsters' bulging, evil, reddened eyes glowed with delight as they sought out plump women and children for food, much like humans would shop for groceries. Many of the dirty, chilling brutes used their claws to pull women and pudgy men from the crowds of panicking people trying to escape their vulnerable homes in the darkness. With their enormous strength, the gorilla-like creatures violently dragged the ones they selected by their hair, some fighting over fattened men and women. The beasts quickly bartered in animalistic grunts, among others, for the ones they wanted. Pulling or carrying their choices, they raped them in the open of the shadowed streets, flinging the fatter women and plumper men into the wagons to keep for food. The beasts pushed the thinner ones aside, where the advancing herds trampled them. There, on the dirty roads or sidewalks, many women and chubby men tried to crawl away in shock until other beasts repeated those terrible, defiling assaults.

One enormous giant kicked in the door of the jail building that housed Amos, the prisoner doing hard labor for trying to molest Zipporah and admittedly raped other women. The monstrous beast reached and felt the pudgy flesh of Amos's belly.

The giant then headbutted the fat man into a daze. Ripping off his clothes in one sweep of its hairy, muscular arm, then bending over him, it raped the plump man mercilessly. Amos's bloodied head struck the wall repeatedly as the creature viciously molested him. The giant clawed at his chubby belly, tearing it open, and began devouring Amos's fatty flesh as he howled from the pain before succumbing to a fate fitting his past actions.

A giant spotted Eliza; her amber hair, shining gold in the moonlight, attracted him to her. That hair color was prized and would befit the other collected scalps on his belt. But the hazel-eyed, fair-skinned teenager was agile and quick on her feet; embracing her terror, she sprinted toward Zipporah's home on the outskirts of town. As Eliza ran, she briefly saw the brutal rape of a girl about her age from the corner of her eye. The giant beast grunted loudly and monstrously, pleasuring itself to the horrifying screams of the young woman. Then the grizzly creature snapped the spine of the girl over its knee, sounding like the crack of a tree branch, before it flung her lifeless body to the side. That horrifying sight made Eliza run faster, her tears spattering into the gloom of night.

Gabriela had been ordered to relay messages between cavalry and infantry brigades; her long, blonde hair flowed wildly as she galloped from town to town. Upon entering the town on the western side, where the gorilla-like beasts were advancing, a large, ugly claw grabbed her leg. Her horse reared, and she nearly fell into a horde of them. Holding tightly to her reins, the skillful rider swung the mustang she rode in a semicircle, knocking three beasts to the ground. Freeing herself from them, Gabriela rode on to deliver her message to Major Benjamin, who commanded part of his battalion in the west. As she skidded to a stop, halting her horse directly in front of Ben, their eyes met. For a split second that felt like forever, they gazed at each other, speechless, her deep blue eyes locked onto his piercing gray ones. Then, with a salute, she handed him the message and broke away, galloping off, her heart pounding not only from fear but also from love.

Bearing a sword in one hand and a dagger in the other, the wild, hairy beasts, quick for their size, spread and continued raping or killing anyone in sight as they began to plunder, spreading throughout the streets and sidewalks of the fortress. The beastly marauders moved fast and broke into homes, killing men and raping their wives in the darkness before a wounded soldier sounded the siren. "Take the plump women and soft-skinned men and as many fattened children to the wagon quick," one gigantic hairy savage beast roared in a deep grunting language only they understood. "Their flesh is tender—good eating!"

Leah daringly balanced on a rooftop, preparing to jump at just the precise moment. She carefully observed four massive, gorilla-like men. Leah waited until the timing was perfect and then leaped into the air, executing a dramatic backward somersault that landed her between the towering brutes exactly where she intended. Once there, her sword gracefully sliced in a swift 360-degree arc, disemboweling all four of them. As they howled from their gruesome injuries, Leah's agile body jumped again, her long, ebony legs wrapping around the necks of two more beastly men standing together. Before they realized what had happened, Leah slit both their throats. As they fell, the weight of one of the lifeless bodies pinned her to the ground. General Helen saw her in distress and sprinted as fast as she could to help, but she couldn't reach her in time. Two more hairy, brutal gorilla beasts approached, and one of them scalped her meticulously braided hair to take for one of his trophies. Leah sneered at the one who slashed her throat as she reached out one of her long arms and stabbed the top of his foot, securing him to the ground before she closed her eyes to death. Helen finished him off with a stroke of her sword while shooting the other with a solar sidearm. Then she kneeled before the body of the brave warrior and gently placed the beautifully braided, long black hair back upon Leah's head.

Mochè spotted one of his division commanders, Sarah, and shouted to her, "General, divide your forces and flank them on the sides before they spread too far. Use your solar weapons to stop them quickly. These giants are cannibals. I know of them; they eat the flesh of women and children. Use caution as they move swiftly for such large giants." Sarah raised her saber in acknowledgment, Mochè not realizing it would be the last time he would see her alive. Then he saw Joseph leading his division. "Joseph," he called loudly amid the screams and cries of his people and the horrible rallying howls made by the barbaric intruders. When he caught his general's attention, he shouted, "Joseph, bring your soldiers to cut them off at the front!" His commander followed his orders and rushed his warriors in single file along the edges of the horde to the front while Sarah's warriors weakened their flanks.

While her soldiers fought fiercely, a giant, hairy, muscular arm pulled Sarah away, slapping her into a stupor. As the grotesque, huge beast stood over Sarah and prepared to rape her, she kicked his groin, and the ogre folded over, groaning in pain.

"So, you feel pain down there just like normal men," she shouted while raising her saber and slashing off his head as he stood bent over. Then distracted for only seconds, Sarah didn't notice two other mammoth men quickly run behind her. One of the behemoths grabbed her by the neck with his immense arm, confining her as the other readied to take her in the same way as the now-beheaded other giant had. Sarah quickly drew her dagger, stabbed the one behind her, and then swung her razor-sharp sword, decapitating the ugly one before her as she shouted, "Nobody violates my womanhood, you bastard!" But Sarah didn't realize the beast behind her was still alive until she watched the glistening metal of his sword slowly appearing from her chest. Then she felt the agony of radiating pain from the saber penetrating her upper body and fell to her knees. With her last breath and final duty to God, Sarah, wielding her sword, sliced off the legs of the giant beast just below its knees. As she heard its anguished roars, Sarah collapsed sideways onto the ground, clutching the sword embedded in her chest. She softly whispered her prayers before facing her end in this realm of existence.

After he left Joseph, Mochè confronted Generals Luke and Helen and ordered their soldiers to spread out and check houses to stop home invasions. Mochè noticed the pillagers dragging another large wagon into the compound. He yelled back at Helen, who had already begun to follow his orders, "Send some soldiers to our supply buildings. Don't let these scavengers escape with any of our women or children; they are trying to capture them for food. They are cannibals! Guard all our stored possessions. Capture them all! I want them alive!"

"As you wish, Manhig," Helen raised her saber in acknowledgment.

Mochè looked up to the heavens and said, "Thank you, Lord, for your blessing of intuition." Following his instinctive feelings, he had ordered his commanders to deploy their soldiers throughout the compound. Thanks to their immediate response to those directions, Mochè's forces were quickly able to crush this raiding swarm of armed and vicious invaders. However, too many of his soldiers and civilians had lost their lives. Many women and men had died in their homes while fighting them, and the brutal creatures molested too many.

Mochè remembered the monks and ran to where Luke had placed them under guard. A small group of invaders quickly broke through the door and overpowered those guarding the four monks. The impostors instantly removed their cumbersome monk gowns, revealing their robust, hairy physiques, akin to the other beasts. They donned the furry animal skin outfits their accomplices had handed them before they departed to continue their assault. The pretending monks weren't expecting to see Mochè. As soon as he entered the holding room, he swiftly drew his razor-sharp sword and skillfully wielded it, disemboweling the first giant invader with a swift swing and thrusting his dagger into the chest of the second. He pointed his sidearm at the remaining two and shouted, "Brother Anthony, kneel before me with your other soldier of Satan!" The grisly, beastlike creatures grunted and then, seeing their comrades bleeding profusely on the floor, exchanged glances before dropping their weapons.

Mochè pressed a button on the radio device strapped above his chest and called, "General Luke?"

"Yes, Manhig," his voice replied.

"I have two more prisoners for you. I'm in the holding room where you brought our visiting monks."

"I'll send some soldiers over to get them."

"Before you do, what is the number of surviving intruders?"

"I'd have to do a head count, but I estimate about half remain alive."

"Have all commanders gather the surviving prisoners near the slaughterhouse, where the street is wider. Bind their arms and legs and have them kneel in the center of the street. They're dangerous animals, not humans; kill whoever moves."

"Yes, Manhig."

Mochè thought of Zipporah and rushed to see her, fearing the assailants had harmed her during the attack. Shockingly, he discovered that when the raiders opened the gate and breached the fortress, a horde of horned, cloven-hoofed demons had slipped in behind them before his soldiers closed it. About three hundred horrific ghouls now marched to a slow drumbeat inside the compound. "Lieutenant," Mochè called, pointing. "Gather those warriors over there and join me. Quickly!" he commanded as the young woman started to run. Within a couple of minutes, about 150 men and women were with him, with many more rushing toward him. Spotting a solar cannon, Mochè shouted, "Roll that out before them!" The thunderous blast killed about 50 of the demons, and the manhig and his soldiers fought the rest hand to hand as some demons dispersed in different directions. He saw Joshua nearby and called, "My friend, please go to Zipporah's home and check on her. Stray demons may have gone there since it's close by. She knows your voice and will come out of hiding."

"Yes, Manhig, I'll hurry."

Mochè resumed leading the battle against the demons.

"Take your platoons to their rear, Captain," he called to a young officer, and she quickly complied. "You, Lieutenant, split your platoon to attack each side of them." Mochè decided to encircle the monstrous, cloven-footed male and female demons as their grotesque faces sneered and raced forward. A painted demon woman raised her sword, bringing it close to Mochè, in an attempt to decapitate him. He swiftly sidestepped her and wielded his saber, splitting her horrible head down the center. The demon's wicked eyes bulged and blinked on each side of her divided face as if surprised.

As Eliza sprinted toward Zipporah's house, her weary, terrified eyes failed to notice the two demons lurking in the darkness. The hideous ghouls quickly seized and lifted her, their monstrous, painted faces grotesque. "No!" Eliza yelled. "No!" she screamed long and loud, struggling to break free from their grasp, kicking at them with both legs while the demons bound her arms with their repulsive, gnarled, cloven-clawed hands. Too exhausted from running for so long, Eliza couldn't resist and bowed her head, succumbing to their ghastly grip. From the corner of her eye, while praying for a swift death, she spotted a horse rider approaching rapidly. Dust from the horse's hooves floated briskly and dissipated into the darkness. Then, in the moonlit night, Eliza watched as the glint of a saber severed the head of one ghoul, then it backhanded and disemboweled the other.

"Take my hand, girl!" a deep voice bellowed. "Hurry!" Eliza gazed into the most beautiful yet rugged eyes she had ever seen, their deep blue color glimmering in a beam of moonlight. She grasped the large hand as the strong arm pulled her onto the horse behind the rider. "Hold on to my waist!" the same voice commanded. They galloped through the darkness until the horseback rider spotted a house. "We'll stop there to rest my horse. I've been riding too long," he shouted back to Eliza.

Recognizing Zipporah's home, Eliza exclaimed, "I know the woman who lives there!"

The rider removed his feet from the stirrups, swiftly lifted his leg over the horse's neck, and gracefully jumped to the ground before helping the girl off his horse. He hadn't been able to see Eliza in the darkness, but now, bathed in a full ray of moonlight, he could see how beautiful she was and recognized her as the one he had secretly admired for so long. "My name is Matthew. I'm a cavalry lieutenant commanding a platoon in General Jeremiah's Army."

Eliza ran into Matthew's arms, tears trickling down her face as she cried, "Thank you, Matthew. I thought I was food for the demons," her body trembling from the shock of the close call she had just experienced. In the brighter light of the moon, she could now see that his beautiful eyes complemented the other features of a remarkably handsome face she finally set her gaze upon, though those chiseled features seemed familiar. He was the handsome young man she had seen at her manhig's sermon. She gently kissed his lips in gratitude. "Come sit while I call my friend."

Eliza approached the door, but it was locked. "Zipporah!" she called softly to avoid arousing any stray demons, but there was no response. She walked back to Matthew and said, "I don't think she's home; no one is answering."

Now able to admire the full beauty of the young woman he had mistakenly thought was just a girl, Matthew nobly said, "I'll stay with you until your friend returns." He removed his short cape and gently draped it around the quivering young woman he had secretly loved but was too afraid to approach. Then, realizing his forwardness, he added, "I-I," losing himself in the hazel-colored eyes of this stunning, amber-haired vision of beauty and recalling the softness of her lips when she kissed him, now entranced as he gazed into her eyes. "I thought you were younger, I mean, a girl, but you're…"

"I'm what?" Eliza giggled, noticing that this handsome, brave young man was nervous.

"Older than I thought, and—" he fought against the anxiety that washed over him. He had been in many battles and had never felt such fear—"you're lovely," the words flowed effortlessly from his lips as he stared into her strikingly beautiful and radiant hazel eyes.

"Thank you, Matthew," her full lips parted in a manner that Matthew found ravishing.

Before Matthew could respond, he heard the sound of footsteps approaching. Quickly drawing his sword, he whispered to Eliza, "Wait here; don't move." He dashed toward the sound and called out in a commanding voice, "Who goes there?"

The running man stopped to catch his breath. He replied, "I am Joshua, second to the manhig."

Matthew approached him and introduced himself after saluting, saying, "I'm sorry, General Joshua, I didn't—"

"Don't be sorry. You did the right thing by asking," he smiled at the tall, well-built young man. Extending his arm for a handshake, Joshua said, "Nice to meet you, Matthew."

"It's an honor, sir."

"Have you seen Zipporah, the woman?"

"She doesn't answer, sir."

"I'll try," Joshua replied. "She knows my voice." He walked up to the door and shouted in his deep voice, "Zipporah! Zipporah?" After waiting, he called out again, "Zipporah! It's me, Joshua!" Then, he heard noises coming from inside the house.

Zipporah appeared and ran toward Joshua's arms, shouting, "Oh, thank God!"

Joshua and Zipporah spoke briefly away from the others as he reassured her about Mochè's well-being. Then he said, "I must go. I'm leaving this lieutenant with you until I can send someone to replace him." It was at that moment, Zipporah noticed Eliza with a young officer. Matthew couldn't offer his horse to Joshua because it was against regulations for a cavalryman to relinquish his horse under any circumstances during a battle, even to a superior officer, unless he was wounded.

As Mochè continued his assault against the hooved demons, a huge horned fiend charged swiftly toward him, its red eyes bulging and pus and snot dripping from its flattened, ox-like nose. In the chaos of battle, Mochè didn't notice the approaching threat. The demon hurled a spear; it flew fiercely and directly at Mochè, who turned too late to dodge the sharpened lance. In that split second, his twisting body froze as he braced for certain death. He then watched as Gershom flew through the air at an unnatural speed, the spear piercing his body. As another warrior moved to destroy the ghoul who had thrown the lance, Mochè dropped to his knees beside the boy, his sword still clutched in his hand. He told him, "You sacrificed your life to save me. Why, boy? You're too young." Mochè began to weep.

Lying on the ground beside the man he had always followed, Gershom spoke for the first time. Yet it was a different voice—deeper and blessed as if an angel could articulate the words of humanity: "I have fulfilled my mission, Manhig. Now, I may return to my Lord." Before departing from the body he had hosted, he told Mochè, "The Lord is pleased with your long devotion to Him. He knows your struggle to restrain yourself from the woman in honor of Him." The boy's eyes now shone with bestowed grace. "He loves you, Manhig, and has decided that it would be best for you to wed and bring other souls into this world. He offers you this gift: keep your priesthood but marry the young woman Zipporah and take her as your wife." His breathing slowed as he delivered his final words: "Now, may she be by your side in my place." Mochè remained kneeling, shocked by the experience.

A blazingly bright light encircled the area, yet it didn't hurt the eyes of those nearby, nor did they flinch. The angel's body began to rise before Mochè and the others, witnessing this divine moment, then dissipated.

Mochè looked up to the heavens and whispered, "Thank you, my dear, faithful companion," as tears streamed down his cheeks. When Mochè rose from his knees, the demons lay defeated and spread dead in the streets. His warriors stood still around their manhig. All had witnessed the miracle and heard the angel speak; now, they began to kneel in prayer.

Mochè noticed the tense expression on Joshua's face as he hurried back from Zipporah's house, his sword dropping to his side in fear. Dreading the worst, he stood in shock, preparing himself for the terrible news.

"The woman is unharmed." Joshua's breathing strained from the exhaustion of running so fast to tell him the good news. "I left a guard in case of stragglers."

Mochè exhaled with relief, frustrated by his mistaken belief. He raised his eyes to the heavens and said, "Thank you, Lord, for answering my prayers. I should never have doubted you." He told Joshua, "I appreciate that you brought this wonderful news so quickly, my friend." Then he asked, "Where was she?"

Joshua answered, smiling, "She obeyed your instructions and waited in the cellar. She wanted you to know that."

"She is alright then?"

"She's fine, sir. The woman was worried about you, so I told her you were unharmed and waited until she calmed down. As I mentioned, I posted a sentry." Joshua, now fully recovered from running hard, said, "Oh, there was already a young couple there. A young cavalry officer, whom I assigned as the temporary guard, and a teenage girl named Eliza. She appeared to be the young woman you rescued from banishment."

Mochè smiled and said, "Thank God. Yes, she is that young one, blessed by God once more."

Chapter Six

Retribution

The sun boldly peeked over the distant mountains beyond the compound, its powerful, golden rays bursting through to clear the gloomy fog of the early morning. Mochè prepared to summon his council to judge the remaining captives. His people demanded swift justice for the wrongs committed by the wicked giant beasts. As Mochè readied to leave for the courthouse, his second-in-command, Joshua, presented reports detailing the casualties among his followers.

Joshua bowed his head in sorrow as he addressed his manhig, "Sir, we lost Isaac and General Sarah," his voice trembling with despair. After steadying himself before Mochè's shocked eyes, he whispered, "Also, the young warrior Leah has perished." Gathering his thoughts, Joshua softly added, "You remember the tall, ebony young woman you recommended for that surveillance mission we—"

"Of course, I remember her courage and loyalty." Mochè's words were unsteady with despair, hoarse from exhaustion. With a tear in his eye, he waved his hand and said to Joshua, "I can't take any more right now. Tell me the rest later."

"Yes, Manhig. There were far too many for such a sudden raid. We all mourn their losses."

"Inform the council I have decided to replace Isaac and Sarah with their seconds in command." It broke Mochè's heart to utter those words, but he was the leader. He repeatedly had to make decisions that weighed heavily on his emotions. "Notify them to prepare for the trial. We can only guard the large number of these beasts for so long."

"Yes, Manhig."

Throughout the night, Mochè had pitched in to help rebuild and repair some of the damage caused by the raid, promptly addressing essential emergency needs. Solar lights provided visibility for the guards as they surrounded approximately two hundred prisoners, whose arms and legs were bound to prevent any escape attempts. They remained on their knees, exhausted from being in that position for so long. The stench of feces and urine from the large group of husky, hairy giants permeated much of the compound. Mochè visited some of the homes of those who had lost someone, comforting them and assuring them it was over, but there were far too many. Laborers began digging graves for the dead in preparation for the following day's funeral mass and Christian burial. He ordered the bodies of the wicked pagan cannibal hordes and the demons to be set ablaze well outside the compound. He didn't want the dust or fumes of their spirits near his people.

Mochè hadn't slept at all the night before as he sat in his judge's chair behind the large oak desk at the head of the council, directing them to proceed. The loss of Isaac by his side and Sarah's lovely yet bold face at the council weighed heavily on his heart. He appointed Deborah, Sarah's second-in-command, to replace her as the general of her army and take her seat on the council. Sadly, Mochè replaced his old friend Isaac with the capable Aaron as head military strategist, who also took Isaac's seat at the council.

Mochè pounded his hammer and declared, "There will be no one to represent the beasts who have taken the lives and virtue of so many of our men, women, and even the innocence of our children. They are not human, and we know their deeds." He gazed at the heavy faces of those crowded in the courthouse, many of whom listened from the doorway and filled the street in front of the building, eager to learn the punishment for those who had wreaked so much havoc. "Our physicians are tending to those harmed physically and mentally, and the council is here only to deliver a sentence," Mochè asserted his authority on the matter. All the attendees could see the distress of their manhig as he spoke those words. Cheers and cries of satisfaction rang out, for they did not want a trial for the beasts who had committed such ungodly acts.

The hammer in Mochè's hand pounded again, and he declared, "There will be silence in this court before God. What we do here is not for revenge or our pleasure. We do it as an act of judgment."

Joseph, a general and council member, stood and declared, "They murdered and committed impure acts against many of our people, which constitutes, alongside assault and murder, adultery. For these combined crimes, their punishment must be far worse than banishment. If we simply banish them, they would regroup and commit the same offenses, if not here, then elsewhere." Out of fear of Mochè's hammer and his anger, the crowded courtroom remained relatively silent, though murmurs of agreement could be heard.

"I agree," said Deborah. "I lost my commander during this plunder, and many brave young warriors died in the skirmishes that followed, including Leah, one of our finest." The new councilwoman gathered her thoughts and continued, "I vote that they remain bound and stripped of their clothes, just as they did to many of our people before committing their despicable acts. Then, they should be paraded before the demons and have their legs bound."

Aaron, newly appointed, rose from his seat and, looking at Mochè, he reasoned, "Manhig, it is a logical thing as we know you frown on executions and the taking of life. This way, we leave their fate in God's hands."

"They will devour them, Manhig." A council member spoke from her seat.

"I agree with Deborah and Aaron," said Joseph. "They are not human, and cannibals who consumed the flesh of many of our people and were ready to take others, and they committed other inhumane crimes. It is only fitting that we allow the demons to consume these ungodly flesh-eaters. If it were up to me, I would have them basted in our finest sauce for the demon's meal!"

Mochè felt exhausted, his emotions completely drained. His people demanded justice that reflected the severity of the crime, and they were right. Although the manhig could pass sentence without the council, he was their leader and didn't want to appear dictatorial. He had learned much from Eliza's unfair sentence, but he agreed with the proposed punishment. "So be it then. I would normally say, may God have mercy on them, but these wicked mutations aren't human; they're followers of the Dark Angel." Mochè struck his hammer before proclaiming, "We will bind them naked and drive them like cattle to the gates of a nearby demon stronghold. They are like demons in spirit, anyway." He pounded his hammer again and declared, "The sentence takes effect immediately. We can't hold this horde much longer. Court dismissed."

Mochè called over Joshua, Helen, and Aaron. "Prepare a party of about five hundred to outmatch those we take. You three are the commanders; I will lead. Be ready within an hour. Send a scout to locate the nearest gathering of demons."

The burly beasts assembled, lying down after trotting about ten miles. Their excessive body hair was matted with sweat as they recovered. The scout had located the closest gathering of demons, numbering about three hundred. The condemned sat licking and rubbing their blistered feet while soldiers moved among them, tying their ankles with strong hemp rope.

"Take one of these beastly invaders aside to make him bear witness to what we will do to anyone who tries to attack our people again," Mochè told Helen. "Select the monk, Brother Anthony, who spoke so eloquently to me at the gate when they first arrived, and we'll release him to spread the word to others like them."

The attractive young blonde-haired general, Helen, walked among the bound, naked, hairy men with a contingent of her soldiers. She remarked, "Look at how they try to cover themselves with modesty," as each beast shielded his groin from her view, "as if they possess virtue after what they did to our women, who will be scarred for life!" she shouted. Her anger surged before her lips curled into a smile. Standing close to one of them, she laughed while glancing down and said, "For such large males, they have tiny genitalia." The shapely-figured general pointed at what one of them desperately tried to conceal. The colossal man, seemingly understanding her, blushed angrily and appeared embarrassed from the humiliation. The soldiers near her couldn't contain their laughter.

"Are you through here, General Helen?" She didn't know Mochè was standing behind her.

"Yes, Manhig," Helen blushed, wondering if the manhig heard her comments.

"Are all the prisoners bound?"

"Yes, Manhig."

"Alright, send some riders to wake the demons. They're probably sleeping after one of their orgies. We can begin to back away slowly when we see them getting close to the condemned."

"They'll be very hungry when they awaken," Helen smiled.

Mochè and Helen rode back to where Joshua and Aaron sat mounted on their horses.

All Mochè's troops remained mounted on the crest of a slope less than fifty yards from the bound prisoners, watching as the demons slowly advanced toward the two hundred condemned individuals. Helen and Aaron stayed mounted beside Mochè while Joshua moved a bit closer.

The huge, muscular, hairy gorilla beasts screamed as the

terrifying creatures drew nearer. Some tried to hop away, but most tripped and fell, prompted by their large, unbalanced bodies. The demons caught up with those who hopped a little further. Their screams turned into screeches as the claws of the horrific, deformed-hoofed, beast-like males and females brutally tore the bound bodies apart alive. Many of Mochè's gathered warriors gagged at the spine-chilling and repulsive sight of demons devouring the flesh of the terrified, hairy prisoners; their screeches transformed into cries resembling those of infants. As the demons feasted, the last remaining beast invader stood beside Mochè, the one who spoke for those who pretended to be monks, now tied like a restrained dog, with a long rope leading to General Helen's hand as if he were her pet.

The grisly, giant beast urinated a high-arched stream of urine from the fright of witnessing the ghastly slaughter of his comrades. Then, the muscled, hairy beast lost control of his bowels, fearing he would be next. The stench of the enormous pile of dung from the giant was appalling. It spread among the assembled troops, all holding their noses against the putrid odor of the digested remains of the human flesh he had consumed of Mochè's followers. "Please," he grunted in his deep voice, "let me go as you said. I beg you." His hairy face showed the terror he felt.

Mochè looked down from his high horse and asked, "So, Brother Anthony, how did you learn to speak so well?"

"I learned to verbalize from a captive we kept. We held her long enough to teach the few of us capable. She resisted at first—a tiger—but we used our methods to make her comply. It took time; she was a wild one." The beast-like creature's fear melted into a smile as he recalled the female warrior captive, unable to restrain the darkness within him. "That's how we learned about you, Mochè, and your people."

"You feigned being a holy man, a monk. That's unholy, Brother Anthony. You're nothing but a wicked gorilla beast devoid of a soul." Mochè rattled the last remaining beast purposely to get more information.

The giant became enraged by Mochè's remark. Even in his fearful state, his uncontrollable wickedness erupted as he bellowed, "We worship Satan, who made us what we are!" The beast, resembling an ape, sneered at Mochè and shouted, "That captive was one of yours." He grinned as he continued, "After she finished teaching me your language, we roasted her alive and devoured her. The ebony flesh of her body was tender and delicious. I ate her face cheeks—a treat for us."

Mochè urged his horse closer to the large creature and demanded, "What was the name of the captive?"

The gruff beast looked around before starting to run, struggling to free himself from the rope around his neck. However, Helen yanked back on the leash. He dropped to the ground, gagging. After catching his breath, he gasped hoarsely and whispered with a sinister smile, "The woman with ebony skin was named Naomi."

Furiously, Mochè shouted to a soldier, "Tie a rope to this creature's ankles!" As his anger intensified, he yelled, "Drag him close to the demons while they're still feasting."

"But you said you'd let me go!" the beastly gorilla shouted as the soldier fastened a long hemp rope to his ankles. "You told me I could leave!" he screamed. The evil beast had no conscience; it couldn't comprehend right from wrong and only questioned Mochè's integrity based on its understanding of human traits, like any other wild animal in the wilderness.

"I changed my mind," Mochè said, nodding to the soldier. "Take him to the demons and leave him there so they can devour him as he did to one of our warriors!"

"No! No!" The creature's cries were long. Its voice faded as the soldier's horse, dragging the bound beast, trotted closer to the demon horde, its colossal body bouncing and pierced by stones and sharp, fallen branches. With his words now faint, Mochè and his command could hardly hear him say, "You're supposed to be a man of God."

Mochè brought his horse close to Helen and whispered, "I don't want anyone to know that these beasts devoured Leah's sister, Naomi." His eyes glared, still filled with anger at hearing that.

"Yes, Manhig," Helen sighed, "it could dishonor their memories."

Mochè's detachment heard only the distant sounds of weeping as the soldier dropped the rope and quickly rode back. Then, the shrieks of the last survivor filled the air.

Helen asked Mochè, "Should I gather all troops to return to the compound, Manhig?"

"No! Let them witness the sentence carried out in full so they can share the verdict they desired with others at our compound."

It wasn't until just before the evening of that gruesome and exhausting day that Mochè arrived at Zipporah's house for dinner, as usual. A male suitor was riding away. According to the council's ruling, single men were permitted to call on her. However, most intimidated by the manhig, chose to stay away from the beautiful young woman, speculating based on all the gossip that he was interested in her. When the departing man spotted Mochè, he kicked his horse and galloped away quickly.

Zipporah heard Mochè's horse and ran barefoot to him after peeking through the small window. "Oh, my love, I've been worried all night and day!" She could hardly contain herself and leaped onto Mochè as soon as he dismounted, her legs wrapping around his thighs and her arms clinging to his neck. "Oh!" she exclaimed, "I lost my composure." The young lady quickly hopped off his tall, robust figure, her eyes wide and sparkling with that glamorous color as she awaited the reprimand from her manhig. "I'm so sorry, Mochè," she said, blushing. "It won't happen again; I just got caught up in my happiness. I have food ready," she added, hoping to change the subject.

Mochè ignored her words and slipped his arm around her shoulder, completely surprising Zipporah, who rolled her eyes upward in astonishment, wondering if Mochè was okay. He then led her to the door and smiled, saying, "I couldn't help but notice a man riding away as I approached."

"Yes, Manhig, I am obeying the council's orders of making myself available to all those young men interested in me."

"How many have there been?"

"A great many, Manhig," seeing Mochè look in the direction the young man rode, she smiled, loving his envy. "You're not jealous, my Manhig, are you?"

"Of course not."

"Thirty-five men have proposed marriage to me," she said, her face serious. "I wanted to get your opinion on them," she continued earnestly. "I have notes on each of the ten I've considered. We can review them together after we—"

"Thirty-five men? Never mind that right now, I-I," Mochè stammered nervously after interrupting her. Zipporah's womanly aroma mingled with the scent of her perfume, soothing him as he affectionately said, "I was just thinking about how wonderful it is to see you after such a long time. I mean, last night and today and everything that has happened." That remark stunned Zipporah even more, but she instinctively caressed his muscular arm draped around her shoulder while in a trance-like state.

After entering the home, Mochè nearly collapsed into Zipporah's arms. "Oh! My love, you're exhausted. Come, sit in the cushioned chair and rest," she said, guiding him to it. Mochè sank into the chair. "I heard about all those who died and the trial. No wonder you're so tired. I honestly didn't expect you so soon, but I'll set the table." Zipporah turned and smiled at the sight of the man she loved, fast asleep like a baby in the pillowed armchair.

It wasn't until two hours later that Zipporah heard Mochè stir restlessly in the chair before he rose and stretched. "How long have I been asleep?" he asked with a smile directed at Zipporah, admiring her beauty as her eyes sparkled and her lips formed an ever-so-elegant grin, her magnificent gaze meeting his. It sent a chill down his spine, yet he still hadn't revealed to her the wonderful gift that God had bestowed upon them both. "Joshua told me you hid in the small cellar. I'm so glad you did;

it was awful out there," he said, staring in a daze as he recalled his night and day.

"I obeyed you, Manhig," she chuckled, adding, "only this once." Then Zipporah became serious and told Mochè, "I held onto the holy crucifix you gave me, praying the entire time." Her eyes were wide yet focused and solemn as she said, "I prayed more for your safety, my love, than for my own, and for those poor people I knew were being killed and hurt outside." A tear rolled down her cheek as she spoke.

"I understand you had other visitors yesterday before your gentlemen callers?"

Zipporah's piercing green eyes rolled with thought until they gleamed, and she said, "Oh, you mean Eliza and that sweet young man, Matthew." She smiled at Mochè, adding, "Don't be jealous, my love. Shame on you. He's practically a boy. Oh! But he saved that dear child, Eliza's life."

"He did?"

"Yes, the poor thing was traumatized in the middle of town by what those ungodly creatures did." Zipporah's eyes widened as she told the story in a lovely way that made Mochè's heart flutter. "Then, while she was running here, demons grabbed her. The child thought she was doomed until Matthew swooped her onto his horse and galloped away to bring her here." Zipporah's enchanting eyes rolled again, imagining how romantic that was. "She told me in private it felt like something out of one of the storybooks her mother read to her when she was little," Zipporah offered a bewitching smile and said, "Isn't that cute?"

"He didn't take advantage of the circumstances, did he?" Mochè asked in a paternal tone.

"Of course not! How could you ask such a thing?" Instantaneously, Zipporah's eyes narrowed like a cat as she replied, "He's very respectful, a true officer." Then Zipporah whispered, as if someone were nearby, "I think he and Eliza…you know, are fond of each other." She beamed a wide smile. "Eliza was making goo-goo eyes at him the whole time they were together. It was so obvious."

"Look who's talking!"

"I love you; that's different."

"Where is Eliza now?"

"I sent her over to Maya's home for dinner."

"Why didn't you let her stay here?"

"Because I wanted to be alone with you," Zipporah whispered seductively. Mochè believed this was the best choice since he needed to tell her about God's blessing and wanted to ask for her hand in marriage in private.

Mochè, feeling nervous about proposing marriage, cleared his throat and said, "I see."

"By the way, where is Gershom, the boy who always accompanies you?"

Mochè frowned as he recounted only part of the story, "He died by my side in the battle with the demons." His eyes revealed his remorse.

Zipporah placed her hands on her cheeks and exclaimed, "Oh no! He was so young," as a tear rolled down from one of her strikingly beautiful eyes.

Mochè gently held her in his arms to comfort her, now openly feeling pleasure from her soft body, still amazed by God's miracle but not yet ready to reveal that blessing to Zipporah. Observing her purity and beauty, akin to a master artist's painting of an angel, and feeling her soft skin, most men would have succumbed to her enchanting charm long ago. But he was no ordinary man; Mochè was the manhig, anointed by God to lead his followers. Having been a priest since his youth, he felt apprehensive. How could he act romantically like a man who had loved a woman for so long? He didn't know how.

Mochè had come to know Zipporah well, cherishing her beauty, unique traits, and the little quirks that everyone possesses. He savored the subtle details about her—how her eyes brightened, causing a slight twitch of her nose just before she parted her full lips to speak, revealing her perfect teeth—only his ears caught a hint of a lisp as she carefully pronounced her words—always admiring the way Zipporah walked, not with strides but floating like a gentle summer breeze, warm and tender—and at times, the way she looked into his eyes broke his heart. These simple qualities, among many others, had become endearing to him, but her impossibly dark green eyes were too beautiful for him to ever fully comprehend. He needed to find the strength to finally express his true feelings. Constantly battling strong temptations that nearly overwhelmed him, and now with God's blessing, he still didn't know how to touch her lovingly, hold her, or what words to say.

"Come, my love," Zipporah said, leading him to his regular place at the table, believing his troubled expression stemmed solely from Gershom's death. "Perhaps dinner will help ease our sorrows," she remarked, wiping away her tears as she spoke.

"All this time, I believed I was protecting him, but it turns out he was sent by God to protect me." Those words just flowed from his mouth.

"What do you mean?" Zipporah asked, looking perplexed as she spoke over her shoulder while preparing dinner.

"He was an angel of our Lord who saved my life." Zipporah didn't hear him; she was preoccupied with the stove, clanging pots and pans.

Halfway through their dinner, Mochè took out a captivating ring from his pocket to show Zipporah. It had a stunning dark green gemstone set into it. "Oh, Mochè, it's so beautiful! Is it yours?"

"It belonged to my mother. It's an emerald jewel," he explained softly.

"I've never owned jewelry," Zipporah said, her eyes in a daze, idolizing a gem so unobtainable to her. "In fact, I've seen very few pieces, but this ring," she couldn't take her eyes off it, "is stunning." She smiled and returned to her meal. When Zipporah glanced back at Mochè, he was still holding the ring, saying nothing and not eating. Concerned, she asked, "Are you okay, my love? You're not eating."

"It's for you, Zipporah."

Her eyes sparkled at the sight of such a glamorous gem, but then she said, "That gorgeous ring? For me? Oh no, I could never deprive you of something so valuable. You've already given me your father's crucifix, a treasured family heirloom."

"Oh, Zipporah, I sincerely apologize," he said, shaking his head. "I realize that I'm not handling this properly, given my limited understanding of these matters," he continued, sounding frustrated.

"What matters, my love?" She smiled at his awkwardness but also at the eloquence of his speech.

After thinking for a moment, Mochè found a way to make her understand his intentions and exclaimed, "Why don't you let Eliza live here after we get married and move into my house?"

Zipporah's body froze, remaining as still as a statue. Her glorious green eyes, which always conveyed so much, were now silent yet wide and serene as though in a trance. Zipporah was in shock, unable to communicate. "Ar—" was all her lips could articulate.

Suddenly, recalling a book he had read long ago, Mochè quickly pushed back his chair and stood tall and straight. He walked over to where Zipporah sat and knelt beside her. As she remained frozen in shock, he declared, "I love you, Zipporah; I always have since the first time I saw you. Will you marry me?" Noticing her expression worsen, he nervously said, "I'm really sorry for upsetting you. Let me get you a glass of water and a—"

Zipporah's small, delicate hand reached for his arm as if it were even possible to hold back such a burly man. Her eyes looked into his as she desperately tried to speak. After a full minute, her gaze fixed on his and her tiny hand attempting to grasp his wrist, she began to articulate her feelings. Although her words fragmented into syllables and were not entirely clear, an agitated Zipporah exclaimed, "How dare you toy with me, especially over such a delicate matter! This is about what I said regarding my gentleman caller—" Mochè interrupted her, impulsively yet gently cupped her face in his hands and pressed his lips firmly against hers, opening them with his and kissing her passionately.

"I'm so sorry for forcing that. I didn't hurt you, did I?" Mochè whispered, asking.

"You're—not joking—with me, are you?" Zipporah asked, her words breaking up with nervousness.

"No, I'm not."

Still struggling to vocalize her thoughts, Zipporah swept his long black hair back and drew his head close to hers, kissing him as she asked, "How—why—now?" She desperately tried to make sense of it all after her numerous failed attempts.

Mochè told her about the boy's death and the miracle of God's gift. He wouldn't admit he was afraid to ask sooner and merely said, "That's why I asked you now for your hand in marriage."

"And you didn't think to tell me this sooner? I could kill you!" But after he slipped the stunning emerald ring onto her petite finger, she fell silent and returned to kissing him, breaking away only long enough to whisper, "I think I'll keep you instead."

Mochè playfully asked, "So, can we discuss the top ten of those thirty-five male suitors now?" Zipporah didn't respond, remaining secure in his embrace, kissing him as she intended to for the rest of her life.

"Mochè!" David exclaimed as he saw his leader approaching their campfire. "We've heard about your horrendous and stressful day."

"How are you?" Andrew chimed in, his curiosity noticeable yet mostly overshadowed by concern. Noticing the dazed look on Mochè's face, he said worriedly, "Sit by the fire, my son. Relax and warm your hands on this chilly night."

"I'm fine, my friends. There's no need to worry about me. I just had a long day." He didn't mention his proposal to Zipporah. Still reeling from kissing the woman he loved, caressing parts of her body that were no longer forbidden, and feeling emotions he had never experienced before, he needed to find the right words.

"No doubt you had a long day from what we heard," David declared.

Andrew realized the best way to help his friend forget that terrible night and day was to engage in a good conversation. "Did you know that centuries ago, many years before David's and my great-grandparents were even a twinkle in their parents' eyes, people used screens to watch things that entertained them?"

That topic seemed to pique Mochè's interest, much to the delight of both David and Andrew. "Was that before they started using AI?" Mochè inquired. "I recall my father mentioning those devices." After spending time with Zipporah and all that had happened, his studies temporarily receded to the far corners of his mind, which remained in a state of love stupor.

"Oh, it began long before people violated God's laws by pushing the limits of AI," David explained. "Initially, they went to places to enjoy such entertainment, and then people brought devices into their homes."

"I know, but I can't envision the places they visited. Where did they congregate in the buildings? Did they stand?" Mochè became even more intrigued.

Andrew took the floor from David and described the scene: "They sat in rows of seats, raised so that viewers could see a giant screen."

"Well, initially there were live performances on a stage, much like in the grand Roman Colosseum of ancient times," David clarified, nearly competing with Andrew now. "At first, it was mostly wholesome and pure," David explained, the diminutive yet stout man standing to emphasize his points. "But it quickly became corrupted and led people away from God's teachings."

"It depicted adultery acted out. People reenacted what these 'actors' did and became adulterers themselves; it influenced them deeply," Andrew frowned. "A sad chapter in the history of humanity."

"Yes," David confirmed. "It was a sin that created a rift between them and God, marking the beginning of the end. That version of what was once referred to as the media of entertainment had many other harmful influences that encouraged people to engage in even worse behavior." David sat back down to warm his hands by the fire.

"My father passed down stories from that same era. He told me that other types of those things called the media drew women to do other barbaric things. After committing adultery, many women got pregnant and would destroy their babies while they were still growing inside them. I could never fully understand that," Mochè said. "The science of that time encouraged it."

"Oh, yes, they did," Andrew elaborated on Mochè's statement. "You see, everything bad begins with acceptance of it, like in the Bible when Eve took a bite of the apple. She enticed Adam into believing it was okay." Andrew shook his head and delved deeper into the subject. "You see, Mochè, whenever tyrants from that long-gone era committed murder, they used softer terms like 'euthanasia,' which means happy death, or 'the final solution' when one dictator exterminated millions of people."

"That same philosophy eventually evolved into the killing of babies, my friend," David said. "They referred to it with a much softer and gentler definition: 'termination,' then, closer to the end of civilization, it became known as 'conclusion.' It turned into a convenience that aligned with the culture of that time. They wanted to have children on their terms rather than by God's. Some women who had undergone such 'procedures'—another soft word—found it impossible to conceive after waiting. Many of them later struggled with depression in their lives." David thought before adding, "It was an unnatural human act, and an unholy one in God's eyes."

"Yes," Andrew said, "It's an unnatural phenomenon, but it began slowly, as all things do; Satan always works in stages, baby steps, as some called it then. First, they took the early embryo. That led to the destruction of late-stage pregnancies and, finally, the killing of newborn babies. Believers in God opposed this, but the masses succumbed to the rights of many." Andrew let out a sarcastic groan, adding, "They claimed to put all those embryos to good use; they mixed what would have been God's children with chemicals and created medicines that ironically only harmed humanity."

"It's a hard concept to believe in times like these," Mochè said, "when we're desperately trying to bring new souls into an underpopulated world of believers to counter so many evil ones."

"Sadly, they no longer believed in God; they felt they didn't need Him," David simplified the situation. "That's when Satan employed his demons. They entered the souls of many humans like they always do when humans are at their weakest."

"Man's inhumanity to man always existed," Mochè declared, his eyes flickering and half-closed from fatigue. "The inhumane, brutal acts against our women last night were committed by animal beasts. There was a time, centuries ago, when humans did worse. I remember that one occasion occurred around their marked year of one thousand nine hundred forty-five. During a war that spanned the globe, a supposedly organized army of humans surrounded a city. With the blessings of the commander of the great country once called America, he allowed thousands of soldiers to be unleashed upon the defenseless females of that once great city. They raped hundreds of thousands of women, some repeatedly." Almost in a doze, Mochè watched the dazzled expressions of his two friends. "Yes, my friends, humanity always did dirty deeds. There were many such mass rapes in the years around that one. The concept of humans killing their young goes back to the barbarism of ancient times. We are nothing more than weak vessels without the grace of God. Humanity always lived among demons."

"It's an unfortunate truth, and during that period, centuries before our time, only a few believers experienced miracles. They were the only ones who encountered angels like those that guide us now," Andrew nodded in agreement. "Well, I think our manhig has had enough cheer for now." Mochè had fallen asleep and was now snoring soundly like a big baby.

Hearing his name, Mochè's eyes snapped open, and he came to, saying, "Yes, I've had enough for one day." Still groggy, Mochè stood up and, while smiling, said, "Thanks for the enlightening conversation, even if it was extremely depressing."

"You mean you've had enough for both a night and a day, my friend," Andrew replied, returning a smile.

Mochè yawned a smile as he walked away and announced, "Oh, I almost forgot to mention, I proposed to Zipporah."

"We thought you would once Gershom became an angel and bestowed you God's gift," David chuckled as he called out to his departing manhig. "That's why we didn't ask you where the boy was!"

Mochè didn't look back; he simply waved his hand. "You guys learn about everything sooner or later; sometimes I think you know more than I do. I wouldn't be surprised if you both were angels."

An intense brightness surrounded him before Mochè arrived at his home in the center of the compound. Engulfed in that familiar light, he realized a messenger of God was present, and he knelt before that divine presence. Whenever an angelic being communicated, it was not through words but deep within him; the world around Mochè fell silent. There were no sounds of conversation, tender words from couples preparing for sleep, or crying children. He knelt in the heart of nothingness, smiling and embracing the instinctive feeling guiding him. The heavenly angel told Mochè that God commanded him to keep his people at the same stronghold for the winter.

Chapter Seven

The Expedition

At dawn, his council already gathered, Mochè addressed them, "Along with far too many others, today Father David, Father Andrew, and I presided over the funerals of Sarah, my dear friend and was an undeniably accomplished general in our army," he stated, a tear rolling down from one of his dark, deep blue eyes. "And Isaac, a friend and father figure to me since before the start of this journey, who also fell while defending us." More tears streamed down his cheek as he recalled the unspeakable tortures inflicted upon Isaac before his death. "Among those we've lost, I buried Leah, a young and glorious warrior of God, just like her sister, Naomi, who vanished from us years ago and whom we now fear is dead." The members could see their leader's distress in his mannerisms and shared in his pain. Yet he sat upright, his voice strong and unwavering—like a true leader. "Knowing that they and the others are now with God brings me comfort, yet I will miss them dearly, as will most of you. This grief we feel is a part of our humanity, and only time, with the help of our Lord, will heal it." The number of his people had slightly diminished due to that beast attack, followed by the demon battle. However, new travelers arrived daily, seeking the man known as Manhig.

After his introduction, Mochè opened the floor for discussion. "I'm open to suggestions and recommendations," Mochè declared, seated in his judge's chair behind the large oak desk at the head of the council. Following the funeral mass and burial of the fallen followers, he had summoned the members to discuss better ways to secure the compound where so many had perished two nights earlier. "I commend the army, its officers, and soldiers for their meticulous performance. We were prepared, and my questions focus on how we can improve our methods to keep intruders out from the start, so we don't have to fight in the place where we raise our families."

"I recommend a continuous presence of cavalry patrolling outside the gates day and night," General Jeremiah suggested.

"I agree," General Deborah quickly declared, the youngest and newly appointed commander in the army, asserting her authority. "Perhaps we should construct smaller, camouflaged forts outside the stronghold to encircle it. This would enable us to deploy our forces and alert our main army even faster."

"Excellent!" Mochè exclaimed, smiling at her diligent expression, confident he had made the right choice in appointing the young brigadier as full general to replace Sarah. "Let's hear more!" The ideas already presented brightened the manhig's spirits and lifted him slightly from his somber mood.

The conversations continued as new ideas emerged, many of which were established over the next two hours. During that time, Mochè realized that, for the first time, he was constantly distracted by the image of the beautiful Zipporah. It felt as though she were standing before him, and his longing for her intensified. He couldn't get her out of his mind after holding her in his arms, feeling her body and kissing her. The thoughts swirling in his mind made him realize he had to marry Zipporah as soon as possible.

Before adjourning the meeting, Mochè announced, "A blessed heavenly being appeared to me last night. God directs us to remain at this fortress throughout the winter. We will use this time to prepare for our departure in early spring." Soft murmurs and cries of relief spread throughout the courthouse. Everyone who had traveled from the Unknown Territory fortress to this massive stronghold understood the challenges the move would entail and felt safe in this fortress they had called home for over five years. "Inform all generals who are not present here to convey that decision from God."

After the meeting, Mochè pulled General Jeremiah aside. Once they were out of the others' listening range, He asked him, "Jeremiah, do you have a lieutenant leading a cavalry platoon named Matthew?"

"Yes, I do, sir. Matthew of the family of Tamstone."

"I don't recognize the name."

"He doesn't come from a military family, sir."

"I'd like to see him. Could you send him over? I'll be here for a few more hours." After a few seconds, he added, "Unless you have him on patrol or assigned elsewhere."

"No, he's with his platoon in my town, inside the compound," Jeremiah replied, looking puzzled and wondering why his leader would inquire about one of his lieutenants. "Has he done something wrong, Manhig?"

Mochè smiled and replied, "Oh, no. He actually did me a great service."

"Ah," Jeremiah replied, feeling relieved, "I'm glad to hear that."

"Is he a good officer, Jeremiah?"

"He's a fine young man and an outstanding officer, particularly for his age."

"A natural, eh?"

"He is, sir."

"Would you mind if I promoted him to captain, provided I find him suitable after we meet?"

"Not at all. Unfortunately, I lost two of my cavalry captains and a major the other night. Matthew is a brave and dedicated young man at just 21 years old. He deserves it." Jeremiah smiled, still looking perplexed, and asked, "May I ask how he served you, Manhig?"

"Of course. He saved the life of a young woman, who is still a teenager and means a lot to me."

"That's Matthew: brave and noble to the core—the epitome of a storybook knight in shining armor." Jeremiah chuckled.

Eliza and Zipporah, on their way to gather items for Zipporah's wedding dress, stopped when they saw Mochè surrounded by a group of children. He was teaching them about the Bible and religion, as he usually did, personally conducting classes each week. His words were loud enough for everyone to hear, yet gentle and calm enough to captivate the little ones as he said, "Today I want to tell you about a special woman named Mary." He smiled. "Are you all ready?" After their unanimous, cheerful responses, he began, "Through Mary, we learn to surrender to God's will in all things." He paused, observing the intrigued expressions of the little boys and girls, then continued, "In Mary, we learn to trust even when all hope seems lost. From Mary, we learn about Christ, the Son of God." Mochè grinned, knowing he had connected with them on their level. "As his mother, Mary was closest to our Lord in his early life and knew of his mission of redemption before anyone else."

Mochè continued to captivate the children with that message and other stories from the Bible. He joyfully shared with the gathering how much Jesus loves them and how important they all are to Him. When it was time to conclude, the children clung to the manhig, wanting more stories. He noticed a little boy gazing intently at his dagger, which gleamed in the sunlight. He asked the boy, "Do you like weapons, young Timothy? Would you like to serve God as a soldier like your dad?"

"Yes, Manhig," Timothy's smile beamed.

"Always remember this, my boy: we battle Satan's non-human demons and beasts in an uncivilized world." Looking down at the eager eyes gazing up at him, he continued, "But the rosary of Mary is our most powerful weapon."

Timothy, still beaming with his smile, replied, "Yes, Manhig. My dad taught me that."

"Next week, kids, we'll resume," Mochè said happily, turning his attention back to the children tugging at him, all eager for more stories, aware that these innocent kids were absorbing God's words.

Lost in the crowd, Mochè didn't notice Zipporah or Eliza, who remained nearby, watching him teach and playfully mingle with the kids as they returned from the schoolhouse after finishing classes earlier that day for shopping. Eliza was now Zipporah's assistant teacher-in-training, and Zipporah regarded her as a younger sister. While teaching many children and some adults separately, they held classes throughout the seven sections, or villages referred to as towns, of the expansive compound on different days of the week.

Smiling as she watched the manhig, Eliza softly said, "Looks like he'll make excellent father material."

"I know," Zipporah giggled. "He will." Her eyes widened with excitement. "I can't wait!" She turned to Eliza, linking her arm with hers. "He sees you as the daughter he's never had," she said, smiling into the eyes of the older teen girl she had come to love.

A tear rolled down Eliza's cheek as she spoke from her heart, saying, "I think of him as the father I never had. He's been so wonderful to me. I never experienced that with a father in my life before." Gazing deeper into Zipporah's eyes, she lovingly told her, "And you, Zipporah, how kind and generous you've been to me. I've never had a friend before."

"Well, now you do, sweetheart," she said with a wide smile, "and a loving father, too."

Mochè walked away from the children, his mind already swirling with ideas for the arduous task of preparing for the upcoming winter months. His overburdened thoughts were also consumed by the journey in early spring, moving further west, getting closer to the place of redemption where they would build another stronghold once they reached the location to which the angel would guide him. While glancing at the distant hills and mountains and envisioning the roads his caravans would travel, he focused on those heavy thoughts to give his mind a break from dwelling on Zipporah and her loveliness.

"Manhig?" General Helen smiled at Mochè, deep in thought as always. He hadn't heard her the first time, but now she could tell she had caught his attention.

"Helen, hello," he smiled. "I thought someone was calling me." Then his expression changed to one of uneasiness and he asked, "Is something wrong? Is there a problem?"

"No, no, Manhig, everything is fine." She paused, reconsidered her words, and corrected herself. "That is, everything is as normal as it can be after we've buried so many of our loved ones."

Mochè knew his generals well and could sense that something was on Helen's mind. "Is there anything I can help you with, Helen?" he asked with a smile. Helen was a remarkable woman: intelligent and an exceptional military leader. Ever faithful to God and protective of His followers, she could be kind and caring but quickly shifted her focus when duty called. Helen was also beautiful in every sense; the demands of her job and training had sculpted her body into a marvel, her face a beauty with wide blue eyes. She sometimes wore her long blonde hair up while in uniform, but off duty, she always let her lustrous mane flow freely, complementing her ravishing eyes. Now, gazing at her strikingly breathtaking appearance in a colorful dress that highlighted the contours of her figure, Mochè wondered why she had never married. He fought to resist the urge to admire her cleavage and shapely legs, which most men couldn't help but glance at.

"No, Manhig. I'm okay," she said, scrutinizing his eyes and noting how they admired her body, feeling inwardly happy that he did. "I was just thinking about Sarah. I never expected her to fall in battle; I always thought she was invincible." Helen smiled to conceal her true feelings.

"We're all mortal beings, Helen. You know that. What's truly bothering you?"

"You're very perceptive, Manhig," she replied, now grinning.

Mochè smiled and said, "I think it's time you stopped calling me manhig. We've known each other since you were a sergeant." He reflected on Isaac and continued, "I asked that of Isaac." Glancing up at the heavens, he added, "But he never would. Neither will Joshua."

Helen smiled and replied, "I don't think I can, sir. It's your position. God appointed you as the manhig, and I feel I must honor that symbol. It's like a military rank."

"Sometimes, it makes me feel really alone, as you can relate to with your rank as a general."

"You'll be married soon. By the way, congratulations on your upcoming wedding, Manhig," she smiled, concealing her envy well. Most of the younger single women in the compound were drawn to the towering and knowledgeable leader, Mochè. It was truly his intense inner spirit that attracted people to him, projected through his stunning blue eyes. "Zipporah's a very fortunate young woman."

"Thank you, Helen."

"Manhig, the thing is…well," she paused awkwardly, which was so unlike her. "I know you and Sarah were close friends, and I-I hope we can be the same."

A smiling Mochè took Helen by the shoulders, softly kissed her on the cheek, and said, "Helen, I already regard you as a dear and faithful friend." Then he commanded, "Stop calling me manhig!"

"As you wish, Mochè," she giggled, enjoying the feel of his hands on her bare shoulder and the pleasure of his lips. But most of all, it was the loving attention he had given her. "Let's see how I can manage to call you that," she laughed, responding to the man she had secretly loved since the day they met without ever revealing her feelings. Knowing she would see Mochè, Helen had chosen her most seductive outfit. She hoped he would find her more appealing than Zipporah and become available to her. Helen had dreamed of the day she could feel his hard, toned body since she first laid eyes on him, and privately, she had often touched herself to erotic orgasms just thinking about being with him. The young general longed to have children with Mochè, the man she adored, wanting to pleasure him as much as she knew he could satisfy her.

As Mochè and Helen stood near the courthouse, a rider approached, his horse galloping. When he saw Mochè, he quickly dismounted, dramatically raising his leg over the animal's neck instead of in the usual way, and ran toward him.

"Well, I see you have some business to attend to," Helen smiled. "Goodbye for now, Manhi—" she changed her wording, grinning wider, and added, "I mean Mochè." She glowed radiantly like a woman in love, still struggling to conceal her secret desire.

The young cavalryman stood and rendered a bold military salute to a startled Mochè, who thought this rider carried urgent news. The young man then bowed and said, "I came as soon as I received word that you sent for me, Manhig. I am Matthew of the family of Tamstone, platoon lieutenant under General Jeremiah." After delivering his eloquent words, the young man stood at attention.

Recalling Jeremiah's amused description of Matthew as brave and noble, Mochè had to suppress his laughter at how spot-on his general's words were. He forced a serious expression and addressed the young man, "Yes, Lieutenant, I wanted to meet you."

Now concerned about why the manhig wanted to meet him, Matthew respectfully stated, while remaining at attention, "I hope I haven't disappointed you in any way, Manhig." The young man's gaze was directed above Mochè's eyes, not directly at them, as was customary for a subordinate soldier.

"At ease, Lieutenant," Mochè said with a slight smile. He continued, "On the contrary, I wanted to meet you to commend you. You did me a great service."

Matthew's stature only relaxed slightly. He was not at full

ease, and his expression was bewildered as he spoke. "I did, sir?"

Mochè extended his arm, firmly grasping Matthew's shoulder, and answered, "You did, son," in a fatherly tone. "You saved the life of a young woman whom I consider a daughter and who is very important to me."

As if a light ignited in Matthew's eyes, he realized the manhig was referring to Eliza, the young woman who had stolen his heart. "Yes, sir. Eliza," he instinctively smiled as he spoke her name. Then he cleared his throat, wiped the smile from his face, and said boldly, "It was my duty as an officer, sir."

Immediately, there was something about this young cavalryman that Mochè liked, unaware he was seeing a reflection of himself at that age. "Come," he said, still holding onto Matthew's shoulder, "let's talk in the courthouse." With his arm now around the young man's shoulders, he led him back to the building near his children's Bible class. Kids were still playing and running around, waiting for their parents.

Losing himself in the children's laughter, Matthew recalled his childhood, impulsively smiling as he said, "I remember you teaching me back in the Unknown Territory, Manhig."

"Yes, Matthew, I remember you now." His advanced, God-given intuition recalled the studious boy who was so different from the others. He was a devoted follower of the Lord, with intelligence and resources far beyond those typical for his age. Seeing the boy transformed into a brave, noble, well-built man, almost matching his prominent height, Mochè felt a sense of pride.

As they sat together in the courtroom, Matthew noticeably relaxed in response to Mochè's soft-spoken words and presence, as if he could see divine power flowing through him. In this man, who was less fearful than his reputation suggested, Matthew found a comfort that reinforced his strong beliefs in everything he did for God. "Do you like the cavalry?" Mochè asked among other trivial questions, trying to get a feel for this young man.

"Yes, Manhig, I do. I feel natural riding a horse; I like their quick responsiveness in battle," he answered, his eyes reflecting the adrenaline rush of it.

"I'm afraid you're no longer a lieutenant in my cavalry, Matthew," Mochè said with a stern expression. His eyes locked onto the young man sitting before him, and he observed as if almost Matthew's soul seemed to lift from his body.

"I-I," Matthew stuttered, filled with despair. "As you wish, sir, but I don't understand," his eyes looked as if he were pleading.

Mochè noticed this young soldier's loyalty even in the face of his own despair. This was the final test he conducted. "Jeremiah, your general, speaks very highly of you." This only confused Matthew more, as he couldn't understand why he would be stripped of his rank yet still receive praise from his general.

"Yes, sir?" Matthew replied almost mechanically, stunned by the shock of the situation.

"I was considering you as captain," he noticed life return to those dejected eyes and continued, "but I no longer believe that's a good idea."

Matthew now realized he was being tested and merely replied, "Yes, sir," in his commanding military tone, obeying his manhig.

"I think it would be best that you serve as a major, leading the captains' companies in a battalion of one of General Jeremiah's cavalry brigades. What do you think?"

The young officer's intense shock was unmistakable, and he couldn't immediately find the right words other than "Thank you, sir."

"You'll be serving under Major Benjamin, one of my best cavalry officers and the second in command of the brigade you will be assigned to. Learn from him, Matthew."

"I know Major Benjamin; he's a friend."

"Congratulations, Major. You deserve this. I'm not doing it because of how you honored me, but because of your commanding general's opinion of you, Matthew. Never betray the trust that he and I have placed in you."

While kneeling and lowering his head, facing the floor, Matthew spoke, "I vow to you, Manhig, I will never disgrace this honor you give me this day. I will forever remain faithful to your orders and those of my superiors, and never renounce God or his glory."

As Mochè stood in the doorway watching Matthew depart, he noticed Zipporah and Eliza walking nearby. In the time it took to wrap up with the children and finish his conversations with General Helen and Matthew, they had completed their shopping and were returning with sacks and boxes. Ready to assist them, Matthew beat him to it. Mochè smiled as he observed the young man, clearly love-struck by Eliza, take all the packages. After calling for a military wagon, he instructed the driver to load everything and bring the two women home. Then, Matthew swiftly mounted his horse with style and galloped in the direction he had come, gallantly waving to the women as he passed the wagon. Leaning against the beam of the courthouse doorway, Mochè whispered, "I think I made the right decision," and smiled before closing the door.

Eliza lived with Zipporah until her marriage, after which she would take the home as her own. When Zipporah informed Mochè of that decision, he immediately replied, "It's not safe for her to live there alone at such a young age."

"Oh, she'll be fine, my love," Zipporah smiled in a way she knew Mochè couldn't resist. "Maya is just a stone's throw away, and besides, more houses are being built in that area every day." Noticing that Mochè still wasn't completely convinced, she reassured him, "Your daughter will be just fine, my love. I see her often, and she has other friends now, too; Rosetta is one of them. You remember her: the Italian girl around Eliza's age who taught me how to make that risotto you love so much? Don't fret so, my love."

"Hmm, I suppose—"

"It's already settled. Stop stressing; Eliza needs to spread her wings. She's at the right age to marry." Zipporah then thought that Mochè wasn't ready to hear that and began to say, "Of course, with your permission, Moch—"

He interrupted her quickly, insisting, "I don't want her to see any unescorted young men in that house if I agree to this."

"Of course," Zipporah assured him, knowing him well and that he was thinking of Matthew.

Matthew often found reasons to visit Eliza, but he never did when Mochè was around. As a true cavalry officer, he carefully scouted the area before knocking on their door. Matthew noted Mochè's schedule for occasional lunches and regular dinners, avoiding those times like the plague. He often visited in the mid-afternoon, claiming he was in the area. Zipporah, a romantic at heart, thought it was sweet but always watched closely when Eliza and Matthew were together. They usually went for short walks. One day, she saw Matthew peck Eliza on the cheek. Over time, that gentle kiss grew into a more passionate one. Zipporah often talked with her young protege and was convinced that Eliza had learned her lesson about adultery. Matthew was a kind and caring young man who would never succumb to that most grievous sin, nor would he disgrace himself before Mochè, as he had vowed. Still, Zipporah knew that Matthew, like all men, could control himself only for so long, and she anticipated wedding bells—likely not long after her own marriage. She had to find a way to break that to Mochè gracefully and in due time.

Gloria, the head physician, approached Mochè a few weeks before his wedding as he walked toward the courthouse where his office was located. "Father, I would usually make an appointment, but my matter is urgent."

"Certainly," replied Mochè, extending his arm and gesturing for her to enter the building. Once inside, he said to Gloria, "Please take a seat and let me know what's so pressing."

"Father, my staff is extremely short on the herbs needed

to make our homeopathic compounds for medicines and treatments."

"Was this caused by that raiding party?"

"Yes, after that recent attack, I had all the sectioned towns conduct a thorough inventory. Many items were destroyed by those raiders, and far too many other supplies were and are still being used for all the injuries and infections we—"

"Forgive me for interrupting you, Gloria, but I understand, and with winter not too far off, time is of the essence."

"Absolutely."

"I'll need several of your staff to identify the right herbs you will need. An escort party will be prepared immediately to protect them. Leave your physicians here," he said, fearing they might be captured or killed.

"If it's alright with you, I'd also like to join."

Mochè regarded Gloria with the respect she deserved for volunteering for such a dangerous mission but replied, "I understand your passion, Gloria, but I can't allow that. You're far too important here, especially now with so many still recovering from their wounds from that attack." She knew Mochè didn't want to explain how vulnerable the party would be to demons and other mutated beasts like those they had recently faced.

A dejected Gloria reasoned, "I guess you're right, Father. Besides the physical injuries, many women and men are still suffering from the immoral things those beasts inflicted on them." She sighed, "I have them on natural antidepressants and remedies to help them sleep as they recover from those horrible things done to them. Many of the herbs for these ailments are among what we desperately need."

"When will your selected staff be ready to travel?"

Gloria considered the supplies and instruments they would need for the excursion and asked, "Would it be best to travel at dawn?"

Mochè considered the vicinity and other factors and replied, "Let me discuss this with Aaron, and I'll get back to you. In the meantime, prepare your people, and I'll assemble an escort party."

Shortly after Mochè began his journey from the fallen city of the East, God blessed his physicians with the knowledge of natural medicines. They thoroughly studied natural ingredients and developed medicines to replace the chemical compounds that immoral companies had profited from and manufactured out of greed, mirroring those found in God's natural garden. Mochè's doctors utilized these blessed medications to cure all diseases. Cancers and other ailments that once killed millions, along with the tainted treatments that exacerbated them, had been completely eradicated and had become merely a bad memory of the past's wickedness. Mochè realized how important this mission was to gather the essential ingredients.

After speaking with Gloria, Mochè sent for Aaron, who arrived quickly. He stood before him, and after rendering a military salute, he asked, "How can I serve you, Manhig?"

"Aaron, I already explained that we'll be working closely together, and it's not necessary to salute me every time I call for you," Mochè smiled.

The tall, slender 52-year-old man, who replaced his dear friend, Isaac, had been a brilliant general before Isaac appointed him as his second in command, so military behavior was usual for him. "I'll try to remember, sir; this position is new to me."

"Okay, I want to organize an escort party for Gloria's assistants to find some much-needed herbs for our dwindling medicines. I want a cavalry unit with battalion strength—a smaller one—four companies of about five hundred cavalry soldiers." Mochè paused and continued, "Choose General Jeremiah's army for this. What time do you want to start the journey?" Mochè was testing Aaron, and he knew it.

"I suggest we send out an advanced cavalry scouting party of platoon strength at early dawn when the light is low enough to conceal themselves if necessary, but still adequate for visibility. They should ride hard to assess the area for any nearby enemies and report back. If all is clear, we should be ready to leave then. But understand this, Manhig: such a mission might take a week at this time of year, possibly longer."

"Very good, Aaron. Go straight to General Jeremiah and ask him to assign an officer of his choosing to lead."

"I'll head out right away, Manhig," Aaron said as he hurried out of Mochè's office.

A cavalry unit assembled to the size Mochè requested was ready at dawn. Approximately five hundred mounted riders lined the wide street leading to the main gate. At the head was Matthew, the commanding officer. Mochè stood beside Jeremiah and asked him, "So, you think Matthew is the best choice?" He privately worried about the young man now leading a battalion for the first time.

"He is, sir. I chose him for this because he's very resourceful," he smiled before continuing, "and it will give him a chance to prove himself before his older subordinates."

"It's your call, Jeremiah. I hope you're right."

As was customary, many people from the seven towns lined the streets to cheer on the departing expedition. Among them were Zipporah and a proud Eliza. Matthew kept his gaze fixed ahead as he ordered the lieutenant beside him to ride to the back of the force and ensure that all companies were ready. The lieutenant rode off and soon returned, confirming the preparedness of his command. Matthew then pointed to the senior guard at the large gate, signaling him to open it. The massive wooden portal slowly lowered over the moat.

Matthew glanced to his side and noticed Eliza blowing him a kiss, which was a bit embarrassing, though only Zipporah witnessed it. Nevertheless, deep within him, the young commander's heart pounded with delighted satisfaction, cherishing Eliza's loving gesture. At the loud thud of the gate hitting the ground, Matthew commanded, "Forward! Slow pace!" Amid the crowd's deafening cheers, he rode through the opening, leading his five hundred cavalry soldiers who guarded the wagons carrying the medical assistants between them.

Later that night, as Zipporah sat with Mochè having their dinner, she seemed somewhat despondent. "What's wrong, my love?" Mochè couldn't help but notice her mood. "Zipporah?" Mochè reached and took her hand in his.

With her head bowed, Zipporah's eyes were tearing. One drop fell, delicately splashing on the table next to her plate. She looked at Mochè, her usually bright eyes now reddened, and said, "I have something to tell you."

"What is it, Zipporah?"

"After I first met you, I never told you everything that had happened to me, Mochè." She didn't use 'my love' as she always addressed him, and Mochè knew what she wanted to express, unable to at the time because of her state of shock.

With her hand remaining in his, Mochè told her, "There is no need to discuss what happened to you before we met, dear woman. Knowing that you, who are beautiful in body, mind, and spirit, love me is enough."

Zipporah sniffed as her tears flowed. "I must. I wanted to tell you so many times before but with the wedding plans and—"

"I know what those despicable, wicked men did to you, my love. My eyes have come across it often in this fallen, heinous world," Mochè spoke in broken words because his mind had retained such awful things so long. "Your lips have no need to say it; I can spare you that. The pain of that which lingers within you, I'll comfort every day of my life. You will heal from these dreadful memories that tear at you while being my wife. When we marry, I will wait until you feel ready."

Zipporah's deep, vivid-colored eyes ceased crying and remained wide, staring into those of the man she loved dearly. Her small hand gently caressed his face as she said, "I never thought I would find comfort in a man until you freed me." Zipporah's loving gaze held his as she told him, "I remember these." She gently touched his lips. "When they passionately kissed mine for the first time, it ignited a fire within my body." She smiled and said, "I've never felt more loving pleasure than when you first held me and felt my body. Each time we madly kiss, my body trembles, not with fear but with erotic ecstasy." Zipporah passionately kissed the man she was to marry. "I feel ready now. Your words have healed me, my love. I'm no longer afraid of giving myself to you."

Matthew's first command faced no significant threats except for a few stray demons and small bands of looters and thieves who quickly fled at the sight of the large assembled cavalry. Other than the scouts Matthew had sent out to scour the countryside for any trouble, most soldiers dismounted while Doctor Gloria's assistants searched peacefully, finding all of the medicinal herbs they needed.

Matthew rested on a patch of grass with his company commanders, surrounded by the vibrant hues of nature during a season when fall colors captivated humanity with their striking transformation. He chewed the tip of a fresh blade of grass, savoring its raw freshness as he lay in contemplation, absorbing the fragrances of late-blooming flora. The early setting sun painted a magical kaleidoscope of orange and deep yellow against a rich blue sky. The tranquility of that moment prompted Matthew to think of Eliza and living with her in the ideal world he had only read about—the place that had once existed. It must have been wonderful to coexist in those splendidly peaceful days before humanity's greed destroyed nearly everything God had created. Matthew pursued his daydream of seeing that young, beautiful woman he cherished in a future setting, smiling as he lovingly watched her with their children, their little faces not yet formed in his mind, relishing any part of that imaginary reflection he could.

"Major!" a captain shouted to him, impelling him out of his loving trance, forcing him to face the reality of the dreadful place now called the world and his duty to God in that wasteland.

"Yes, Captain?" His powerful voice lacked any hint of the precious setting where his mind had just wandered.

"Distant cries of combat, sir!"

"Hand me your binoculars, Captain, quickly now." As his eyes scanned the flattened plain below the hill where he stood, he heard the distant, echoed cries of a single man fighting. Looking closely, he noticed what looked like a lone figure battling a horde of cloven-footed demons. As the gentle breeze carried the sounds a bit closer, he listened as the large, dark-skinned man shouted in a language he didn't understand. "Captain!" he yelled, "quickly prepare thirty riders to escort me into battle." Turning to another captain, he shouted, "You are in temporary command. Send a rider," he pointed down the incline, "if anything at all happens here while I'm gone."

"Yes, sir," both captains replied respectfully, almost in unison.

Matthew galloped toward the cries of the man who was single-handedly battling numerous demon beasts, with his thirty riders trailing behind. Remarkably, the tall, large, ebony-skinned man had already defeated at least twenty of God's enemies before Matthew and his men arrived. Matthew's party swiftly eliminated the rest in just a few minutes. "Are you alright?" he called out to the large black man, unsure if he would understand the language.

The man dropped a beautifully decorated shield, unlike anything Matthew had ever seen, along with a lengthy spear with a wide, tapered, razor-sharp blade at its tip. He stood as tall as Matthew, wearing a feathered headdress and speaking with a dignified accent that Matthew had never encountered before. "I am Nikanyiso," he said, pointing. "My heirs come from a distant land over there."

"Are you harmed, Nikanyiso?" Matthew couldn't pronounce the name as the man did, with what sounded like clicking sounds.

Nikanyiso laughed, revealing his full mouth of white teeth at Matthew's poor pronunciation of his name. "You can call me Nick, like most people do," he replied to the tanned white man with a handsome and noble face. The man clasped his hands together and said, "While I appreciate it, I didn't need any help.

My ancestors were great warriors, and I honor them by using their fighting skills and dressing as they did in battle." He was muscular, with a striking face that radiated dignity. He removed the ornate headdress and handed it to a woman who was running toward him from a thicket of wild bushes with two young children following her. "This is my family: Rachel, my wife, and my son, Joseph. And this little one is my daughter," he said, lifting the small child into his arms, "Mary."

"I'm Matthew, the commander of this cavalry battalion." He nodded at Rachel and smiled at the kids before asking, "Is there any way I can help you, Nick?"

"Thank you," Nikanyiso bowed slightly. "I am searching for a man called the manhig. A holy heavenly being has guided us this far."

Matthew smiled and pointed to Gloria's team of assistants spread out near his encampment. He told Nikanyiso, "If you can wait until my people are finished, I will take you to him." Matthew looked to the sky and said, "In the morning, we will travel." Nikanyiso nodded in agreement. "Join my commanders for our evening meal," Matthew said, extending his arm in a gesture of friendship, showing Nick his encampment.

"I will hunt our dinner," Nikanyiso declared.

Matthew held the man's arm, saying, "No need, my friend. We have plenty of fresh meat already brought in by my hunters."

"Ah, I see you are great warriors as well," Nikanyiso said, his eyes admiring the weaponry of Matthew's soldiers.

"Yes, we are trained by Manhig, who was taught by the blessings of God himself."

Nikanyiso declared, "I wish to serve God through Manhig."

"As do we." Matthew grinned at the fascinating man he stood facing.

"Then we will serve together, my friend in Christ."

"That we will."

Chapter Eight

An Autumn Wedding

After Matthew introduced him, the tall, ebony-skinned man bowed before Mochè and respectfully proclaimed, "Manhig, I have traveled far, guided by a heavenly being, to see you." Lowering his head in respect, he continued, "I am a descendant of great Zulu warrior chiefs from generations past and centuries ago."

Mochè smiled but immediately grasped the muscular man's upper arm, lifted him from his kneeling position, and said, "You are welcome here, my friend, but we do not bow before anyone except the Lord."

The man stood near the same commanding height as he did and answered, "The humility of an outstanding leader whom I will always follow and obey. My name is Nikanyiso."

"It's good to see you, Nikanyiso," Mochè pronounced the name flawlessly, impressing both Nikanyiso and Matthew, who stood beside him.

"To speak my name like a Zulu, truly, you are blessed by God," Nikanyiso called out to his wife and children, who had been riding in the wagon with Gloria's staff. As the shorter woman trotted along, followed by the boy and little girl, Nikanyiso introduced them: "This is my wife, Rachel, and my son,

Joseph." The tiny girl's legs worked hard to keep up with her brother, taking longer to reach their father, who then said, "And this is my Mary."

Mochè swooped up Mary and greeted her first, saying, "Hello, Mary. Are you a servant of God like your father?" Mary nodded with her thumb in her mouth. Then, Mochè turned back to Rachel and said, "I'm sorry, Rachel. Welcome! I always fall for the little ones first," he smiled. "Not like this young man." Bending down, he extended his arm to shake hands with eight-year-old Joseph and asked, "Hi, Joseph. Are you as good a fighter as your father?" That prompted a roar of laughter from Nikanyiso.

"I'm learning, Manhig," the boy said, his face sporting a serious expression.

With his arm extended to welcome his newest followers, Mochè instructed Matthew, "Major, find Aaron to locate family quarters for these fine people." Before the young commander left, he pulled him aside and asked with a smile, "How was your first battalion command, Matthew?"

Matthew smiled and replied, "It went well, sir. We completed our mission with minimal issues."

"How did it feel, though, son?" Mochè's smile grew even wider.

"Magnificent, Manhig," Matthew beamed with joy.

"Great! Go now and get these people set up. Oh, there's a particular young lady who's been pestering me with questions about your return."

Now blushing and looking sheepish, Matthew said, "I'd better see General Aaron to get these people settled at once, sir. I'll take them to the holding room over there," he pointed. Then he quickly mounted his horse and rode off, saluting while still blushing. Nikanyiso and his family headed for the holding room as instructed.

Mochè laughed heartily and rejoined the group. "I'm over here!" he shouted when he heard Gloria, the head physician, calling for him.

"Father!" she exclaimed excitedly, then corrected herself, "I mean Manhig," her face reddened at her mistake, "sorry. I—"

Still laughing cheerfully at Matthew's lovestruck response, he told Gloria, "I'm still a priest, Gloria. You can call me Father," aware that those of his followers, who always addressed him as a priest, were now questioning whether they should keep doing so since he was getting married.

"Oh, okay!" she smiled and asked, "How did everything go? I rushed here as soon as I heard the command had returned." Turning her head in amusement, she added, "My staff isn't here; I think I passed them in my excitement. They must have already been on their way back to their towns."

"Well, Matthew told me right after he dismounted that the mission was successful. They found everything you wanted."

"Oh, wonderful!" She sounded as joyful as a schoolchild leaving the classroom. "Did they encounter any problems, Father? Was anyone hurt?"

"Matthew hasn't given his full report. It's customary for him to do so with his commanding general. However, he noted that aside from a minor skirmish with a group of demonic beings, nothing significant took place." Mochè considered that for a moment and then told her, "They did come across a new family of followers, though." His own statement prompted him to realize a few things, and he advised Gloria, "You should have someone check them for any diseases; we don't want to expose the communities to illness."

"I'll have someone do that as soon as possible. In fact, I'll do it myself while I'm here. Are they in a holding area?"

"Yes, they're in the one a block away waiting for Aaron." Mochè thought for a moment and said, "I should go with you to check them for demonic possession since they all had contact with demons." Demons could cast their weapon of possession from a close distance, especially if that human's soul was weak from combat or in spirit. Mochè noticed that Gloria wasn't listening to him; she remained in her private mental space, savoring the joy of having all her new herbal remedies once again.

"I see you're in your glory, Gloria," Mochè chuckled at his pun. He was in a good mood. "Come, I'll walk with you over to them."

Before he and the head physician reached the holding room, they watched in horror as the building's door blew off and floated in the air before crashing to the ground. Nikanyiso stood between the broken beams of the devastated opening that had once been a doorway, looking completely unhinged. Wooden splinters, fragments, and other remains of the building's entrance clung to his body and hair. "Doctor," Mochè yelled to Gloria, "Stay here until I'm finished." A terrified Gloria ran to the side of the walkway and crouched down, hiding from the horrifying sight of the large, fierce black figure with glowing red eyes, poised to attack anyone in sight.

Mochè spotted a squad of twelve soldiers marching nearby and let out a loud whistle using his fingers to his lips to catch their attention. When the soldiers recognized him, they rushed over. He commanded them, "Tackle that large man and restrain him. I need to cleanse him of demonic possession at once!" Mochè prepared his holy water, crucifix, and anointing oil. Knowing this would be a larger-than-usual battle, he unfurled a long, wide brown scapular and blessed it with the holy water that dripped from his fingers. Mochè draped his rosary around his neck and was ready to confront the father of demons, Lucifer, his enemy.

The soldiers looked terrified at the enormous man hunched over, his body twisting in every direction, and his face contorting into the grotesque mask of a savage monster. Their sergeant shouted, "Encircle him widely and then close in!"

Nikanyiso's large teeth grew longer and sharper, stretching over a long red tongue that dripped with saliva, transforming into those of a wild beast—a wolf. His reddened eyes bulged, nearly popping from their sockets as he snarled at the soldiers forming around him.

"Move in quick!" the sergeant roared. "Grab him and hold him firm!"

Now a hairy beast, Nikanyiso hurled the first one like a little girl's doll. Another warrior hopped to the rear of the raging man-turned-beast and seized him around the neck, but he was airborne before the first soldier landed with the crackling sound of broken bones. The other soldiers backed away, their pleading eyes fixed on their squad leader.

Now, groveling on its hands and knees, the demon's repulsive head snapped around, seeing Mochè walking toward him. It growled, barking and sputtering specks of frothy foam.

As Mochè walked closer, black smoke swirled around the fiend that was once Nikanyiso, whose hulking body began to contort unnaturally. It bent and twisted into bizarre shapes as if made of putty. Loud, bone-snapping echoes reverberated as the beast slowly transformed into a mixture of bulging, surreal forms, growing in size and eventually evolving into what appeared to be a giant dragon, towering forty feet over the holy man, who stood firm before it. The frilled-necked creature's ghastly head lowered, almost touching Mochè; its reptilian eyes locked onto him, sharp fangs flaring, the mouth on its snout gaping as wide as Mochè stood, with froth dripping onto him. The priest's long legs leaped over the scaly, spiked tail that curved and slithered like a serpent, stretching far into the crowd that had gathered to witness the unfolding spectacle. People panicked at the horrifying sight and sought shelter wherever possible, some curling into a fetal position.

The massive beast stood on its hind legs, reaching sixty feet high, and threw its colossal head back, bellowing loudly as long orange and yellow flames spurted from its nostrils. It lowered its head to confront the priest again, roaring and unleashing even more flames, this time aimed directly at Mochè, who remained standing, unharmed by the fiery blaze spouting over him.

When Matthew heard what was happening, he ran back to the manhig, sword in hand, ready to fight the beast, but Mochè waved him away.

"Once again, you annoy me, priest!" The demon's voice burst furiously, echoing through the streets and rattling the nearby buildings like an earthquake. Again, it roared thunderously, "I take this soul as mine!" causing even more vibrations from the tremors generated by its mighty howl and stomping feet.

The giant dragon spread its wings wide and flapped them. Tucking in its spiked tail, it took to the air and then flew high above the town. It soared toward the sky and suddenly dove into the gathered crowd. Flying close and directly over them, spitting glowing, yellow, and orange spurts of fire among them, the hysterical followers flattened themselves to the ground, some running in panic. Grown men cried in fear among the sobs of women and children before the dragon circled once more and then landed next to Mochè.

The beast's head came close to Mochè's face and spoke to him softly, almost in a whisper, "See the young blonde woman, your physician, crouching to the side, her dress raised high?" Dripping saliva, the beast continued, "Look at the voluptuous, milk-white legs she exposes for your pleasure. Have sex with the beautiful, blue-eyed doctor. She reeks of lust for a man, and your weakness is for women. You can enjoy the feel of being inside her." The beast bellowed loudly again in that same hideous laugh, reverberating throughout the town once more.

But Mochè stood calm and walked closer to the beast, saying, "You know you can't beat me, Lucifer." He then sprinkled holy water onto the dragon's snout, inflicting a blazing burning fire as the creature's short arms fought it. Screaming in pain, the demon cried out from its torment while slowly shrinking in size, slapping its horned tail against the unpaved street, flapping its bat-shaped wings, and howling its sounds from Hell. A dozen tiny demons sprang from the pores of the mighty dragon, running and jumping like evil trolls.

"Sergeant!" Mochè shouted to the man, now crouched in horror. He pointed and ordered, "Have your squad destroy those wicked little goblins now! Don't touch them with your hands!" Then he turned back to the giant beast, smiling, and said, "You hate this, don't you, Satan?" Mochè teased as he quickly anointed the monster between the eyes, reciting his holy words for the rite of exorcism. "You can't defeat the power of Christ! Leave this righteous man now, Fallen Angel! Beastly Demon from Hell!" he commanded repeatedly until Nikanyiso's body reappeared, but still showing his red demon eyes. Mochè pressed his crucifix against the man's forehead, and dark, murky smoke erupted from Nick's nose, tormenting the demon within him. After tucking the holy water and anointing oil into his pocket, the priest delivered a powerful left punch to Nikanyiso's head, followed by a right. The left-right combo knocked Nick down, bringing him to his knees before he finally collapsed to the ground, purring like a kitten. "Sergeant!" he shouted. "Have your strongest soldiers hold him down now!" As the military squad restrained Nikanyiso, tendrils of bleak smoke spiraled around him, gradually turning grayish-white before vanishing. Mochè anointed Nick's lifeless body once more and completed his prayers of exorcism, freeing the man from the death-like grip Satan had on him.

After the beast was obliterated, leaving only dust in the street, which a soft breeze gently swept away, Mochè returned his brown scapular, rosaries, and other blessed items to the belted pouch of his black pants. He stood facing the heavens, thanking God for blessing him throughout that harrowing ordeal. Crowds of people gradually regained their composure, holding and calming their children.

Mochè took Nikanyiso by his shoulders, putting him in a sitting position, and asked, "How are you feeling, my friend?"

The stunned man replied, "Did I doze off for a second there?" His family ran to him from the holding room to comfort him. Rachel had held the little ones' eyes shut so they could not see the horrifying sight their father endured. Mochè blessed the three of them, quickly checking for any signs of possession.

Still regaining control, people stood in shock and amazement at the miracle that unfolded before them. Most had never witnessed an exorcism. They all knelt in prayer at the power God had given to their manhig.

Matthew approached his leader and knelt before him, bowing his head as he stated, "I will follow you anywhere, Manhig. Even to battle the fires of hell if you ask me." A weary Mochè simply placed his hand on the young man's shoulder to acknowledge his intended bravery.

Gloria rushed to Mochè from her crouched hiding place and, while crying, told him, "I will definitely continue to call you Father." She hugged him tightly before departing, still not fully recovered from that harrowing experience.

Zipporah and Eliza had heard about what was happening and rushed from a nearby classroom. They witnessed the enormous dragon as Mochè's sacred words of exorcism destroyed it. Stunned, Zipporah and a weeping Eliza clung tightly to opposite sides of him, unable to utter a word.

It was a beautiful autumn day, with the countryside adorned in vibrant shades of yellow, orange, and various greens. The sky above Mochè and Zipporah cast a mélange of magical, blooming rays upon them as if God had blessed their union from the heavens. Among the last fresh flowers of the season, the couple faced both priests, David and Andrew, who officiated the ceremony.

Every follower who was physically able helped prepare for the wedding of their manhig, especially after witnessing or hearing about the great exorcism. Everyone came not only to accept Zipporah but also to know and love her. All the towns in the compound now widely embraced her, not just for becoming the wife of their leader but also for her marvelous and patient teaching skills. The followers now cherished Eliza, the other former outcast, as Zipporah's assistant and appreciated the lovely young woman she was. Most recognized the error of their ways in making hasty judgments and learned a valuable lesson.

Zipporah, wearing a plain white gown, adorned her long blonde hair with a crown of flowers that enhanced the dark green eyes, which seemed to pierce her groom's heart as she gazed at him. Wearing her cherished emerald ring that matched the color of her eyes, she displayed the elegantly carved crucifix hanging from her long, slender neck. Never before had his followers seen Mochè in a priestly black suit. With a slight smile on his face, he stood captivated by the stunning young woman he was marrying, unable to fully comprehend that this long-awaited moment had finally arrived. Eliza looked breathtaking in her floral dress, which showcased her splendid legs, as she gracefully stood beside her adopted sister and father.

Matthew sat on the grass beside Benjamin, near the front of the crowd, unable to take his eyes off Eliza. Occasionally, her gaze would meet his, sending chills down his spine. Benjamin noticed the long blonde hair he recognized as Gabriela's nearby. It was the first time he had seen her in a dress. Two thin shoulder straps supported the dark blue garment, revealing her cleavage and complementing her striking eye color. The hemline rose higher with her legs folded beneath her, exposing Gabriela's shapely lower extremities and delicate feet. Her open-toed shoes rested on the grass beside her legs as she turned to look at Ben. Without blushing, Gabriela swept her long hair back glamorously, her eyes on Ben as she smiled at him. As their gazes met, Ben smiled back.

All the followers spread across the nearby hills, watching and listening to the blessed words of the sacrament of matrimony as they unfolded through the many loudspeakers surrounding them. When David spoke the words, "I now pronounce you man and wife," men, women, and children erupted in cheers, clapping to celebrate the ceremonial conclusion. Nobody could possibly know that David and Andrew had secretly rolled dice to determine who would receive that honor. Mochè swiftly lifted an ecstatic Zipporah and hurriedly carried her through the openings in the crowd as they made way for the couple to pass between them.

Benjamin lost sight of Gabriela in the crowd now rising to leave. Matthew pushed through the throngs of anxious young men wanting to escort Eliza. Keeping her close, he smiled as he kissed her lips. Then he took her arm and guided her to the awaiting parties.

Each town held a feast, and the manhig and his new bride attended every one. After they conversed and tasted the food provided by each town, Zipporah expressed her desire to see her new home. Her big eyes twinkled at her new husband as she spoke.

Mochè opened the door to their new home with one hand while supporting Zipporah in his other arm. As he lifted her over the threshold, she giggled with happiness. He told her, "I had it built for our wedding. I know it's a bit lavish, but everyone insisted I bring my new bride to a nice home."

"Oh my God! I've never seen a lovelier home in my entire life," she said, as a few tears trickled from her lovely eyes and rolled down her cheek. Distant memories of the humble living accommodations her parents provided for her as a child resurfaced—always having to move to another place to escape the wicked followers of Satan. Now, she had a beautiful home with the man she loved.

"Not nearly as lovely as it should be for you, my wife."

"I've never visited your other house before," Zipporah giggled softly, letting her happy tears flow, but wryly added, "It wasn't appropriate for a young, unmarried woman to visit the manhig's home." Twirling around like a child, she cheerfully said, "All it needs is the necessary touch of a woman."

"I appoint you in charge of that, then," he said, comically stepping around her and evaluating her before humorously adding, "You seem to be a woman, my love."

"I will take charge tomorrow."

"Are you ready for tonight?" Mochè hesitantly questioned, reflecting on Zipporah's earlier mention of her memories of fear after being in the hands of the gang that raped and pillaged.

"I've never been more ready," Zipporah's eyes glowed wide, assuredly as her eyebrows raised in a seductive manner.

"Then enough of this!" Mochè vented his frustration and swept her off the floor, carrying her toward his spacious bedroom. "You'll be too tired tomorrow to make the necessary touch of a woman after I finish with you!"

"Ooh!" Zipporah squeaked playfully, her marvelous eyes sparkling mischievously like a young girl's. "Be gentle with me, oh great, Manhig," she giggled timidly.

Mochè stopped in his tracks and asked, "So all that time you were trying to lure me with sexual innuendos, hints, and touching me, it was just all bark and no bite?"

"Yes," Zipporah chirped nervously as Mochè kicked the door shut behind him with his boot.

"Wow!" Zipporah exclaimed, cupping her cheeks with both hands to support her head as her late-morning coffee cup rested on the table. "We've been up most of the night." She reached across the table and took the large hand of the man she loved as he enjoyed his breakfast. Smiling enticingly as a fulfilled wife, she remarked huskily and tantalizingly, "Your hands have been everywhere on my body; I never knew they could move so quickly." She smiled, licking her lips seductively. "So?" she asked, "what's the verdict? Will you keep me or toss me to the wolves?"

Mochè blushed before answering, "I think I'll keep you." He laughed. "You wore me out; I don't think I could handle any more."

"It took long enough, you beast." Zipporah sat laughing, enjoying their first meal together in their new home. "I never knew making babies would be so much fun," and as she blushed, she added, "How could I know I would become so sexually wild? I was so wet—you know—down there. I never knew these things about my body, my love."

"Didn't your mother ever explain these things to you?"

"No," Zipporah's eyes shone with the innocence of a child. "I guess she expected my husband would."

Mochè elaborated, "I've heard so many things in the confessional it's as if I received an education."

"Before we married, my womanhood became moist and sometimes wet whenever we kissed, and," she blushed, "whenever you fondled me there and in other places."

"Those are normal ways a woman reacts to sexual pleasure." Mochè recognized that the men who had abused her were savages and that those horrific experiences could have prevented her from ever experiencing the pleasure she had now found. He was glad that Zipporah could overcome her past trauma and finally enjoy the bliss of matrimony.

Zipporah giggled as her eyes grew wider and she entered a daze. Remembering the night she declared, "Wow, I never knew about all those things you did to me. I felt like an acrobat and sometimes thought I was losing my mind in all the excitement." Glancing at Mochè's expression, she asked, "What? I'm a married woman now; I can speak such things."

"I know, wild woman, I just never thought you would say them," Mochè meekly answered. "I think I might have created a monster."

Zipporah winked at him seductively, her green eyes beaming as she said, "Or I may have, my love." Then she seized her coffee mug and took a sip, winking at Mochè again, her eyes peeking over the mug.

"Jeremiah?" Mochè spotted one of his generals on his way to his office at the courthouse before taking his honeymoon. "Can I see you for a moment?"

"Of course, sir."

Once seated in his courthouse office, Mochè got right to the point and asked, "Has Matthew given you his report yet? For the first command he led?"

Jeremiah smiled and answered, "You've taken a liking to that young man, sir, I see." Jeremiah leaned forward, laid back his head in thought, then said, "It's no wonder; the young man's a born leader and a fine example of what every officer should be like." He sat back in his chair and told his leader, "He did give me his report as soon as he first returned." Smiling again, Jeremiah explained, "I delved further into the matter as I'm certain is why you're here. Two of my trusted captains in that battalion reported that their major, Matthew, performed and acted meticulously. He was cautious but determined and followed protocol on everything."

"Good to hear, good to hear," Mochè smiled delightedly.

"You did right by promoting him, Manhig," Jeremiah said, reinforcing his statement.

The newlyweds spent their week-long honeymoon primarily exploring the stunning beauty of autumn leaves and the nearby vistas of rolling hills, expansive plains, and cascading waterfalls. Mochè consistently carried weapons for their defense, teaching Zipporah to fire various types. He admired her serious expression as she aimed, looking both dignified and proficient.

Smelling the fresh country air and the scents of the season's last flowers, they sat beside a small cascade of spring water and listened to the sounds as it splashed and hit the rocks. Mochè whispered romantically, "I wish I could take you to all the wonderful places I've read about in books." Then he returned to the reality of his time and said, "If only things were different and we lived back then, before they ruined the world."

Noticing her newlywed husband's distress, Zipporah shouted over the splashing water, "Let's go skinny dipping instead!" As she began to remove her clothes, she urged, "C'mon! Let me see your glorious body in natural daylight!" She added, "Take my hand, my love!" Watching her magnificently sculpted naked body glistening from the water in the sunlight invigorated Mochè. He joined her and embraced her tightly as the water splashed off their bodies, knowing he would cherish that moment for the rest of his life. They made love under the waterfall while Mochè supported Zipporah's body, her legs wrapped around his waist. They did the same in lakes and ponds, even in open grassy prairies. Holding their breath and swimming underwater, Zipporah seized her love, enveloping her legs tightly around his body; her passionate screams transformed into bubbles as they copulated beneath the water.

As they sat recovering, Zipporah caressed her husband's

wet body, telling him, "Now I know why so many young women sneak down to the stream to watch you bathe." Zipporah giggled heartily.

"What?"

"Yes," Zipporah couldn't stop laughing now. When she composed herself, she continued, her voice breaking up between her howls of laughter, "They line up like ducks in a row to peek at your glorious nude wet body." She had to hold her lips to stop her hysteria.

"Why didn't you ever tell me this before?" Mochè asked, taken aback.

"I was one of them after we first met," Zipporah laughed. Then her face folded and appeared stern as she said, "After I claimed you, I scattered all of them away." Seeing his shocked expression, she smiled while glancing at his groin, "Don't worry, my love, you have nothing to be ashamed of—at all!" She giggled again, but this time, she blushed.

"Now I have to have a soldier guard me." Mochè sat restlessly.

"Oh, let them have their peeks!"

"Then what Zipporah told him registered, and Mochè toyed with his wife. "Maybe you're right; perhaps I'll put on a performance for the young ladies."

Zipporah's eyes widened in fear. "Forget everything I said; I wouldn't want any of them to entice you and take you away from me."

"Naw! It's okay; maybe I'll charge admission. I can—"

"I excited myself with my own words," Zipporah chipped off his words and swept her arms around her new husband. "Let's do it again!" Mochè knew his wife was trying to change the subject. "Hurry, my love; I can't wait."

During that glorious week, they couldn't get enough of each other. Every evening, they returned exhausted, only to reignite their cravings for one another in bed. Mochè nicknamed Zipporah 'bunny' privately because she wanted to make love as frequently as a rabbit. Most outings concluded with Zipporah enticing Mochè to return home, which she enjoyed the most. It thrilled her to see her new husband so relaxed and free from his work, and she dreaded the end of such splendid times.

After their return, Mochè resumed wearing his many hats in managing the stronghold, while Zipporah became engrossed in her labor of love, adding 'a woman's necessary touch' to their new home by decorating it with Eliza's help. She also aided Eliza in settling into Zipporah's old home, where she had lived ever since Mochè rescued her. Zipporah held fond memories of that place, where she had shared many meals and conversations with the man she loved; she often reflected on those moments and felt glad that Eliza would live there.

"Well, I think we're going to need a small wagon for this shopping spree," Zipporah laughed at Eliza. "I need so many things, and you definitely need new curtains, as well as a new table and chairs," she thought sentimentally again about the many meals she had shared with Mochè while sitting at that table. Zipporah and Mochè always chatted about simple topics that often shifted to more engaging ones. They talked for hours, and she remembered those moments fondly. "You know, maybe the table and chairs could be renewed and varnished," Zipporah smiled, hoping Eliza would agree.

"Oh, I definitely think they could," Eliza replied, knowing her sister well and almost sensing her feelings.

"Great! We can put that expense to good use for something else," Zipporah beamed.

"I'll park the wagon here; it's in the center of where we'll be going," Zipporah said. "I'll get someone to carry your kitchen furniture for repair; it's right over there," she pointed. "Oh, by the way, I'll have Mochè send someone over with a folding table and chairs until they finish restoring yours."

"He's always so wonderful to me; I hate seeing him go through the trouble knowing how busy he always is."

"That's what fathers are for, honey," Zipporah took Eliza's

arm as they walked together.

After her marriage to Mochè, whenever Zipporah traveled through the compound's streets on her errands, the men who once scorned her now bowed before her, and the women who had envied her and called her foul names now curtsied in respect for the wife of their manhig. Once considered outcasts, Zipporah and Eliza now strolled gracefully as they did their shopping.

"Manhig, we need fresh meat to supply all the new arrivals. We have nearly ten thousand among us," Joshua declared at the council assembly. "It's getting cold, sir. Winter comes upon us soon." Mochè listened to each member speak, his mind secretly wandering and thinking how nice it would be to share a warm bed with the woman he loved for the first time during those cold months.

"I agree, sir," Joseph, his general, replied. "Like all the other generals, we're training more and more soldiers."

"Do we have enough grain and feed for the animals?" asked Mochè.

"Yes, sir,"

"How is the storage for hay and grass for the horses?"

Another council member and general, Deborah, declared, "The doctor reported that she has all the medicines prepared, and we have enough jarred vegetables, fruits, and such stored away. The slaughterhouse informed my adjutant that they have poultry. We have all the supplies and necessities to carry us throughout the winter, except for red meat. That's the main concern, Manhig. Our poultry supply alone won't get us through the winter."

"This time of year, there are plenty of wild pigs, boars, sheep, cattle, and goats—the list goes on, sir," Mark explained.

"Okay, I'll ensure that fifty of our best hunters are ready. I'll also organize an escort party of cavalry and wagons to transport the gutted animals. Everything will stay fresh in the cold air." Mochè didn't like the idea of sending any of his people out for long excursions during the dangerous cold months. "Let's do this immediately to ensure the expedition returns within two weeks."

Everyone unanimously voiced their agreement, one by one. Mochè struck his wooden hammer against the block to adjourn the meeting. As Mochè rose from his seat, Joshua asked him privately, "May I lead this expedition, Manhig?"

Placing his hand on his second-in-command's shoulder, Mochè replied, "You're far too important to me here, my good friend; you know that." He gazed into the eager man's eyes and said, "I need you here to assist me if we're attacked. You know how vulnerable we are in the colder months when pillagers roam in droves looking for food to steal to sell in the open markets of gangs."

"You're right."

"Joshua, unfortunately, you will have other opportunities to fight."

"Who will you send, then, sir?"

"I'm thinking about it. This hit me too fast with so many new mouths to feed."

"Jeremiah speaks highly of the young officer, Benjamin."

"Yes," Mochè seemed to be contemplating, then said, "He's an excellently trained officer, and perfect for the task of leading such a large force. I've intended to promote him to a brigade commander for a while now. It's my fault I didn't get around to it with my wedding and everything else that's preoccupied me. However, I also wanted to give young Matthew some field experience as a second-in-command. Though I don't know if he's ready to be a second for something this important."

Matthew stood at attention before his leader. Mochè had reconsidered after understanding the truth about why he was hesitant to send the young man. Zipporah had enlightened him to this.

As they shared their evening meal, just like they always had, both seated in their usual spots, Mochè brought up the topic. "I don't think the boy is ready yet. I admit he's an excellent officer, but he needs more hands-on experience." Zipporah simply smiled, her eyes wide in a way that always tugged at Mochè's heart. Looking at her, he asked, "What?" knowing she had something to say. Their love for each other was so strong that they had become like one, and he understood her body language and facial expressions very well.

"Oh, nothing, my love," she slowly swayed her head on her long, graceful neck.

"I know there's something you want to say."

After a long pause, observing his wife completely ignore him as she ate her meal properly and ladylike, using good manners as always, Zipporah looked up and asked, "Oh, is there?" Mochè didn't need to say anything; she recognized his expression well. After wiping her lips with her napkin, she said, "Well, if you must ask, I'll tell you what you already know." She smiled at him and continued, "You're being overly protective of the young man, my love."

"That's ridiculous!"

"No, dear, you don't want to admit it, but he's the son you never had," Zipporah beamed. "In fact, he is the mirror image of you at that age," she laughed. "It's so obvious. Everyone who knew you back then can see it."

Mochè sat back in his chair, shocked. "I-I"

"No wonder your daughter loves him; she sees you in him. You have to let him spread his wings, dear, just like you did," Zipporah looked at her husband lovingly. "Who else would you send with Major Benjamin? General Helen, who makes goo-goo eyes at you whenever she's near?"

Mochè, deep in thought, asked, "How could you possibly think that?"

"I know it, my love," she said, smiling. "Women's intuition; it's never wrong." Zipporah took a sip from her coffee mug. "That woman's in love with you." She knew her husband was naïve in such matters, which was why she had ceased to tempt him when he first refused to marry her. Zipporah would never be a part of adultery, nor would she even consider dishonoring Mochè in any way.

Mochè, shaking his head, speechless, finally said, "She's a fine general and nothing more."

"Her love for you seeps from every pore of her body."

As Matthew stood waiting for his Manhig's orders, Mochè sized him up and now realized his wife was right. He did think of this young man before him as a son. Although their ages were not that far apart, he could still be his biological father. Mochè now faced that and recognized the resemblance to himself at that age. "I want you to accompany Major Benjamin, who is commanding the escort party for the hunters, Matthew."

Everyone was aware of this mission and its significance; discussions about it were widespread throughout the towns. "I'm honored, sir. Thank you for your confidence in me. I won't disappoint you, Manhig."

Mochè smiled at the young man who reminded him of himself at that age: eager, brave, and a gifted commander. "I want you to help Benjamin choose a small brigade of about 1000 cavalry riders and 150 of the fittest infantry who can run fast and for long distances to escort the professional hunters. I already instructed Benjamin to take no longer than two weeks for this mission."

"Yes, sir!"

Mochè declared, "I want you to help Benjamin prepare the brigade with essentials, including weapons, winter clothing, food, and other necessary supplies. This is a large command, Matthew, and you understand its importance. Major Benjamin will lead, but I want you to be his second-in-command. Rely on his experience and training. Ask him questions and depend on him; he's an excellent officer." Mochè grasped the young man's forearms in a military-style embrace and continued, "If Major Benjamin falls or is wounded, you will have to make all decisions once you're out there." He turned and gazed into the distance, imagining what it would be like in the cold. "I know you won't let me down, son," he thought, then added, "Tell Benjamin to take Nikanyiso with him so he can further assess him as a warrior and the tracker he claims to be."

"Yes, sir!"

"Matthew?"

"Yes, Manhig?"

"Be careful out there." Mochè turned again to gaze into the distance and the perilous lands where Benjamin and Matthew would soon journey.

When Zipporah told Eliza that Matthew was second-in-command of the expedition everyone was talking about, she panicked and cried, "I must go to him before he leaves. I've never expressed my feelings for him. I should have, but I never did, trying to act hard-to-get." She wiped her eyes and told Zipporah, "You taught me that."

"Well, it worked, didn't it?" Zipporah comforted Eliza and softly said, "I'll take you, sweetheart. We'll go together."

When Zipporah asked to see Matthew, the sentry at the army's gathering point—filled with typical chaos before heading into a possible battle—or perhaps multiple battles—responded respectfully, "He's very busy, ma'am."

Zipporah stood firm and repeated, "I would like to speak to him."

Realizing he was addressing the manhig's wife, the soldier replied, "I'll send for him right away, ma'am."

Within a few minutes, a surprised Matthew appeared. As soon as she saw him walking toward her, Eliza instantly ran into his open arms and, while hugging him, whispered, "I love you, Matthew." She softly kissed his lips as Zipporah strolled off to the side to give her adopted sister privacy.

Wide-eyed in shock, Matthew took her hand and led her to a corner near the post. Now aware of his true feelings, he responded, "I love you, too, Eliza. I have since we met."

As they passionately kissed, Zipporah cleared her throat from the short distance where she stood, indicating people were watching.

Now blushing and realizing she was making a spectacle, Eliza softly said, "Please come back to me, Matthew," as tears rolled from her stunning, heartbroken hazel eyes.

"I'll come back to you, my love. I swear it!" Looking back at his post, he said, "I have to return now; Ben and I are preparing everything."

As Eliza backed away, crying, she blew him a kiss. Then she ran to Zipporah's arms.

The large assembly of cavalry, all wearing heavy animal furs over their uniforms to protect them from the cold elements, mounted at the broad street before the huge wooden gate lowered, covering the moat at Benjamin's command.

"Nikanyiso, ride next to me." Ben saw the tall, ebony-skinned man standing, wearing his Zulu headdress, while carrying his decorated shield and holding his long spear.

"I prefer to run, Major, if it is your will. It will keep me warm from this bitterly cold land."

Benjamin smiled and answered, "As you wish."

Matthew glanced at Eliza, who stood beside Zipporah. With a grin, she blew him a kiss, tears in her beautiful eyes nearly breaking his heart. He smiled and waved at her.

Riding slightly ahead of Matthew, Major Benjamin didn't need to search for Gabriela; he had already confirmed that she was assigned to the escort party as a dispatch rider and scout. Amid the cheers and rallies of the crowds to the sides, Benjamin led the brigade out after giving his order. The people understood the dangers of the cold: roaming bandits, demons, and other wicked hordes that lurked in winter. Their cries of support grew louder as their brave warriors passed by. The infantry followed last, riding in wagons alongside those reserved for hunted meat, crossing over the moat.

General Helen approached the manhig who stood watching his army leave, privately worrying for the young man. She smiled widely, saying, "I see you're nurturing your boy, Mochè." Zipporah carefully watched every movement the other woman made from her vantage point with Eliza. "If something happens to Major Benjamin, it will be a big command for such a newly promoted major, don't you think?"

"He'll handle it." Mochè smiled and turned to face Helen. "Remember when I gave you your first large command when you were a major?"

"Touchè, Manhig," she bowed in a humorous gesture. Zipporah continued to study the woman, Helen.

After two weeks in the harsh elements of unknown territory west and north of the compound, Benjamin evaluated the meat brought in by the hunters. The wagons were full, so he sent everything back to the fortress with all his infantry and most of the cavalry to protect the valuable cargo. He and Matthew would stay behind and follow their rear to guard their trail with the remaining cavalry.

"Major John, maintain a continuous cavalry patrol at all times," Ben said, giving his final orders. "Always encircle your encampments with sentinels." The broad-shouldered officer acknowledged with a military salute and departed with the precious meat supplies sufficient to sustain the stronghold throughout the entire winter.

Adhering to the strict military protocol, Major Benjamin consistently dispatched platoons of cavalry scouts to establish a perimeter around their encampment, safeguarding it and reporting any suspicious activity. As anticipated, they encountered bands of looters, various gangs of robbers, slave hunters scavenging through the winter, and numerous demon patrols searching for human flesh to consume. All succumbed to Ben's experience and training, bolstered by Matthew's intuitive military tactics. They defeated tribes of demons and vicious hordes of other wicked, mutated, beastlike creatures scattered in different directions.

As Matthew helped prepare to break camp, he thought about the slower, heavy wagons laden with the necessary meats from different animals, pulled by large oxen, that were probably already far ahead on their way to the stronghold. He contemplated how happy most of the brigade, deployed to guard it, would be to return, as he privately couldn't wait to see Eliza.

From a distance, Ben saw two horses racing furiously toward him. Taking out his binoculars, he recognized them as his scouts. With all his infantry and most of his cavalry already ahead, he anticipated that he and the remaining 200 cavalry troops would need to ride hard if his scouts reported a force attacking them and they had to escape quickly.

The two riders jumped off their horses in haste. Holding their reins, they rushed to give their report. "A large force approaching, sir," one shouted to Major Benjamin in his manly bark. Matthew stood listening at the crest of a high elevation.

Benjamin called out, "How many, Lieutenant Gabriela?" he recognized the young blonde dispatch rider.

As Ben walked nearer to her, Gabriela spoke quietly. "Too many for us to count, sir," she reported as they spoke for the first time. Ben relished the voice he had imagined hearing for so long.

"We wanted to report this to you before we were spotted," the first scout stated.

"We couldn't see what type of weapons they carried, so we thought it best to inform you of their presence as soon as possible," Gabriela said to Ben, their eyes locking. The young woman stood, starry-eyed, imagining ways to touch him, even considering purposely tripping on a stone to fall into his embrace. She felt a deep passion within her and knew with certainty that she loved him.

"Good thinking," Ben commended her. "Switch horses; yours are too tired," he addressed both scouts, noticing the excessive sweat dripping from their animals. "Hurry!" commanded Ben, "Take us to where you saw them."

Concealed between two evergreens in a cluster, Matthew used his long, folding telescope to observe. "My God," he whispered, "there must be at least a few thousand of them, Ben."

Ben whispered back, "Matt, make sure the moonlight doesn't reflect off your glass. Use one hand to shield it."

"I learn something new from you every day, my friend," Matthew chuckled as softly as he could.

Ben confirmed through his scope, "At least that many, Matt." Now pointing, he said, "Look over there, my friend."

Matthew slid his telescope to where Ben was pointing. Shocked, he softly exclaimed, "There's even more."

"Do you want me to take a closer look, Major?" Nikanyiso asked, smiling. "I move as quietly as a serpent slithers."

"No, Nick. Stay with us. We have to get back as quickly as possible," Ben quietly ordered.

Resting his telescope on a large rock for support, Ben quietly said, "I'll estimate their strength." Zooming in closer, he gasped and murmured softly, "My God in Heaven, they're the same gorilla-like creatures who raided us—at least 9000 of them—maybe more." Pulling himself from his brief stupor, he whispered, "Nikanyiso, quickly gather the others! We must ride hard to catch up to the meat wagons and our main force."

Ben turned to Gabriela and the other scout and said, "You both did excellent work." But he stared into the woman's eyes, recalling how beautiful she looked in a dress that revealed her alluring lower extremities. For the first time, after hearing the voice that matched her beauty, his keen intuition sensed her soul, and he now understood that he loved her.

Chapter Nine

The Great Battle

"**W**e'll have to hold our chats indoors as we always do in winter, my friends," Mochè declared, warming his hands by the fire. "It's getting too cold already."

"And that, coming from a tough guy like you, mighty Manhig," David joked.

"The next thing he'll tell us is that we'll need to have them a little earlier, now that he's a happily married man," Andrew chuckled.

"If you two aren't angels, you're definitely mindreaders," Mochè laughed.

David seemed serious as he stroked his long gray beard and stated, "I was just reflecting on a story that happened over two centuries ago, my ancestors passed down to my grandfather. It's such a simple one, but I always remember it."

"Are you going to share it with us or just sit there grinning?" Andrew teased his friend.

"Well, my ancestor was a little boy sitting in a park with his mother," he paused to explain what a park was before continuing, "She had taken him there to watch a puppet show when he was about four or five." Andrew knew what a puppet show was, but Mochè did not. "My father said she bought him ice cream—a flavor I had never even heard of." Basic flavors of ice cream were one of the few luxuries of the past that they still enjoyed at the stronghold. "Could you even imagine living in such simple, happy, peaceful times as those? Then everything changed right after that. My heir witnessed the fall of the last civilization when he became a man." David stopped caressing his beard and frowned, tears welling up in his eyes.

Mochè watched the distress wash over his friend and explained, "We could have coexisted in this world. There could have been peace and harmony today." Shaking his head, he remarked, "The leaders of that time blew it."

"Politicians," replied Andrew. "Those who governed were called politicians; my great-grandfather told my grandfather about them. They ruled before either of them lived."

"I studied those once referred to as politicians, and unfortunately, to put it short but not sweet—it's all bad," Mochè explained. "They were corrupt individuals ruling in a pseudo-democracy reminiscent of the ancient Romans."

"They had a monetary system at that time and took money from the large corporations that once existed," Andrew interjected. "Greed fueled the politicians. They led the world to its end."

"How ironic for someone who was supposed to lead or govern that they 'led' the world to ruination. Remember when I mentioned the media?" David asked. "Just connect the dots and consider greed one of the seven deadly sins when you think of politicians."

"All types of media worked hand in hand with politicians," said Andrew. "Especially the news media. They hired what they referred to as reporters. They were nothing but deceivers who fed lies to the great populations long before the end. Differing versions of reports led to disagreements and then to fighting between people. They were also pawns for corrupt corporations to sell products that typically didn't work or were even harmful to them, like the medicines they used back then—all chemical compounds."

"Finally, another thing I learned about when I was younger: chemical medicines," Mochè proudly announced. "They altered the natural gifts that God bestowed upon them and created chemical equivalents."

"Righto!" Andrew exclaimed. "And by what driving force?"

"Greed!" David and Mochè yelled, almost harmonizing.

"The news media fueled hatred among people. It escalated into street violence driven by greed. That animosity, nurtured by the news media and their outreach strategies, contributed to the decline of cities," Andrew recounted. "All for profit."

"And to a ruined world where we now struggle to survive," Mochè gazed at the darkened sky. "Satan deployed his demons well, long before the world fell. They infiltrated the media and entered the bodies of politicians who allowed them."

"Well, my friend," David looked at Mochè. "Now, you must procreate and bring more life to us."

"And I know he'll enjoy every minute," Andrew chimed in with his friend as they both laughed while teasing Mochè.

"I'll try," Mochè chuckled.

Just then, they heard a commotion nearby. All three men listened carefully. Sometimes, fights or domestic quarrels erupted, but this was different. It was the usual sounds of daytime, which typically died down by evening. "Something seems wrong," Andrew reasoned aloud as Mochè quickly rose from the cold ground of the evening to see what was happening.

"The hunting party is returning," Mochè finally told them as he left to see his expedition commander, Benjamin, and his second-in-command, Matthew.

"How many do you estimate?" Mochè asked. "Those beasts apparently had others of their kind who knew their allies had come to see me, the well-known manhig," he said, shaking his head in frustration, his expression revealing his emotions. "I should've sent trackers to find out where they came from."

"I counted at least 9000, Manhig," Major Benjamin replied. "Possibly more."

"Nine thousand of those same monstrous mutations we fought?" Mochè looked visibly shocked. "My God!"

"Yes, sir, but may I suggest something?" asked Ben. Mochè was already walking to the assembly he had ordered.

"Speak quickly, son."

"They're too large to ride on horses, so many of them are traveling in wagons pulled by several oxen, which is slowing them down. The others are trotting sluggishly but determinedly alongside," Ben explained as he and Matt kept pace with Mochè. "We estimate that at their current rate of advance, it will take them at least a week and a half to reach us. The mutants use blunt weapons and lack advanced armaments. Sir, we have an advantage here. If we act quickly, we can prepare to fight them before they get to our stronghold."

Mochè stopped to listen. "Go ahead," he said, remaining standing. He heard what Ben was saying and comprehended its importance.

"Manhig, we can send out machinery and even laborers to dig ditches as traps with spikes at the bottom, as many as possible. We can also have our commandos build hunting blinds to attack them with our laser and solar rifles from above. At every other tree, we post automatic solar guns," Ben explained. He caught the interested expression on Mochè's face and continued, "When they see their comrades fall into the traps, they will panic and spread out. I would suggest a wide perimeter to encircle them all so no strays escape.

Matthew added, "Our solar cannons will blast them from the front and on separate flanks at the rear. The armies deployed at the perimeter can eliminate any of them who run. Sir," Matt continued, "they might get close to our stronghold, but we can stop them."

Mochè appeared extremely impressed and turned to his officers, asking, "How do you know these things?"

"We discussed these military tactics together, sir, on our way back," Ben answered. He didn't want to take all the credit. Both Ben and Matthew were instrumental in planning many of the defenses they discussed with the manhig.

"Benjamin, you know your stuff, and you did well, Matthew, as a second-in-command. You both did excellent work. Go and eat, then I want you both to meet with me when I discuss this with Aaron and my generals."

"I'm not hungry, sir," answered Ben,

"Neither am I, Manhig," replied Matthew, almost synchronizing with Ben, both still maintaining Mochè's long strides.

"Okay then," they couldn't see the proud smile on their manhig's face as he walked briskly, "come along."

"Majors Benjamin and Matthew have already presented me with some excellent plans they've worked up," Mochè spoke, addressing the council. He glanced at Ben and Matt, standing to the side, and beckoned them to come over. As the young majors stood beside him, he instructed, "Benjamin, please tell the council what you shared with me."

Benjamin and Matthew laid out their entire plan before the astonished eyes of every member, elaborating on certain points and resembling generals. They shared the blackboard and drew maps, each using a pointer to indicate suggested positions for terrain and specific weapons to deploy for each. "And we must inform the communities about the ditches to prevent harming any of our own. We recommend digging the ditches and constructing the spiked bottoms, but hold off on placing them until we're sure the mutations are nearby," Ben finalized.

"Or, we can cover them with wooden planks and remove them when necessary," Matthew added.

"Well," said Aaron, "as a general and chief strategist, I'm quite impressed." It wasn't easy to make an impact on Aaron. "These young men demonstrate exceptional battle strategy, and I commend them on many levels."

General Jeremiah applauded, prompting a wave of handclaps and cheers from the room. "Although we face a significant battle ahead, they have provided us with a potential upper hand if we wisely heed their advice. As their commanding general,

I urge the council to set a date to honor these young officers."

"Sir, if I may," Ben interrupted, saying, "Our scouts, Gabriela and Mark, also did excellent work out there. They were the riders who first spotted the force, sir." Matthew nodded in agreement.

Jeremiah smiled and said, "My young officers demonstrate honesty and, more importantly, embody the virtue of humility. So be it." He paused and continued, "If we succeed and survive, that is, may I see a show of hands for approval of decorations for our two majors and their scouts?" The response was unanimous, and Ben and Matt were invited to join the council to finalize the plans.

As both young men answered the questions from the council and generals, reiterating some specifics of their proposals, Ben and Matt continued to impress, especially Mochè, who stood proudly beside them the entire time.

"Our military now has," Aaron said, glancing down at his papers, "about 7,500 fully trained soldiers."

"They outnumber us, then. Remember what havoc they inflicted upon us after they entered our gate," General Helen stated. "Many of our people still suffer from the contemptuous things they endured." Helen viewed the expressions of the council members and remarked, "Any new soldiers should know that they are nothing more than cannibalistic animals who rape and pillage. Remembering General Sarah, she announced, "We should take no prisoners." She shouted, "Kill them all!"

"I agree," General Deborah said. "They raped several of my dear friends, both women and men. They are twisted versions of savage beasts with no souls."

"Our new soldiers must also be aware of how gigantic those mutated animals are," replied Joshua. "Generals, prepare any newer soldiers to employ strategies with that consideration."

"Here, here!" yelled Elisheba, Aaron's wife and a council member who was a general heading an infantry and a cavalry brigade. She offered her support. "They are creatures of Satan."

All eyes were on Mochè, waiting for his decision. Recalling his last encounter with the alleged final remaining captive, who revealed he killed Naomi, the warrior and Leah's late sister, he felt no pity. "I agree," Mochè finally said. "They are godless creatures who we must eliminate to prevent them from wreaking havoc on other innocents." Mumbles of agreement and some cheers circulated among the gathered members. "We must also find their stronghold and destroy the women who bear others like them." Mochè didn't like hearing his own words, but he knew they were true.

After the meeting, Mochè called General Elisheba, the last general to leave the courthouse. "Elisheba, have a few companies of your cavalry ride out to the cloistered convent. Tell them they must evacuate and escort them here to our compound, where they'll be safe—hopefully."

"Their mother superior is a tough old bird; she might not comply."

"Ask Mother Angelica to do it as a favor for me. If she still doesn't agree, tell her I will personally ride out there and bring her and the other nuns back."

"Yes, Manhig," Elisheba chuckled. "That ought to do it."

Then Mochè called Matthew over. Privately, he told the young man, "I'm advancing you to lieutenant colonel, Matthew. You've made me proud. I'm having General Jeremiah assign you a light cavalry brigade."

"But, sir, respectfully," he said, not wishing to show disrespect. "I would outrank Major Benjamin, who is an experienced cavalry officer." Matthew searched for the right words. "He trained me, sir, when I became a lieutenant."

"He was the officer who recommended you before you left with the expedition, son."

"He did?"

"Yes, I understand that you're both friends, but he believes you have a divine gift." Mochè looked at Matthew. "I am promoting Benjamin to full colonel and will be a senior heavy brigade leader—that's long overdue. Your brigade will be attached to and fall under his command. Benjamin is an exceptionally experienced officer. His parents were generals whom I knew well, and they sent him directly from school to our military academy." Mochè paused, recalling Benjamin as a child and his fortitude and dignity, qualities he maintained into adulthood. A remarkable product of his parents, Mochè remembered them fondly. "What he learned came through training; what you know is instinctual. Benjamin always prioritizes God and our military, yet he possesses the wisdom to recognize that your talent is a gift from God. Learn from Benjamin, Matthew. Always draw on his resources to enhance your gift. You'll learn a lot from him."

"Yes, Manhig, I already have." Matthew knelt and thanked his leader. Mochè pulled him up and reminded him, "We only kneel before God, son. You deserve this."

Zipporah lay embracing her husband beneath the thick covers of their bed; her alluring bright eyes sparkled as her small feet tenderly warmed Mochè's. Then the glow of her deep green eyes dimmed as reality pulled her from any carnal thoughts. "You'll be going into battle again, my love," she said in the light cast by the flickering flames of the fireplace; her soft feet stopped affectionately caressing her husband's. Zipporah's face now appeared devastated as she continued to speak. "It just dawned on me." She pulled herself into a sitting position, much to Mochè's disappointment. "My God, I don't know what I would do without you," she expressed the words she was thinking. Mochè said nothing, only gazing deeply into her beautiful eyes as if he could see her soul, within which lay worry and despair.

He softly stroked her cheeks and replied, "I'll come back to you, Zipporah. I always do and always will."

Zipporah's eyes widened with passion as she pulled her husband back under the covers.

When Matthew found the only time he could spare while preparing for the upcoming battle to stop the raiders from repeating their past atrocities, he rode out to Eliza's home. Knowing that Mochè was deeply engrossed in coordinating everything for what was likely the biggest confrontation he had ever faced, Matthew realized he wouldn't be anywhere in sight. Casually leading his horse down the incline, he noticed a wagon. As he drew closer, he recognized it was Zipporah's.

Eliza heard his sounds and, after peeking through the small window, flung open the door and ran to Matthew, who was now walking toward her while holding the reins of his black stallion. She jumped into Matthew's arms, her legs wrapping around his thighs and resting there as if she intended to remain like that forever. When she finally came up for air after kissing him for so long, she told him, "Oh, Matthew, I thought you'd never come. You and Ben are the talk of the entire compound. I'm so proud of you!" She then returned to kissing him, even more passionately now.

As Matthew twirled around with Eliza's body still wrapped in his arms, he spotted Zipporah and her friend Rosetta standing in the doorway, smiling. He dropped Eliza and, taking her hand, walked toward the two gleaming young ladies. "Hi, Zipporah," he said. "Rosetta," he nodded.

Zipporah rushed up to kiss him. "Oh, Matthew, we're so proud of you." She saw his expression and whispered close to him, "Don't worry. I won't tell Mochè you came here." She winked at him. "Though I think you have his approval now," she laughed. Rosetta stepped up, blushing and unsure what to say, and pecked Matthew on the cheek.

"Come in, dear; sit for a bit. I know you must be busy."

"I am," Matthew replied. "I can only stay for a minute," secretly wishing to spend that time holding the young woman he now loved.

"Mochè explained Benjamin's and your feats to me," Zipporah remarked. "Everyone is deeply grateful for your quick action and planning."

"Any second-in-command would have acted the same, ma'am," Matthew replied, "and Major Benjamin always adhered to protocol," demonstrating his honesty.

"Nevertheless, you reacted remarkably as a second," Zipporah smiled. "He told me, based on your reports and those of Major Benjamin and your subordinates, that if you hadn't sent out continuous scouts and returned to us so quickly, we would have never known and would have been overrun." Matthew's mind was too focused on Eliza to mention that the scouts were Ben's idea.

"You and Benjamin are both heroes, my love," Eliza interjected. "Accept it."

"Eliza, the manhig mentioned that he wants you to be at his home with Zipporah. He said a large, hidden cellar can accommodate both of you," Matthew explained.

"He worries too much that we might be overrun. We have every confidence in him, his army, and you, Matthew. Congratulations! He told me you now lead a light brigade." Zipporah smiled, but she hid her fear well to avoid upsetting Eliza.

"We could be overrun, ma'am. Better to be safe than sorry."

"Okay then, we'll be in the cellar, Eliza with me." Turning to Rosetta and holding her hand reassuringly, she continued, "Rosetta will be with us as well; her new husband is assigned to the soldiers guarding the outside of the compound, and we don't want her to be alone. There's plenty of room for you too, dear," she said to Rosetta. Zipporah grinned again and told Eliza, "Run outside to be with Matthew, as I know you both want to be alone."

Eliza now cried in Matthew's arms. Her hazel-colored gaze reflected his as she spoke, "I love you, Matthew. Please be careful out there." She hugged him tightly.

"I'll come back to you, Eliza." He kissed her softly. "I love you far too much to die now."

Mochè stood before his thousands of followers, all spread across the grassy hills. They wore coats in the chilly weather, some basking in the few rays of sun that beat down on them. He began his sermon, "My dear followers, we have reached a point in our journey that will define us. There was a great lineage of what were once called popes who preceded the fall of Peter the Roman and the destruction of the church that was once great. As a replacement for those past leaders of that Church of Christ, God anointed me to lead his renewed church—to lead all of you, my dear friends in Christ. It is with great regret that I must inform you that those ghastly, unnhuman beast raiders that most of you remember are coming at us once more. They are the same giants from our ancestors' Holy Septuagint encountered when our religion was forming. The fallen angels who bore children with human women. Their offspring were the Nephilim or giants. Destroyed in the flood of Noah's time, the likes of a similar breed have once again descended upon us for the sins of our forefathers who delved too deeply into science and the transformation of mankind." Mochè paused to look among his followers.

"In these final days, we savor each moment as if it will last forever. But let us not grow too comfortable in those diminishing heartbeats we live in, for we do not know when God will call us home. And remember, there is a place in paradise for all who truly believe in Him and pray for His divine mercy. I pray that God grants all our warriors the strength and endurance to withstand what lies ahead." Mochè quoted Deuteronomy 20:4: 'For the Lord your God is He who goes with you to fight for you against your enemies, to give you victory.' Then, he quoted Psalm 144:1: 'Blessed be the Lord my Rock, who trains my hands for war, my fingers for battle.' Mochè could see the frightened faces of many around him, yet the eager and commanding presence of many others. He continued, "Many of us will fall in battle. But remember our Lord's words from John 15:13: 'Greater love hath no man than this, that a man lay down his life for his friends.' Also, recall John 3:16: 'For God so loved the world that He gave His only begotten Son, that whoever believes in Him should not perish, but have eternal life.' I will see all of you again, here or in the ever after!"

Scouting reports indicated that herds of beasts were getting close, causing widespread panic due to fears of a repeat of the last dreadful incident. Terror spread as residents from all towns scurried to help build defenses against a presumed break-in. They boarded up their windows and doors and constructed barriers in the streets, which now resembled ghost towns. Mochè had stationed more soldiers at the large gated entrance, both outside and inside it.

Everyone in the stronghold trembled when the first faint sounds of pounding drums resonated in the distance as the herd of gorilla-like beasts drew nearer.

"I'm terrified," Eliza told Zipporah as they closed the cellar lid and climbed down the stairs to join Rosetta, who was already waiting and trembling with fear. Eliza remembered her dreadful experience at the hands of those gorilla-like beasts, her eyes wide with horror. "There are over 9000 of those awful creatures our soldiers will face," Eliza verbalized her worries for Matthew. However, her beautiful hazel eyes softened as she recalled first meeting the handsome young man who had spared her the unthinkable. That memory brought her some comfort, though she was now desperately worried for him. Zipporah shared the same fear but concealed it better to encourage the younger girls with her.

"Don't worry, girls," Zipporah said as she embraced Eliza and Rosetta. "Mochè gave me this," she pointed to the automatic solar rifle leaning upright in the corner, "and I know how to use it."

Mochè primarily based his battle strategy on the insights of Ben and Matthew, while also integrating his own military training and extensive experience. He consistently dispatched scouts to gather updated reports on his army's positions and the enemy's locations. His goal was to eliminate those dreadful creatures, preventing them from fleeing to harm more defenseless people, as they typically did, recalling the horrors they inflicted on his followers. Mochè assigned his second-in-command, Joshua, to the southern sections, nearer to the fortress, so he could serve as Mochè's eyes and ears in that area, traveling between the armies stationed there. Mochè sat on his white stallion next to Helen and Aaron, both mounted and ready at the front, waiting about four miles from the stronghold entrance. Suddenly, they heard cries in the distance. The sounds grew louder and transformed into painful howls and screeches as the hairy beasts fell into the deep traps concealed beneath grass-covered sheets.

"They're not very bright," Helen called to Mochè, smiling amid the ongoing agonizing screams of pain. "They're doing exactly what you expected," she smiled, displaying her admiration and hidden love for him.

"I took that into consideration when I made my preparations, but don't underestimate their immense strength," he smiled back. "Be cautious when you encounter them. I don't want to lose you, General," he said, recalling the loss of Sarah and Isaac, unintentionally igniting a spark of hope in Helen that he might share the same intimate feelings for her that she had for him.

"Manhig, we fired our solar cannons at the enemy beyond the traps." The young man looked visibly shaken. Mochè had eagerly awaited this captain's report from a couple of miles ahead of them, near the trap site.

"Pull yourself together, son, and give me your account."

"We blasted all the cannons, not wasting any power. All fired accurately at their targets. The commandos continually fired their weapons from the higher positions of the blinds built into the many trees, which were also successful." The captain still displayed his apprehension and fear as he continued, "They took out a great many, sir, but there are far too many of them, Manhig. They're advancing quickly."

"How many do you estimate we destroyed with the traps, tree setups, and cannons?"

"Sir, many. Hundreds, possibly even quite many more. They

kept falling into the traps, killed by numerous weapons fired at them from higher elevations, but they still advanced. The enormous holes are filled with their bodies. The beasts are marching right over their dead comrades."

"Did they spread out?"

"No, Manhig, they're coming right at our front here. I've never seen a herd this size before."

A scout reported to General Helen, "Ma'am, Lieutenant James reporting," he saluted her. "The brigades you commanded, deployed from the outer perimeter, are on their way."

"Thank you, Lieutenant," she said, then turned back to face the front.

"Ma'am," he saluted and departed.

"Rider!" Mochè called to another dispatcher. When he recognized her, his voice softened as he directed, "Gabriela, tell Colonel Benjamin and Colonel Matthew to bring their brigades in now." He whispered to her, "Use caution, dear. You know I worry for you." The young blonde woman saluted, kicked her horse, and swiftly rode away.

Mochè dispatched scouts to the other cavalry units to begin deploying their troops in an organized manner, thereby preventing chaos on the battlefield. Mochè aimed to minimize radio communications for this battle, relying more on scouts and dispatch riders. Benjamin and Matthew's brigades, attached to General Jeremiah, were part of the forces forming a broad perimeter along with Generals Deborah, Joseph, Mark, and Elisheba.

Generals Helen and Aaron remained mounted next to the manhig on either side of his stallion—their limbs had pieces of armor attached. Chest shielding was too cumbersome. The traps had been set days earlier, and now the sharpened stalks of golden bamboo, native to the area for over a century, stood upright and straight, their top edges as sharp as razors. Hundreds upon hundreds of hairy barbarian raiders marched toward their gruesome deaths, unaware of what was unfolding. Their simple minds led them to believe it was pagan gods, displeased with their poor performance during the attack, who cast them to their grisly fates. The hordes rushed even faster as hundreds more fell into the deadly craters. The spikes pierced the huge men's body parts, heads, faces, and groins, leaving a grotesque diorama of hideous figures impaled with razor-sharp poles protruding from them at odd angles. Only when the holes were completely filled could the beasts wearing animal skin furs advance, walking over the traps filled with the remains of their comrades.

As a precaution for his armies, Mochè had tied colored ropes to indicate that the area was dangerous, preventing any of his troops from entering nearby to fight. Now, he was bringing his cavalry and infantry in closer to try to stop the wicked herd advancing toward the front of the stronghold after passing the traps. Helen's and Jeremiah's cavalry advanced to engage at the front. Generals Deborah and Joseph would attack the barbarians approaching them from different flanks, positioned apart toward the end. Mark and Elisheba formed the last line of defense, less than a mile from the compound. Constant scouting reports ensured that the beasts didn't split up. The fighting at the front began to grow fierce.

Colonel Benjamin sat at the head of his brigade, waiting for orders. Nikanyiso, eager for battle, jogged around his horse. Beside Ben was Matthew, his brigade behind him. Both scanned the land with their telescopes for any signs of the enemy or dispatch riders.

"I see that attractive young blonde woman approaching, Matt," Ben announced cheerfully. "I know who she is," he added with a smile.

"I also have her in sight," Matthew replied, dismissing Ben's unnecessary remark.

The rider's horse galloped at blinding speed, leaving a trail of smoky dust in her wake. She slid her mount to the side in front of them and turned in her saddle. "Colonels," the young woman saluted both before saying, "Second Lieutenant Gabriela reporting, sirs," completing the formality of introduction even though they both knew her name. "The manhig requests that you bring your forces to the front now."

"How far away is the enemy?" Ben inquired. Even in the heat of preparing for battle, he longed to hear her voice.

As her flustered horse danced in a circle, she reined in the mustang, showcasing her skill as she replied, "Very close, Colonel. When I left, they were less than 15 minutes away. I rode hard, sir, so I estimate they'll arrive at the front in about ten minutes, maybe less."

"Were the other cavalry informed?" asked Matthew.

"Yes, sir, riders were sent to all cavalry brigades."

"No time to waste, then," Ben turned his stallion back to his command and shouted to a captain, "Prepare all battalions! Immediately!" He then turned back to the dispatcher and instructed her, "Ride swiftly back to the manhig. Tell him we're moving quickly."

"Yes, sir!" she saluted and galloped away.

"Gabriela looks lovely riding a horse, don't you think?"

"Ben, stop staring at the Lieutenant's bouncing backside and let's get ready, you lovesick puppy!"

"She's beautiful and an excellent equestrian and such a magnificent sight, though," Ben whispered as he began to gather all the reports from his subordinates.

"Besides," Matthew explained as he readied his weapons and grasped his sword, "you know the regulations state you must obtain her permission and that of your commanding officer before you can court a young woman, and then only with another couple present."

"Is that what you did with Eliza?" Ben smiled satirically, observing his friend blush. "How about we give each other permission, and you and Eliza can be our escorts? That would be better than asking a stuffy general."

"Ben, if we survive this catastrophe, any general would be happy to give you permission, and you can do the same for me."

Ben turned back again and shouted, "Riders forward! Fast

pace!"

Matthew yelled the same order to his brigade. As he turned and watched his cavalry ride in perfect unison alongside Ben's, he commanded, "Full gallop ahead!" Nikanyiso trailed the cavalry, running, with the feathers of his shield and headdress fluttering in the rush of his speed.

Matthew's and Ben's brigades charged down a trail, passing the waiting cavalry and infantry troops stationed at the rear and center of the anticipated path of the hairy, gorilla-like raiders. As both their brigades approached the front, Ben and Matt saw the grim faces of the beast-like apes while other brigades emerged from the flanks ahead. They had just begun to engage General Helen's command. Ben spotted Mochè shouting orders to the ranks. Then, he observed the manhig dismount and race toward the enemy alongside the infantry. There, he could immerse himself in the thick of battle to relay specific instructions through his chest-mounted radio transmitter.

Ben and Matt led their cavalry riders past the infantry at the front and into the horde of beasts. The battalion of foot soldiers employed the ancient Roman technique, known as the 'testudo formation,' in which they covered themselves with their shields while their long spears protruded. The mutant beasts inadvertently crashed into the sharp edges jutting out, and their enormous bodies slid down the long poles. Many spears snapped from the weight of bearing them, and the giant creatures ran in circles, bleeding profusely. Other beasts panicked and darted in confusion with the broken spears sticking out, knocking over many of their own and creating chaos among them. But the pandemonium didn't last long, and they quickly regrouped and charged ahead, frothing with rage.

Matthew's horse reared back among a thick cluster of the hairy gorilla beasts as they swung swords in one hand, daggers in the other. Waves and waves of beasts poured toward him and Ben. Removing his solar mortar rifle strapped to his shoulder, Matthew blasted it to make a hole in the herd. Hairy, giant figures blew apart, bloody limbs and heads flew in the air from the multiple mini-bomb explosions. Small patches of hair from the beasts lingered and floated in swirls amid the smoke of the small detonations. Those ghouls who had stood at the front now held their robust stomachs as their entrails poured out and spilled to the ground.

One of the giants held his bloodied intestines in one hand, swinging a sword in the other as he charged at Benjamin, who fought mounted on his stallion. Ben's legs held tightly to his horse's body; shifting his rifle to his left hand, he drew his saber with his right and sliced the brute's head clean off. It rolled as its body appeared to be walking in circles momentarily before keeling over.

Nikanyiso speared the giant men, gracefully stabbing or slicing one after the other. He squatted and swung his lance, tripping six of the raiding beasts. Some of the uncoordinated mutations fell onto their own swords or daggers.

Matt fought close to his friend, Ben. They watched each other's backs, calling out to warn the other of charging groups of the fur-covered animals they battled. Ben repeatedly fired his sidearm, swinging his horse in a circle, taking out about fifteen beasts before holstering the weapon. Then he removed his mortar rifle and blew apart another twenty of the beasts with a single blast. That opportunity for a clear opening between the beasts happened spontaneously, and Ben took advantage of it. He never could have killed that many with his soldiers nearby. Though it seemed the more ape-beasts they killed, the more that came. He and Matthew led their cavalry riders further into the chaotic fight. Nikanyiso sprinted along into the heart of the clash of thousands.

Mochè, at the center of the struggle, commanded his generals over the radio, "Many are escaping through us! General Deborah, move your army in now to flank them!" He watched the tremendous number of beasts passing by him. With his sword and dagger in hand, he fought while he spoke. "General Joseph, move in now to flank them on your side! Hurry! We have to stop them!" For the first time, he noticed that these creatures kept drinking something from a pouch they shared among themselves. "They're taking some potion to help them fight better. Some sort of drug," he muttered. He called his commanders in the field via radio and told them, "The beasts are consuming a potion to strengthen themselves. Destroy the pouches you see them passing around."

As Mochè fought, he noticed Helen in the near distance struggling against men twice her size. Like giant bees, the large horde swarmed around her. She fired her sidearm with one hand while wielding her sword with the other as the beasts closed in. One of the hairy giants grabbed her leg, pulling Helen from her horse. "No!" Mochè shouted, "Not today!" He remembered Sarah's face the last time he saw her alive when the beasts compromised his fortress and charged furiously, like a madman, toward the herd surrounding his general, determined not to let his friend die. He jumped into the center of the horde, battling fiercely like the savage he had become. Standing next to the fallen Helen, he swung his sword in a wide arc and then backhanded it in the same fluid motion, decapitating or disemboweling ten of the ugly creatures. Backing away from the muscular, formidable man, the beasts thought he was insane. This gave Mochè a moment to lift Helen from the ground. "Are you okay?" he asked, holding her in his arms to steady her.

Stunned from her fall and near death, Helen stood dazed in Mochè's embrace. The battle raging around them felt like a mirage. In that fleeting moment of bliss, she could feel his breath on her face and his eyes close as he stared into hers. It was the first time she felt his muscular body pressed against her, awakening emotions she had never known before. With her womanly love radiating from her, she longed to kiss him and express her deep affection. Then, from the corner of his eye, Mochè spotted one of the monstrous ghouls charging toward them. He shielded Helen with his body and tried to move away. It was too late; the beast stabbed Mochè with its dagger. Before he fell, he managed to drive his sword into the ogre's stomach before dropping it.

"Soldier!" Helen screamed. "You two," she pointed, "take the manhig; he's been wounded!" She helped them, now tearing, blaming herself for that moment of passion that caused this. "Be careful with him! Get him to the hospital quickly!" Knowing Mochè would be in good hands, Helen realized she had to stay with her army and returned to the fight with tears in her eyes.

Matthew saw Mochè fall from a distance and galloped through the fighting toward him. Jumping off his horse, he commanded the soldiers who held him, "I'll take the manhig!" As Matthew held Mochè, lifting him onto his horse, he felt a pain as though a mule had kicked him in the back. He tried to steady himself but fell to his knees, then to the ground, lying beside his manhig. Nikanyiso rushed to find a medic.

General Deborah attacked the brutes fiercely at the flank. Her army broke through with fury, but many of those beasts spread out and moved toward the fortress. "Rider!" she called. "Go quickly to General Joseph and warn him that over a thousand of the savages got through my forces and are heading his way."

Deborah began to turn to direct her subordinates. As she did, another dispatch rider approached, appearing panicked, and told her, "General Helen reports she couldn't hold the front." Her breathing strained as she continued speaking. "It's a horrifying sight, ma'am. They're drinking something that makes them go berserk. General Helen has suffered too many casualties to assist you. Ma'am, they're taking many of our soldiers aside and raping them before they slaughter them in horrific ways. I've seen it!" Trembling, her deep blue eyes widened and bulged in fear; she said, "Then the monsters cut the flesh from the top of their heads to take their hair." Bowing her head, she said, "Our manhig was wounded."

"Oh, no!" Deborah answered, now feeling anxious.

"Yes, ma'am, and well over a thousand that broke through

the front are coming this way."

Remaining calm, Deborah told the scout, "Stay here for a moment." She thought as quickly as she could, recalling all the military advice she could muster from her former commander, Sarah. Deborah rode close to the shaken blonde-haired rider and said, "Go to General Joseph on the other side and warn him that well over two thousand beasts are coming toward him, not the thousand I thought." Deborah paused, thinking, then commanded, "Go now!"

The young dispatch rider galloped across the countryside, her long, blonde hair flowing in the wind from the hard ride. The booted feet of her long, slender legs kicked the horse to go faster up each incline. As her mustang leaped over the highest hill's crest, she pulled it back promptly, the horse skidding to a halt when she saw the terrifying sight of hairy gorilla creatures directly before her. She had ridden into the middle of a vast herd of beasts. Panicking, the young woman tried to turn the agile mustang, but one of the giant creatures grabbed her boot, yanking it off as she fell from her horse. Fighting her terror, she pulled off her other boot to try to run barefoot. A large, hairy claw grabbed her and pulled at her body, ripping off her uniform coat and shirt amidst her screams as she kicked and punched.

Another massive beast grasped her belt and swiftly tore off her military field pants and undergarments in a single motion. The beast pushed the nude young woman to the ground, opening his fur coat and readying himself. Completely restrained by the beast, the blonde woman screamed at the sight of the mammoth's evil red eyes glaring, preparing to satisfy its primal need. Unable to move or even budge, she cried while stiffening every muscle of her body, trying to prepare for the humiliation and pain of what was about to happen to her. Fighting to resist, she gazed at the dreadful creature about to take her, terrified, remembering the fate of a young woman she had watched.

The first ape-like beast pushed away the one who now crouched over her. He grunted in the language of beasts, "I saw the blonde trophy first," he muttered in that primitive tongue as he sniffed around the naked young woman like an animal. "She's not a virgin, but I'll enjoy humiliating her anyway and take the blonde hair!" Fighting desperately from going into shock, the young woman began slowly crawling away on her hands and knees. Her terrified eyes, watching the giant get angry, grunting again, "You can devour her when I'm finished—not before!—I saw her first!" He spotted his prized colored hair wiggling away, grabbed the woman, and flung her over his hairy shoulder. Pulling back her long, golden hair, the young woman squirmed, kicking and punching the beast amid tears of her fear.

"No! I want to take her and the trophy!" He punched the beast that carried the woman, causing the massive creature to fall. As its huge body lay on the grass in a daze, the other lowered its colossal body over his young blonde trophy, grunting as it prepared to take her. She kicked the giant in the groin, and he fell over, moaning.

The young woman fought her fear and stood up on the frigid hilltop, crouching and desperately looking for a way out of the surrounding herd. Now losing all hope, the tired young woman's nude body went limp as she awaited her fate, finally allowing the shock to conceal her mind from what would happen.

As the two gorillas began bickering again, a mounted rider seemingly appeared out of nowhere. The rider swung his saber in an arc, killing both the beasts battling for the woman's flesh. He reared his stallion to make an opening in the herd, urging his horse past the distracted, onlooking beasts, and swept up the young woman with his arm. In a daze, she instinctively positioned herself behind the rider, and they rode together over the grassy knolls of the countryside as swiftly as the wind. Without wasting time, the cavalryman galloped away from the horror that haunted the young woman's mind. Too frightened to cry, she clung tightly to the rider's waist, escaping thoughts of her near-gruesome fate, her long exposed legs glistening in the sun as her bare feet naturally grasped the legs of the rider.

Field doctors could finally treat the wounded after the monstrous creatures tore through the front lines of Helen's forces. Injured by the edge of an enemy's sword, Ben removed the armor piece from that limb and wrapped his bloody arm in a bandage. As he did, he ordered, "Major! Take both Colonel Matthew's and our brigade back to the stronghold. I'll meet you there." Ben intuitively knew that the herds would be on the way to the stronghold. Then, he mounted his stallion to search for Matthew, unaware that his friend had been injured and taken to one of the hospitals. Separated amid the chaos of battle and believing that one of the generals had ordered Matthew back to reinforce the stronghold like some other officers, Ben scoured the landscape, searching for his friend to ensure he was alright. He rode swiftly and determinedly toward the compound, avoiding the hordes of ghoulish, mutated creatures.

In the distance, he saw a smaller figure that he thought might be human. Ben pulled back on the reins of his horse to stop. Taking out his telescope, he focused it. As the blurry shape sharpened, he realized it was a human woman among the horrid ghouls. Ben kicked his stallion and galloped straight at the person, crashing into the horde of creatures before skidding to a halt. After killing two of the giants who held her with a wide swing of his saber, he pulled hard on his horse's reins, rearing it up to create a gap in the herd of beasts, and swept up the young woman he now recognized. Trembling and crying in fright, she seemed to be in shock, clinging tightly to Ben's body as they rode away.

When they had ridden far from that herd of gorilla-like beasts, Ben pulled back the reins to stop his horse and quickly tied it to a tree. He removed his remaining armor pieces and flung them to the side, then cradled the naked young woman in one arm and, using his other hand, removed his bedroll from behind the saddle. Ben gently laid her on the soft grass and wrapped his warm, padded bedroll around her, sheltering her virtue and warming her from the cold. Rubbing her shoulders to help keep her from succumbing further to the effects of shock, he spoke softly, "It's me, Gabriela, Colonel Benjamin."

Now recognizing him, she sat up, searching around in fear as if for something. She embraced the squatting young man with jet-black hair in silence, unable to speak. When Gabriela finally calmed down enough to say just a few words, her body shaking wildly from shock, she nervously exclaimed in fragmented syllables, "I've never been so scared!" Those broken words were all she could muster before her tears flowed freely. Still frozen in shock and unable to move, Ben quickly dressed her in his spare uniform slacks and a sweatshirt from his bedroll to cover her nudity and keep her warm. The clothes fit loosely, and the legs of the pants were far too long, so Ben rolled them up to expose her bare feet. He tore his scarf in two and wrapped each piece around Gabriela's feet to keep them warm.

Shrouding his uniform coat around her shoulders, Ben softly told her, "I'm afraid we have to go, my love." He lifted her once more and placed her on the saddle before mounting in front of her. "Hold on tightly, Gabriela." And she did as they rode together to the stronghold. Now, as if enveloped in the safety of a mother's womb, her wrapped feet grasped his lower legs, and her hands clasped together, locking her arms securely around Ben's waist. Her head tilted and rested on his upper back as her baggy clothes and long blonde hair flowed in the wind of their swift ride.

Generals Mark and Elisheba sat on their horses, positioned close to each other, as their two armies combined forces to protect the compound a mile behind them. "We're the last line of defense," Mark said, breaking the silence.

"Based on the number of beasts remaining that the scout informed us about, we have eliminated almost six thousand of those vile creatures," Elisheba replied. "I'm worried about my husband at the front. Our manhig was wounded, but I haven't received any news about him."

"Yes, but look at how many of our troops were needed to defeat those nearly six thousand." Mark smiled, "Don't worry about Aaron; he's invincible."

From her telescope, Elisheba watched a dispatch rider galloping fast, heading their way. "He's probably riding to tell us that the beasts are advancing on us."

"Whatever remains of their herd, we'll easily destroy," Mark said calmly as he watched the rider approaching at lightning speed. Then, through his scope, he realized it wasn't a dispatch rider but General Joshua, Mochè's second-in-command, who led the southern armies.

Bloodied from battle, Joshua slid his horse sideways; he looked terrified. "They outsmarted us!" he shouted. "The thousands of gorilla beasts didn't attack where General Deborah expected. They divided and spread into two separate hordes. They went around you, heading for our stronghold!"

"Colonel!" Mark shouted. "Turn our forces and head for the compound!"

Joshua turned to a scout and yelled, "Rider! Quickly deliver a message to General Deborah and then General Joseph. Inform them of what happened and tell them to bring their armies to the stronghold! Tell them the beasts will likely breach it." Joshua turned back to Elisheba and, while thinking, he said, "There must be a more intelligent leader at the rear of the horde of those hairy creatures."

After hearing the news that the beasts had separated and were headed toward them, the company of soldiers Mochè had posted inside the compound rang the bell and activated the siren. It was a signal that the stronghold was compromised. They made last-resort plans for as much defense as they could offer to the terrified citizens. Soldiers dragged out the many pre-built wooden structures to hold back the raiders and to fight from behind. The captain in charge assigned snipers to higher elevations to eliminate the intruders as soon as they entered. However, he realized the number approaching them was unstoppable, but he continued his effort as it gave some hope to the thousands of people there.

As the stronghold's interior was hastily fortified, the commander outside the fortress positioned her snipers in the tree blinds. Aside from the three solar cannons already stationed at the gate, this would be solely a commando defense. The rest of her company remained concealed behind the trees, armed with automatic rifles, some of which were mortars. She knew her company was heavily outnumbered, and standard battle tactics wouldn't suffice in a situation like this. It was a futile effort, but it was the last line of defense.

"Doctor!" Mochè shouted from his hospital bed as soon as he heard the siren. "Come right away!"

"Yes, Father?" Gloria answered calmly as she rushed over. The hospitals were filled with wounded soldiers, many in critical condition requiring surgery, while others had less severe injuries, such as minor stabs and sword wounds.

"Bandage me as best you can. I have to join my armies."

"But your sutures are fresh, Father; they will tear."

"I can't lie here in luxury while my armies are battling. Do it, Gloria!"

"I swear, you are the worst patient I've ever had."

"It's a sin to swear, Gloria," Mochè forced a smile, grimacing in pain from the tight bandage the doctor was wrapping around his waist. He then gently held the doctor's wrist and said, "Seek shelter below if they get in. Your services won't be needed if they do, and you should be safe, my dear friend."

With a tear in her eye, she replied, "Be careful, Mochè," using his name for the first time and realizing they might never see each other again.

In a different hospital in another town, Matthew sat up, wincing in pain. "Wrap them tighter!" he demanded.

"Sir," the young nurse said, her expression reflecting the seriousness of his injury, "you shouldn't even be on your feet. You have broken ribs and a sword wound."

"Did you not hear the siren?" His face showed determination as he continued, "We're doomed if we don't stop those ghouls!"

"I understand. Let me help you. I'll give you something for the pain."

Matthew slowly limped down the street, strapping on his saber and sidearm. Once the sentinels lowered him outside the compound in a small cart by a rope and pulley, he called to a soldier, "Fetch me that horse, Lieutenant!" As the man led an Appaloosa over to him, Matthew glanced at the horse's saddle and asked, "Is it armed?"

"Yes, Colonel. It's a nice horse. Just brought in by a cavalry rider, and it has a mortar rifle and a solar rifle on the sides," he pointed out. "The poor lad didn't have a chance to use his weapons."

"Help me onto the horse," Matthew grimaced in pain as the Lieutenant carefully assisted the injured man into the saddle. "I'll use his weapons to honor him," he shouted, painfully galloping on the black-and-white spotted horse toward the sounds of the approaching herd of beasts.

General Deborah galloped, leading her army back to the stronghold as fast as she could from the west flank. General Joseph led his forces from the eastern side. Both armies rushed back in a fury to support the troops of Elisheba and Mark, who had split up, each now attacking a side of the divided gorilla beasts. Mark's army struck well over a thousand surprised beasts, who never expected their arrival at the western point of the stronghold. However, a considerable number of the apelike creatures made their way through. Elisheba engaged the same size of beasts on the eastern side of the compound, also taken aback by their presence, where it was least expected. Both Generals Mark and Elisheba dispatched infantry troops to help reinforce the compound.

Mochè began giving orders to the company of soldiers stationed outside after lowering himself beyond the high, sturdy wooden gate at the front; he didn't want it opened for any reason. Some of General Mark's cavalry arrived just in time to assist the small detachment being organized outside the stronghold by the manhig.

The engagement outside the large gated entrance of the tall wooden barrier of their blessed home raged on. Now bolstered by Mark's and Elisheba's armies, Mochè led a stronger force into battle against the hairy gorilla beasts, diminishing their strength.

Matthew painfully swung his sword only when necessary, relying more often on his other weapons. As he rode amid and fought the massive hordes of beasts, he recognized Mochè. Knowing he was wounded in battle, seeing his manhig fighting among his armies lifted his spirits. At an opportune time, when he neared him, he called out, "Manhig, it's good to see you, sir!"

From the corner of his eye, Mochè noticed his young officer. He shouted, "Likewise, young Matthew. I heard you were injured." Both men grimaced as they braced against the pain they endured.

As the fighting continued, the beasts, desperate to enter the fortress, threw ropes to climb. They were hungry, and the cannibals had only preyed on fallen soldiers and some of their own when necessary. Such large men had to eat frequently and craved the fresh victims inside the fortress. Human flesh was a delicacy. Their large, muscled arms labored as their strong, hairy legs pushed hard to scale the barrier. The dull iron sounds of the hooks clanging against the wood of the fortress front frightened both soldiers and townspeople alike. All remembered what these beasts had done to them, and many were still suffering from those wounds.

However, when the small herd leaped from the top of the wall, they landed in a large, wide woven net made of heavy hemp rope that lay spread out before the gate inside the fortress. The soldiers at the sentry stands used a large wooden pulley to slowly lift the weight of the loaded net, causing the twelve beasts inside it to fall into a heap, flopping like fish out of water and struggling to break free. The captain inside the compound ordered the lead rope of the net to be tied to a sturdy pole, leaving the ghouls suspended in the air.

Then the remainder of Generals Elisheba and Mark's armies entered the conflict, closely followed by General Deborah's forces, who arrived simultaneously with General Joseph. None of the armies were needed; aside from a few stragglers and those who hung helplessly within the compound, the enemy had been defeated.

"General, our army has captured 20 of the beasts; many are lying on the field wounded," one of Deborah's brigade commanders reported as she surveyed the compound after tending to her army. General Deborah had gathered all her wounded, like the other generals, and sent them to hospitals or allowed medics to first stabilize some in the field.

"They aren't human, Colonel; send detachments to destroy all of the wounded beasts where they lie. As for the ones who are still alive, it's up to the manhig. Bring them here." While recalling their last raid, she turned back and told him, "Bind them tightly; they're incredibly strong."

"Oh, I forgot. Three of those speak, ma'am." He pointed to the hanging, netted ape-beasts. I heard them talking in our language."

"I'll let the manhig know," remembering the four who dressed like monks and spoke the language of the followers. She frowned at the memory but observed the creatures with care, wondering why God would allow such wicked mutations to exist.

"So, which of you speaks?" Mochè asked, his hands clasped behind his back. That posture eased some of his pain. Much to Gloria's delight, he returned to the hospital, but he went outside when Deborah's runner informed him about the speaking mutations. Mochè wanted to find out where their women were. Deborah and Helen stood beside him, observing the ghastly things as all of them remained silent, none responding to their manhig's question.

"Perhaps we should boil one of them in oil, Mochè. Maybe the others will speak after seeing that sight," Helen said, smiling. "We can make a nice stew with the meat of the gruesome thing. Why waste good food?"

"Let me have my way with that pretty woman, and I might talk all you want," a voice called out from the bundled beasts. They heard a loud sniffing sound before the same deep voice said, "Hmm, I smell a virgin. Nice and ripe. Such a shame someone like her, so beautiful with such a shapely figure, remains one." His deep, wicked-sounding roar of laughter was horrifying. "She emits an odor of attraction for you, Almighty Manhig. Maybe you should give her what she wants." He let out another spine-chilling animal-like howl.

"Don't let him rattle you, Helen. That's what he wants," Mochè whispered.

Embarrassed and blushing, Helen calmly told the speaking beast, "Not long ago, I escorted about 200 of your kind to their doom. They trotted completely naked, and just before the demons we left them with consumed them alive, I pointed out how small their genitalia were for such large men," she teased. "Who could you possibly please with such tiny tools?" she chuckled. "Maybe mice?"

"Touché, Helen," Mochè whispered again, this time trying to hold back a belly laugh.

The net full of beasts wobbled as a brawny, hairy arm reached out, identifying the one Helen had insulted. His roar was thunderous as he called her despicable things. "When I get out of here, you'll pleasure me before I eat you alive, woman."

"Good job, Helen, you got his attention." Then he told the beastly creature who now glared at him between an opening of the roped net, "But you're not going to get out of there, so do you wish to speak now?" The ghoul remained silent. "It gets cold at night. Oh, I recall how much giant creatures like you excrete your meals of human flesh. Pew, I still recall the odor. Must be getting pretty hungry, eh?" Mochè grinned while thinking, then said, "Well, I'll just leave you to wade in your own feces and eat each other for now. Let out one of those animal cries like you did if you're ready to speak."

Mochè began to walk away when another one grunted, "Wait!" as the first one told him to shut up. "Will you let me out if I talk to you?"

"Of course."

"Use caution, Manhig. They will do anything to escape," Deborah advised.

As a wide perimeter of torches glowed, guarded by soldiers standing shoulder to shoulder with their solar rifles, each beast dropped one at a time. As one fell, a soldier forced it to its knees, binding its arms behind it with heavy rope and tying its ankles tightly. Mochè separated the three who had learned to speak. He knew some could talk. The last survivor from the previous raiders of his kind had explained how some of his fellow animalistic cretins learned speech. They captured one of Mochè's followers. When he heard about the despicable acts they committed against the young woman who had taught them by force, he had that survivor killed. One of these three beasts who could verbalize was more willing to divulge what the manhig wanted to know.

"Are there more like you?"

"Only some, mostly old and feeble."

"Are your women there?"

"Yes."

"Will you take me to them?"

"Never!" it snarled, exposing its sharp teeth. "They are giants like us and resourceful. They will devour you all after torturing the people you send." Mochè knew he was trying to intimidate him. He sprinkled the mutated brute with holy water and watched as the hunched, hairy gorilla howled in agony, confirming the creature's wickedness and demonic presence. He realized there was nothing he could do to make the beast reveal the location of their nesting place, and he wouldn't resort to torture, not even on an animal. Mochè learned as much as he expected. Being unruly beasts, they left a trail still fresh with the horrible scent of their bowels, which even he could detect. It wouldn't be difficult for the dogs.

"Including Deborah's 20 captured ape-men, all other generals had gathered over a hundred. Along with the 12 from the net, that makes well over 130 surviving raiders," Aaron addressed the hastily assembled council. The generals present still wore their battle gear.

Unable to attend, Moche returned to the hospital. Joshua, his second, read to the council from the manhig's letter: 'These mutations are evil and the result of the sins of our forefathers who delved too far with the manipulation of human life. There is no other judgment than to eradicate them from the face of the earth by fire, leaving their dust to blow in the wind in the hope God will direct that remaining trace of them back to Hell.'

"So is the ruling of the manhig," Joshua said. "Acting on behalf of the manhig in his absence, I command it to be so. General Helen, you have lost more troops than any other army. I honor you with the task of carrying out the orders."

General Helen stood up and saluted Joshua, saying, "Thank you for the privilege."

As Helen stood outside the fortress, with battle gear and remnants of war scattered around her, a solar backhoe dug a broad and deep pit under Helen's orders. A group of husky laborers assisted in trimming the edges of the large hole. Helen then ordered, "Start a fire of ample logs to make it grow hot and have steady blazing flames."

Later, when she observed the hot coals burning in the inferno, Helen ordered, "Throw them in one at a time."

Helen recognized the one who had insulted and embarrassed her. She walked up to him where he stood in line, his arms and legs bound, and softly told him, "Enjoy the tropical climate, lover boy." As his eyes bulged with rage and he struggled to break free, his large muscles expanded while he screamed sexual expletives. Helen used all her might and pushed the giant into the fiery pit, hearing his insults quickly shift to horrifying shrieks of desperate pleas for mercy among the others screaming from pain as they slowly burned alive. Most of the beasts clung to the sides of the hole where it wasn't yet as hot, desperately trying to climb the wall of softly dug earth but slipping. Helen merely yelled below, "Bye-bye, big boy! Now you know what it's like to be roasted!" recalling what happened to the warrior Naomi. She turned to her soldiers and ordered them, "Let the fire burn completely out. Guard them closely so none get out." While finishing those words, a ghoulish burning shape leaped out, flames ravaging its skin as it twirled in agony. General Helen kicked the skeletal figure with the heel of her boot, and it broke apart, falling back into the giant hole. "Let the pit remain open so their ashes scatter as our manhig wishes," Helen shouted her orders, her battle uniform tattered from the fury of combat.

Chapter Ten

Winter's Journey

After the battle that defeated the gorilla beasts, Zipporah, Eliza, and Rosetta emerged from their basement hiding place, carefully checking first to ensure the fighting had stopped. From the cellar, the women couldn't hear what was happening. When Zipporah cracked open the hatch a little to listen, they heard the townspeople's cheers and knew it was over.

Rosetta rushed home to see if her husband had returned yet. He had been detached to the company of those soldiers guarding the compound. Zipporah took Eliza's hand, and the two women ran together to find their men. They weren't back in town, so they quickly walked to the large wooden gate where soldiers were still returning. Standing on tiptoes to look between the crowd, they couldn't spot either Mochè or Matthew. They waited until the last troops returned and still didn't see them.

Seeing the frightened expression on the young woman whom she considered a sister, Zipporah said to Eliza, "Let's go to Mochè's office at the courthouse. They'll know where he is, and he'll definitely be aware of Matthew's whereabouts."

Now in full panic mode after seeing the lock on the courthouse door, they spotted Aaron leaving the council, and Zipporah called out to him. Breathless from fear and running, she managed to shout, "Aaron?"

He turned and, upon seeing their faces, yelled while pointing, "They're both alive! Head to the hospital!"

"Oh my God!" Zipporah attempted to conceal her tears from Eliza, but the teenage girl was already crying as she matched Zipporah's quickening pace.

They smelled the odors of disinfectants, ether, body fluids, and other medicinal scents permeating the air even before the two women entered the hospital tent. Holding hands tightly, they walked together, facing the horrific sights of men and women screaming in pain as the staff rushed around the large open area, treating the wounded. Stretcher-bearers continued to bring more casualties to the rows of cots in one of the extended infirmaries Mochè had ordered set up in advance in each of the seven towns. Some serious injuries required attention on the battlefield before medics could transport them. A warrior cried out in pain as doctors amputated her arm above the elbow to save her life, discarding the limb as the hand and fingers of it still moved in gesticulation atop a pile of other arms and legs on the bloodied floor until orderlies or nurses found time to take them away.

Another soldier resisted the medics who were trying to remove his leg. "Let me die," he screamed. "What kind of warrior will I be without my leg?"

"Steady him, nurse," a doctor instructed his assistant. Without glancing at the injured man he was treating, he said, "The technicians will make a new limb for you that's just as good, soldier."

Eliza spotted Matthew lying sideways on a cot near Mochè, gazing at the canvas wall. She and Zipporah practically flew to them.

As Eliza approached Matthew, she noticed his back turned to her, with a bloodied bandage covering his wound. "Matthew," she whispered, unsure if he was awake. "Oh, my God," she sobbed.

"It's nothing, my love." He heard her voice through the weeping and spoke softly so Mochè couldn't hear him. "I can't turn, though. Come, let me see your beautiful face."

As she held his hand tightly, a doctor walked over to examine his stab wound. "You're very lucky, Colonel. You must have been moving when you were hit. The blunt end of the sword fractured your ribs, and just the tip of it tore your flesh. It could have been much worse."

"See, my love, you mustn't move until you're completely healed. I'll come by every day to take care of you."

"Yes, he was moving," Mochè shouted from his cot as Zipporah knelt beside him, caring for him. "He was trying to get me on a horse, the young fool! He was trying to save my life. I remember, lad," pride clear in his voice as he spoke.

"How could you do this to me, Mochè? I was scared out of my wits." Tears rolled down Zipporah's face. "Oh, God, I love you so much!" She wiped her tears and ordered, "Don't you ever do anything like this again!"

Helen, who had come to visit the man who had saved her on the front line, noticed Zipporah and stepped back outside to wait. She brushed shoulders with Colonel Benjamin as she exited, and he entered.

The colonel, his arm in a sling from the sword wound sustained while battling at the front, had come to visit two of the hospitalized patients: his friend, Matthew, and the young woman he had brought in, Gabriela. He approached Matthew only to find him occupied with Eliza, so he stood on his tiptoes, searching for the young blonde woman who lingered in his thoughts. As he stood searching the tented room, he felt a gentle tap on his back. Ben turned to see the same angelic face that haunted his dreams.

"Colonel?" Gabriela's fair-skinned face, slightly windburned from riding for so long, greeted him. "Hi," she said with a smile. "Oh, you're wounded," she cried out, holding her hands to her cheeks, displaying the same emotional response as if he were a loved one—a boyfriend or husband.

"Gabriela," he paused for a few seconds, becoming tongue-tied before he continued, "Oh, this is just a small wound. I thought you'd be in bed—I mean a cot." He nervously corrected himself to avoid sounding misleading.

"No," her blue eyes looked up into his. "They released me earlier today," she smiled again. "Thanks to you—I mean, sir."

Ben watched as her full lips parted, feeling a pang in his chest. He said, "There's no need for rank in the hospital."

"Good," she smiled again, saying, "I wanted to thank you properly, Benjamin." She stood on her tiptoes, her arms reaching around his neck, and kissed him softly on the lips. Then she stood gazing at him, blushing.

"I thought you said you were a perfect gentleman with the young lady," Matthew called out to Ben from his cot.

"Oh, Colonel," she saluted, but Matthew waved it off. "I wanted to thank you for recommending me for a decoration, sir."

Seeing her up close and not mounted on a horse, Matthew thought she was indeed a beautiful young woman. Observing his lovestruck friend's expression, he admitted the truth, "Colonel Benjamin had more to do with that than I did."

She turned back to Ben, her eyes widening to reveal a beautiful indigo hue in the tent's lighting as she whispered, "Thank you, Benjamin." His heart beat faster as her splendid face transformed into a heavenly smile.

Gabriela and Ben strolled outside together. She whispered, taking his hand in hers, "I really appreciate everything you did for me out there, Benjamin. It was very gallant of you." Then her expression changed, becoming more serious as she said, "I thought for sure I was…" She couldn't bring herself to say the thoughts that still traumatized her. "I saw what they did to another young rider." A tear rolled from her lovely eye, and she began to tremble. Ben wrapped his one good arm around her shoulder to comfort her. She whispered even more softly as he held her, "Even when I was dazed and in shock, I remember you called me 'my love.' Did you mean that, Benjamin?" Her big eyes gazed deeply into his once more.

"Yes, I did," he replied swiftly, needing no time to think.

Gabriela immediately stood on her tiptoes and pressed her lips to Ben's. At first, it was a gentle, tender kiss, letting Ben feel the softness of her full, shapely lips. But Gabriela wouldn't pull away from his mouth, wrapping her arms around his neck. Being careful of his wound, she pressed her body close and held him tightly. Opening his mouth with her lips, Gabriela kissed Ben excitedly, licking his lips. She moaned as her tongue rolled with his, the fingers of her hands exploring his muscles. Ben removed his sling to fully experience the softness of her body, which he had only dreamed of before. In their secluded spot, wrapped in each other's arms, they each uncontrollably released the repressed passions they had held back for so long.

Eliza and Zipporah visited the hospital daily to see their men. They nurtured and cared for them, cherishing every moment spent together. They felt relieved to see them recovering well after so much worry and many tears.

On the third day the ladies came, Mochè walked with Eliza to a private corner. Looking fondly at her, he softly said, "My daughter, it's only fitting that you live with Zipporah and me. For now, leave your home empty and move your things to our house, which should have been yours long ago. Moments like this remind us of the importance of family. I worried about both Zipporah and you during the attack. I don't want you living alone out there any longer. You can have your privacy," he glanced in Matthew's direction as if he knew that Matthew often went to see Eliza, "but I want you to live at home. Always remember you are now Eliza of the family Ignatius." Eliza wept at the love he expressed, recalling his formal adoption of her, which she cherished.

When they were alone and lying on their cots, Matthew asked Mochè, "Manhig," he hesitated for a moment and then continued, "I respectfully request that I may have the hon—the privilege—the—"

"Are you trying to ask permission to court my daughter, Colonel?"

"Y-Yes, sir."

"Hmm, you choose a convenient time, young man; how can I refuse you now?" Mochè glanced at Matthew and added, "Alright, son, I trust you'll exercise discretion with her. But don't you ever try to save my life again!" Mochè then burst into laughter. "Why not use Colonel Benjamin and the young woman he fancies as escorts?" Matthew wondered how he knew.

After ten days, Mochè declared, "Enough of this!" Ignoring the pleas of Zipporah and Eliza, he rose from his cot. "I must leave before the scent of those animals fades."

"But your wound hasn't fully healed, my love!" Zipporah pleaded.

"I need to get started. Although their scent is strong, I can't wait too long."

"That's it; I'm getting Doctor Gloria!" Zipporah ran out in search of her.

"We have to destroy their women so they never spawn males who can commit any more ungodly acts!" Mochè shouted back at her.

"I'll go with you, Manhig!" Matthew called from his cot.

"You won't do anything of the sort, young man," Mochè replied. "You'll stay here and heal properly!" He then looked fondly at the young man, who reminded him of himself at that age, and quietly told him, "Unfortunately, now you know you'll face other battles, Matthew." Mochè knew the final one lay ahead in their destiny, and there would likely be others before that time.

No one could stop Mochè—not Zipporah, Eliza, or Doctor Gloria. His mind was made up. But before Mochè set out on the hunt for the women, Zipporah announced to him, "The Lord has blessed us with a baby, my love."

Shocked and stunned by the sudden news, Mochè fell to

his knees and gently pulled Zipporah's stomach toward him, kissing it, seemingly overwhelmed by the revelation. "It's wonderful."

"You seem surprised, my love. We lie like rabbits making love so often; what did you think would happen?" Zipporah giggled, her eyes radiant in the light that shone on them. "Remember how you always call me bunny?" Zipporah's eyes glowed. "Soon, you'll be able to drink the milk from my breasts, as is our tradition," she giggled. "If I provide enough, that is," referring to the follower's misinterpretation of Isaiah 66:11: 'So that you may be suckled and satisfied from her consoling breast, so that you may drink deep with delight from her generous nipple.' The literal words of this passage evolved into a marital ceremony over time, commemorating a wife's breastfeeding time.

Mochè rose and embraced her tightly and said, "I love you, Zipporah. It won't be long before I return. And when I do, we'll prepare a giant feast to celebrate."

Zipporah smiled at her departing husband and softly asked, "You won't cheat on me with General Helen while I'm pregnant, will you?" It was a question intended to be delivered in a whimsically sarcastic tone, while still conveying its intended message. Zipporah knew he was leaving with Helen to hunt for the female beasts, and her intuition told her that Helen had strong feelings for him.

He softly vowed, "In my entire life, I will never love another woman except you, my love."

Mochè led a cavalry brigade atop the grand wooden gate, which had been lowered to cover the moat. He felt he would need such military strength for the intended mission, unaware of what to expect while venturing into unknown territory for an extended period. Helen rode slightly behind him to his left. Nikanyiso, who had proven himself to be a courageous warrior and tracker, ran alongside his manhig. Among the recovering followers, those able lined the sides of the wide main street, rallying them on in the usual tradition. Closest to the gate were a distraught Zipporah and Eliza, clutching each other in fear, both secretly worrying about the impending fate of the man they both loved. Dogs ran ahead, sniffing the scent of the beastly raiders still fresh in their sensitive nostrils.

Once they were far from the compound, Helen rode closer to Mochè as their horses traversed the slopes and meadows of the rugged land. "You're still in great pain, Mochè; I can tell by how you ride." Looking at him with loving pity, she asked, "Why didn't you allow me or another general to take charge of this expedition so you could take more time to recover?" Helen didn't express her true feelings because she privately wanted this time to be with him, away from Zipporah.

His eyes reflected the torment of each stride of his stallion. Mochè replied, "I wanted to see this done personally." He grimaced slightly from his horse's trots and added, "Taking defenseless female lives, even those of the beasts we pursue, troubles me. I would never impose such a task on another officer."

Glowing with love and admiration for traits like those in him, Helen couldn't restrain her words: "Those are just some of the reasons why I love you, Mochè." She lowered her head in embarrassment at her uncontrolled feelings and urged her horse even closer to him. Her lips nearly brushing his ear, she whispered, "I know I can never have you, my beloved; just know that every part of me aches for you." She kept her stallion near his.

Mochè was speechless. Realizing his love for Zipporah was impregnable, this beautiful young woman riding beside him was chiseling away his defenses. Finally, he told her, "Men are weak in body, Helen. Please don't tempt me further, for your beauty is irresistible."

Those words frightened Helen because, before he uttered them, she had felt secure in his ability to resist. Now, she confronted the reality that she was successfully chipping away at his strength. They were on the brink of committing the ultimate sin of adultery. Although her physical desire pushed her recklessly, she didn't want to reduce the man she loved to that.

Helen spurred her horse and distanced it from Mochè, praying to God for strength.

As the sun set, Mochè halted the brigade and loudly addressed: "Captain Tamar, we'll camp here for the night and resume at dawn! It's getting too cold to travel!" He didn't want to proceed in the darkness of unknown territory and the brutally frigid temperature. "Post guards in a perimeter and change them at regular intervals," he instructed her. "Have everyone check for frostbite."

Mochè and Helen walked away from the main brigade force as the soldiers set up camp. As the only high-ranking officers, it was customary for them to pitch their tent apart from the rest of their army.

As Helen undressed, Mochè ordered her, "D-Don't disrobe!" Seeing the nakedness of her thighs and legs by the flames of the campfire, he stuttered nervously. "W-We—never know who might descend upon us in the darkness."

"If I keep myself tightly wrapped in my bed pack, hiding from your sight, may I at least rest my body without cumbersome clothes?" She giggled, "I'll fight them in the nude if necessary." Helen looked into his eyes and said, "We've always disrobed together with other generals. Why does it bother you now?"

Midway through the night, the fierce and blistering winds howled, and the temperature dropped even more. In the biting cold, Helen called to Mochè, "I'm freezing." Her words faltered as her body trembled. "May I warm my body against yours, like the other soldiers nearby are probably doing?" Her teeth rattled. It was a common practice when patrolling in the harsh winters.

Also shivering, Mochè quickly and spontaneously unzipped his bedroll, and Helen's bare body slid into it. They rubbed against each other to stay warm, unable to speak, their bodies tumultuous with ferocious shaking.

They slept quivering until they both awoke in unison from the perspiration of their shared body heat. Helen fought, but couldn't resist the moment she had mentally awaited so long.

Impulsively, she pressed her lips against those of the man she yearned for. She uncontrollably licked his lips and cheeks.

As their heat of passion erupted, feeling her nakedness slipping in the moist sweat against his, Mochè fought to hold back but succumbed to the soft skin of Helen's nude flesh. His uncontrollable hands advanced and fondled illicit places as Helen screamed and twitched from pleasure. He touched the flower of her womanhood, opening the lips of her femininity and feeling the tears dripping from it; Mochè began licking them away.

Helen squealed in ecstasy from the exhilaration—a euphoria she had never felt before. In the wild passion of a lioness, pushing their blasphemous conduct, she scratched his bare body, pleading for him to take her. Helen's fingers grasped the core of his virility and guided it. Mochè, poised and ready to penetrate her virginity, suddenly heard the sound of a rider approaching from a distance, interrupting him.

Clinging to Mochè, her passion unfulfilled, Helen watched him dress quickly, his nakedness captivating. Their sexual aroma still permeated, and her body trembled, but she forced herself up and reached for her uniform. Then, gazing deeply into his eyes, she said, "I love you so much; I can't help myself, Mochè."

With a troubled expression, he told her, "My God, what did we almost do? Finish dressing and join me outside."

Once outside the tent and alone, Mochè muttered, "You tempt me once more, Satan, father of demons. But the Almighty God has halted you again." He looked to the heavens and spoke, "Thank you, my Lord, for sparing me from the unthinkable." Then he heard the thunderous, roaring howl of Satan—a deafening screech in the quiet of the night—marking his failure by the hand of God once more.

Mochè and Helen, still warm from their passion, with the depths of her femininity still wet and yearning for his body, stood together watching the scout ride back at a quick pace. He swiftly dismounted and reported, "Manhig," he saluted, "the camp of those beastly women is nearby."

"How far?"

"Half a day, Manhig."

"Helen," he now looked upon her differently and with fondness, as if she were a lover instead of his general, "assemble the brigade right after they've eaten; we can make it there by the afternoon."

At the stronghold, Matthew was still recovering. Nevertheless, he and Eliza began courting alongside Ben and Gabriela. Both women wore dresses for the occasion, and Matthew continued to dream of Eliza's shapely legs, which he first saw at her father's wedding. "So tell me, Gabriela," Matthew started, attempting to divert his attention from his wicked thoughts as Eliza smiled, folding one leg over the other to raise her dress slightly, aware of Matthew's meandering eyes. "So tell me, Gabriela," Matthew repeated, now blushing as they sat together, enjoying their wine and beer while having dinner at a tavern. "Was Ben truly a perfect gentleman while he was alone with you out there on the prairie for all that time?"

Now that the trauma was well behind her with Ben's help, Gabriela didn't stop Matthew from having a little fun with his friend, even though he didn't really know what happened or what condition she was in—nobody did but Benjamin and Gabriela. Ben only said her horse had run off, leaving her alone. "Yes," Gabriela forced a smile. "Benjamin was a perfect gentleman the entire time and on the way back," she said, blushing and giggling, "even though I didn't want him to be." She kissed Ben lovingly, who was sitting close beside her.

Matthew kissed Eliza, who snuggled against him and whispered, "I love you, Eliza. You'll never know how much I do." He put his hand on her bare thigh, feeling her soft flesh there as he had never done before.

Seeing that prompted Ben to get more passionate, and he softly told Gabriela, "You already know how madly in love I am with you." He kissed her shapely lips.

"Tell me again, Benjamin," Gabriela replied, her deep blue

eyes widening. "And this time, kiss me like you mean it," she added, her full lips slowly parting, eager.

Although not allowed during their initial courting, the two couples parted ways, intending to reunite at the same place in a couple of hours. They wished to walk privately to uncover more secrets about each other rather than in front of any prying eyes or ears.

Matthew and Eliza already had a head start with their blossoming romance. "Let's go to that place we discussed," Eliza whispered, her cheeks flushing as she spoke. Matthew agreed, unable to resist after noticing her naked legs and remembering the feel of them.

Benjamin had never described in detail the story of how he found Gabriela. He didn't tell anyone about her nudity or how she was nearly molested by those beasts. He loved her too much even to joke about his heroism or Gabriela's vulnerability during that time. The woman he loved was a victim of those horrible creatures, and Ben would never allow her to be ridiculed by other soldiers for what happened to her. He had heard many stories told by both male and female warriors, boosting their egos by mocking the embarrassing situations in which other victims found themselves. That experience did draw them closer, though, as fellow soldiers and, more profoundly, the intimacy they now shared.

Now walking together in the chilly evening air, Ben felt the grasp of her small hand through their mittens as they held each other. He didn't dare suggest going somewhere warmer; it wouldn't be proper.

Gabriela pulled him down and whispered in his ear, "Why don't we go to a warmer spot?" Her eyes lit up in a way that ignited Ben's libido.

"I know one," Ben admitted. "When I commanded guard duty near the gate, there was a small station building. It's been vacant since they built the new, larger one."

"Let's go to it." Gabriela's eyes were wide and almost pleading. She pulled his tall figure down again, whispering softly, "I want to feel your body against mine, Benjamin, not in these bear suits," she giggled.

Ben made a fire in the cozy room's wood stove. The small blaze quickly warmed up the vacant station as burning wood glowed, and they opened their fur coats.

"I remember how beautiful you looked in your dress that day at the wedding. It revealed the contours of your lovely figure—your full breasts and shapely legs."

Gabriela's soft hands pulled Ben's face close, kissing his lips excitedly, licking around them before saying, "I wore it for you. I've loved you even before we first spoke."

"As I did you," whispered Ben.

"I wanted you to see my legs," she smiled, giggling seductively as her big eyes stared into his. "Little did I know then that you would soon see my entire body." She slowly and alluringly slid down her floral-designed evening dress and stood before him in the warmth of the stationhouse. "Now you see my nudity again. Remove your clothes," she commanded, shocking Ben. Gabriela whispered, rubbing up against his body, "You've already seen my body twice; now I want to see yours."

Ben nervously bowed to her will while saying, "You're beautiful, and I love you not only for that reason, but more for what radiates from you. It's almost as if I can feel and touch that glow that emanates from you, and I love it." Ben spoke sincerely.

Gabriela pushed Ben down onto the hay floor and gracefully sprang onto his lower abdomen, facing him with her thighs snugly holding the sides of his body there, her feet sliding as her toes massaged the tender sides of his legs as he lay comfortably, using bundled straw as a pillow for his head. Her arms stretched down, caressing his chest muscles, and she began to speak softly. "You never bragged about what you did for me," she said, her expression serious. "Nor did you ever tell anyone what I looked like when you first saw me," she continued, blushing yet sincere. Her thighs began to slowly move forward and back, her body feeling his as she asked, "Why? Other men would have."

"Because I love you too much." Her body rocked back and forth more vigorously to those words, and Ben gasped with pleasure as Gabriela softly moaned.

Gabriela's fluid movements slowed to her faint moans of ecstasy, and then she softly told him, "Don't worry; I won't let you do anything against our laws." She smiled. "As difficult as it is for me, I won't disgrace us by committing the ultimate sin." She remained sitting on Benjamin's thighs, her body flung back erect, but still oscillating, groaning to the pleasure of those movements. Gabriela's beautiful eyes widened, and she smiled, fascinated by how much Ben's anatomy responded to her.

The couple continued lying on the straw-covered floor, their clothes piled nearby, passionately embracing and soaked in sweat near the warm, glowing fire. They lay, feeling each other in intimate places and losing track of time. Gabriela swept her long hair from her face. Now wild and tousled, it made her look seductive. "This is the first time I've been with a young man. Does my body please you, Benjamin? I mean with as much as I can do without—you know." Ben's inability to speak and the way he caressed her flesh indicated that he did.

Gabriela whispered softly once more to the man she was certain she loved, "If this goes any further, you'll have to marry me, you know," as her toes caressed the sides of his legs. "I can only restrain myself with you for so long. My God, it is so difficult. I want to feel you as a wife does her husband."

"It wouldn't be the worst thing that has happened to me," he whispered in response to Gabriela's gleeful moans. Then Ben pulled away and said, "Matthew and Eliza!"

"Oh, my God! We forgot," and she stood up quickly, sliding on her panties.

"But Ben, admiring her shapely nude figure in the light cast by the flames, announced, "Another ten minutes won't matter!" He pulled Gabriela back amid her laughter as she flung her panties away with a toe of her bare foot.

Mochè and Helen rode together, hard and fast, not speaking about what nearly happened the night before. Mochè halted the cavalry. Pulling out his telescope, he watched women emerge from what appeared to be an enormous crater in the ground. "Soldiers!" cried Mochè. "Arm yourselves and prepare to eliminate those ungodly female beasts so they cannot spawn again! Charge!" Nikanyiso, dressed in his garb and wielding his long spear, ran swiftly, almost keeping pace with the horse-mounted troops. As they got closer, Mochè caught a clearer glimpse of the women and yelled, "Halt!" While waving his hands from his saddle, he screamed, "Everyone stop!"

The cavalry slowed down and then skidded to a stop as all the horse-mounted riders clearly observed the women they were about to kill.

"They look human, Mochè," Helen quietly called to him, now close by his side.

"Remain with the troops. I will approach them alone so as not to frighten them."

"What if it is a trap, my love?" Those words slipped out of Helen's mouth, thankful no one was near enough to hear them. "Use caution!" she shouted, worrying for him.

Mochè rode among the naked women, observing them and sizing them up until one moved closer to him. "Have you come for the mutants?" asked the woman who now stood before him.

"We've destroyed all the mutations," Mochè replied, surprised that the woman could verbalize.

"All of them?" Her large brown eyes widened in shock.

"Yes."

"Oh, thank God!" she fell to her knees, bowing before Mochè.

Mochè dismounted and approached her. "Don't be afraid," he said to the trembling woman. "You're human, aren't you?"

"Yes, we are," she answered. Looking to the heavens, she called, "Praise be to God; he has answered our prayers after years of bondage." She looked into Mochè's deep blue eyes, as if seeing his soul, and admired his beauty, asking, "Are you an angel?"

Mochè took her arm and raised the woman from her knees, saying, "I am not an angel; only kneel before God or one of his messengers, not me."

"I am Chenoa. My ancestors migrated from there centuries ago," she said, pointing to the north and further west of where they stood.

Mochè asked, "Chenoa, where are the females of the horrid beasts?"

"They scattered when the mutants left. It was the first time they all departed at once, except for a few," she said, pointing to a handful of frail elderly gorilla beasts. "Even they still have their way with us," she said, looking at them with disgust. Then she referred back to the female gorilla beasts. "Yes, their women feared for their lives whenever they were nearby. The beasts were incredibly cruel to them."

"To their own women?"

"Yes, it was sad. The mutant males only used them to bear beastly, mutated giant children like them. The male mutants were violent creatures who abused their women. Once their females can no longer mate, they kill them and throw their bodies to the wolves," Chenoa cried. "Like they do with us. Though to us, they consume our bodies when they kill us. They relish the flesh of humans."

Mochè stood before Chenoa with countless questions, but only asked, "Why are you here?"

"They force themselves on us to breed only female humans; they consume most of our male infants, allowing only enough to survive for breeding."

"What's the purpose?" Mochè couldn't comprehend.

"They use us only for pleasure," Chenoa said. "It is their way. They prefer us for that purpose more than their women. It satisfies them more because we're smaller, and it gives them a sense of dignity to humiliate human females."

Mochè declared, "My God, what kind of lunacy has fallen

upon us in these end times?" He spoke to no one in particular, venting only what the woman was telling him. Then Mochè commanded a sergeant, "Destroy those old beast animals who prey on these women. At once! Throw their bodies to the wild animals!" The sergeant saluted and carried out his orders.

Chenoa explained several more things to Mochè and a shocked Helen as they sat and listened to her. There were seventy human females of varying young ages, most capable of speaking, but they kept that ability a secret from the giants. Only a handful of human men remained, allowing just enough virile males to live for mating purposes to ensure the birth of more female humans. The twelve remaining young men hid when they heard Mochè's forces approaching. Their belief in God, passed down through generations, was also a secret.

Helen and Mochè comforted Chenoa, assuring her that she and her people were welcome to come and live with them. When Chenoa shared that joyful news with her people, they all emerged from hiding in the massive crater. It was warm inside; caverns and underground springs had existed within the vast cavity for centuries. Mochè assumed the crater had formed from some kind of enormous impact long before. There was no need for clothing, and most of the women frolicked around naked, much to the surprise of the male troops. Their male soldiers' staring eyes disgusted Helen and the other female soldiers until the remaining men revealed the finely chiseled features of their nude bodies. That top-tier group of the remaining men sent shivers down the spines of most of the female warriors.

Mochè realized how problematic this could be and instructed Chenoa that all her people must wear clothes, recalling Zipporah after her rescue and remembering those earlier days when he first fell in love with her. "Your remaining men must now abide by the laws of God regarding adultery," Mochè told Chenoa. He quoted the biblical verse, 'But I tell you that anyone who looks at a woman lustfully has already committed adultery with her in his heart.' He reflected on his own heart regarding what he had done with Helen and felt great remorse, knowing how Satan tempts those closer to God more than those whom he already commands. "I realize it will be difficult for both your few remaining males and many females because the beasts have abused you, and your people have become conditioned to mating." Mochè looked upon Chenoa warmly and said, "That is the way of animals; now you have to learn to live by God's laws for humans."

Mochè and Helen rode away from the crater together. Mochè wanted to speak with her privately. Nikanyiso trailed them from a distance. "I'm leaving you here, Helen, to oversee the preparation of these people. I want you to organize them for travel," he told her. "That young captain will assist you; she's a good soldier. I'm riding ahead with half of the brigade and Nikanyiso."

"But isn't it better if we stay to—"

Mochè interrupted her words. He knew that Helen wanted to travel back with him, but the thought of Zipporah and the days when he first loved her revived his devotion to her and dispelled any foolish temptations from his soul. Mochè spoke to Helen only about their time together, reminiscing about battles and the moment he first saw her as a girl in her teens. Since then, he admired her immensely and didn't want to overshadow those cherished memories with trivial physical desires.

They hadn't realized how far they had wandered from their encampment, already a couple of miles behind them. As they spoke, Helen, succumbing to Mochè's gift of flamboyant language, leaned over, kissed him, and said, "I know you love Zipporah and that she is with child. I understand, Mochè." She smiled.

Right after she finished speaking those warm words, a horde of over a hundred mutations and animal-hoofed demons suddenly emerged and charged toward them from a close distance. An arrow sprang from the herd and struck Mochè between his left shoulder blade and chest as they closed in; that terrible drumbeat began.

"Nikanyiso!" Helen screamed as the tall black figure rushed forward almost as swiftly as a desert windstorm. "Take the Manhig's reins and bring him to the stronghold on horseback!" She turned, now close enough to see the painted faces and bodies of the deformed, grotesque mutants and demons. "Now!" Helen shouted. "He's seriously wounded and only Gloria can help him!"

"Don't do this, Helen. Please obey my orders and escape with us, woman. I order you!" Mochè struggled to speak; he understood what she was about to do by herself.

"There's no time! If I don't block their path, they'll overpower all three of us!" she quickly yelled, not looking back.

"Please, Helen!" he strained to speak.

She ran close to Mochè and quickly kissed him on the lips, saying, "I've loved you since I was a measly sergeant in your ranks!" As soon as Nikanyiso jumped behind Mochè's saddle, Helen kicked the horse with her booted foot. "Goodbye, my love; may you live long and bear many more children." Then she turned, sword in hand, to face her final battle. Mochè heard her last words before he fell into a state of near-unconsciousness.

Nikanyiso's journey back with Mochè was a dangerous one. He had to stop several times to give his manhig a chance to rest. He quickly removed the arrow from his body during their first stop, but it became infected. Nikanyiso's large hands dug into the snow that had started falling during their trek as he searched for the herbs he needed for Mochè's ulcerated wound. Nikanyiso managed to stop the infected bacteria from spreading. The muscular man worked tirelessly, wearing his fur skin for warmth. He built an earth lodge by creating a simple lean-to with a fire beside it. Nikanyiso hunted for food with his spear, using the furred skins to warm Mochè and keep him from shivering due to fever.

In his fiercest delirium, Mochè battled the demons alongside Helen. Then he cried out over her loss and screamed, "Why didn't you ever come to me before with these feelings?" His dreams propelled him further into madness, and he heard Helen's voice telling him, "Many women desire you, Mochè, but they honor you by not approaching you as I did." She smiled at him, and he reached out his hand to express his sorrow for her death. Recalling his temptations for her, he succumbed to her in one illusion. He wept for Helen's loss in another mad delusion, where she said, "All the women who wanted you, including me, were shocked when you fell in love with Zipporah." Then he went back to sleep, fighting his mind to prevent more nightmares.

The sentries quickly opened the gate when they saw it was their manhig, now appearing seriously wounded. Two soldiers came and carefully took Mochè off the stallion. They didn't wait for a wagon but carried him to the nearest hospital as an exhausted Nikanyiso huffed and trotted behind.

Doctor Gloria rushed to the hospital where the soldiers had taken him as soon as she received the news. She was amazed at the incredible job the large, muscular man performed. "Nick, you did remarkable work; you've saved the manhig." His eyes showed his happiness before he collapsed to the floor.

Mochè opened his eyes to the tears of Zipporah and Eliza once more, but this time in a different hospital. "Oh, Mochè, my love, I won't scold you this time. I'm so happy you're alive." She turned to the man lying in the next bed and said, "We can never thank you enough, Nick." Eliza's tears dripped onto the cold compress she was rubbing on her father's forehead. He still had a slight fever even after more than a week since his return. Nikanyiso had been treated for exhaustion and dehydration and was being discharged that day.

After his bizarre hallucinations during their journey back, while Nikanyiso cared for him, Mochè finally snapped out of his brain fog and regained his mental clarity. He focused on the reality of those defenseless women and the brigade he had left behind. Then he remembered what had happened to Helen. "They killed General Helen!" he shouted.

"What?" Zipporah and Eliza exclaimed almost in unison.

"She's the one who saved Nikanyiso and me when a herd of demons attacked us by surprise."

"This is true," confirmed the ebony-skinned warrior, standing dressed and ready for his discharge papers from the hospital.

When Nikanyiso left and Eliza stepped outside the hospital for some fresh air, Zipporah knelt beside Mochè's bed and whispered, "Now I feel terrible for accusing her of wanting you."

Mochè took Zipporah's wrist and said to her, "Don't feel that way. You were right; she tempted me, but the grace of God intervened and stopped her."

"I know many women desire you; I discreetly overhear their discussions."

"Lust is a sin."

"You're a beautiful man, my husband. Have you lost interest in me?"

"Never, my love. You're the most beautiful woman I've ever seen and the only one I will ever love. In fact, my mission took me somewhere that brought back memories of our time together after I first found you. It was a captivating thought and rekindled how deeply I love you." That made him think of his brigade back there. "I need to get dressed! My brigade!"

"No, you're not getting out of bed! This time, I'm standing my ground!" Mochè looked shocked. "Your troops returned yesterday. A captain has been waiting to speak to you."

"Who stopped her?"

"I did!" Zipporah's deep green eyes widened, appearing glorious—a sight Mochè had missed during his expedition.

"But why would you do something like that?" Mochè was astonished to hear his beautiful wife sounding like a tyrant.

"Because, my love," she bent to peck his cheek, "you had delusions and acted like a stark raving lunatic. Besides, she made a temporary report to the council."

"Were there any women with them?"

"Yes, many of them," Zipporah smiled. "And, like me when I first arrived, they refused to wear clothing. Is that what reminded you of me, my love?"

"Sorceress!" Mochè joked, pulling her down for a more passionate kiss, unconcerned about who was watching. "Tell that to those gossipers you eavesdrop on!" Then he remembered, "Oh, I'm sorry; I forgot that you're pregnant!"

Blushing in embarrassment from their public kiss, Zipporah told her husband, "I'm pregnant, not disabled. I'll have someone send for that captain now."

Mochè pulled her closer, more gently this time, whispering in her ear, "Then wait until I get you back home, my love." Zipporah's face flushed even more as she trotted away, a gleam in her eye.

"Captain Tamar reporting, Manhig," the young woman with medium-length light brown hair saluted before standing at attention. Tamar, tall and thin, had attended the military academy.

"Take a seat, Captain, and make yourself comfortable," Mochè, now sitting up in his hospital bed in a room converted into an office, pointed to a padded chair. The young woman felt a bit nervous; she had never reported directly to the manhig before. "Tell me what happened after I disappeared."

"Sir," she sat down hesitantly, secretly enjoying the soft chair's feel, her eyes glowing, "we—"

"It's comfortable, isn't it?" Mochè smiled as he interrupted.

"Yes, it is, sir. I've never sat in a chair like this before," she smiled unconsciously, snapping back to an upright position and wiping the grin from her face.

Mochè replied, "Sit back and relax, Captain. You deserve it. I heard you did great work out there." When he noticed the young woman looking more composed, he asked her, "So, tell me what happened after I left."

"Well, sir, I sent out a scouting party when you and the general didn't return. After waiting as long as I deemed safe, I ordered a defensive perimeter and had the brigade prepare the women for travel." Tamar looked a bit embarrassed but explained, "Sir, you will need to deprogram those women and the few men who were slaves of the beasts."

"What do you mean?

"They have been conditioned their entire lives to service the beasts with their bodies and the men to mate. I had a difficult time restraining them from—" Tamar cleared her voice, "—committing adultery. Those people tempted my soldiers, both male and female, sir."

"I will do that immediately. What else happened?"

"We didn't have enough wagons for the freed slaves, sir, so I instructed the carpenters to build another. Crude as it was, it served its purpose." Mochè listened intently, impressed by his officer's performance. "Then I led the brigade back, always adhering to protocol, sir. Again, it was difficult with the way the women acted."

"Did you see any traces of General Helen?" Mochè pondered and added, "Or encounter any opposition?"

"We discovered traces of dried blood on rocks in one area of the grounds, a couple of miles from the encampment. It appeared to be evidence of a prior skirmish, but there was no sign of the general, sir." Her eyes raised in thought, and then she elaborated, "We fought a small herd of the hooved demons, but I noticed others among them that I didn't recognize. It was their attire; possibly a different tribe? I couldn't tell for certain, but I could provide a description for one of the artists to render a drawing. Besides that, sir, we encountered raiding parties trying to sneak in and steal. We captured some and returned them as prisoners."

Mochè smiled. "Exemplary work, Captain," he declared. "Have an artist illustrate an example of that new tribe you encountered." As she rose to leave with his permission, Mochè continued, "I'm promoting you to major. You'll soon be assigned a battalion." He smiled at her again and added, "Rest up now and take a short leave. I'll send your promotion order to your commanding general. General Deborah, is it?"

"Yes, Manhig," the young woman beamed joyfully as she rendered a military salute. "Thank you, sir. Thank you very much."

"You are most welcome, Major; you truly deserve it."

When Mochè felt ready, he addressed the assembled council the following week. Sadly, he noticed the vacant chair that had belonged to Helen. It revived memories of her, especially that last encounter that lingered in the distant corridors of his mind—those places where people conceal their innermost secrets. He still had nightmares about feeling her tender kisses and then watching her go to face the enemy alone. An immense respect and fondness welled from his heart for her. He knew he could never fully recover from that memory, and his loving camaraderie for her was eternal. "I wish to address the matters concerning General Helen first," Mochè declared before the members, appearing distant and remorseful. "We will hold a grand assembly outdoors for all who wish to honor her at the funeral mass I will conduct. Our churches are too small for the number of people I know will attend." This was both a statement and a subtle message that he wanted all followers to be present. Bowing his head before the members, he stated, "Miriam will succeed her here in the council chamber and as general of Helen's army."

Mochè aimed to ensure he covered everything and added, "I have quarantined the women away from the few men who were captives of the beasts. We must condition them to our ways, especially considering their persistence in not wearing clothing and their need to commit adultery." Mochè paused in deep thought until he appeared to perceive something and compassionately described, "I want Doctor Gloria to form a task force of women to treat them with love and understanding for the ordeals they endured. She has experience in these areas. They must remain isolated, but I think they will eventually abide by our ways."

"It will be as you wish, Manhig," Aaron spoke for the others. "But realize that most of those women were born into that abuse and might never recover. Unfortunately, it's a way of life for them."

Joshua took the floor and spoke about a different issue: "It has been brought to our attention that a new band of wicked followers of Satan exists in these lands." Joshua presented an art rendering to the members to pass among those seated. "Major Tamar came upon these people while on her returning expedition to bring to us those poor women who had been captives of the beastly giants for years," he explained as he handed the copy to Mochè, asking, "Do you know what tribe they are, sir?" asked Joshua.

"Yes," Mochè's demeanor shifted to one of deep concern as he held the artist's sketch in his hand. "I am aware of them, unfortunately. They are Baphomet worshippers, individuals of Satan reborn from centuries past." Looking sternly at the council members, he asserted, "We must send out scouts before we travel in early spring to destroy them. We don't want to encounter them on the tremendously arduous journey that awaits us."

Before Mochè closed the meeting, he addressed the council, saying, "I propose that Nikanyiso, the warrior, be honored for his bravery against overwhelming odds in bringing me back here safely." He paused as a single tear rolled down his cheek. "Additionally, I want a posthumous decoration of our highest order to be awarded to the Late General Helen for her courage in holding off an enemy of demons, allowing her fellow followers to survive." Mochè bowed his head in respect. Facing the members again, he declared, "Meeting adjourned," pounding his hammer against the wooden block on his large oak desk.

The blossoming relationships between Matthew and Eliza and Ben and Gabriela deepened as the brutal winter winds pounded the compound, that sheltered place where their love sprouted and grew.

"I've touched your flesh while we lay together in nakedness," Matthew told Eliza. "I must ask your father for your hand in marriage. My unrestrained thoughts of you propel me greatly, and I love you too much to wait any longer. You are my only true love, so I must seek his blessing in the spring before we leave."

"But I never allowed you to commit the ultimate sin, Matthew," Eliza said, her wide eyes filling with tears, recalling what Caleb did to her. "You don't know about me, Matthew. You don't know what I've done. It breaks my heart to gather the courage to tell you, but I should have done it already."

"What foolish chatter is this, my dear?"

Her stunning hazel eyes shone as they met his, and she gazed lovingly at Matthew. "I'm so sorry I never told you before. I love you too much and didn't want to lose you. I was selfish, but even the mere thought of losing you caused me pain. You think I'm pure, but I've been with another man," she hung her head in shame. "It was the manhig who saved me from banishment. He looked upon me with love and compassion and adopted me as his daughter." Tears streamed down her face. "I can't marry you, my love. It would bring shame to your honor and your family."

"I've heard people talk, but I challenge anyone to say it in my presence!" Then he took Eliza in his arms and whispered, "I know Caleb forced himself on you; if I had been there, I would have killed him with my bare hands." He held her tightly, embracing her closely. "I love you and will never love another. I want you to be my wife. Will you marry me?"

Eliza was frozen in surprise, unable to speak, before she finally whispered, "Yes, my love, I will." She wondered how her father, the manhig, would decide on such a sensitive matter to him.

"You never inquired about my background, Eliza."

Now assured of his love for her, Eliza giggled softly, saying, "I thought you were just born a brave and noble warrior, my love."

"My father was a blacksmith, a sword forger; my mother died when I was an infant." Matthew's wide eyes stared into the distance, lost in memory. "I held my first saber when I was a young boy. It felt poised and natural," he said, a hint of a smile now gracing his lips. "My father trained me to properly use that weapon each day when I returned from school."

"How did you lose your mother?" Eliza's concern and empathy for the young man she loved deeply were unmistakable in her finely featured face.

"She was killed in an attack when we ventured outside a temporary stronghold before we reached the one in the Unknown Territory. My dad and his sister, my aunt, raised me."

"Oh, how terrible," tears started to trickle down her cheeks.

"The manhig taught me Bible school there. He was kind and helped me cope with living without a mother."

"You are such an excellent fighter and strategist. Did you attend the academy?"

"No, I rose through the ranks quickly after finishing school. I became an officer at an early age. Benjamin taught me when I was assigned to him," Matthew fondly recalled Ben 'showing him the ropes.'

"I'm so sorry, Matthew. I should have asked these things before. Being so worried about what you would think of me I didn't." Eliza snuggled in his arms, pressing her chest against his. She lowered her blouse, exposing one of her ample breasts just as a mother would prepare to feed her baby. Eliza said, "When I bear you a child, I'll feed you in place of your mother." She placed his hand on her breast. Matthew fondled the nipple, watching it become erect, fascinating him.

"I will ask your father for your hand before we depart for our new place in early spring," Matthew pondered and declared, his demeanor now firm. "Anyone who speaks or gossips about you will have to face me, my love!"

The fierce winter winds pounded the stronghold, and other brutal elements prevented Mochè from preaching outdoors during that time. Andrew, David, and Mochè shared services within the warmth of indoor churches. Whenever Mochè conducted services indoors, he stood at the foot of the sanctuary near the altar and his chair, where the consecration of the Holy Eucharist occurred. He told those in attendance, "Whenever you receive God in the bread and wine of His sacred body, I or the other two priests stand here," he pointed. "Just as with a woman's womb, this spot is within the womb of the holiness of God. Even whenever you receive Him outdoors, I perform that sacred consecration of the bread and wine in that same blessed sanctuary of the womb of God's holiness beforehand."

Ben held Gabriela's hand firmly as they walked together through the meadows on an unseasonably warm late winter day. Early flowers began to bloom, and Ben plucked one from the sprouting grass. He placed it between his love's tender ear and her gorgeous blonde hair, which streamed softly in the gentle rhythm of the warm breeze, feeling magical for the time of year. Both were off duty and dressed casually, laughing at simple things and stopping occasionally to kiss or admire one another. Then Gabriela stopped, placing her hands on Ben's chest. Keeping them there, she looked earnestly into his piercing, dark gray eyes, now sparkling in the sunlight.

"I want to tell you about me, Benjamin." Her arms moved and stretched as her hands gently grasped his upper arms, as if holding him in place to listen to what she dreaded telling him. Her expression displayed that anxiety. "You've told me about your noble family. Your father and mother were generals, and you are their only child. Your parents are respectable." Her eyes drifted away from his to a distant mountain, where they would soon be going. "Mine were not, Benjamin."

Ben gently took her hand and placed it back in his. "I never intended to flaunt my family, Gabriela. Please tell me about yours," he said softly and encouragingly as if she could share anything without it mattering to him in the least.

Gabriela's big eyes gazed back into those of her love as she began to speak softly, almost in a whisper. "My father was a wicked man," she said, her eyes widening as she recalled. "He often beat my mother." A tear rolled down her cheek as she continued, "I was a young child, but I can still remember the horror of it all." Shyly and hesitantly, she admitted, "He also abused me, Benjamin, in many ways as a child," her eyes widening in fear at the thought, afraid to glance at Ben. "He forced himself on me when I was only 11 years old," she whispered, now crying in shame. She hesitated, wiping her tears before saying, "I'm not a virgin, Benjamin—by my own father." Another tear rolled from one of Gabriela's lovely eyes onto the frown her beautiful and full lips had now formed. "I know you won't want to touch me anymore, and I understand." She wept.

Ben pulled Gabriela close and embraced her. "It's alright, my love. I'm here now, sweetheart, and I won't ever leave you." He bent down to kiss the top of her golden hair.

"Does that not bother you, Benjamin? That my own father did that to me?"

"Of course, it bothers me. He was an evil and pathetic excuse for a man," he told her softly, gently stroking her thick strands of hair with his fingers.

"There's more," she said. "When my mother discovered what he was doing to me, she tried to stop him, but he beat her—" her voice faded, "—to death," her eyes widened again in terror at her own words. "My father fled when he realized he had killed my mother. He ran from the compound, leaving me to roam the streets looking for food." Gazing at the stunning scenery in the distance, Gabriela, in a daze, explained, "It was the manhig who saw me," her lips curling into a smile at the memory. "My clothes were in tatters, and I was afraid of his imposing figure at first, as I was of all men, but he used his magnificent charm on me," she grinned, serene and tender. "He was so kind and caring that I trusted him immediately. He took me by the hand and led me to the first tavern we came to. Sitting down beside me while I enjoyed the biggest feast I'd ever eaten," she laughed. "I can still envision it." She remembered the prominent figure of Mochè next to her as a child, watching her eat. "The manhig bought me new clothes and took care of me for several years. He taught me about God's love and how He brought me to him. The manhig wanted to adopt me, but the council advised I needed a lady to teach me the ways of womanhood." Gabriela smiled and said, "I didn't want to leave him; he was a father to me—the only one I'd ever known. I still call him Dad—privately. Please never tell anyone that," she paused for a moment.

"I won't," Benjamin replied with a loving smile.

In a daze, Gabriela explained, "The manhig eventually hired a kind widow named Kathy to raise me as a lady. Dad—I mean the manhig," she smiled, "came over every day to visit me." Her eyes showed sorrow again as she said, "Kathy died when I was 17 years old. I miss her so much." Gabriela stared in a daze.

"What happened next?" asked Ben.

"Kathy had been a teacher," Gabriela explained, "so I had already finished my schooling and joined the military as a private. At first, Dad didn't want me to join the military. He wanted me to be a teacher. They promoted me to a cavalry corporal when they saw how well I could ride." Her eyes glowed as she reflected. "I had never ridden a horse before, but I intuitively rode like the wind," she smiled.

"It was a gift from the Almighty."

"Yes, that's exactly what I thought, and that's when Dad—I mean the manhig—accepted my decision." She giggled and said, "But he still worries about me." Gabriela smiled seductively at Ben and said, "You're the first boyfriend I've ever had, Benjamin."

"I thought young men would be breaking down your door, so I never asked to court you. I mean, you're so beautiful," Ben blushed.

"I wish you had. I never wanted a man until I saw you, Benjamin. I was afraid of men." Like drops from heaven, her placid blue eyes gazed up at Ben as though they could see his soul and she whispered, "I've watched how you are to people—respectful, kind, noble, and…handsome." Gabriela's fair skin flushed even more from embarrassment. "I observed you closely, Benjamin, when you had no idea I was watching. I longed for you so strongly it hurt." Then Gabriela returned to reality and asked, "Does my past bother you, Benjamin? Please tell me the truth."

Benjamin bent down to kiss her lips and whispered softly in her ear, brushing his lips against it, fully aware of how much that delicate and petite, shell-like organ of hearing excited the woman he cherished. "What bothers me is how deeply I love you and how I can't control myself around you. I never want to lose you, Gabriela."

"Oh, Benjamin, so it doesn't bother you?" Her lovely eyes stared into his, seemingly surprised. "I prayed it wouldn't." Then reality struck again, and Gabriela asked, "But am I the kind of woman you want your parents to meet? I have no family name, working-class or otherwise."

"Who should I ask for your hand in marriage, Gabriela?" He ignored everything she had told him.

"Oh my God! You want to marry me?"

"As soon as possible," he kissed her with passion. "It was your idea; remember in the stationhouse when I fought hard to restrain myself from committing the unthinkable—the intimacy of my desire for you almost overwhelming me."

Gabriela's two stunning, heavenly blue eyes looked up at Ben, radiating, and she blushed at the memory of being the un-controllable one. Happily, she said, "Oh, Benjamin, I love you and I'll be a good wife to you." Then, hesitating, she added, "I'm afraid you'll have to ask the manhig for permission. He is the only father I ever had."

"With sword in hand, I will face that battle!"

Surrounded by the soldiers guarding them, almost the entire stronghold spread across the cold countryside to show their respect for their fallen general. Only those who were sick or recovering from battle wounds remained in the compound, attended by the few soldiers who stayed with them. Mochè spoke eloquently for his dear departed friend and comrade in Father David's and Father Andrew's company, "As you know, we hold our masses indoors during the colder months." He looked at the crowd gathered before him, bundled in furs and warm coats, and continued, "I knew most of you would want to honor the woman you knew as General Helen. I knew her as a friend and comrade in arms."

Mochè quoted John 14:1-3: 'Let not your heart be troubled. You believe in God; believe also in me. In my Father's house are many rooms. If it were not so, I would have told you. I am going there to prepare a place for you. And if I go and prepare a place for you, I will come back and take you to be with me that you also may be where I am.' Mochè paused before continuing, "Helen is now in one of our Lord's rooms, waiting for us until we can be with her again."

Mochè then quoted from Ephesians 1:7: 'In him we have redemption through his blood, the forgiveness of our trespasses, according to the riches of his grace.' The manhig explained the meaning of that passage to the massive congregation. "Helen was a faithful servant of God and served Him with honor and distinction. Helen has earned her place in Paradise. I pray that God bestows his loving divine mercy and forgiveness upon that young warrior of the Lord, and may He forgive her any minor offenses she may have committed, as none among us is without sin."

Mochè ended the service by saying, "Greater love has no one than this, that someone lay down his life for his friends." As a tear rolled out of one of his stunning eyes, he said, "General Helen died saving my life."

The manhig directed extensive preparation for the disassembly of buildings under the guidance of an architect who had recently joined the community. Peter, the new architect, explained an innovative method for their removal that would be more effective than the methods used in the past. Although it remained a significant undertaking, this approach would simplify reassembly once they arrived at the new place. During that cold winter, all followers contributed to the effort. They felt deep remorse for leaving the homes where they had lived for so long, but envisioned the new stronghold where they hoped to settle again. Everyone prepared to embark on their journey in early spring to another location, now heading south, closer to the place of redemption.

Having difficulty recalling Helen and his near-ultimate sin with her, Mochè sought to formally confess his sins to Andrew and David.

Chapter Eleven

The Journey

After Mochè's formal confession at church, he sat beside the sanctuary with David and Andrew in the empty building. Mochè felt compelled to formally confess his near-adultery with Helen, but he also wanted to discuss it with his priest friends.

"Mochè, as a friend and not a priest, I urge you to exercise discretion with the women you meet in the future," Andrew advised. "You are the manhig. All will fall if you do, my dear friend."

Mochè bowed his head in disgrace. "I know; I don't understand what came over me," he thought, adding, "Maybe it was a repressed subconscious attraction to Helen, or perhaps the stress from that expedition. I don't know. I only thank God He stopped me. I still can't tell if I would have actually committed the ultimate sin against our laws. Could I stoop that low?"

"Everyone who is close to God faces greater temptation. You know that better than anyone," David reminded him. "By your own words: 'Our place is not a refuge for sinners, but only for those who follow God's will.'"

"And what about Zipporah?" Andrew reflected. "You have a beautiful wife, Mochè, and a baby on the way. You are truly blessed."

"I know, I know," Mochè kept saying softly. "Satan has tempted me always with women; he often tells me so. God has stopped me for the last time; now I stand on my own legs with stronger love and devotion to Him and Zipporah. Satan wants me to fall so he can command our people. His wishes only strengthen me."

"He is truly repentant, David. He made his confession and received the sacrament of penance. Enough of this, then," Andrew stated, rubbing his hands briskly as the temperature inside the church dropped. "Could you throw a log in the stove, David? It's getting chilly in here."

"Okay, you're right. Let's stop badgering the poor guy," David smiled as he stood up. Closest to the woodpile, he grabbed a piece, stomping on the insects that fell from it, and carefully placed the cut hardened wood inside the glowing inferno. "But let me say this before we change the subject: we must use Mochè's experience anonymously to teach others about the ease of succumbing to the dangerous criminal offense of adultery."

"Yes," replied Andrew, "We must stimulate our flocks more than ever as we draw closer to the end. They must remain strong so they can nurture their families to live according to our laws, always reminding them that our former world fell due to sin."

Stroking his gray beard, David reflected an expression of repulsion before saying, "As our followers grow, many have lost sight of even the understanding of what defines sin. Many commit adultery within our very compound."

"Especially now that we are about to embark on a long journey," replied Andrew, recalling the temptations that often arose during previous long-distance travels. "Eyes see more from outdoor wagons than behind the closed doors of our civilized compounds. Men are more inclined to prey upon women, and many women allow it when their men guard the caravans, go hunting, or participate in expeditions. Many will commit adultery right under our noses when we travel."

"I will enforce our laws no matter where we are!" Mochè barked. "Now, please change the subject!" The discussion shifted into one of their typical fireside chats, although it took place indoors. Their conversations meandered as they often did, this time veering, somewhat inexplicably, toward a massive energy once harnessed by the world.

"The significant force your great-grandfather learned about is called nuclear fission," Mochè addressed Andrew, who had raised the topic. "I studied it during my training. It can be a brutal weapon with the capability to kill millions. Yet when tamed, it can supply electricity and energy to heat homes." Mochè sneered, "They limited solar energy and made it nearly unattainable from greed."

"So, nuclear fission was kind of like a friend and an enemy," joked David.

"Yes, people who lived back then believed it would bring about the end times. They didn't realize it was their own actions causing it," Mochè replied glumly. "Explosions may come and go, but the destruction of mankind came from within—the sins of humanity."

Mochè lay in the comfort of his bed with Zipporah's petite, warm feet massaging his, her stunning green eyes gleaming in approval as if she could read her husband's mind about his immediate intentions. "It's okay, my love, you won't hurt me," she whispered seductively. Most of their belongings were packed, except for essential items like the bed and sheets they lay on, and their table and chairs. Moving her legs carefully due to her pregnancy, Mochè prepared himself for the intimacy of their marriage.

"Maybe the other way," Zipporah grinned as she turned over, revealing her resplendent pregnant body bent in prayer position as her milky white breasts hung gracefully, her backside raised, waiting. They both abruptly stopped, pausing all movements at the sound of a loud knock on the front door. Eliza was sound asleep in her room down the hallway. Mochè rushed to the door, fearing the worst—a major problem of some sort.

Mochè opened the door to find Matthew standing before

him. "I must speak to you, sir. I'm truly sorry to intrude on your home, but the council building was already removed when I went there."

"Come in, son," Mochè said, taking Matthew's arm and leading him inside. "What happened? How bad is it? I need to get dressed at once," he said, having thrown on his nightgown in his haste.

"No, Manhig; it's nothing like that, sir."

"What is it then?"

Zipporah walked into the large kitchen, dressed in her bathrobe. When she saw Matthew, she said, "Why, Matthew! Come and sit at the table." She pulled out a chair. "I'll make some tea."

"Can someone please tell me what's happening?" yelled Mochè.

That snapped Matthew back to attention, and he stated, "I've come on a personal matter, sir." Then it dawned on him that he had awakened his manhig. Standing erect, he said, "I didn't know you had retired for the night, sir. Please forgive me." He turned to Zipporah and bowed, saying, "Ma'am."

"That's quite alright, Matthew. We had just retired," Zipporah motioned for him to sit, then turned to glare at her husband, her gorgeous green eyes squinting like a cat. She knew why the young man was there; Eliza had informed her of his impending task. Eliza had heard the commotion and cracked her door to listen. Kneeling there, she knew why her love had come. Her admiration and love for Matthew's noble deed gave her a chill.

Mochè waved his hand, gesturing for the young man to sit. Zipporah sat very close to her husband. "So then, tell me, what personal matter is so important?" Mochè's intuition perceived what Matthew was about to ask.

"Manhig, if it is your will, I would like to remain standing to address you on this matter." Mochè couldn't resist the flamboyance and charm of this young man, which reminded him so much of himself at that age. "I've come, sir," Matthew hesitated for a split second, "to ask for your daughter's hand in marriage." His eyes were directed toward the ceiling as he spoke. Eliza giggled to herself at the suspense of it all.

"Well then, that is certainly an important matter. You'd better sit down for something as significant." Mochè waved his hand once more to signal Matthew to a chair. Zipporah whispered in Mochè's ear, "Eliza is a woman now, my love," her lips brushing against her husband's ear, knowing how much he liked it, and it calmed him, "and she also has the desires of one—whether you like it or not, my darling."

"Well, sir, as you know, I now hold a high rank," Matthew began speaking as he seated himself. "I have quite a bit of credits saved, sir, and I plan to buy Eliza a nice home when we reach the new place. I will ensure that she wants for nothing." Still eavesdropping, Eliza felt a wave of anxiety wash over her, almost making her wet herself.

"I see," Mochè said, his eyes remaining steely. "It seems you have everything figured out." Still thinking, he asked, "How does my daughter feel about this matter?"

"Well—"

Before Matthew could answer, Eliza came running from her doorway, screaming, "I want to, Father! Please allow us!"

Mochè, having composed himself after the shock of Eliza running barefoot out of the shadows, answered, "How can I oppose that? You have my permission, son. Once we reach the new stronghold, you may marry my daughter."

Eliza ran to Mochè and told him, "Thank you, Father." She kissed his cheek before dashing into her love's embrace.

"Thank you, sir," Matthew said. "I'll take good care of Eliza; I'll lay down my life for her if necessary."

"Now that wasn't hard, my love, was it?" Zipporah whispered in Mochè's ear again, this time saying, "Later, we can pick up where we left off," as her lips brushed against his tender ear once more. She stood up and declared, "Well, I think this calls for a celebration. I'm not sure what I have left in the kitchen, but I'll find something here," she said while looking around. As she finished speaking, the front door banged again.

"I wonder who that is? I'd better go and see."

"I'll go, ma'am," said Matthew as he gracefully dashed to open the door for Colonel Benjamin. He looked at his friend and then at Mochè. "Did you—"

"Come in, Colonel," Mochè beckoned to him.

Benjamin recognized Matthews's horse twenty minutes earlier and waited, rubbing his hands to warm them against the chilly early spring air. His anxiety gnawed at him, and finally, he couldn't wait any longer; he knocked on the door, wondering how the manhig would react to his appearance on the doorstep. As everyone would be busy preparing in the morning, he had no other option.

"Take a seat, Colonel. I believe I know why you are here. It appears that springtime is in the air."

"Sir, Gabriela told me you were more of a father to her than any other man she ever knew, and I—"

"Yes, I love Gabriela as much as a father can love a daughter. I'll save us both time, Colonel. I've already reviewed your record and finances, and I know you come from an excellent family that educated and raised you to become the fine man you are. I know your parents well."

"But how did you know, sir? I mean, how did you know I wanted to—"

"Gabriela mentioned that you both want to marry. I guess to soften me up a bit. Do you know she has had a tough life, son?"

"Yes, sir, I do, and I plan to correct that, with your permission, of course, sir."

"You have that, son, along with my blessings. Gabriela told me how you rescued her. Why didn't you come forward for a commendation?"

"I didn't find it necessary, sir." That remark revealed much to Mochè about the young man's character.

"You're a fine young man, Benjamin. It's about time my dear Gabriela found someone who can provide her with a better life. Take good care of her, son."

"I will, sir, and thank you."

"Well, I suppose it's a double celebration," Zipporah said, standing up again, teary-eyed from the romance of it all. "Let me get back to finding something to drink for it. Ah! Here's some apple cider."

Earlier that spring, Mochè guided his people to complete the disassembly of the last buildings. His and Zipporah's home had been the last taken apart right before they departed. Now, dismantled homes and buildings rested, neatly packed in specially built, larger, and stronger reinforced six-ox-teamed wagons. Laborers would reassemble them at the new place. Mochè had Peter, the architect who joined the followers, use new structural plans to take apart each building in a way that would minimize problems during reconstruction, thereby greatly speeding up the process. While the followers slept in large tents, they undertook the labor-intensive task of packing all their other belongings into the large wagons for the journey ahead.

Before they departed, Mochè addressed his followers, saying, "May God bless us on this new path we take, knowing we are coming closer to Him. It will be challenging, and many may fall along the way. Others may succumb to the temptations that Satan inflicts upon us all, especially while we travel. Know that he does so because we are getting closer to God."

The convoy was immense, stretching long and far. Now with a battle strength of nearly ten thousand, the seven separate armies formed lines miles long beside it for protection, with cavalry riders trotting alongside and special patrols assigned to move back and forth to provide surveillance and additional information. Assigned soldiers guarded the specially packed wagons, which carried disassembled buildings and those that transported cargo, supplies, and followers. The nuns from the cloistered nunnery traveled in covered wagons separate from those of the followers.

Gabriela resumed her position as a dispatch rider. She rode like the wind, and Ben often enjoyed watching her bouncing behind from his telescope as she galloped. Knowing he did,

Gabriela enhanced that performance by assuming more exotic positions when she was sure only her Benjamin was looking. As a higher-ranking officer, Ben had a private wagon, where Gabriela secretly slept at night. They coordinated their breaks, lunches, and dinners to spend time together as often as possible.

Eliza had to use more caution, as her father always checked on her before he went to sleep. When she was certain he was fast asleep, she rushed to Matthew's wagon behind Ben's on the long line. Once, Eliza fell asleep in Matthew's arms and had to quietly sneak back into her bed. Both she and Gabriela couldn't wait to marry so they could be with their men without hiding.

Not yet fully accustomed to the followers' rules, the rescued women slaves traveled separately in wagons. Wives observed their husbands closely to prevent them from succumbing to their wicked temptations.

Anyone wishing to join Mochè was confined until he could check for demonic possession and their true intentions.

Rosetta slid down her dress and stood nude before a se-cluded pond in the quiet woods. She had walked there from the wagon she shared with another soldier's wife to bathe during the caravan's first quick stop at the beginning of the journey. Her husband was one of the soldiers assigned to the front of the long line and remained there for weeks at a time. Putting her toe in the placid water to test it, she turned startled at the sound of footsteps on the dried leaves. One of the male slaves stood close before her, fully nude, his sculpted, hardened body glistening from the sun that peeked between the branches of the large cherry tree beside the pond. Rosetta froze in awe at the perfectly chiseled body now brushing against her, his hardness touching her naked body as he began mindlessly fondling the beautiful, young woman as he had been conditioned to do. Her morality urged her to run, but she remained still, entranced by the virile male slave, enjoying the feel of him. As his sturdy arm held the dazed woman, he slowly lowered her shapely body into the shallow water, mounting her. Trembling from arousal,

Rosetta's long, slender legs spread wide as the toes of her feet grasped tightly to his buttocks, and the virility of the Adonis slowly entered her wet feminine lips. His rhythm hastened, forcing splashes in the shallow water, as Rosetta struggled to stop her impassioned moans from becoming screams of ecstasy.

While Mochè personally led a scouting party with Nikanyiso by his side, he noticed in the distance what appeared to be a very large man. Taking out his telescope, he examined the colossal figure more closely, fearing that other monstrous gorillas might be lurking or that giants, reborn like the Nephilim from his biblical ancestors, might be nearby.

"Nikanyiso!" he called to the tall warrior trotting ahead of him, "Stay by my side. We don't yet know what kind of creature he might be." Exercising caution, Mochè carefully guided his party closer to the man. "Arm yourselves, soldiers," he ordered his warriors to be prepared.

When they came close, they realized how enormous this man was. Aaron, the chief military advisor, rode slightly behind his manhig, terrified by the massive figure. "Who are you?" Mochè called to the mammoth man. "Can you verbalize?"

"I can," the giant man appeared to be frightened.

"We are not here to harm you," Mochè called again to assure the man of his good intentions. "Soldiers, put away your weapons, but keep them close." Then Mochè called to the giant of a man once more, "What is your name?"

"I have no name," the man said in a deep voice resonating off the nearby cliffs.

"You appear to be looking for someone?"

"Yes, I'm looking for Manhig; do you know where he is?"

"You're speaking to him."

"Oh my God," the behemoth figure fell to his knees. "I have been searching for so long."

Mochè dismounted before him. Kneeling, he was noticeably taller than Mochè stood. He extended his hand to the large man's bulky forearm. "Rise; do not kneel before me, only before God," Mochè pointed to the heavens. The giant stood tall, towering over him.

"An angel guided me this way." The big man blushed with embarrassment, saying, "I'm not very smart and kept losing my way."

"What do you want, my friend?"

The giant began sobbing when he heard Mochè addressing him, "I have never had a friend before. Nobody ever called me that. Everyone who has seen me since my family died has been afraid of me. I only want to serve God through you. The angel told me that."

"Well, you'll have many friends if you join us, that is. Have you been baptized?"

"No, my family has never met a priest before." Mochè realized the simple man didn't know that a holy person or a believer could have done that. Even if he had already been baptized by someone in his family, Mochè would do it again.

"Bend down so I may consecrate you," Mochè said as he removed his holy water and oil from his belted pouch. He reflected on how he wouldn't want to exorcise a demon from a man so large. The memory of his last encounter with Nikanyiso remained vivid in his mind and would linger for a long time. The man bowed his head, and Mochè continued, "I'll give you a name from our Holy Bible." Using his holy water, Mochè pronounced, "I baptize you, Goliath, in the name of the Father, the Son, and the Holy Ghost." Mochè made the sign of the cross on Goliath's forehead to ensure he was free from demons. "Come with us, Goliath. You are one of us now."

"Thank you, Manhig. I will be your humble servant for as long as I live."

Much too large to ride a horse, Mochè paced his stallion slowly so Goliath could keep up. Surprisingly, he seemed swift on his feet for such a large man. Mochè leaned over to Aaron and whispered, "Ride ahead to the caravan and stop it. I want all the followers to meet Goliath. Announce to them all to show no fear in his presence, as it upsets him."

"He'll need to do something truly remarkable before I stop being scared of him. As you wish, Manhig," Aaron replied before galloping off toward the caravan."

Mochè always visited Zipporah immediately upon returning from his outings. His love for her grew with each passing day, as did her belly, which carried his child. "My love," he said, embracing her carefully to avoid hurting her womb, "I have a new student for you and Eliza."

"Mochè, my love," Zipporah chuckled. "I'm not made of glass. You can hold me properly." She glanced around for the child who needed schooling. "Where is my new student?"

"Look beyond the last wagon. He is coming now," Mochè pointed him out.

"Oh, my God," she said to her husband, "I'll need the wood-workers to build an especially large chair for my new student."

"He had no name, so I gave him one: Goliath."

"How appropriate, my love."

Mochè halted the convoy and had his followers camp for a few days, perhaps a week. Time was of the essence, but he wanted to check the food and medical supplies. Hunting parties were formed to gather meat, fresh early summer berries, fruits, and greens from the meadows, allowing his people to rest from their arduous journey. Patrol scouts spotted a large stream in the meadow near the center of the long line of wagons, vehicles, tanks, and riders. Cattle drivers, sheepherders, and tenders of other animals led their herds to access fresh water. The cavalry riders also brought their horses, all of which were done in an organized manner. Mochè's workers siphoned the fresh water and filled all the containers in every supply and personal wagon. Goliath carried the giant barrels two at a time, easing the workload for the others. Like the younger boys, the simple-minded Goliath had a crush on his beautiful schoolteacher. He was already learning to speak better and had even picked up some basic arithmetic.

Everyone awoke to a warm, sunny day. A pregnant Zipporah

led the women to the stream, where they could wash the road dust off their bodies, as most people did when they stopped by a lake or pond. Guarded by two female soldiers who accompanied them, ladies of all ages stepped into the cool, refreshing water, giggling and laughing. Already disrobed and about to enter the flowing water at the stream's edge, Zipporah suddenly remembered that she had forgotten to bring her fragranced soap. She called out to her friend Rosetta, "I have to go back." Smiling over the sounds of splashing water hitting the rocks, Zipporah told her, "I forgot my soap. Silly me." She raised her hands and threw a robe over her body.

"You can use mine," Rosetta called back, floating naked while splashing the refreshing water over her large belly, showing signs of pregnancy from the male slave months before.

"No," Zipporah blushed, continuing sheepishly, "my husband likes the scent of my soap." Then she lowered her voice to nearly a whisper, saying, "I always try to please him." She smiled like a woman in love.

"I wonder why?" Rosetta smiled with an insinuating expression.

Zipporah flushed an even brighter red as she laughed and waved her hand at Rosetta—a friendly gesture that urged her to respect her privacy in front of the other women.

Rosetta completely ignored her and shouted, laughing as she did, "If I had a figure like yours even while you're pregnant, I wouldn't care about what anyone thought I did with my husband." Unlike her friend, Zipporah, Rosetta tried to hide her pregnancy from her husband by gaining weight.

Zipporah turned and waved her hand again to her friend, now feeling even more self-conscious. As she moved away from the stream, she heard leaves rustling in a cluster of bushes near the water, frightening her. After hearing grunts and groans, Zipporah began to walk faster until she realized it was a pair of those freed slaves having sex under the cover of shrubs. Clapping her hands broke them up, and the naked couple ran away. A relieved Zipporah shook her head but smiled, understanding how conditioned the released captives had become.

Then, Zipporah heard screaming coming from where her friends were bathing. Turning, she watched a small group of scantily clad men and women deftly running down from a slope. The assailants swiftly slit the throats of both guards from behind, showing no emotions. Blood pulsated from the necks of the two soldiers, now unable to vocalize a warning. They fell to their deaths at the feet of many others who now rushed down the incline and began lifting and carrying the struggling and screaming women away over their shoulders.

One of the men looked at Zipporah and began trotting in her direction, but she clutched her belly and ran back to the encampment as fast as she could, screaming, "Help! Help! Please!" The near-naked man ran back to his horde.

In a hastily prepared circle of his division commanders and Aaron, Mochè expressed his thoughts straightforwardly, "There's a likelihood that the women have already been raped and killed. We must bear that in mind." He lowered his eyes after sharing that grim assessment. "Sorry to be blunt, but we live in an ungodly world and have repeatedly faced such primal acts."

"Perhaps they kidnapped them to use as slaves," Aaron noted, recalling the women they had rescued during the previous winter.

"My wife is too upset to attend this meeting, and in her current state, I wouldn't force her; however, she did describe the attackers to me. They were not the painted, hoofed demons but a different type."

"Could they be those who worship Baphomet from that artist's drawing we saw?" Joshua asked.

"I hope not, but whoever they are, they're brutal and murder with ease. We must leave at once!" Mochè ordered.

"I agree that the raiders have plans for the young women and may have already fulfilled them," General Joseph said, "especially seeing how they slaughtered the older and pregnant women in the stream and took only the younger, prettier ones."

"They slit open the pregnant young woman, Rosetta's belly, and took the child from her bleeding womb," General Miriam said gloomily. "Probably for a pagan ritual."

"Either way, we must go quickly," declared Mochè fiercely, for losing any of his people was painful to him. "And we're wasting time," he gazed into the distance, deep in thought. "I'll lead three brigades of cavalry. Assign Joshua to one and tell Benjamin and Matthew to prepare their two." The manhig stood and then turned back to instruct, "Aaron, you'll ride with me, but assign General Mark to deploy his army to our rear to watch our backs. We won't know what we're riding into until we get closer." Mochè rubbed his chin in contemplation and added to his orders, "Prepare wagons to accommodate the twenty women in the hope they have survived." He turned to Aaron, "Have all military double up on patrols guarding the caravan before we leave!"

"Yes, Manhig," Aaron stood with the assembled commanders, rendering the military salute to their manhig before he departed. Mochè now had the doleful duty to inform Zipporah and Eliza that their friend, Rosetta, had been one of those murdered. He knew they would take it badly and worried about Zipporah's pregnancy, but he thanked God for His blessing of sparing her.

As many followers as possible gathered to watch the assigned military brigades ride out of the encampment. Those mourning their losses did not join them but gathered in prayer with Father David. Meanwhile, Andrew walked down to the stream. Smelling the sweet scents of nature along the gravel path he traveled, he intended to administer the blessing of the last rites to the women now draped in blood-stained blankets along the water's bank. Before him lay an esoteric panorama: a paradox of devastation that unfolded under the loving embrace of God's nature.

Andrew leaned over a small pond formed in a bend of the flowing stream, cupping water in his palm to refresh himself with the sweet-smelling, fragrant splashes. He noticed a slightly wavering reflection on the otherwise glassy surface. As he looked closer and the mirrored image stilled, he saw a young woman—the one he had always loved. "Sarah?" he asked. "Is that you?"

"Yes, my love," her image smiled. "I never stopped loving you, Andrew. I have never married."

Andrew moved closer to her; his tears fell like droplets from a sun shower as he softly told her, "I never wanted to ruin your life, my love. Not a day goes by that I haven't thought of you, my dear woman." He gazed deeper into the water's reflection and said, "You're still young and beautiful while I'm old. How is this happening? Surely it must be an illusion or a dream?"

"No, Andrew," Sarah smiled lovingly, "you're not dreaming; I'm real. Look more closely at the water. You are young and beautiful, just as I remember you from our last time together."

The old priest leaned further over the stream and beheld his reflection. He appeared handsome once more, with a tight-skinned, chiseled face like the one he used to have. Straightening up, he felt his body tall and erect. Bending back down, he asked, "How is this possible?"

"Come to me, my love. There is no time here as you know it," she replied, extending her soft, milky white arm from the water. "Take my hand, my love. I'll guide you to eternity with me." She smiled, her beauty radiating into Andrew's soul.

Andrew placed his hand into the gentle, fair-colored one he hadn't touched for nearly fifty years, and his body faded and merged with Sarah's.

As two cavalry platoons led by sniffing dogs approached, Mochè halted them. Knowing they were near, he whispered to the soldier handling the animals, "Soldier, tend to the dogs here so they don't reveal our position." He gestured to his tracker, Nikanyiso, who knelt beside him and hand-signaled the other warriors to dismount and follow him. Looking down a small hill with his field glasses, he spotted the captured women. After quickly counting them, Mochè turned to Aaron and softly said, "They all seem to be there, but we must move swiftly." He handed his binoculars to Aaron, telling him, "Look for yourself." Then Mochè commanded a soldier with a stern whisper, "Get me a scoped rifle! Quickly!"

As Aaron watched, the women shivered from fear, kneeling with their wrists bound and naked as they had been in the stream. They convulsed from terror; the heathens painted their nude bodies for what he assumed was preparation for some ritual. As the women trembled in fear, their eyes widened, pleading and piercing, fixed on something they watched. Then, as Aaron scanned the field glasses slowly away from those women, he sighed in shock at what he saw. The wicked people had tied and gagged the remaining painted young woman, like the others, but forced her nude body over a large, rounded, gold-painted object—apparently a pagan symbol. Her eyes were red and swollen from crying as a giant painted man wearing a horned skullcap savagely violated her. "They appear to be preparing the one whom the barbarian is molesting for some type of pagan sacrifice, Manhig." He saw the flames of a roaring fire rise near the altar and returned the glasses to Mochè, saying, "I can watch no more. They are going to burn all those poor souls alive before a pagan altar, a type I've never seen, Manhig. All their evil warriors kneel before a statue I don't recognize."

"I do," whispered Mochè, peering through the rifle scope, sighting the huge man's head, and carefully lining the crosshairs. He didn't want to hit the young woman who was moving back and forth to the rhythm of the violent thrusts of the colossal pagan male who was far too large for the petite young woman. It was apparent the giant was hurting her with his violent movements, leaving Mochè little time to aim and fire to free her. Mochè's finger slowly squeezed the trigger to take the headshot. The blast of the powerful sniper rifle resounded, tearing apart the giant's skull and spattering blood and bone from the bursting head—his horned helmet flew high in the air. A gory blur swept across the crosshairs of Mochè's scope before revealing a pulsating, dark red, bloody mass that squirted in throbs onto the woman's back. The enormous, muscular man's lifeless body fell onto her and then slid to the ground. "They are worshipping Baphomet, the statue with a goat's head and legs and a human's body. You can see the torso and large breasts of a woman with the genitalia of a man. Baphomet is a form of Satan who defiles God's creation of humanity that the Dark Angel and his band of wicked fallen angels hate." Mochè commanded in a loud holler, "Move the platoon forward! Now that they know we are here, I want to destroy all these godless heathens. Radio Mark and have him move in from the rear. Tell Benjamin and Matthew to charge upon them with Joshua and us. Have all warriors use advanced weapons against these wicked people until they are close. Let none of them escape! Move in now!"

Mochè's cavalry descended upon the wicked Baphomet worshippers, quickly surprising them and gaining the upper hand. Their warriors were too busy enjoying the preparations for the imminent human sacrifices, indulging in an orgy of naked painted men and women engaging in licentious acts with one another. Mark attacked from the rear in the open meadows, cutting off any escaping herds that fled for their lives. Benjamin and Matthew each attacked from opposite sides with their brigades, trapping the enemy on both flanks before they could escape among the rises and rows of blossomed cherry trees. It was a brilliantly executed military maneuver by both officers. The advanced weapons were no match for the wicked followers of Baphomet. Their mortar rifles alone blew apart many of the enemy. Mochè's combined force slayed every remaining man and woman of the surprised evil tribe with their swords and daggers.

After the battle, Mochè sat upon his stallion in deep thought, wondering if there were any more followers of Baphomet or whatever wicked creatures lay in store for his people.

Aaron slowly and quietly trotted his horse alongside Mochè and asked, "How did you learn so much about Baphomet,

Manhig?"

Mochè glanced at his chief military advisor and said, "I remember studying that subject," recalling how many years ago, when he was a very young man, "so many years ago, Aaron. God prepared me for everything I would ever encounter," he continued, privately wondering, 'except women.' He remembered what he almost did with Helen, but was thinking more of his beautiful wife. "Hurry, let's get back to the encampment." That vision of Zipporah urged him to be with her as soon as possible. "Is everything prepared for the return, Aaron?"

"Yes, Manhig; the women are loaded in three smaller wagons," he responded. "I put two female soldiers to ride with them as you requested for some comfort on the trip."

"Bring the dear young woman whom they violated directly to Doctor Gloria," Mochè instructed him. "They've all been traumatized and will need medical assistance, but that child of God will require the special type of help Gloria can offer."

"Yes, Manhig. I will do as you wish."

"I'm riding ahead to return to the convoy with Benjamin and Matthew's brigades, Aaron." Looking into the distance, he added, "You shouldn't encounter anything more than bands of thieves, possibly roaming demons. The scouts haven't reported anything threatening. Besides, you have an army with you."

"We'll be fine, sir. Return to your lovely wife; I know you're worried about her, sir."

"You are very perceptive, my friend. It won't be too much longer before my child comes," Mochè smiled and rode off to help Benjamin and Matthew reassemble their brigades.

Mochè's mount kept pace with Benjamin and Matthew's horses as they led their brigades, all secretly eager to get back to their women. A rider quickly approached from their left, causing both officers and Mochè to wonder what was wrong.

The scout abruptly halted; the dust of his skidding horse blew high as he saluted and then began riding beside their path. "A larger band of thieves is preparing to attack our center, sirs."

"How many, sergeant?" Mochè asked. "Are they mutations or human?"

"Only about 150 riders, sir. They appear to be human."

"Enough to kill many of our soldiers and get off with much of our needed supplies," Matthew instinctively replied, then called, "Colonel Benjamin, it's best if you prepare your brigade to form a semicircle with mine!" Then Matthew thought and conceded, "Sorry, Ben, I didn't mean to outrank—"

Ben interrupted him and responded, "You made the right call, Matt. That's exactly what the manhig or I would have done. Let's do it. Move your brigade to the left side." Seconds later, Ben added, "I have them sighted with my scope!" He shifted his brigade from the rear to the right and, using Matthew's forces, began forming an arc to ambush the unsuspecting gang. Both brigades quickly confronted the surprised bandits, with their commanders and Mochè entering the fray.

During the fighting, Mochè noticed their advanced weapons, recalling Andrew's prediction, passed down from his father, about other larger evil settlements having similar armaments to those of his followers. Just as he was about to strike one of the evil warriors with his sword, Mochè suddenly stopped upon noticing the man who bore his father's face.

"You outsmarted me this time, my brother, but you won't do it again!" the man shouted.

"What did you say?"

"You appear surprised," the bandit's stallion reared up on its hind legs. "What, didn't our dear father tell you about me?" Mochè held his saber pointed down in his hand as the man yelled again. "I'm named after our father, Solomon," he smiled. "You rescued my daughter, Eliza, who fled from me when she was a child with my whore of a wife, Beth." He let out an evil laugh and said, "Farewell, Damian, I'll kill you another time."

"We've brushed them away, killed many of them, sir," proclaimed Matthew, who arrived back first. Seeing his manhig's dazed expression, he asked, "Are you alright, sir?"

Mochè snapped out of his stupor and said, "Yes, I'm fine."

"Are you sure, sir?" Matthew asked hesitantly while sheathing his sword. "You appear as pale as if you've seen a ghost," he added respectfully.

"For a moment, I thought I did, son."

Mochè quickly galloped to his wagons, where Zipporah and Eliza were waiting, worried for their men. When Zipporah heard the sound of hooves, she realized her husband was returning and nearly raced to greet him, with Eliza close behind.

"Oh, my dear husband, you are unharmed?" Both her and Eliza's eyes were still swollen and red from mourning Rosetta's death.

"I'm fine," Mochè answered, recalling the horror of seeing his father's image in the brother he never knew he had. Cradling both of them in his arms, he said, "It's so nice to come home to a family." He then knelt to kiss Zipporah's belly. "You, too, my child."

"Thank God you're safe, my love," Zipporah answered as she and Eliza cried from relief and joy that he and Matthew were safe. For the first time, Mochè saw Eliza both as a woman and as the spitting image of her late mother.

Sadly, Mochè pronounced, "I will preside over Rosetta's funeral in the morning. I'll speak to her husband later." After talking with them and comforting his wife and daughter about Rosetta's death, he once again reassured them both that he and Matthew were unharmed. Mochè then took Eliza aside and sat with her. Smiling with his arm around her, he said, "We haven't had much time to talk, my daughter."

Sensing something was troubling Mochè, Eliza held tightly to the man who had formally adopted her and replied, "Father, if this is about Matthew, know that I would never dishonor you before we marry."

"No, no, my child," he lovingly stroked her hair as he always did, holding her tightly. "I know that, my child." Still in her embrace, he continued, "I was merely reflecting on how you lost your mother, Elizabeth. She was a dear woman. I remember her well and know she's with God now," he said, continuing to caress her hair.

"Yes, she was always wonderful to me," Eliza recalled her mother's loving care. "My biological father left us with nothing, and my mom struggled to support us until you helped us." Her beautiful eyes stared into emptiness as she reflected on those difficult times. "I was too young to remember him, only how frightened my mother was of him. He often beat her; I remember that. His name was Solomon. Oh, how I dreaded my mother crying out that name to stop him from hurting her." Eliza spoke as if releasing repressed anger, her arms weakening and dropping from holding Mochè, falling to her sides in despair.

Mochè quickly held her and whispered, "Sometimes, it's good to confront the things that haunt us, my dear child. I've wondered about your biological father, but I never wanted to upset you, as it seems I have done now."

Eliza felt secure in his strong arms and whispered, "You could never upset me. You're too wonderful to me for that." She raised her arms once more to hold him tightly. "I love you, Father. You are the only father I've ever had."

Benjamin, tired from the expedition, strolled to his quarters. He felt someone tap his shoulder and turned to see Gabriela's radiant, smiling face. "I've already heard about your exploits, Benjamin. I'm so proud of you. Everyone's talking about what you and Matthew did: "rescuing those unfortunate women and then during the attack," her deep blue eyes glowed as she spoke. Then she asked, "Did you find any of those women attractive?" Gabriela blushed, aware that they had been found naked.

"Never!" replied Ben. "You know I only have eyes for you." He dropped what he was carrying and slowly pulled her close into a tight embrace, his fingers gently stroking her long hair, which he relished so much. He said, "You are the only one I long for, and the body I find comfort in."

As Gabriela held him tightly against her, she exclaimed, "Oh, Benjamin, I longed to feel your touch on every part of my body when you were away. I've missed you so much. The devil tempts me, I know, but I cannot help it," and her lips kissed his passionately. "I have to ride now, but I'll come to you tonight, my love."

"Hold me back when we're together, for I'm out of control. Prevent me from doing the unsacred thing before we marry." Ben had missed the woman he loved terribly.

"I'll try," she smiled while mounting her mustang. Her eyes widened like two blue heavenly droplets. "I'll try my best," Gabriela called before galloping away, glancing back at him through the long strands of her golden hair, smiling.

Later, while cuddling with Zipporah, Mochè whispered to her, "I met the brother I never knew I had. Eliza is my biological niece," he explained, his voice trembling.

Zipporah ceased all her gentle movements and lay in shock, finally asking, "What do you mean by this?"

Mochè then explained the skirmish in which he encountered his unknown brother. Seeing the shock in his wife's widened eyes, he told her, "I sensed his vision of evil and felt the presence of the Dark Angel within him. Please never tell Eliza about my meeting him; it would be too disturbing for her right now. She shared with me the horrible memories she has of him." Mochè dwelled in deep thought and added, "Her mother was such a wonderful woman."

Stunned by that story yet warming his feet in hers, Zipporah whispered, "Maybe that's why you've always felt an intuitive love and devotion to her, my love."

He kissed her lips and said, "You are a wise woman, my wife. Yes, there has always been a natural bond between Eliza and me. Now I understand why."

When all was quiet in Mochè's wagon, Eliza slipped out of the wagon assigned to Gabriela and her to lie with Matthew.

Soon after Mochè returned to his family, he went to visit Andrew and David. "What's wrong, my friend? Why are you weeping?" Something had clearly upset David, who was normally as unemotional as a rock. Now, he sat in a chair next to his wagon, appearing like an old man, motionless, not even rubbing his gray beard as he did by habit. David remained silent as he regained his composure. Mochè looked around and asked, "Where is Andrew?"

"He's gone," David finally answered. "He just disappeared."

Mochè sank into an empty chair beside David, which seemed to belong to Andrew. "Did the guards conduct a thorough search for him?"

"They searched everywhere as I did before I called for them."

"He couldn't just have disappeared into thin air."

"They found these down by the stream," David pulled from his pocket Andrew's rosary, wrapped around an old, small, framed photograph.

Mochè smiled before saying, "He told me he had an actual photograph taken a long time ago. He came across a photographer, if I'm pronouncing these words correctly, who owned a device called...I've forgotten the name of the instrument. May I see it, David? He never showed it to me."

"Of course, Mochè. Please forgive me for behaving this way," he said, handing the rosary and picture to his friend.

"My God, how young and handsome he was," Mochè said in awe. "Look at the meticulously combed long jet-black hair Andrew had," he continued, complimenting his dear friend's appearance. Looking at the woman beside him in the photo, he remarked, "That must be Sarah, the young woman he often spoke of. She was stunningly beautiful."

"We were young once, too, Mochè."

"He's with God now, David. The Lord sent her as a messenger to take him before us," Mochè shed tears. "Because he obeyed his priestly duties to his flock, even forsaking the love of a beautiful young woman," Mochè said, handing the items back to David. "As do you, my friend."

"How do you know for sure he is with God?"

Mochè looked up at the heavens and saw the bright light radiating. He replied, "I see them."

For the first time since he began speaking, with his spirit now renewed, David smiled and said, "I'll leave these beads and the picture he cherished for you when I go to see Andrew again."

Not long after the encounter with the Baphomet worshippers while journeying to the new place, Zipporah smiled and told Mochè that she was in labor. She said it calmly and quietly, knowing her husband would panic. "Mochè, my love, I'm ready for a doctor to come."

"Why, my dear, do you feel sick?"

"No, my silly, darling husband, your child is coming now," she answered; her dark green eyes had a splendid glow as she smiled widely. At those words, Mochè jumped from his wagon and ran to find Gloria.

"She'll be fine, Father. I just checked on her yesterday, and I knew it would be soon," Gloria said as she escorted the shaken, tall, and muscular man back to his temporary home on wheels. Glancing up at him as she strode alongside him, she told Mochè, "For such a tall, strong guy, you're a big baby." Facing forward again, she added, "Just like every other grown man."

"Why didn't you tell me it was coming?" Mochè asked, almost frantically.

Gloria merely glanced into his eyes for a split second and replied, "If you could see yourself in a reflection, you wouldn't be asking that question."

Mochè paced the ground outside his temporary home until he heard the sound of a crying baby, and his heart seemed to drop from his chest. "Oh, my God," he whispered.

Upon opening the curtain at the rear of the wagon, he saw Zipporah glowing with a surreal beauty unlike any he had seen before. "Come, my husband, and meet your son," she said as she held the baby that Gloria was wiping clean.

When Mochè finally held his newborn son in his arms, he

asked Zipporah, "What forename should we give him, my darling wife?" He thought for a moment and said, "I would prefer not to use my father's name," recalling his recent encounter with his wicked brother who bore that same name.

"Gershom," Zipporah said with a smile, "after the holy angel who announced God's permission for our marriage."

"Yes, after my faithful companion," Mochè agreed. "There is no better way to honor him. Hello, Gershom, of the family Ignatius. Welcome to the world." He pondered his words, thinking, even though we live in troubled times, you are a new soul of God, my son.

The long journey lasted five months and finally ended in the late summer of the year they had set out. The angel guided Mochè's people to an elevated area of a valley at the foot of high bouldered hills. Natural rock formations provided cover on all sides except for a small area at the front corner. Inside the natural structure was a vast flat area. Instead of a moat, as used to secure the entrance in the last stronghold, a narrow natural opening between the rocks became their entry point. That slot was wide enough for their wagons to pass through and for the armies to exit and re-enter ten abreast. It simply needed a large gate.

Mochè saw the new fortress as a blessing from God, as if He had created the fortress behind the big rocks, with elevated flat protrusions for guards on all sides. Fresh water flowed down from natural mountain springs high in the hills, and a river from the large body of water they had crossed ran through a spacious meadow at the foot of the natural fortress.

As the trees and bushes around them showcased their form in the prime of their season, enhancing the beauty of God's creation, Mochè guided his people in dismantling the long, separate lines of seven towns while the armies guarded them. Then, the labor of building commenced once more.

The number of followers grew during the journey and now totaled sixteen thousand. Another architect, Jeffrey, had joined the caravan. He assisted Peter, the structural engineer, who had dismantled the buildings using an innovative method for easier reassembly. Together, they created construction plans to accommodate the growing number of followers.

Laborers gathered all the organized cut wood pieces from the buildings of the last fortress, along with the stored wood from the Unknown Territory. They built a new lumber mill by a stream flowing from the wide river's tributary, similar to the one at the first grand fortress where they had stayed for ten years, and felled trees for additional wood.

Mochè instructed the workers to build a new cloistered nunnery at the far end of the river for the nuns, where it would be more secluded, allowing them to maintain their privacy and safety.

Among the existing houses, the architects designed four-story buildings. They created shafts for sanitary disposal and basic elevator systems that utilized electricity generated from the sun and the water flow of the nearby river. Their scientists developed innovative and revolutionary methods to harness more solar energy, thereby increasing efficiency. Mochè approved the plans, and construction of the towns commenced. Rebuilding progressed much faster than before, using the marked wood pieces Peter had stored on the massive convoy. Goliath played a crucial role in unloading the heavy fitted lumber. Since it required cranes and sometimes a crew of six laborers to move each piece, the giant managed to handle two at a time by himself. Goliath also became an asset in various construction projects.

Walking together with Aaron, Mochè stopped so they both could check the construction site. Seeing Goliath working so hard, Mochè called out to the giant, "Goliath, may I see you?"

"Yes, Manhig?" Goliath promptly came and stood towering over both Mochè and Aaron.

"I notice you work too hard and don't take breaks like the other laborers."

"I labor in the harvest of the lord," Goliath responded, his words surprising Mochè.

"Go then, my friend; you are truly blessed." Mochè turned to Aaron, saying, "From his heart and not his mind, he refers to Matthew 9:37-38. Is that remarkable enough for you to not fear him, Aaron?"

Aaron nodded and responded, "It certainly is."

Everyone worked diligently and reassembled all the buildings within the prepared natural rock formations. With Goliath's contribution, possessing the strength of many, they miraculously completed everything by mid autumn.

All the precious cargo arrived with minimal losses, including the bee hives, the oak wine and beer casks, and the syrupy substance that would be converted to wine for sale at the new taverns and used as the blood of Christ in church. Gardeners carefully replanted the transported grape vines in the fertile soil by the water, hoping they would regain life again as they had before with God's grace.

Lying with Zipporah under the sheets, Mochè pulled his mouth away from her elongated, dark nipple. Some milk squirted and splashed onto his face. Giggling, Zipporah said, "Oops! I'm sorry." She covered her cheeks with her hands and laughed at her husband's expression as her breast milk dripped from his chin. "So, my love, what's the verdict? Do I taste as good as I look?" It was the first time Mochè had taken milk from his wife's breast, fulfilling the tradition of intimacy, built on their misinterpretation of that bible passage.

"You taste as sweet as you look," Mochè answered her with a smile while wiping his chin with his fingers. "But I don't want to deprive my son of his nourishment."

"My breasts are filled with milk, and when you do that, it relieves the pain I get from such an overload—look how big my breasts have gotten!"

"Well, in that case, I'm glad I can help."

"Want some more?" Zipporah giggled while blushing, then whispered, "I love how it feels when you do that—it excites me." She pulled Mochè's head back to her breast.

Zipporah caressed his legs with her toes in a way she knew would turn him into putty. She always engaged in gestures like that before sharing something important. Gently restraining his wandering hands as he lay atop her, she softly said, "I am with child again, my love," a tender smile gracing her face. Mochè again removed his lips from her breast, and his eyes widened. But he remained speechless as Zipporah maintained her smile and continued, "You remember how often we acted like rabbits on our journey; this blessing from God is the result." Before allowing Mochè to respond by calling her bunny, Zipporah used her toes to grasp both his legs. Seeing the pleasure on her husband's face, her petite hands slowly pulled Mochè closer, her body ready to receive him. "I'm a bunny rabbit—what can I say?"

Hours later, she whispered into her love's ear, "It's time for your daughters, Eliza and Gabriela, to begin their new lives with the young men they love." Zipporah looked into her husband's glorious eyes and said, "I know you wish to hold on to them longer, but the time has come. You told them they could marry once we settled here."

I remember them as little children—both my daughters— where did the time go?"

"Time is precious, my love. Allow them to savor each day as if it's their last—just like we do," she smiled, though a tear rolled from one of her splendid eyes, knowing that every forthcoming day could be their last.

A week later, Matthew and Benjamin stood before the altar of the newly assembled church in their town. After nervously waiting at the front of the church, they watched as their manhig held each of the two women's arms and slowly marched toward them to the superbly played piano music by Professor Moran, the new music teacher at the school. Eliza and Gabriela looked stunning, each smiling magnificently and glowing in their specially tailored wedding dresses, exhibiting their marvelous figures. The ceremony began after the grooms joined their fiancées, holding hands and facing Mochè, who presided with the assistance of Father David.

Each couple gazed into their significant other's eyes as Mochè asked them to recite their vows individually. He then stood before each couple in turn and declared, "I now pronounce you husband and wife. You may now each kiss your bride."

After completing their vows, both couples marched back down the aisle, arms linked as the music softly played. Ben whispered into Gabriela's ear, "Now, you have a family, my love; you are Gabriela of the family of Joyce. And you can clearly see how much my parents love you." The young blonde bride was speechless, shedding nothing but happy tears.

In the beautiful, warm autumn, the couples celebrated their honeymoons separately but sometimes reconnected to share dinner at the compound or by campfire, always having weapons nearby whenever in the wilderness.

"It's such a lovely time of year," Gabriela told Ben as they lay naked on the soft grass of the meadow. Gabriela felt somewhat intimidated by what would happen for the first time. They had come so close often before, but now that it was permissible, Gabriela worried she might not satisfy her husband properly at the memory of her childhood trauma. She engaged Ben's eyes while in the passion of lovemaking and whispered, "Be gentle with me, Benjamin." But nature took its course in the heated, impassioned entanglement of their responding bodies. Ben felt Gabriela's moisture with his fingertips, hearing her moan softly and knowing the magnificent woman he had loved and lusted for so long splayed, ready to receive him. Guided by Gabriela's fingers, he gently and very slowly entered her for the first time. Gabriela's eyes widened in the ecstasy of what they both had only dreamed about before. Gabriela's and Ben's joyous screaming squeals resounded to the grassy knolls up from where they lay entwined together in their bliss of grappling and rapid bouncing. Gabriela and Benjamin consummated their marital vows over the following hours of stimulating euphoria.

Afterward, as they lay happily fulfilled, Gabriela hesitantly asked, "Can you…do it again?"

Ben leaped back onto his new wife. "I can do this all day long."

Gabriela and Ben couldn't hear Matthew and Eliza's blissful sounds as they rolled from the slight inclines of a similar area. "Oh, Matthew," Eliza said, her face radiating satisfaction, "it's so wonderful to finally enjoy each other as we desire."

"That's because you drive me crazy with your magnificent body that I've been restraining myself from having," he roared in ecstasy.

"We came so close so many times," she breathed heavily, kissing every inch of his muscular body before lying upon him once more, indulging in their marital bliss. Eliza shrieked with joy at her fulfillment, her delight echoing each time. They sought special places, like behind the Indian grass of small ponds, lakes, and streams. Once there, Matthew slowly undressed his love before enjoying her shapely body to their complete satisfaction.

Gabriela and Ben found a hidden crystal cavern. As they crouched beneath the droplets, some hanging lower than others, Ben took her hand and led her to a waterfall sprinkling from above. He undressed Gabriela and held the cheeks of her soft derrière, her legs grasping him around his thighs, and made unrestrained love standing under the water that stimulated them even more.

The couples gathered together on the last night of their honeymoons, the young women gleaming at each other, knowing that everything had gone well for them both. They spoke of places they went, but not the private things they did there.

A couple of months later, Mochè stood before the massive crowds of the followers he now led. As all assembled along the river and the hills above the large meadow outside the new stronghold, he addressed them through a loudspeaker. Many listened, sitting on the rocks and boulders of the compound itself. "My dear followers, I have already consecrated our new home in the name of God." Mochè paused and looked upon the captivated faces of his people. "The time of our redemption is getting closer, my dear brothers and sisters in God." Glancing at Father David, who sat close to him and his family as always when he spoke, Mochè continued, "Father David and I have calculated that the anniversary of the birth of our messiah comes upon us." Smiling now, he roared happily, "I order that we all celebrate that special day with an enormous feast!" The crowds howled their praises and joy, clapping to their manhig's words. "Banquets will spread throughout each town of our new home place."

While joining a scouting party, Mochè peered through his telescope to observe the large crowds of people in the distance. Focusing the glass further, he noticed what appeared to be a well-organized army of strangers. He could see the advanced weapons they carried. "They seem to have armaments similar to ours," he told Joshua, seated on his horse beside him.

Aaron, seated on his spotted Appaloosa at Mochè's other side, asked, "Do you think they have harnessed solar power, Manhig?"

"I'm not sure, but they certainly have scientists and technicians to design as many firearms as they possess," Mochè replied. "Here, take a look," he said, handing the scope to Aaron. Mochè sat in deep contemplation, recalling the more organized evil gangs his old friend mentioned during one of their fireside chats. Recently, Andrew had visited Mochè in a dream, reminding him of what he had explained a couple of years earlier: "There are bands of wicked followers of Satan who have scientists just like we do and have manufactured advanced weapons like ours. Although we've never encountered them, they are out there. My father told me how the evil ones had also prepared for the end times when I was a boy." That dream was why Mochè formed the scouting expedition he now rode with.

Joshua, already looking through his scope, said, "I see what could be a solar-powered rifle. I hope I'm wrong." He turned to Mochè, saying, "Their force seems to be of army strength, Manhig."

"I know," Mochè resumed looking through his telescope after Aaron finished using it. He spotted a rider who seemed to be their leader, pointing and giving directions. Zooming in closer, he observed the leader's face, focusing on it for a full minute, and privately confirmed it was his brother.

That night, as he rested comfortably in his wife's arms, Mochè had a dream. He was playing chess with his father and made a bold and exemplary move. "Perfect," he said, smiling.

His father smiled back and patted him on the head, but corrected the boy, "Damian, you did well, but always remember all perfection comes from God; his will we only aspire."

Then the boy saw the face of his father change to that of a younger man, and his dream became a nightmare, seeing the face of his wicked brother, screaming, "Farewell, Damian, I'll kill you another time!"

Mochè screamed in his sleep, mumbling foreign words that Zipporah couldn't fully understand. She only recognized one part of the Latin from the fallen church that he yelled, "ultimum judicium," as she cradled his shivering body against hers, comforting him.

Soaked in sweat, Mochè whispered, "I must battle my own brother before God's last judgment."

The following warm autumn night, Mochè went to speak to David by the river, knowing he was lonely after Andrew had ascended. As he greeted his old friend, David said, "Even though it's not the same stream, the river reminds me of Andrew." David forced a grin. "Especially over there," he pointed to the mill at the stream's tributary that flowed from the river.

"My wife has sent food for you, my friend."

"God bless Zipporah's heart," he replied, accepting the wrappings infused with the aroma of his favorite meal.

"She is concerned about you and would like you to come

and live with us. We now have two spare rooms since Eliza got married."

"Sit," said David; "let's talk." It felt like old times at the fireside. "You made the right decision by marrying that woman." He looked to the heavens and corrected himself, "Or I should say He did," David smiled. "Andrew and I both told you way back then, remember?"

David and Mochè began discussing the past again. Their favorite subject was always the fascination with how easily the great decline ultimately led to the fall of civilization.

"Sorry to resurrect what I've always said about those great darkened days, but it was primarily the evil force known as the media," David replied. "They steered people toward immorality. That card toppled all the other leaning cards in the deck. It happened gradually, as everything does, but their damage became irreversible."

"I agree with that," said Mochè, "but I remember hearing stories of people who toyed with Satanism. They once formed churches and temples to honor him, depicting him as anything but the evil being he is and always will be throughout eternity. They revered that false image, not realizing it led to the possession of their souls."

"The father of lies," David declared with a smile, "John 8:44."

"Well, now we have a large, organized army of that same wickedness, birthed from the great decline of civilization, plaguing us in these fallen times," Mochè stated. "Remember what Andrew said about large groups of wicked followers of Satan who have scientists like we do and may have created advanced weapons and technology as we possess?"

"Of course I do," David answered. "We spoke of it often. Andrew's father passed down that knowledge from his great-grandfather. But what do you mean we now have them?"

"I've seen them," Mochè replied, appearing mystified. "They're close to us, David." Mochè then told his old friend about his evil brother, requesting that he keep it a secret.

Chapter Twelve

A New Place

After living in their new place for two years, a holy one, or angel, appeared to Mochè. It was the same spiritual entity that had guided Mochè from the very beginning, delivering a sacred message from God. Amid a blaze of bright light surrounding the manhig, the angel conveyed God's command. While enveloped in that celestial glow, Mochè learned that this place was their last fortress—the site of the final battle between good and evil upon God's created earth. The time was drawing near, and Mochè called for a council meeting.

The manhig addressed his council from his large desk, bringing the meeting to order with a single tap of his hammer against the wooden block. "Over there," he pointed to a small glass-covered frame he had placed on the wall, visible for all members to see, "is a centuries-old map I've carried since the beginning. I never knew its significance until now. It's from the last large cathedral in the now fallen great city of the East." Mochè stood and walked to the framed, drab-colored geographic chart. "This is an antique map written in the script of an ancient language, but the priests there had deciphered it. We are close to here," he pointed at a spot on the map. "I don't question the Lord's decisions, only that his messenger told me that where we are now will be our last stronghold; we will move no more. We have reached the place of Armageddon, where we will fight the last battle between good and evil with Christ before judgment." Mochè watched the startled faces of all his council members and listened to their murmurs and mumbles. "We now know the exact place but not the time. No one knows the day or hour when these things will happen, not even the angels in heaven or the Son himself. Only the Father." Mochè quoted Matthew 24:36, then he tapped his hammer again and said, "Meeting adjourned."

Everyone was living once again in the only civilization they knew. All followers enjoyed God's blessings each day, unaware of when the last would arrive. Husbands and wives nestled closely at night, cherishing the bonds of their marriage while procreating to bring as many new souls to God as possible before the end.

The year before, in early summer, Zipporah had given birth to another boy, whom they named Eliezer. Mochè knew it was the name of Zipporah's father and wanted to honor her by remembering that man. He had heard many stories she told about him, being a professor and follower of God.

"Be careful, my love," Zipporah said every morning before her husband disembarked to lead scouting parties, surveillance missions, or hunting expeditions. Mochè wanted to keep a close watch on his brother and the army that wicked man had been forming since he recognized him as the older brother he had never known—an evil being. He always wondered why his father never revealed the existence of his malevolent brother. When he spoke to his older friend about it, David felt it was due to embarrassment or perhaps because he didn't want Mochè to dwell on their differences and disturb his studies. Yet it still tormented the far corners of Mochè's soul.

As he held Zipporah close to him, the way he did every morning before he left, he told her, "Don't be afraid for me, my darling wife." He kissed her lips softly, and Zipporah relished it. "Take care of my boys," he smiled, patting the head of his firstborn's soft crop of blond hair, like his mother's, and kissing the cheek of his baby son, Eliezer. Little did Zipporah or Mochè know that their stronghold had already been compromised.

Gabriela and Eliza became pregnant around the same time, just months after their honeymoons. Gabriela gave her husband a beautiful daughter, while Eliza presented Matthew with a son. As their friendship deepened during this period, Matthew and Ben often spoke to distract themselves from the stresses and pressures of frequent fighting, whether in skirmishes with demons or grand-scale battles.

While off duty and sitting together under the shade of a large elm's wide-spreading branches, adorned with saw-toothed leaves, the friends began discussing various topics: everyday matters, such as the happenings in the compound and the stunning vistas and scenery near their new home.

Matthew shifted the conversation by saying, "We've been friends for a long time now, Ben," and Ben nodded with a grin of agreement. "Ever since you showed me the ropes," Matt chuckled.

"We've fought many battles together," Ben's eyes glanced into the distance, reflecting on them. "Fighting side by side brought us closer."

"I've read in the building of books much about the ways of the last civilization," Matt smiled, listening to the sounds of a mother blue jay feeding her babies in a nest high above them in the large tree. "It wasn't all bad, as many people think—I mean before Satan began to rule." The building of books was one of Mochè's original ideas. The manhig took a great many antiquated books on various subjects from the great city of the East and carefully stored them. From the beginning, Mochè had scribes copy those old texts for anyone who wanted to expand their knowledge.

"I can't tell you how many times I sat in that building when I was in the academy," Ben mused.

Matthew's face glowed as he told Ben, "The people living in the last civilization had ways to relieve stress and relax."

"Hell, we do that right here in the stronghold every time we sit and drink beer and wine," Ben chuckled. He knew his friend wanted to make a point and was only teasing him.

"No," Matthew's eyes glanced in space as if imagining, "they went to exotic places and just lay in the sun." He chuckled, "Can you imagine that? Just lying there in comfort; what a way to relieve stress."

"I like my way better!" Ben laughed, "No, I've read a lot about what you're talking about. It brought couples and even families closer."

"That's what I mean," Matt interjected—"exactly! There were so many ways to keep couples close to each other. Just a few weeks ago, I read about how fathers were more involved in their wives' childbirth at that time. In our fallen world, we wait in a different room until the baby's born."

"Men were also more involved in helping their wives with the newborns. Of course, they didn't have to rush out to fight hooved demons back then," Ben laughed.

"I read that only some men and women centuries ago adhered to our custom when the wife nursed. We do it as a tradition, but to them, it allowed the man to feel closer to his wife and more involved with her birthing." Matthew looked at his friend and said, "I find that true when I practice our custom with Eliza. Do you?"

"Do I what?" Ben perked up. He was thinking about how much he loved Gabriela and wished to be close to her in every way.

"Hello! Wake up!" Matt knew Ben was daydreaming. "Do you find that applying our custom of drinking your wife's breast milk brings you closer to each other?"

"We-I have not done that yet," Ben stammered, blushing.

"Why not?"

"I don't know."

"Ben, I know you love Gabriela."

"I do," Ben's eyes now focused, thinking about his beautiful wife. "I'm truly blessed, but I don't want to do anything to her only because it's a tradition. Does it hurt Eliza when you do it?"

"Just the opposite. I also read that many mothers centuries ago had pain from an overload of milk in their breasts, just as our women experience. It depends on the individual. But in that long-ago time, they had breast milking machines which relieved the mother of that ordeal." Matthew continued, "We have no such machines, and the flimsy syringe Eliza was using doesn't remove all her discomfort."

Ben became interested just thinking about the subject. "Maybe I'll try it," he spoke softly to his friend.

"It depends on whether or not Gabriela has an abundance of milk. Some women don't have enough. Eliza's breasts became really large with milk," Matthew explained.

"Judging by the size of Gabriela's, I'd say she has more than enough, and she has complained of pain. I never knew about these things or that I could actually help her."

Matthew whispered, "It ignited an erotic passion in Eliza and me. Don't mention this to Gabriela, as it might be embarrassing if Eliza found out I told you of this sensitive intimacy we share beyond it being a ceremonial gesture."

"You know I would never betray anything you tell me confidently. Do you drink the milk directly from her breast as with our custom?"

"Yes, I suck it from her nipples as the words of our Bible say. The longer I do, the more it fuels her desires. It made us feel closer to each other, Ben, especially in these days when we don't know which will be the last."

"I often watch Gabriela breastfeeding," Ben admitted, blushing. "It's a very captivating experience indeed. I won't know until I try it, and Gabriela may hate it."

"The book explained that while some couples centuries ago loved it, others abhorred it." Matthew spread his arms. "I don't understand why anyone would dislike doing it—a way for a husband and wife to bond in the sanctity of marriage."

"I always felt a passion when watching Gabriela, but she never asked me to indulge in that tradition."

"Well, discuss it with her first, then gently ease into it. That's what we did." Matthew looked at his friend skeptically and said, "Maybe in a sane world, this would seem strange to some," raising his shoulders in question before continuing, "but not in ours." He shrugged and added, "Maybe that's why not so many practiced it centuries ago."

When Ben arrived home that evening, he observed how naturally and motherly Gabriela appeared while feeding their daughter. Sitting upright, with her toes splayed against the bend of her bare legs, she resembled a flawless portrait of mother and child. Even the room in which she sat carried the pure scent of a clean young infant. After Gabriela gently placed the baby back in her cradle, Ben walked closer to her.

Giggling, Gabriela said, "I know that look so well, my love," and she fell into her loving husband's arms, "Take me, Benjamin, do whatever wicked deed you wish to me," she still giggled, but now much more seductively.

When Ben sat her down on their bed and put his lips to her breast nipple, now long and erect, he began sucking and then drawing and swallowing the milk from her breast. "Do you like this?" he asked in his excitement.

Plunging her fingers into his long crop of hair and clawing it sensually, Gabriela screamed in a rush of sexual passion, "Oh, Benjamin, I love the feel of your lips drawing my milk from my nipple." She impulsively drew one arm behind her, pushing her chest forward, the other remained raking and pulling his hair with this new stimulation she felt, urging him on as her legs wrapped around his waist. "Eliza told me about this, but you've never done it to me before." Her face reddened from the wave of excitement that overcame her.

They fell from the bed and rolled together on the floor of their new home, enjoying each other's every sensual movement. "Don't stop, Benjamin. Keep doing it, but draw harder. Oh, my love!" Gabriela's body trembled, and she screamed, "Harder!" biting her lip to control herself, grimacing from the exhilaration, "You're turning me on so much!—making me crazy!"

Gabriela pushed Ben's body back. As he lay flat in shock, but a satisfying daze, she swiftly slid off his pants and mounted herself over him, her fingers guiding him to enter her, she allowed her breasts to hang so he could reach them with his mouth while she bounced wildly.

Solomon, Mochè's brother, had deployed a company of about a hundred warriors to laboriously scale the high rocks behind the stronghold before dawn and attack the compound in the morning. Their purpose was surveillance, but more importantly, they wanted to kill as many of Mochè's soldiers as possible to rattle him.

Solomon now rode ahead of a battalion-sized force in the distance of the gated entrance. Startled at the sound of the siren and the loud bell ringing, Solomon now knew his invaders had been spotted. He watched from his binoculars as a giant of a man and others emerged from hidden caves, hurling his soldiers off the rocks to their demise.

Mochè quickly mounted the stallion Aaron brought to him and led a standby cavalry battalion. "Quickly!" he shouted, "Open the gate!" and the cavalry charged outside the stronghold.

When Ben and Matt heard the emergency warnings, they quickly donned their uniforms and led their brigades, which had already assembled in response to the blaring siren and clanging bell. Their brigades headed for the battalion where their manhig was already in motion. Dividing his forces, Ben directed Matthew's light brigade to go straight, while he led his larger, heavy brigade to the right toward the higher ground.

Mochè turned from his galloping horse to observe the brigade maneuvers unfolding, thinking he couldn't have done better himself. He caught up to Matthew and yelled, "So, young man, you leave my daughter quickly this fine morning," while smiling among the flora around the fortress, which were already displaying the flower buds of early spring, their bouquets filling the morning air. Ben's brigade joined with Matthew's, and he now rode alongside Matt and his manhig.

"Yes, sir, I had nothing better to do after hearing the siren and bell," Matthew joked. "Are they actually attacking us with such a small number, Manhig?"

"No," Ben answered the question directed at his leader. "They're assessing our response time and the armaments we bear," Ben turned in his saddle and pointed behind him. "See how swiftly our sentinels eliminated their raiding party? Their leader isn't a fool, it seems. This will only be a skirmish," Ben assessed. "But notice the weapons they're employing."

"Very good, Benjamin," Mochè was pleased with both young men. "You both responded quickly and in good military order, and you see well with your young eyes."

"Yes, the weapons," Matthew replied after witnessing the accumulation of broken bodies, some appearing to cry out in pain. He couldn't hear their distant wails over the thunder of galloping horse hooves. "Their armaments seem similar to ours."

"Have some of our soldiers collect weapons from their fallen comrades; I want our technicians to inspect them." Amidst the fighting, Mochè glanced to the right and saw another cavalry force positioned on a hill. Those riders appeared different and stayed on horseback, while what remained of Solomon's deployed detail turned and rode away. "Take charge here, Benjamin. I'm taking a platoon to see what those others want."

As Mochè rode closer to the cavalry poised on the incline, he noticed that the men and women were naked and painted. "Oh, my God," gasped Mochè, taking a closer look at one of them. "It can't be," he murmured in shock and disbelief.

The female cavalry leader rode closer and asked, "Why do you look so surprised, Mochè?" She laughed wickedly. Her completely naked body bore pagan designs from her face to her bare feet, including the toes that curled and grasped the horse's body. Below her hanging breasts was a painted image of the Leviathan cross, the mark of Satan; other small images of witchcraft and sorcery were drawn around her erect nipples. The men assembled behind her seemed to be mutants, some resembling half-demons.

"Helen, is that you?"

"Of course," she said, her tongue licking across her full lips erotically as she rode around Mochè's horse, her blonde hair blowing in the breeze, scrutinizing him closely, her breasts bouncing with the rhythm of her trotting stallion. She rode close to him, her lips puckered sensually as she blew her breath onto his face, then whispered, "Do you still lust for me as I do for you," she asked, her eyes wide and painted with makeup enhancing their beauty, making an obscene gesture with her hand to her groin. She swiftly and unexpectedly reached out her slender neck and kissed Mochè's lips. "You left me wet with desire that last night we were together—like a wild animal in heat!"

"You're possessed by demons," Mochè spoke his realization.

"Of course I am. They had their way with me until I began enjoying it. I chose that one to service me," she pointed to a muscular mutant seated on a horse. "He's the only one among the other imbeciles who can pleasure me. I tried them all." She rode up to the husky male and simply caressed his breast with her long, painted fingernails, then said, "See what I mean?" She giggled. "And so quickly, too. Just like a mechanical toy." She looked at the mutated males behind her and said, "They're not human and so stupid, but when they learned I had military experience, they made me their leader. I trained them all to be warriors and even began to teach some of them to speak. With their limited minds, they could never learn to speak as cloquently as you, Mochè," Helen reached to fondle his muscular arm, but Mochè pulled it away abruptly. "I stopped teaching them because they began telling me nice things with their measly, bumbling wording when I bedded them—those lies men—even mutated ones—offer so freely when they only want one thing.

I had those who knew how to verbalize castrated and ate those remains of their manhood—or should I say mutated malehood," she giggled.

"I don't know why I ever allowed you to tempt me so far," Mochè appeared disgusted at the sight of the woman he used to admire.

"Silly man, like all men," Helen laughed wickedly again. "I secretly slipped you a love potion to make you desire me—a small dose since I wasn't a demon yet, as you call us," she chuckled. "I was pure then, a virgin." She rode close to Mochè again, licking his closed lips. "How else could I have gotten a rock like you to crave me? I almost succeeded. You were ready to take my virginity." She looked up to the heavens and shouted, "But He stopped me!"

"If there is still an element of goodness within you, Helen, let me exorcise the demons and return you to yourself and the love of God."

"Never!" she screamed. "I worship the other now! He gives me the things I now desire!" She appeared in thought. "Give yourself to me first, Mochè, and I'll let you expel those who are within me." He knew she was lying.

"You know I can't do that!"

"Oh, I forgot; your wife and child," she paused, thinking again. "Perhaps I should slaughter Zipporah and devour your child before your eyes after I defeat your army!" she yelled, her horse still trotting around him. "I eat children now, my love. Young babies are the tastiest. I destroy the life those imbecile mutations put into my womb and eat them as well," she licked her lips, the same that touched Mochè's, and he felt repulsion. "Your eyes show your surprise."

"Disgust, not surprise, demon woman!" Mochè had heard enough and realized he could never exorcise her among the men guarding her; she harbored a powerful demon within her, perhaps Lucifer himself.

"Many of your followers still pledge allegiance to me as a general," she shouted back at him. "My army is scouring the countryside to find warriors to join me and ultimately defeat you. Then you will bow, kiss my feet, and take me to your bed. Groups are organizing as we speak. Even your own brother has vowed to kill you—but I'll spare you if you take me as your mate!" As Mochè led his platoon back to the brigades, Helen screamed diabolically, "I give you one last chance to take me as your woman." Watching the trail of dust behind him, knowing he wouldn't accept, she yelled even louder, "Remember what I promised to do to your wife and child!"

Later that beautiful spring day, Mochè assembled all his followers by the river in the open space, displaying the rolling hills behind it. Assured by his scouts that his enemies were far away, he conducted his service. Mochè wanted to share with his people what he had told his council about this place. Three loudspeakers were necessary to ensure that the massive gathering of about twenty-five thousand followers could hear. He began by announcing, "The same holy angel who has guided me from the great fallen city of the East since the beginning of our journey has come to me once more." He glanced at some familiar faces and continued, "Many of you who have been with me the longest remember our perilous travels and the numerous battles we encountered on our odyssey with God as our guide. We have lost many along the way, but each day we procreate, we renew God's people with new souls." Mochè heard the cries of infants and children, their parents trying to quiet them, and said, "Hear them among you. New lives to bring to our loving Father. He has always protected us, and now He brings us this blessed message. God has consecrated this fortress where we now stand as the final place. There will be no other place for us from here as we had expected, except the womb of God's loving embrace for all of us judged as righteous." Mochè looked to the heavens and elaborated, "While I was swaddled in that heavenly bright light, His messenger declared that this location would be where the last battle between good and evil upon God's created earth will take place." After hearing his words, Mochè raised his arms to silence the murmurs of men and women and declared, "Live your lives each day to the fullest. Enjoy them as if they were your last." The great leader looked upon the vast crowds of his followers and asked, "Those among you who are able, keep procreating and bring forth more blessed creations of God. Women enjoy your husbands, and men take your wives. All, let us keep our laws sacred to avoid banishment in these end times. For now, we know the place but not the exact time." His deep blue penetrating eyes glowed in warning, "As we get closer to God, the Dark Angel will tempt us all the more."

As his people, now renewed with the Holy Spirit, began to rise, believing the sermon was over, Mochè raised his arms once more to stop them. His voice crackled with remorse, and his expression conveyed the gravity of the final announcement he would make that day. "My friends in God, a horrible thing has happened. Instead of the death we believed General Helen had faced, a worse fate has befallen her." Mochè bowed his head and spoke from his heart, "It pains me to tell you that General Helen has been possessed by Satan himself, just as Nikanyiso had been years ago." He paused momentarily, observing the fearful expressions on his followers' faces; some seemed to question what he had said, especially Miriam, who had been Helen's second-in-command and succeeded her as general of her army. "Helen, my dear friend, is now a demon. She commands a large cavalry and an army opposing us, following the Fallen Angel's will. If you encounter her, run; she is not the same person you remember. Don't speak to her because you would be speaking to Satan, the father of all lies." Mochè quoted Corinthians 11:3: 'But I am afraid just as Eve was deceived by the serpent's cunning, your minds may somehow be led astray from your sincere and pure devotion to Christ.' After the Lord's Prayer, Mochè looked at the crowd and proclaimed, "Go with God, my dear friends, and pray for Helen's soul."

As Mochè held his youngest son and walked away with Zipporah, who grasped his oldest son's hand, General Miriam approached him.

"I'm sorry to interrupt, Manhig," she nodded politely to Zipporah, who smiled back. "But is it not possible to exorcise the demon that imprisons Helen as you did with Nikanyiso?"

Holding his general's shoulder, he softly spoke, "Were you there when I fought that demon?"

"Yes, I was. I saw what tremendous strength it had," Miriam said, a tear in her eye, which distressed Mochè even more.

"I know you were close to Helen, Miriam, but she has too many strong mutants guarding her for me to restrain her," he sighed. "When I exorcised the beast within Nikanyiso, I had a squadron of soldiers assisting me," he noticed the disappointed look on his general's face. "Know that if an opportunity ever arises, I promise you I will try. I already pleaded with her, but Satan controls her with all his power, preventing me from reaching her now."

Mochè strolled to the river just outside the new stronghold's open gate, where numerous soldiers, positioned on various levels of rock platforms, guarded the fortress's front. Lookouts scanned all directions with binoculars and telescopes. He spotted David and walked over for an evening chat, as he always did after dinner with Zipporah and his family. David had become reclusive after Andrew's disappearance, avoiding sitting at Mochè's table and sharing meals with him and his family. Now that he was alone, Mochè and Zipporah felt sympathy for him and often invited him to their home.

"Your antisocial behavior is getting annoying, my old friend," Mochè chuckled, "you're making me carry your dinner to you once more."

"Oh, Zipporah spoils me, Mochè," he sniffed the wrapping of his meal. "It's not that I don't want to come over; it's just that I want to be outside in God's glorious countryside as much as I can before it—" David smiled, cutting off his words. "I still talk to Andrew here by the water."

"We understand, David. I spar with your spirit only to keep you on your toes, my friend."

"I liked your sermon today." David looked around at the budding trees and flowers, inhaling the fresh scent that permeated the air. "Life is so beautiful. If our forefathers could have only appreciated God's glorious world and followed such simple rules, it would have been a very different world from the one we live in now," he smiled.

"Yes, it does seem simple," Mochè smiled back at his old friend.

"I remember when you secretly told Andrew and me about the place of the final battle between good and evil and judgment from our Lord afterward. Now, we sit at that place."

"Yes, we are here, but we still do not know the time." Mochè mused.

David shook his head, saying, "I'm sorry to hear about what happened to Helen. It's terrible. Can I help you in any way to release her from the demon?"

"No, the beast within her is too strong to fight while she remains guarded. Among other things, she revealed that she secretly gave me a love potion. That's why I felt such an intense sexual attraction to her during that expedition years ago." Mochè didn't elaborate on the inappropriate way she now painted her bare body, the immoral comments she made, or the obscene gestures she displayed.

"That explains a lot, my friend. Oh, my dear God in Heaven, forgive me for judging you as harshly as I did." David looked to the sky and continued, "I'm sure Andrew now knows and is also sorry."

"You both had no idea; besides, God stopped it." Sensing that David wanted to be alone, Mochè said, "I bid you a fine evening, my friend. As always, I'll see you tomorrow." He turned back to see David's smiling face and continued, "Perhaps you'll surprise us and show up at our door to join us for dinner."

As David sat by the sound of flowing water, enjoying the tranquility of the spring evening while praying and meditating, he heard soft footsteps on the gravel and stones by the riverbed. Turning quickly, he asked in horror, "My God, woman, what have you done to yourself?"

"Do you desire me, Priest?" Helen's wide blue eyes gazed into his. "I know all your private thoughts." She walked closer to David, flaunting her nude body adorned with Satanic markings, so close that he could smell her feminine fragrance. "I know your secret lust for me," the toes of her feet spread apart his robe and massaged his leg, rising higher. David quickly brushed her leg away.

"Begone, Satan!" David reached into the pocket of his robe, pulled out his Holy Water, and sprinkled it on Helen.

She laughed as her flesh sizzled, and then her voice transformed into the deep roar of a monster, asking, "Is that all you have, Priest? You're too old, but I grant you the power to satisfy me as a man does a woman. Do it now, or I'll take your life!" the beast within Helen growled.

"Never! I obey the laws of God!"

Helen swiftly reached out her arm, skillfully slitting David's throat in one brisk movement. Bending over him as blood gurgled from his neck and his eyes bulged, Helen's long painted nails gently stroked his long gray beard. She softly said, "You could have had the feel of a woman for once in your miserable life, but chose death instead. Foolish man, as all men are."

Before Mochè entered his home after speaking with David, the presence of an angel appeared to him, saying, 'God commands that you must find the strength to slay your father's son, Mochè. For if you hesitate, he will destroy you as he now follows Satan and is already lost.'

Chapter Thirteen

Vigilance

Three years had passed since David's death. Mochè and Zipporah, along with the entire town that respected the fallen priest, mourned him deeply. Mochè had conducted a sacred funeral in which everyone joined to pray for the soul of the holy man who had followed the manhig from the beginning. During that service, Mochè clung to the rosary beads wrapped around the small, framed photo of Andrew and Sarah that David had left for him, recalling both his old friends dearly. That incident drove all the townspeople away from any fond memories of the once-beloved general and made them regret the days when they admired her. Even those who had been close to her, like Miriam, distanced themselves from her memory.

When Mochè learned of David's death at Helen's hands, following a sentinel's report of a woman fitting her description leaving the river, he was furious. He personally assembled Matthew's cavalry brigade and galloped in search of her. Upon spotting her leading her army, he charged into the center of her mutated males and females, catching them off guard. After penetrating the heart of her cavalry and killing many of her warriors, Helen's forces fell into temporary disarray. He rode close to her, cutting her off.

"I've outwitted your mindless muscled mutations," Mochè yelled to rattle her, and it worked.

Hissing at him, she growled, "I'll get you for this, Mochè!"

"I decapitated that big mutated moron who pleasured you so well," he said as his stallion reared up. Its hooves nearly hit Helen's startled face as her eyes glanced at the mutilated figure of her demon lover's head that Mochè dangled before her by its hair. "I guess you'll have to find a 'bigger' man," Mochè glared at her.

"I'll have you as my lover; you'll see. I told you that you would kiss my feet. Now I swear you will kiss my naked body!" She made an obscene gesture.

"Ugh! Your naked painted body repulses me!"

"David was just the beginning!" Helen yelled in her high-pitched voice. "Wait until I breach your fortress and slaughter Zipporah and your children in the comfort of their lovely, red-painted home with a white picket fence!" She had evidently learned about his home and second child, making Mochè wonder if she had placed someone within his stronghold—a traitor among them. "Then you'll come to my bed!"

"Find another big-muscled mutation to satisfy you, harlot! It will never be me!"

Helen's eyes widened, and she hissed again, "I'll have you, Priest!" Now sounding deep and resounding like Lucifer, whom he had exorcised many times, the demon roared, "I licked David's blood from my blade!"

"Farewell for now, Demon Helen, formerly known as General Helen, a bold and valiant warrior of God." Mochè laughed, "Now you battle poorly like a child as a pawn of Satan."

As he rode with Matthew back to the stronghold, he remarked, "I want to speak with you later, Matthew."

"Of course, sir. Send for me, and I'll come at once," Matthew wondered if he had done something wrong.

With nearly a hundred thousand followers, God commanded Mochè to expand his massive stronghold. The Lord inspired his architects to devise a plan to blast through the stones of the mountain, leveling it to construct an extension to the existing fortress. When they flattened an adjacent area, they would have twice the living space they had.

"Are you certain the explosions will not damage our existing stronghold in any way?"

Peter assured him, "No, Manhig, Jeffrey, and I've carefully surveyed the grounds, and they are solid. We will deploy our explosives carefully and only in certain places we have strategically marked so as not to affect our existing site."

"I expect the vibrations will be tremendous. You're certain they won't cause our people harm?"

"No, sir," he pointed toward the homes closest to the bordering grounds, "Those living near our blasting area might have a few coffee mugs broken, but nothing more than that. I'm sure, Manhig."

"Okay, then, I'll have someone assemble a team of skilled workers and laborers. How many do you estimate we'll need?"

"We know you want it completed as fast as possible," Peter said, looking at Jeffrey. They whispered for a few seconds together, and Peter answered, "At least three rotating shifts with 75 laborers and 25 skilled workers for each, Manhig."

"Okay, you'll have them. I assume you've already selected your assistants and foremen?"

"Yes, Manhig," Jeffrey replied. "We will need much more lumber from the mill."

"And you will have it!" Mochè answered as he left for his next stop.

After Mochè had his scientists and technicians analyze their adversary's weapons, his team worked diligently to create newer, more advanced armaments than those of their new enemies. They disassembled every component of the captured solar handguns and rifles, studying them carefully. The team's head manager presented his report directly to his leader.

As he stood before Mochè in his courthouse office, the head

of that department explained, "Manhig, they indeed harnessed the power of the sun but at a much different wavelength." He showed a technical diagram to Mochè and continued, "You see, their intensity is slightly greater than ours."

"Hmm, I see," Mochè answered the anxious man before him, rubbing his chin in thought before he continued. "Is there anything we can do about it?"

"Yes, sir," responded the head scientist, Doctor Robert, as he pulled out another mechanical drawing. "We're employing their method but significantly increasing its power. See the—"

"I trust you, Doctor," Mochè interrupted. "Great work, Robert. Let me know as soon as you have some prototypes."

"We should finish soon, sir."

Doctor Robert had completed the development of prototypes for new weapons two weeks after his discussion with Mochè. Following their testing in an open area by the river, Mochè happily approved them.

"The newer solar mortar rifles have performed excellently, Manhig," Aaron informed him as he and his manhig walked alongside Joshua after assessing the progress at the building site. "They possess nearly double the blasting power of the older models."

"The generals also report that the automatic rifles fire significantly faster than before," Joshua stated.

"I commend Doctor Robert for his speedy work." Mochè was pleased that his armies would have superior armaments compared to those of his enemies. "I know his staff worked around the clock."

Mochè parted ways with the other two men and met Doctor Gloria at her hospital, the largest of the seven. He was eager to see her progress after providing her with additional scientific technicians and equipment to enhance surgeries and support the development of natural medicines in the growing communities.

Gloria was ecstatic and couldn't wait to show him the new surgical ward that the manhig had funded. Like pulling back the drapes for a musical recital that all the schools had recently started, Gloria drew back the curtain of the entrance to the large area to display her new equipment. "It's glorious, isn't it, Father?"

"I see you're in your glory, Gloria," Mochè said, smiling, recalling using the exact pun years before. "It looks too complicated for me, Gloria, but I know you'll do wonderful things with all these new gizmos," he smiled as he spoke.

After chuckling at his pun, also recalling he had used it before that awful exorcism years ago, she answered, "Oh, I will, Father. You can't imagine how many more lives I can save now with all these—gizmos," she conceded with a giggle, embracing Mochè's choice of words. Gloria stood on her tiptoes and kissed Mochè's cheek. "Thank you, Father," she said.

Everything regarding the expansion and protection of the stronghold was moving forward. Mochè stood with Zipporah and his sons, watching the construction as it began. He held Eliezer in his left arm while his wife held Gershom's hand. Goliath was single-handedly picking up boulders that it took a crew to do.

"Do you see that big man, Gershom?" Mochè pointed with his right forefinger. "He's very strong, isn't he?"

"Yes, Papa," the boy replied. "But he plays with all the little children. He's very nice."

"Yes, he is, Son. He's a very good man of God."

Zipporah turned to admire Mochè. "You're still a beautiful man, my love," she declared. "In fact, those few gray strands sprinkled among your hair make you look even more," she paused, thinking, "sexy—that's the word." Her beautiful eyes glowed in a way that had always tugged at Mochè's heart since the day he first met her, which now seemed so long ago. "It excites me," she whispered softly so the children couldn't hear.

"If you keep talking like that, we'll end up taking our boys home for a nap."

"Why do you think I'm saying such things?" she giggled.

"Remember what you keep saying about bringing more souls forward?" She appeared like a child caught sneaking a cookie from the jar. Then she leaned in closer, whispering huskily into his ear, her full lips deliberately brushing gently against it, "Let's go home and start on another."

"Okay, kids, we'll all come back another time to see the workers again."

Hours later, Zipporah and Mochè sat at the kitchen table with Gershom, enjoying their late lunch while Eliezer played with his food in his wooden highchair. Zipporah calmly said, "I think we made a good start earlier. What name would you like if God gave us a girl?"

Mochè leaned closer to her and whispered, "It's best not to speak in front of Gershom; he can understand."

Wide-eyed and speaking in her usual voice, she asked, "Why? He'll become a man sooner than we think; he should know." Zipporah lowered her voice and whispered, "Besides, if he didn't awaken from his nap to our wild screams, I think we're safe." She kissed her husband's cheek and continued in her regular voice, "I sense we'll have a girl this time, so you better think of a name," she said while playfully tickling his private area with her toes from under the table as Mochè blushed. But he seriously considered whether he would ever see his boys as men.

"Devil Woman," he chuckled. "I could never resist you, bunny." He felt her roaming toes and knew he would soon be back in the bedroom.

Zipporah's eyes glowed as she sipped from her cup of coffee. "I know, my love," she said, "nor can I resist you. Always remember the rabbits we are," she raised her eyebrows playfully. However, Zipporah's expression grew serious, and her demeanor changed with a thought that struck her. "My love, please don't mention this to him, but Matthew is troubled by what you told him." Her eyes conveyed concern as she spoke. "Eliza told me this confidentially."

"Did my daughter mention what I said to him?"

"Eliza said you mentioned a while back that you wanted to speak with him, but never called for him." Zipporah's deep green eyes held their gaze. "He's concerned that he may have disrespected you somehow."

"Ah! Yes," Mochè recalled. "I've been so busy that I neglected to send for him." He didn't want to tell his wife that he was preoccupied with Helen's threat against her and their children. Mochè had been conducting a private investigation, speaking with many of his subordinates about general topics without revealing the nature of his suspicions.

"May I ask why you wish to speak to Matthew?" Zipporah asked with wide eyes.

"No, you may not, General Zipporah," he joked.

"So, Lieutenant Colonel, I'm relieving you of your rank," Mochè said casually to Matthew. "That's why I wanted to see you."

"May I ask, Manhig, did I do something wrong?" Matthew couldn't conceal his disappointment.

"You did outstanding work as an officer and brigade commander, as did Colonel Benjamin," Mochè glanced up quickly to see the surprised expression on Matthew's face. "If you consider that an offense, then so be it. Both of you have embarrassed many of my generals several times with your superior performances and exemplary service. I already promoted Benjamin to full general as a penalty, and he will command an entire army with you as a major general and second in command." Mochè scribbled on parchment, unaware of the glow on Matthew's face. "General Mark is retiring, and I'm appointing Benjamin to replace him with you as his second." Mochè now observed Matthew closely and explained, "The council agreed with this decision. It seems you two work well together."

"We do, sir. I've learned much from Benjamin."

Mochè smiled as he finished writing and handed the new orders to Matthew. "Benjamin already has his papers."

"Manhig, I don't know how to thank you for this privilege. I-I—"

"You are a brilliant commander, son. I studied military tactics under former academy instructors and generals as a young man. Benjamin did the same at the academy, Isaac and I set up long ago." Mochè glanced to the heavens, fondly recalling his old friend and teacher. "For you, it came naturally—a gift from God. You were created for this job, Matthew."

"Thank you, sir. I promise I'll never fail you."

Gabriela held her pregnant belly and poised herself over Ben, her toes gently massaging his legs in a way she knew he liked. "See, I told you I still could," she smiled. "We have to celebrate your promotion, my love."

"Are you sure it's okay for the baby?" asked Ben, his face contorted at the lovely feel of her. "I mean, you're quite far along."

"That doesn't change a woman's desires, Benjamin," she smiled as her body slowly moved, her toes now grasping his legs, anchoring her motions. Then Gabriela stopped, her deep blue eyes squinting suspiciously, her breasts larger than usual and hanging; she asked, "You would never cheat on me while I'm in this state now that you're a general, would you, Benjamin?"

Gabriela's beautifully shaped figure resumed moving and labored rapidly, continuing until she received the response she sought. "Never, my love," Ben squeaked in reply to his wife's question, assuring her.

"I love you, Benjamin!" she screamed out. "Tell me you love me again, and louder, or I'll pounce on you even harder!" she yelled in her wild ecstasy.

As Ben stroked her hair, he clung to it tightly as if holding on for dear life against her brisk bouncing and movements. "I love you, Gabriela!" he screamed as his petite wife slowly eased up.

"Uh-oh!" Gabriela stopped moving and softly said, "Benjamin, you better call a doctor; I just went into labor."

Even though the slaughterhouse was brimming with meat, Mochè prepared a large hunting party. He wanted the butchers to continue salting their meat to satisfy the throngs of people arriving to join them. In addition to protecting the hunters, Mochè aimed to use this opportunity to scout the locations of his enemies. Knowing Benjamin and Matthew were at the stronghold would also allow the newly appointed generals to watch for anyone suspicious or asking questions about the expedition. His thoughts of a traitor still lingered in his mind, though he hadn't told anyone yet.

Mochè borrowed a heavy cavalry brigade as escorts from General Benjamin's army, whom he trusted entirely, knowing he would never betray his people.

"Be careful, my love," Zipporah said, her worry always apparent before he set off on any expedition. "You have two children and another on the way." Her eyes glowed with love for him as their boys stood beside her, waving after Mochè had kissed them both.

"What?" Mochè, already mounted on his stallion and distracted when his wife spoke, finally discerned her words. "Another one?"

"Yes, my love," she replied as Mochè leaped off his horse without using the stirrup of his saddle.

"And you tell me now?" He held her tightly to him, not wanting to let her go.

"Yes, my love," her gorgeous eyes glanced up at him like those of an innocent child. "This way, you won't waste time and can hurry back to me."

"I love you, Zipporah. I won't be long, and I will hurry back to you," he said, kissing her. He knelt and kissed her stomach, saying, "I'll come back to you, too, my child."

"Daughter," Zipporah smiled as she corrected him.

As always, Mochè brought extra wagons in addition to those for their hunted game: two for injured soldiers in case they encountered a battle, and another two with bars for transporting any captives. He was more determined than ever to interrogate all prisoners to gather information about the possibility of a traitor.

As Mochè led the cavalry away after dawn, Zipporah and her boys waved from the cheering crowd gathered along the wide street leading to the gate. Eliza and Matthew stood beside them. Crowds of people assembled in the vast open prairie near the river and on the rocky hills above it.

Now that Goliath had learned to defend himself with weapons, Mochè took him along. He was excited to go and trotted beside Nikanyiso, who wore his shield and headdress while carrying his spear, following their manhig. The metal forgers needed to cast a larger sword for the giant of a man.

Mochè spotted Helen and some of her naked male followers resting and couldn't resist engaging with them. When Helen was a competent general, she would never have made such a blunder by exposing her forces to the enemy in more than one way.

Helen lay curled on her side in a fetal position; her back-side turned toward Mochè and his army. Peering closer through his telescope, Mochè saw a large, muscular mutation holding onto her. Everyone lay sprawled across the grass, apparently after some pagan orgy. He thought for a few seconds, recalling what a good general she had been, now resorting to such lewd behavior. She was a beautiful woman if one could look past the pagan-painted symbols on her nude body.

"Bring me a lasso on a rope, Lieutenant," Mochè command-ed, wanting to capture Helen. He could take her to the strong-hold and exorcise the demon without her men protecting her.

"Colonel Maria, I'm only taking two platoons with me to take the woman. Move one regiment closer in case we have to engage them, but do so slowly and quietly."

"Yes, Manhig," the colonel signaled with her hands to direct the regiment closer. Then, she raised her arm to signal the riders to slow down.

Mochè slowly led the small detail across the short distance without issuing any verbal commands. Prairie birds chirped and flitted from tree to tree as they gathered seeds in the quiet solitude of the warm morning. The sounds of crickets and the buzzing of bees collecting pollen from the flowers resonated in the stillness. He observed Helen's backside shift slightly as she slept, her figure still as voluptuous as it had been on that expedition years before. As the horses of his platoons paced ever so slowly, Helen sat up, rubbing her eyes. She began to caress the hardened chest of the mutant beside her, gently putting her leg over his and softly brushing it with her toes. Mochè watched the woman's movements closely, realizing that Helen displayed a passion for that mutated strapping one, likely a replacement for the one he had decapitated. Remembering how selective his former general had said she was in finding someone who could pleasure her, this muscle-bound goon definitely hosted the body she craved. Mochè had to quietly trot his horse to her before she alerted her army, probably nearby.

Suddenly, Helen sat up erect and turned, her blue eyes accentuated by dark makeup, widened. She hissed when she saw Mochè, her eyes transforming into malevolent beacons as she glared at him. After kicking the man beside her awake, she seized the sword that stood firmly embedded in the ground and alerted her male protectors surrounding her. Then, Helen charged directly at Mochè, the breasts of her naked body bouncing in synchronization with her long strides. "You'll never learn, Mochè! You can't defeat me!" she screamed as she advanced. Her protectors were now running alongside her.

Mochè twirled his lasso swiftly, fearing that her army would soon be alerted. He threw it, but Helen deflected it with the blunt end of her sword. He then flung the lasso over her lover, securing it with the rope. Mochè smiled at Helen, saying, "I'll take your Romeo away instead!" He dragged her lover, its hefty body bouncing over rocks and mounds of dirt as it dragged behind Mochè's horse. "Farewell once more, Demon Helen! You'll have to find another mutated demon to service you. Take your time and choose wisely," he shouted to her as he and his platoons galloped back to their main force. He could hear the faded curses coming from Helen as she screamed from a distance.

"Put this, whatever you want to call it, in the prison wagon! Cover its nudity!"

"Will they come after us, sir?" the colonel inquired.

"No, Colonel Maria, Helen's army is drugged and recovering from one of their unrighteous binges."

"Why do you take the male, Manhig? He is nothing more than a moron and a mute who can't tell us anything."

"It might lure Helen close to us." He smiled at Maria. "Like a spider to her web."

"I see, sir," she smiled back, "and what a demonic spider it is at that!"

A month after Gabriela delivered, Ben and Matt took their wives to a pub for dinner and drinks. The two men followed Matthew's new book about spending their available time with their wives. Zipporah offered to watch their babies, and Matt and Ben gladly accepted her generous proposal; they both needed a break from their procreation efforts, as their manhig constantly suggested in his sermons. Coming home tired from the added patrols Mochè had ordered and into the waiting arms of their wives had drained them both. Talking about it often, Matt and Ben felt sure their wives needed a break more than they did. Even though they were fortunate enough to hire cleaning personnel, their wives refused to have nannies. Instead, they wanted to care for their babies themselves, which must have been tiring. Taking their wives out would undoubtedly help them exhaust the seemingly endless energy of the two women.

The place they had dinner featured an additional room for dancing, now approved by the council as a venue for both their married and unmarried followers. Lessons were held at the schools in the evenings, and the women loved the idea; however, most men dreaded it, especially the hardened warriors.

Seen as a way for young men and women to meet, couples to court, and married individuals to enjoy themselves, it ultimately served as a means for all to procreate. Bringing new souls into the world to combat the evil ones was deemed urgent as the clock ticked. Ben and Matt agreed to the dancing since it provided a way to tire their wives even more, allowing everyone to get a good night's sleep. Going out to dine and dance encouraged young women to wear their finest dresses, with Eliza and Gabriela donning outfits that rose above their knees, showcasing their shapely legs after their pregnancies.

After almost an hour of dancing, the couples drank beer and wine, sitting at their table.

"Wow! That was great!" Gabriela expressed her elation, seeming perked up rather than tired.

"It was!" Eliza agreed, "especially the fast ones!"

Ben and Matt looked at each other until Ben finally expressed what they were both thinking: "Aren't you girls tired?"

As soon as Ben finished speaking, Gabriela edged her chair closer to him, and her foot slipped out of its shoe, beginning to creep up his leg. Gabriela's wide blue eyes shone indigo in the evening light, racy and inviting. She licked her lips seductively as Ben felt her toes slowly stroking his upper thigh to his groin—that magical spot. When her toes sensed his arousal, she leaned in closer to Ben, whispering in his ear, "You're not getting off duty tonight, General." As she licked inside his ear, her toes feeling his pleasure grow, Gabriela asked softly, "Are you ready to go home, dear?" Giggling faintly, she reminded him, "You made me the monster I am, sweetheart. C'mon, let's go home. Zipporah has the kids for the night." Gabriela winked at Ben, "We can do whatever we want without changing diapers. I left Zipporah some of my milk; the rest in my breasts is for..." she winked again.

"We're leaving now," Ben told Matt.

"So are we," Matthew answered. Ben hadn't noticed how much Eliza worked on his friend; only Gabriela did. "Waiter! Check, please!" Matt called.

As Mochè and his cavalry resumed escorting the hunting party, Goliath and Nikanyiso came running back from their scouting mission. Once they calmed down, Nikanyiso asked Goliath, "My friend, would you please bring me something to drink? I'm too exhausted to go myself."

Mochè sensed that Nikanyiso had something he wished to share privately; he never tired. "What do you want to tell me, Nikanyiso?"

"Manhig, the enormous man, walks far too loudly to be a scout," he said sadly, looking at Mochè. "I regret being the one to say this about such an otherwise wonderful person."

"Don't worry, my friend. We'll find something else for Goliath," he said, rubbing his chin in thought, then added, "I brought him along only because I didn't want him to work every day. He refuses to take a break."

"I know; he seems dedicated," replied Nikanyiso.

"Why did both of you run back so quickly?"

"Oh, I almost forgot," said a smiling Nikanyiso. "We heard very loud growls. They sounded like an animal that once roamed my ancestors' lands long ago," the concerned warrior explained with a smile. "But they can't be that. They never lived in this country."

"Take me near to where you heard them."

Nikanyiso raised his arm, saying, "Not too close, Manhig; we haven't seen them, but they sound very large."

"What a roar they have; there seem to be several," said Mochè. "Let me take a look." Nikanyiso spread apart the tall blades of big bluestem grass on the incline so Mochè could peer down at the prairie and see them through his binoculars. "Oh, my, these are creations of God I've never seen before," Mochè said as he looked closer. "The larger one eats while the smaller one brings fresh meat," he laughed, "just like Zipporah feeds me. The one with the long mane of hair must be the male, and the other the female. Here, take a look, Nikanyiso." Mochè handed him the field glasses.

"Wow, the beasts are huge, and there are so many."

"I remember Father Andrew telling me stories that his grandfather passed down about places called…" He strained, trying to recall. "I can't remember their names; the word sounded odd, but they were places where people went to see animals from all over the world. These creatures must be survivors from those long ago. That was centuries past, though."

"Maybe they are the ones my ancestors knew about?"

"Perhaps. They look fierce," Mochè thought for a full minute before saying, "Let's return to the group. I want to capture a male and a female to bring back to our stronghold."

"Why would you desire that?"

"Can you think of better watchdogs to safeguard our fortress?"

As the brigade camped for the night, Mochè sat around a campfire with Maria, Nikanyiso, and Goliath. "I like Nikanyiso's idea the best, but it will be a big job digging all those holes for traps," Mochè said. "Even though we have a heavy brigade, I'm not going to order seasoned warriors to dig," he smirked. "And then how can we get them out? We have no rope netting to capture them as we did with the beasts who climbed our stronghold's gate."

"I could dig many holes easily," Goliath said. "But wouldn't it be easier to open both ends of the barred wagon, lure them in, and then slam the gates closed as soon as they're inside?"

Mochè looked at him, stunned with surprise, and said, "That's a very good idea, Goliath."

"I used to watch children play games like that when I was young," Goliath chuckled happily.

"What should we use for bait? We need something that lives. Animals like that enjoy hunting their own food and then playing with it," Nikanyiso explained. "It's their wild nature." All eyes turned to Helen's muscle-bound goon, peering from the prisoner wagon. It seemed to understand what they were saying and released a long stream of urine out of panic, grunting and moving its hands in fear.

"Thou shalt not kill," Mochè reminded them.

After a long silence, Nikanyiso finally spoke up, saying, "Manhig, it wouldn't really be us killing the muscled moron; it would be the animals, wouldn't it?" He glanced around at the others by the fire and added, "We would only be slamming the doors."

"Helen's boyfriend is a demon mutation, sir," Maria stated. "It's not human."

"Hmm," Mochè sat, pondering, "I wanted to lure Helen with it, though; not those beasts."

"With all due respect, sir, from what I've heard about Helen, she probably has already found another mate," Colonel Maria clarified what her manhig was likely thinking.

"It's unfortunate what happened to her," Nikanyiso said.

"The beasts roar a lot and so loudly," Nikanyiso remarked, keeping his distance from the barred wagon that held the mated pair of lions. He wouldn't admit his fright, but the usually fearless man confessed that they intimidated him a bit.

"I hope they don't squeeze through the bars, my friend," Mochè taunted Nikanyiso, then broke out in laughter.

"We're almost back at the fortress," the colonel called to the frightened Nikanyiso. "We should arrive before evening."

"I can't wait to hug my wife," Nikanyiso murmured softly.

"The hunting was a success," Mochè announced. "The hunters took more than enough meat for our many people, and the slaughterhouse butchers can salt the remaining for the winter. Just think: we had a skirmish with Helen and brought back two prizes to guard our homes to boot. And we did it all within the same week."

"Too long a time for a brave man to be away from his wife," Nikanyiso said in his same soft voice.

"You seem to be getting braver the closer we get to home," Mochè joked, feeling the same way about longing for Zipporah.

Gabriela sat upright in a chair, nursing her baby son. Ben always savored watching her in this natural motherly role as she fed their boy. Gabriela knew he did and how much closer it brought them, so she now did it in the nude to enhance the atmosphere and what she anticipated would follow. Their two daughters explored the kitchen nearby, one walking while the other crawled but struggled to stand. After having two baby girls in a row, Ben was ecstatic to finally have a son.

As she nursed, Gabriela's eyes gazed at Ben as if she understood his desire. Smiling seductively, she told him, "You're next, Benjamin; don't worry." Her voice was soft, and her eyes widened contentedly, aware that her husband still longed for that precious gift from her that now bound them. Once she finished and placed the baby in his crib, she announced, "Okay, my two darling girls, it's time for a nap." Gabriela leaned down to pick up the youngest and took the hand of her older daughter, leading them to their bedroom while winking at Ben and purposefully brushing her naked body against him as she passed.

As Gabriela leaned over Ben, enjoying the feel of his body, he asked her, "Are you sure you have enough milk for the baby?"

"Have you noticed the size of my breasts, my love? I can feed five grown men," she giggled, but purposely sexy to encourage her man to feed, which satisfied her intensely. She knew it also relieved her husband's stress of leading an army in the harsh conditions outside the semblance of civilization in the stronghold.

Gabriela rested her body sideways and exposed one of the elongated nipples of the darkened areola of her large breast. That act made him feel closer to his wife and more involved with the birth of their child. Gabriela moaned in pleasure as her fingers combed through Ben's hair lovingly.

"Take more milk from me, darling. Oh, please don't stop and let me hear your slurping sounds," Gabriela let out a shriek of ecstasy. "I have plenty for the babies."

That warm bond nurtured their love and closeness for each other, even as the world drew to a close, whenever it should come. Just as a baby finds comfort in a mother, Ben was able to ease his pains and dispel the horrible sights he had witnessed in the many battles he fought and those that lay ahead of him. In doing so, Gabriela found solace and a way to comfort both herself and the man she loved during the now numbered days leading up to the inevitable. That priceless act now preceded the pleasurable acts of their matrimony.

As time passed, Mochè wanted to teach his two sons how to hunt. Not knowing how much time they had left on God's earth before the end, it was something he felt compelled to do as a father. But first, he had to teach them how to use a weapon. He decided it would be best for them to learn the bow and arrow first. Zipporah waved goodbye from the doorway, holding their baby daughter, Soleil, by the hand. She blew a kiss to her men and called out, "Have fun, boys!" before closing the door to read a story to her daughter. Soleil was named after the sun because it shone brightly the afternoon she was conceived.

Three cavalry riders sat ready on horseback nearby to warn Mochè of any intruders. He didn't take his sons far, but instead close to the fortress by the river. As he knelt beside his eldest son, Mochè said, "You're the oldest, so you go first, Gershom." Nodding to his youngest, he told the boy, "Don't worry, Eliezer, you'll get your turn, Son." His father carefully observed Gershom's stance as he stood, holding the bow in his hand. To reassure the boy, he softly asked, "Did you know you were named after an angel?"

"Yes, Papa, Mom told me that."

"You remind me of him so much," Mochè said, remembering the boy he didn't realize was a holy angel always by his side, protecting him.

Seeing the arrow in position, he advised his son, "Now pull back the bowstring slowly."

"It's hard, Papa!"

"You can do it, Son; pull back and aim at that tree," he pointed so the boy could see it clearly.

Gershom's arm strained as he pulled, sending the arrow straight into the tree. "I did it, Papa!"

"Yes, you did, Son!" The boy repeated a bullseye shot three times in a row. "Now, let's give your brother a chance."

The smaller Eliezer stood boldly, holding the bow. Knowing that the small boy couldn't pull back the bowstring by himself, Mochè winked at Gershom, who smiled back. Kneeling closely to Eliezer, he said, "Let me give you a little help." Placing his hand over his son's tiny one to steady the bow, Mochè grasped the bowstring underneath his son's hand, and the arrow flew and hit the tree. "That's how you do it, Eliezer. Pretty soon, you'll be able to do it all by yourself, just like your brother."

When he was confident that Gershom no longer needed help, Mochè sat back, admiring his boys. Now assisting his brother, Gershom looked like a natural. While enjoying time with his sons, his mind wandered to the day he first met their mother, recalling how he had fallen in love with her so quickly. He loved her dearly but wouldn't admit it until God intervened. The bow and arrow reminded him of his battles, fondly remembering the wonderful archer that the late warrior Leah had been in what now seemed so long ago.

By evening, the boys returned exhausted, their father carrying the archery gear. "Well," called out Zipporah, "I see my warriors are back." She smiled at her husband. "Dinner's ready, my love. Take the boys and wash up." Soleil sat in her highchair, already at the table.

As the family sat together eating, Zipporah's wandering leg brushed against her husband's leg; her toes caressed underneath his jeans while her eyes innocently focused straight ahead. Then, her toes traveled higher on the outside of his pants to that special spot she wanted them to rub. When she felt he was ready, she leaned over and whispered into Mochè's ear, "Ready to make another, my love?" She smiled seductively, then added,

"It's the rabbit in me." Zipporah smiled, looking as virtuous as a sculpted angel.

"Why do you always talk to Papa about rabbits, Mommy?" little Eliezer asked while Zipporah blushed.

"Because Mommy moves as spryly as one does sometimes, Eliezer."

After their exhausted three children fell asleep, Zipporah lay in her husband's arms, their bodies sweating profusely. Her big eyes glowed with satisfaction as she declared, "Wow, that had to be a boy!"

Her feet warmed Mochè's in hers, occasionally straying higher. "Did I move as spryly as a rabbit?" her soft, full lips brushed against his ear. "Do I still please you, my love?"

"After all the years I've loved you more than anything else in this world, you still need to ask me that question, my wife?"

"Just checking, my love," her deep green eyes shone as beautifully as they had the first time Mochè had seen them, under a dirty mask of mud and sludge. "Ready to go again? Maybe we'll have twins," she smiled, her eyes glowing as they did when she first looked upon Mochè that day years before.

They wrapped together once more as they did so often, both privately wondering how much time they had left before the end.

Helen, the demon, waited patiently in the shadows of the stronghold until she heard the sirens blast and the tolling of the large bell, knowing the emergency warnings would clear her path. As the loud signals blared, Helen quietly stepped into the streets of the stronghold, swathed in evening darkness. Dressed in a light hooded garment that completely concealed her nude body and masked her identity, she strolled along the vacant streets, with several of her goons positioned at her sides and behind, also disguised. Helen's lips curled into an evil grin; her plan was underway. She watched as people scurried to their homes, realizing that Mochè was already on his way to the council building, leaving Zipporah and his children alone at their house. Helen had breached the fortress several times before for surveillance. She knew exactly where the man she loved lived with his happy family, having observed them previously. Now, Helen would enact her vengeance upon Mochè by destroying what he cherished more than her: Zipporah and his children, as she had threatened to do.

After quickly removing her light coat and revealing her nudity, Helen commanded one of her guards, "Quickly, kick in the door!" With her dagger in hand, Helen told the mutated goon next to her. "I won't soil my bare feet on the door of the woman I will kill as soon as I enter. The kids," she grinned wickedly, "Just wait until I roast them over a fire on skewers like piglets before I devour them."

Chapter Fourteen

The Breech

Three weeks before Helen breached the fortress, sneaked through the streets, and went to the door of his home, Mochè waited for his son-in-law at his office. As soon as he arrived, he stood up and placed a hand on Matthew's shoulder, guiding him away from his courthouse office and into the refreshing open air. He had summoned him for a matter of great importance. As they walked, he whispered, "Let's talk away from prying ears about something personal."

"Certainly, sir."

"Matthew, you're the father of my grandchild and part of my family now, as you know. I'm afraid you're the only one I can fully trust with something of grave importance." He turned to see Matthew's absorbed expression. "The former general, Helen, now a demon, as you know, has planted someone inside our stronghold." Mochè grimaced, "There is a traitor among us."

"Sir?" Matthew stopped walking and stood, startled.

"I believe it is someone in the military or the council—or both—holding a higher position. They would need to be close to me to obtain the kind of information I think they have."

"How so, sir?"

"Simple details such as the color of my home and fence, and the fact that I have more than one child, any soldier would know. But now, when we go on specific expeditions, they expect us and are aware of our exact positions. They must be receiving intelligence from someone of a higher rank or within the council, or a person possibly eavesdropping."

"I understand, sir," Matthew was already contemplating.

"Matthew, you're a wise young man. I want you to personally strengthen our stronghold and launch an investigation using people you truly trust, not telling them what you suspect. Carefully and respectfully evaluate everyone, but find this traitor living within this place where we raise our children."

"Manhig, I pledged my loyalty to you years ago. Now, I vow before you that I will protect our family and your people with my life, and I will find the person who betrayed you and God."

As they walked together before departing from each other, Mochè wanted to lighten the mood. He said, "I understand my daughter is expecting her second child."

"Yes, sir," Matthew answered, seemingly joyed.

"Gabriela just had her third. You better work harder, son. You wouldn't want your commander to humiliate you, would you?"

"Absolutely not, sir," Matthew chuckled quietly.

Three weeks later, Matthew reported to Mochè's office. Noticing his expression, Mochè knew he finally had something to share and gestured for Matthew to step outside. "Have you received any more information, Matthew?" Until then, Matthew had only been able to uncover crumbs of information, but nothing relating to anyone in particular.

"Yes, Manhig, we should go somewhere private to speak. What I have to tell you is important."

"Let's go down to the river to talk at once."

When seated alone on large rocks by the river, where the flowing water and the chirping birds were the only sounds, Matthew told Mochè, "I'm afraid it's General Mark, sir."

"I sensed something suspicious when he mentioned that he wanted to retire," Mochè said with disgust. "He isn't even 50 years old yet."

"Mark kept his trail concealed; he was wise and extremely cautious. However, I tracked it down to him. I never saw Helen up close when we battled her, so I didn't realize she always walks around completely nude without a care. I thought those painted pagan symbols covering her body were tight-fitting clothes during the times I saw her from a distance. I never paid much attention to her." Matthew's expression revealed how rattled he was as he said, "I recently watched them commit adultery right before my eyes."

"Calm down, son. Someone might overhear us."

"She mounted Mark like a wild animal. Her powerful legs wrapped around him, restraining him still as a toy doll—and Mark is a strong man. Her movements were furious and rapid. She howled like a wolf as she pounced on him repeatedly. I thought she might kill Mark with the violent way she discharged her passion."

"I understand, Matthew; it's not a picture I want my mind to envision."

"Sorry, sir, but I never knew a woman could act in such a way—like a beast."

"Helen is no longer a human woman, son. Go on."

"Mark believes she loves him."

"The fool, she's using him. In her present state, no one man can satisfy her."

"I trailed him for a while. They met here late last night. I moved closer to where we now sit, hiding behind that boulder to listen to them speak." He pointed to a large rock. "I overheard their plan." Matthew looked panic-stricken. Mochè had battled beside the young man many times, and Matthew had never even shown a glimpse of fear.

"What is it, Matthew?"

"Helen has entered our fortress several times; I heard her say so. Her people have dug a tunnel at the corner beneath the hill of rocks, the one blind spot of our stronghold. She moves freely throughout our compound and has walked along our streets in disguise, wearing a long, hooded coat that conceals her face." Matthew paused. "Manhig, tonight they are planning to invade us. I heard her say she wishes to slaughter everyone you love." Matthew bowed his head. "She learned what happened to her lover after you encountered her back on that hunting expedition." Mochè now realized he had succeeded in luring Helen after all.

"Do you know if anyone else is involved in this? Any of my other generals? Solomon?"

"Not to my knowledge, sir. I've been investigating this for a few weeks. She wants you for herself."

"With what number of soldiers does she expect to enter?"

"I scouted her encampment with Benjamin. We roughly counted her mutant followers to be well over a thousand."

"I didn't realize she had that many."

"The majority of her forces will launch a divided attack at the front and the left flank, the corner where we are most vulnerable." Matthew pointed to the area. "The rocky hills don't completely cover that side. That will serve as a distraction while Helen and a platoon of her goons climb through the tunnel."

"You did excellent work, Matthew, as always. Send Eliza and my grandchild to my home so they can hide with Zipporah and my children in the concealed cellar. Tell Benjamin to bring my dear Gabriela and their kids as well. There's plenty of room; it's a large basement with ventilation. I constructed it for times like this, as many others did inside their homes. It's completely hidden under the kitchen floor. God forbid Helen reaches my home; she'll think they left to hide. Now, let's make our plan."

"You have these gas lights I set up to give plenty of light. There is a portable toilet facility in the back room and a faucet for fresh water," Mochè explained before hugging Zipporah, Eliza, and Gabriela close to him. Then he knelt and embraced all the children who loved him, telling Gershom, "You are the oldest. Protect everyone." He smiled at his son's proud face as if he had been appointed to a special assignment.

Zipporah walked up to her husband and held him tightly, telling him, "Be careful, my love." Her eyes glowed gloriously in their vivid color but appeared strained with fright.

"You know I always come back to you. We will live together eternally, my love."

Shortly after sunset, Helen's army attacked precisely where Matthew had indicated to Mochè. The emergency siren blared as the giant bell chimed. People inside the compound fled to their homes to seek shelter. Matthew had concealed his platoons of the best climbers above that location on the corner, planning to strike the enemy from a higher elevation. When Helen's forces charged the followers' fortress, Matthew's commandos eliminated many of the muscle-bound mutants within fifteen minutes with their new high-powered weapons. The survivors scattered as Ben's cavalry advanced from behind those assaulting the front entrance. The mutants who struggled to climb over the high gate fell victim to hidden sentinels who tossed them off one after another with bone-cracking sounds as their mutated bodies hit the solid ground.

Unaware that her army had been repelled, Helen stood before the tunnel her mutants had dug. She passionately kissed the former general, Mark, telling him, "I long for you, my love, and I can't wait until this is over so I can be with you again and show you my true affection." Pushing his head against her voluptuous breasts and holding it there while she caressed the back of his neck with her long nails, she told him, "I will do things to you that other men can only dream about." Knowing she needed his short-term help, Helen moaned, allowing him to feel the softness of her bare skin before squatting down with her male protectors as Mark climbed through the tunnel they had secretly dug. Helen followed closely behind the traitor who led the way.

Knowing her destination, Mochè allowed Helen to enter unhindered. She donned a long, hooded light jacket that completely concealed her from head to toe, hiding her face as well. Mochè's soldiers cleared the streets in preparation. Matthew had dispatched soldiers to sneak up from behind and quietly take out the platoon of muscular thugs one by one, covering their mouths as they did so, ensuring that each loss would go unnoticed. By the time Helen arrived at Mochè's door, unbeknownst to her, only four of her male lovers remained behind her.

After quickly removing her light coat and revealing her nudity, Helen commanded one of her guards, "Quickly, kick in the door!" Holding her dagger tightly, she told the goon next to her. "I won't soil my bare feet on the door of the woman I will kill as soon as I enter. The kids," she grinned wickedly, "Just wait until I roast them over a fire on skewers like piglets before I devour them."

After the door burst open, Helen stood in shock as she saw Mochè sitting in a chair at his table. "Hi, Helen," he greeted her, "you look lovely this evening, all dressed up, wearing nothing and painted so beautifully." Mochè smiled widely as one of his soldiers rushed up from behind her remaining guard and slit his throat. "Sorry you missed Zipporah and my children. She would have loved to brew a pot of tea and chat with you."

Recovering from the shock of seeing Mochè casually sitting there and realizing she was alone, Helen squatted. Her blue eyes glowed in a shadowy corner as she curled and squinted like a cat, hissing at Mochè. Then she leaped like a leopard and crashed through the shuttered window. "Go after her," Mochè commanded the soldiers outside. "Shut down the compound immediately."

Shortly afterward, Mochè called off the search when a soldier reported to him, "She clawed up the gate like a tigress, climbed over, and leaped to the other side, Manhig." He shook his head and exclaimed, "She landed between the chained lions we keep for protection. They scratched at her leg, but she growled, frightening them. Then she ran away into the darkness. I have seen nothing like it in my life, sir."

Mochè opened the hatch in the floor of his house and found his wide-eyed wife, her rifle pointed directly at him. "Please don't shoot me, my love. I surrender to your mercy," he said, raising his arms.

"We couldn't hear anything from here," Zipporah said, sounding disappointed because she wanted to hear everything Helen said. "It's soundproof down here as well." She lowered her rifle. "You can add that to your list," Zipporah replied with a sarcastic grin.

Chapter Fifteen

Judgment

"Manhig," a follower asked from the assembled masses by the river, eager to hear their leader speak, "When will our Messiah return? I ask this respectfully, but we have waited so long."

Mochè raised his arms and spread them wide to symbolically embrace the nearly two hundred thousand followers in the hills behind him and alongside the far-reaching river. "Keep your faith, my friends; the time is at hand. The great battle foretold to us will soon arrive. We are near the end of the seven-year tribulation. You have witnessed the evil before us unfold over those last years. It will end when we face the last battle against evil."

"Why do you keep asking us to procreate, Manhig?" another woman yelled from the back of the crowd. "Why bring new babies into a world with so little time left?"

"Have you learned nothing from my sermons? With each new baby comes a precious soul for us to teach love and counteract their wickedness," he pointed outside the stronghold. Then, carrying his microphone, he walked toward a nearby flock of followers and asked a young woman holding her child to stand. "May I hold your child?" he whispered, and the young lady nodded in agreement. Raising the toddler, he said, "Our power over evil strengthens with the love this child receives and will someday administer." Smiling, he handed the little girl back to her mother's arms and asked her to be seated again, explaining to his assembled masses, "There was once a time, many years ago, when the wicked plotted the destruction of God's children. They conditioned humanity to annihilate itself through violent wars, skirmishes, and brawls waged by humans against humans for power struggles and greed." Mochè gazed out over the vast reaches of his people. "It was a time when masses were exterminated, and men, women, and children were thrown into blazing fires or buried to hide the traces of their sins. Did they learn?" His voice rose as he answered his own question. "No!" he yelled. "While women destroyed the living babies within their wombs, they experimented on human life!"

Mochè ceased speaking to listen to the terrifying cries and observe the fearful expressions on the faces of the crowd of followers. "When they took human life so freely, it stripped away the dignity of humanity," he said, bowing his head. "We procreate to bring new souls forward, strengthening our love for God and each other and elevating the grandeur of humanity once more."

"They implanted devices in the minds of those who could not be persuaded to compel them to accept their science." Mochè pointed outside the fortress's perimeter again and continued, "The scientists of that long-ago time created the wicked demons and mutations that attack us at the commands of Satan." He paused, looking sternly at the crowded prairies, boulders, and hills where his throngs had gathered to listen. "Those events occurred worldwide. When human life was nearly exhausted at the hands of the evil one, God sent His angels to gather believers from all the fallen cities of the ruined world to these lands. Then, by His will, the angels guided them to me," Mochè paused, looking at his people. "And you demand that God bow to our will and appear on demand?" His gaze remained grim as he stated, "That would be nothing more than a puppet show. It would be a display of force, like those tyrants who polluted the minds of our ancestors. Our righteous God is a just God. His Son will come soon. Be prepared!" Mochè placed his mic on its stand and walked back to gather his family.

Several years had passed since Helen, his former general, breached the stronghold. Yet Mochè still stood tall and erect, maintaining the physique of a younger man and the commanding presence he had always possessed. God had bestowed these attributes upon him, enabling him to remain strong and lead his followers to the place of judgment after the final battle between good and evil—the Armageddon. Work on the massive extended fortress was completed less than two years after it began, and it now accommodated the growing number of followers who were joining him. Goliath, whose stamina was fifty times greater than that of the other laborers, had worked feverishly on the project and was instrumental to its completion. Among the new houses, many mighty complexes were erected by his architects, some standing six stories high.

"Wow, my love, that speech sent shivers up my spine," Zipporah softly told her husband. She remained a beautiful woman throughout the years of marriage spent with the man she had loved since the moment she first saw him. One would have to look closely to see the faint beginnings of crow's feet forming under her glorious eyes, which still radiated their deep green color. She stood on her tiptoes to whisper in Mochè's ear, "The boys are going hunting, and the others will be at that school show." Zipporah raised her eyebrows and winked, "I don't know what we could ever do in that big house all alone."

"I might have something in mind," Mochè leaned down to whisper into the ear he loved brushing against with his mouth. "You never tire out, do you, bunny?"

"No," Zipporah quickly replied with a smile, "it's the rabbit in me. Besides," she began, brushing her body against his, "you started it with that fiery speech." She innocently looked up at her husband and said, "The shiver up my spine, remember?" Zipporah's smile widened as her eyes sparkled.

"It doesn't take much to trigger you, does it?"

"No," she flashed her eyebrows, "never with you, my love. Even though my ability to bring new life might slow down a bit soon, your seed is still strong, and God might bless us once more. Remember Sarah from the Bible?" Her eyes sparkled again. "We could go on for years." Then Zipporah grew serious and softly said, "I told you long ago that I love you, Mochè." Her gaze met his, revealing her eternal deep affection. "I said that back at my first little house. Remember? At that same time, I also told you that I felt it the moment I first saw you, and I knew then with certainty that you loved me."

"I remember everything," Mochè stared into space, recalling it all. "You've given me six wonderful children, my dear Zipporah," he said emotionally. Perking up, he kissed her, saying, "The harder you work, the more you get." Zipporah's eyes lit up once more as Mochè called to his sons, "Gershom! Eliezer! Gather the others!" He glanced down at his wife and whispered, "Time's a-wasting."

Gershom and Eliezer were nearly young men, while Soleil was almost a teenager. The boys inherited their father's deep blue eyes and stood tall, whereas Soleil was strikingly beautiful, inheriting her mother's hair color and having eyes like dark, heavenly green glowing stars. Following her, a boy arrived, strong as Zipporah had predicted based on his manner of conception. They named him Damien, after his father. Tabitha arrived a year after Damien, and Luna, named for the full moon that shone during her conception, was three. Mochè took Zipporah's arm and led his family home for lunch before they went their separate ways.

After her unsuccessful attempt to destroy Mochè's family, Helen repeatedly rode close to the fortress, where she had missed her opportunity. Soon after her failure, the stragglers who survived the raid and only half of her mutant army trailed behind the nude demon, as she became known. Using her dagger, Helen had castrated Mark, the general she blamed for her defeat that night, and then had him impaled on a long wooden spike before the fortress for all to see. Helen sat on her stallion with her cavalry guarding Mark, ensuring he died slowly and painfully. Mark's eyes teared and bulged from the immense pain. He was unable to speak as the wooden pole protruded from his mouth, ran through him, and exited from his bloodied rectum—his body perched on that stake positioned grotesquely at an odd angle. After the nude demon rode away at dusk, Mochè sent a platoon to retrieve Mark's body to give him a Christian burial. Mochè fought the dreaded memory of when Helen almost succeeded in seducing him.

Gradually, Helen's mutant army expanded over the years. Other cloven-hoofed demon tribes also settled nearby. Her obsession with Mochè grew deeper during this time. Spurned by the man she had always wanted, the sexual desire of the crazed leader intensified as well. Any of her male, muscle-bound mutants she chose had to fully satisfy her, or she'd have them executed. Helen performed lewd shows with the mutated males and females in the open meadow to tempt the followers of God. Her cavalry lined up behind the live displays to protect them. Mochè forbade his followers from watching, and occasionally, he sent a cavalry brigade to break up her performances.

Long after their children had gone their separate ways and their daughter, Luna, was fast asleep during her afternoon nap, Zipporah cuddled closely to her husband, her toes gently caressing the sides of Mochè's legs. Her eyes glowing with amusement, she whispered, "You always loved that," as Mochè reached his fingers to touch her lips.

"I've loved everything about you, my precious wife," he replied, fondling her voluptuous lips. "I love the sensation of these every time they touch and kiss my body," he smiled as he kissed her.

"Well, I think we may have made a child as big as Goliath

this time," she giggled like a little girl.

"I hope so," Mochè chuckled. "We've toiled like sweaty laborers for hours," he groaned, feeling the gratifying depletion of his energy as he gave her a cynical smile.

Zipporah rested in the arms of her loving husband, staring as if into space. Her wide eyes gradually focused before she said, "Many among us fester with adulterous ideals, Mochè. I overhear women discussing such matters." Rising on one elbow, with her hand supporting her face, she looked at her husband and continued, "I've heard several of them claim they have committed the ultimate sin. Helen's lewd acts compelled them to do the unspeakable." Her eyes widened as she added, "Now they are luring unwed men to engage in the same acts Helen does with those mutated men, and those of the other transmuted males and females."

"Years ago, when I talked with David and Andrew around the evening campfire, Father Andrew told stories about people watching similar acts on what they once called," he had to think, "device screens; I think that was the term his great-grandfather used."

"I don't understand; what were they?"

Mochè fondly remembered his priest friends and all the conversations they had shared over those many years. "They were box-like objects, some large and others small, that had screens. Displayed on them were images of people doing the same things that Satan commands Helen to do with her male protectors, and the acts done by her transmuted males and females."

"I still don't comprehend how humans could fit inside them," Zipporah said, squinting her eyes and grimacing as she struggled to make sense of what Mochè was saying.

"There were recorded projections within those devices, not real people. It's complicated, my love," Mochè knew his wife was intelligent, but such concepts had been difficult for him to fully grasp when he first learned about them. "Corrupted people created those contraptions a very long time ago. I still don't completely understand how they functioned, only that it led to great sins when those who watched them began reenacting the sinful acts depicted in them. It resulted not only in the decay of their souls but also in the degradation of humanity."

"Did that lead to the end of civilization?" Zipporah's eyes appeared troubled.

"Oh, that was one of the foremost impieties of that era, which swiftly began dismantling the last civilization," Mochè reflected. He then continued, "The funny thing is that many other cultures collapsed due to similar degeneracies before that one. You'd expect they might have learned."

"I remember that fiery speech," Zipporah blushed, "you know, the one that stirred my excitement. God had had enough."

"I have tried for years to offer the only civilized way of life I knew to save their souls," Mochè frowned as if defeated.

"You've done a wonderful job, my love. That's why I admire and love you so much," Zipporah kissed his cheek to lift his fallen mood. "But why, near the end, would followers succumb to so many sins?"

Mochè leaned on his elbow, gazing deeply into her stunning eyes as he said, "Satan tempts us the hardest when he knows his true Master will soon bring this place of sin to a close." Then he lay back, whispering, "We all face judgment; for several of my followers, unfortunately, it will be His wrath."

Now, secure once more in her husband's arms, Zipporah asked, "Will we be together when we…you know…we leave this—"

Mochè cut off her words, "We will be together eternally, my love, as the angels are."

"Then let's try some more," Zipporah said as she snapped out of her foreboding disposition and positioned herself over her husband. "It's better to be safe than sorry," she added as the rhythm of her movements began again. "Why do you think our Lord made this so pleasurable for a husband and wife other than to procreate?"

When they stopped and lay beside each other, exhausted,

Zipporah began stroking her toes against Mochè's leg again, noticing the pleasure on his face. After hearing the loud sounds coming from inside their home, her toes grasped his flesh as she whispered, "They're back!"

"Hurry! Get dressed!"

"Oh, I love the thrill of sneaking around like this," Zipporah giggled as she slid on her panties. "Let's go to the cellar tomorrow when they're home. It will be so exciting. It's comfortable down there once you get used to it. We can find a secret spot."

"I think my wife's gone crazy now," Mochè said to Zipporah, who giggled like a child as she dressed.

As Helen's cavalry of mutants grew, so did Solomon's. The demon hordes expanded tremendously as well. Satan summoned the most wicked from all corners to unite. It seemed they emerged from the very depths of hell itself to aid Mochè's malevolent brother, who had even assisted Helen during some of her performances solely to spite Mochè. Helen and Solomon rode together, showcasing the increasing number of soldiers behind them to torment the man they both loathed: Helen because Mochè wouldn't be her lover, and Solomon because their father had favored Mochè. The hooved demons also paraded in the same wide, long meadow. Their horrendous drumbeats pounded dreadful sounds throughout the towns of the stronghold at times, alarming Mochè's already frightened followers.

Helen's sexually vulgar spectacles grew increasingly obscene. Her exhibitions featured multiple muscled goons simultaneously. Refraining from sparking a premature engagement with her now heavily armed, large force, combined with that of Solomon's army and the demon masses, Mochè had finally had enough. He ordered his longbows to fire at her forbidden performances. But Satan protected her, and the razor blade-tipped wooden projectiles inconceivably missed her body, hitting only her goons. Helen pulled out an arrow from one of her mutant protectors and held it over her mouth. She swallowed the droplets of blood that trickled from the tip of the blade. Running up close to the corner of the fortress, she screamed, "You can't hurt me, Mochè!" Helen danced around, closer to the stronghold, "See?" she yelled. "You will succumb to me sooner or later! Come to me and I will do incredible things to you!" She smiled seductively, licking her lips, "Much more than that hag you married." Then she walked back to her cavalry and ordered more of her males and females down from their horses to resume their orgy.

Tempted by Satan and unable to resist any longer, many of Mochè's male and female followers left the stronghold to indulge in the pleasures Helen offered. Groups of civilians and soldiers abandoned his flock, leaving their wives, husbands, and children to satisfy their desires with the obscenities she provided—acts they had never seen or participated in before. They could no longer resist and fell prey to her bodily temptations.

"See Mochè," Helen called to him close to the fortress as she performed with two of his followers, "Ahh, see how your men enjoy me?" Howling with pleasure, crooking her forefinger, she cried out once more, "Come, you can too." She groaned with satisfying contentment, "You will sooner or later. My master told me you would—like you almost did on that expedition." The Dark Angel cast an alluring glow around Helen, making her appear even lovelier as she enacted sordid and vulgar things to his former followers. "Do you remember that time?" Her eyes widened to a dazzling blue as she seductively asked, "Do you recall how you couldn't resist the feel of my soft flesh? Hmm, I've longed for you since even before then."

"You drugged me, Demon Woman!" Mochè yelled back at Helen's hisses.

"Satan tempts my people more than ever as we come to the end. How can I stop this nonsense, Joshua?" Mochè stood beside his friend and second. "God forbid my family hears her wicked words."

"We could attempt to capture her, but those goons would probably engage. And if they didn't, where would we keep her so her words are unheard?”

“If only we could muzzle her like the beast she has become,” Mochè replied rhetorically.

“A marksman could shoot her, but that also would provoke an attack prematurely, Manhig,” Joshua sympathized. “And Satan would protect Helen as he has done with the arrows we shot at her.”

“I don’t think God will take this much longer. The signs are falling into place.”

“If I’m pregnant all the time, I’ll never get to ride again,” Gabriela told Ben as she lay atop him. “This will be our fifth, Benjamin.” Her words broke up from her swift movements. Ben focused on the long nipples of his wife’s large breasts, now wobbling near his face as her body bounced faster.

“I see what you’re looking at,” she smiled. “Little Benji wants my milk, don’t you, baby?”

“You love me doing it,” he told her as her fair skin blushed at the truth and her strides quickened. “Besides, you only have three months to go,” he said, huffing as Gabriela moved harder and faster.

“Three months, and then you will start planting another,” she groaned loudly with elation. “Don’t stop; keep going. I’m just moving my belly, sweetheart.” Then Gabriela resumed her position until she fell off him from the satisfying exhaustion.

The couple recovered in each other’s arms, embracing. When her breathing slowed, Gabriela seductively asked Ben, “Is my little baby ready for mommy to feed him?” She knew it was a way to ignite another round. But before she did, Gabriela’s demeanor turned serious, and in a soft voice, she told him, “When the time comes, I want to be with you, Benjamin.” She looked at him with loving passion. “I want you to leave the field at the end of the battle and come to me before it happens.” Gabriela glanced at her stomach and groaned, “If I’m able to ride in that last battle, I’ll gallop to you, my love.”

“We’ll be together, my dear wife,” Ben replied, a tear glistening in his eye. "Just bounce your lovely backside if you ride so I can recognize you," he said, forcing a smile.

As Matthew and Ben walked together, reviewing their army, Ben let out his repressed frustration, saying, "Sometimes I wish you had never told me about those books."

"What are you talking about?"

Ben glanced around to ensure that no one could hear him. Then he replied, "Those things that you read from the house of books—what you explained to me years ago."

"Oh, why?"

"Well, for starters, it made my wife a nymphomaniac." Ben didn't elaborate; the acts between him and his wife were personal. "Gabriela is nearly perpetually pregnant. Matthew, we're already on our fifth child, and if we continue this way, it will be six unless—"

"I know what 'unless' means," his voice conveyed deep remorse for what was to come at any time. "We don't have to speak of it." Matthew smiled again, "It's wonderful that you'll have five. Eliza and I are working on our fifth now. Isn't it amazing how God gives man and wife such pleasure to bring him new souls?"

"Remember how we talked about the things we did before we married?" Ben's eyes gazed into the distance, remembering.

"We never succumbed to the ultimate sin, though. We restrained ourselves," Matthew fondly recalled his days of courtship. "Why do you think God gives the drive to young couples He knows will marry?"

"I remember how difficult it was to contain myself, but you're right: I knew from the beginning I could never live without Gabriela as my wife."

Matthew looked at Ben admiringly and said, "You have to take these things in stride, my friend. Bringing new souls into His world is a natural act between a husband and wife." Matthew had a glow about him, wishing to see his wife.

"I guess you're right, my friend," Ben conceded, aware that

his friend didn't have a clue as to how sexually aggressive and unpredictable Gabriela could be in the bedroom.

"Let's dismiss our troops and ride home for lunch to see our wives and children. Our soldiers can do the same." Matthew smiled at Ben.

"I'm in here, Matty!" Eliza shouted at the sound of her husband's footsteps. "I'll just be a few more minutes."

She looked magnificent as he approached her while she sat, her back relaxing against the comfortable padded chair. "Your son takes so much of my milk today," she smiled at the man she had loved for years.

Matthew heard the faint suckling sounds as he came close and kissed each of their foreheads. "He grows strong from your milk, my love."

Eliza smiled, aware of her man's desires. She had learned to recognize that expression so well and always longed to see it to pleasure him as much as possible in the remaining time they shared. "Let me put the baby down for his nap; now that his stomach is full, he'll sleep soundly." She smiled wider and asked, "Would you like to see me in the bedroom, dear?" She asked enticingly, the side of one foot caressing her other leg seductively.

Matthew took her hand and led her to their bedroom. Gently sliding down the shoulder straps of her dress, the light garment fell to the floor, and Matthew admired the beauty of her nudity. She had never looked lovelier to him, and he picked her up and placed her naked body on the soft mattress. As he had done so often before, he gently took her in his arms to her moans of pleasure.

As he lay with her, both savoring the moments of their satisfaction, Eliza whispered in his ear, "I know my breasts have comforted you. I instinctively do it for you fondly, as if you suck the milk from the mother you've never known. Her loss deprived you of that experience as an infant, and I give you that loving gift now, as I said I would before we married."

"I know that, dear, and I love you that much more for our bond, which can never be closer."

"And I love that even being a noble warrior, you are a sensitive and loving person who can say such a tender thing to me. I crave the closeness this precious gift has given us as if we shared in the birth of our children." Eliza's wide, glowing hazel-colored gaze met her husband's magnificent blue eyes.

"I have loved being your husband since the day we started sharing our lives together. God blessed me the day I first laid eyes on you."

With tears streaming from her eyes, Eliza recalled softly, "You swept me onto your horse, and I've loved you ever since."

"I'll come to you before it happens, my love. No matter where I am, I will come," Matthew confirmed his love and devotion.

Eliza held him close and tightly, whispering, "Our souls will live together eternally, my love."

Mochè felt a slight tremor beneath his feet. It then intensified just slightly. A bright light enveloped the manhig, its intensity so great that everyone around him could see it. His eyes closed as he sensed the spiritual being enter, and he now understood that the time had come. He rushed to the courthouse as Joshua gathered the generals and council members.

"We have little time left, so we must be quick," Mochè spoke from his judge's chair behind the large oak desk at the head of the assembled council and his generals.

"My scouts report that Helen and Solomon have over a hundred thousand mutations and other wicked warriors, spreading across the countryside before us. The hoofed demons number about fifty thousand strong," General Matthew stated on behalf of Benjamin, who now held a seat in the council. "My commander, General Benjamin, already sits at the head of our army and awaits my return. He remains there because our enemies seem prepared to advance on us at any moment, Manhig," Matthew rendered a military salute to his leader, thinking it might be for the last time.

"Then their forces equal ours," yelled out another council member.

"No!" Matthew shouted in response. "We are a hundred and fifty thousand soldiers strong, and ours is of God!"

"Aaron, are all the army generals ready?" Mochè asked, waiting while Aaron listened as each one confirmed.

When everyone established their preparedness by radio already in the field or seated before him, Mochè ordered, "General Miriam, you will swing wide to their left as they try to engage the corner of our fortress." She listened intently. "As their forces advance, make your way to attack their rear."

"Yes, Manhig!" Miriam formally rendered her salute.

"General Tamar, you will swing right and join with General Miriam at the rear."

Tamar, who had replaced Elisheba two years earlier, answered by radio from a position in the meadow, "Yes, Manhig!"

"General Matthew, tell General Benjamin he must attack the front with General Deborah, as General Luke engages the left flank and General Jeremiah's larger force attacks the right flank. Have all your chariots attack the demons; they are scared of them, as you know. The enemy cannot break our front; that is where they will center their attack. We must hold it as long as possible." Then Mochè gave a heartbreaking order, "General Joseph will evacuate the stronghold when the battle commences. We have wired the front entrance gate for demolition, so allow some of the enemy to break through and enter only there. They will crumble and perish beneath the boulders and rocks at the mouth of our beloved homes. The Lord has willed this and told me." He looked at his general and commanded, "General Joseph, you will also divide your army." Mochè paused. "One half to hold off any invaders who break through from approaching the river near our fortress, and as I already said, to evacuate and bring the other 7,500 human souls who do not fight down to the river's side and among the boulders on the hills that overlook it and guard them there. That is where we all must go after our battle. That is the place of our judgment."

Mochè rose tall and commanded, "General Joshua will ride with me. We go to battle for the last time in this world!" He pounded his hammer against the wooden block, aware it was the last time he ever would. "We prepare to meet evil on the open field of battle."

After Mochè ended the meeting, he rushed to see Zipporah. Almost flying into his arms upon seeing him, she held him tightly and whispered, "I know, it's now, my love." Tears flowed from her dark, wide green eyes. As always, she wore the magnificently hand-carved wooden crucifix around her thin, long neck and the priceless emerald ring that once belonged to Mochè's mother on her delicate finger. "But how can this happen when the flowers blossom so beautifully in the open prairies and hills?" As tears kept pouring from her lovely eyes, she whispered between her broken words, "It can't be at a time when the air smells so sweet with the aroma of life blooming in the meadows," Zipporah cried, trembling in her husband's arms. "Look," she said while crying, "I just planted new flowers in our front garden."

"We always knew this day would come, my love," Mochè comforted her. "We have loved and appreciated the beauty God has given us for so many years." Holding her tighter, he tenderly asked her, "Do you remember our honeymoon and the lovely sensation of God's splendid flows of water and the gentle sprinkling against our naked bodies?"

"I do, my love, as if it were only yesterday," she sobbed.

"So many picnics we shared alone at first as we made love on the grassy knolls, and then those we enjoyed as our children came and grew?"

"I remember all those glorious times, but they passed so quickly. I believed we had more time; I prayed for it." Zipporah asked, "Hold me for just a few more moments before you leave, my love, so I can relive them in your arms, even if only for that brief time."

"Father," Gershom began as Mochè quickly prepared himself for battle, "Eliezer and I want to fight alongside you."

"I do too, Daddy!" shouted Soleil from behind her brothers, her voice joined by Damien's.

"Those are brave and valiant words, my children, and I'm very proud of you all." Mochè smiled, then reached and held them tightly in his arms. "But I have other plans for you, my three bold sons and daughter." With a commanding tone, he told Gershom and Eliezer, "I commission both of you, my eldest sons, as lieutenants in my army." The two older boys stood erect and proud. "As officers, I order you to escort my wife and younger children to the river's side and protect them once there," he looked at all of them lovingly. "Soleil, you are the sergeant-at-arms who will assist in escorting this command. That's an official order!"

"Mochè," Zipporah's tears still flowed, "Please come back to me one last time so we may go together, my love?"

"I'll always return to you. I told you that long ago, my darling wife."

Matthew had run as fast as he could to see Eliza back home and hold her one last time in case he didn't survive. "I don't have much time, my dearest beloved wife." He huddled with her and his children and told Arthur, "Son, you are the oldest. Take your mother and your brothers and sisters to the river's side. I will see you there later," he spoke confidently to assure them. The little boy stood straight and saluted his father.

When Matthew reached the front of the army and positioned his horse beside his commander, he asked Ben, "General, are the infantry, tanks, and other vehicles assembled? Have you any last orders?"

"Everything is ready, General."

As Matthew and Ben poised on their stallions, awaiting Mochè's order to attack the approaching armies, Matthew told Benjamin, who sat beside him, as always, even at the end, "Well, old friend, I guess this is it." He smiled at his best friend and comrade in arms. "Thank you for training me so well."

"It's been an honor, Matt," Ben formally addressed his friend and saluted. "God blessed you with your skills; I merely honed them a bit," Ben smiled back.

"The honor has been mine, Ben," Matthew formally saluted Benjamin. Leaning closer, he whispered, "If I don't make it back, will you please ensure that Eliza and my family are safely at the river?"

"Of course, Matt. Please do the same for me?"

"You're too stubborn to die at such an important time," Matthew forced a smile.

"Nick," Benjamin called down to the tall and muscular black warrior who always ran alongside them into battle, "you may have the honor of leading my army today." Matthew smiled at his commander's order—a slight grin that concealed his anxiety about the coming battle, and more importantly, its aftermath.

Nikanyiso wore his feathered headdress and shield, grasping his long spear in honor of his warrior ancestors. "Thank you, General; it has been a privilege to serve under you." He knew it was his last battle and that his wife, eight children, and five grandchildren were safely at the river.

Goliath worked stationed by the river as General Joseph began sending civilian followers there. Goliath carried those who couldn't manage and lifted them two at a time. Still having a schoolboy's crush on his teacher, he blushed while he greeted Zipporah and her children.

"Goliath, my best student, I see you serve a noble cause today," Zipporah said. Then she turned to the sound of a wagon approaching, thinking it was her husband. She recognized Gabriela pulling up, tightening the reins to a complete stop.

"Zipporah?" she called out, and Zipporah trotted over to the wagon. "Would you please watch my dear babies for me?"

"Where are you going, sweetheart?"

"I must ride as a dispatcher; it's my duty." Gabriela's fair skin flushed before she spoke her truth: "I'm worried about

Benjamin, and I want to help him in any way I can." Her eyes were pleading. "I want to be with him."

"Do you think riding so soon after you delivered is a good idea?" Then she realized how foolish she sounded with so little time left. It sobered her to the reality at hand. "I'd be happy to watch your little ones, Gabriela. Come, bring them here. They can stay with Eliza's children and mine until you return."

Gabriela huddled her kids close to her, sobbing, "Mommy will come back for you, my darling babies."

"I'll take good care of them, sweetheart, so don't you worry," Zipporah called to her.

Gabriela untied her mustang from behind the wagon, mounted, and waved before galloping away. Zipporah glanced back toward the wide, long meadow and heard the dreadful sounds as the last battle between good and evil unfolded. She could hear the mighty blows from cannons and tanks among the earth-shaking sounds of thousands of galloping horses. Zipporah's body trembled as she listened to the roars of those awful rifle and handgun crackles amidst so many other thunderous single and automatic rattling booms. All the sounds of war now came from the same open field where Helen used to taunt her husband. Zipporah's mind replayed all those lustful and vile words that wicked woman spoke about Mochè. She prayed that God would destroy that evil person and protect her husband.

The ground itself trembled as if in fear as the thousands upon thousands of horses galloped and vehicles roared and bounced upon it. Mochè and Joshua led the final battle against the evil, with Matthew and Ben galloping beside them. "Be careful of Solomon," Matthew shouted to his manhig over the thunderous resounds of horses and weapons blasting. "He rides directly at you, sir!"

Although they wielded new sidearms and automatic rifles, some equipped with mortar-expending carbines, Benjamin had instructed their cavalry to use them sparingly and engage in close combat with swords and daggers. Their infantry held the advantage of aiming with their stable weapons positioned effectively. The clangs and clanks of the dull-sounding metals against one another dominated the atmosphere of the immediate battlefield's front where the armies clashed first.

Mochè kicked Solomon off his horse as he charged at him. Struggling to survive among the spooked horses ferociously rearing up all around him, Solomon roared, "Nice try, Brother!" He found the reins of his horse and swiftly mounted just in time before a tremendous riderless stallion nearly pounced on him. Solomon drew his solar rifle from its saddle pouch and carefully aimed it at his brother. He fired but missed, hitting one of his evil soldiers instead.

Ben blocked a demon's spear with the blunt end of his saber just before it struck Matthew's back, and his friend obliged with a nod. The two friends had always looked out for each other in every battle they fought. The fighting at the front grew increasingly fierce, prompting cavalry riders from both sides to dismount and engage in hand-to-hand combat. A repugnant, vile demon roared and grunted in the language of beasts, saliva dripping from its distorted mouth as it charged at Matthew with a long, razor-bladed spear. Ben intervened once more, leaping to the side of the hideous creature and breaking the demon's wooden lance, kicking it in half with the heel of his boot. He then severed the gruesome head of the beast to prevent it from casting a demonic possession. While gripping his dagger, Matthew held up two fingers, indicating that he owed Ben two.

While fighting in the fiercest battle he had ever encountered, Ben felt a solid object hit him and fell to the ground. Stunned by the hammer's blow to his back and still dazed, he watched as Matthew's saber split the head of the beast that stood, raising the mallet for the final blow. After regaining his composure, Ben stood and held one finger to Matthew, signifying the updated score of aid to each other.

Ben and Matthew stood back to back, fighting against the greatest hordes of well-supplied troops they had ever faced. Wave after wave of mutants, demons, and Solomon's army of the wickedest gangs he had spent years assembling from distant lands surged forward. Helen rode a white stallion, leading her army of mutated male slaves. Her naked body, painted with satanic symbols, and her beautiful face twisted into a sneer as she engaged Mochè's armies, finally seeking her revenge. Helen's large breasts bounced wildly, unable to keep pace with the uneven strides of her horse's galloping gait as her evil eyes searched for her adversary.

Armed with a dagger and sword, Ben struggled against the pain of the hammer blow to his back and fought for his life, but fell to the ground as a sword appeared from nowhere, piercing his side.

"It's not as bad as it looks, my friend!" yelled Matthew over the cacophony of intense howls and roars from the raging battle.

"You still owed me one, my friend," Ben muttered jokingly, but cringing in pain.

"Here," Matthew said, moving closer to his friend, "hold this tightly against it." He pulled a large cloth bandage from his belt pouch. Amid the chaos and explosions, he spotted a dispatch rider with long blonde hair flowing in the breeze. She rode high in the saddle, bringing her mustang to a skidding halt before jumping off, still grasping the reins. Matthew called to the woman running toward them, "Gabriela!" He waved to her, "Take him for treatment!"

"No!" Ben defied. "Go to the river to be with our children!"

"Oh, my darling love!" she comforted Ben, disregarding his words.

As Matthew fought, circling around his friends and protecting them both from the turmoil of combat taking place, Gabriela tightened the bandage around Ben's waist. Matthew yelled to Ben over the noise of battle, "I'm paying off my debt to you now, my friend!"

"I can ride," Ben softly told Gabriela.

"Oh, Benjamin, you foolish man; I told you to be careful." Tears rolled down from her deep blue eyes as she cried, tending to his wound.

Matthew lifted his friend onto a wandering stallion and said, "Gabriela, guide him to the riverbank. Doctor Gloria has set up field hospitals there; you'll see them! Hurry!" Blood was already seeping through Ben's bandage.

Gabriela swiftly took the reins of Ben's horse, holding on tightly as she galloped away under fire, leading Benjamin's horse to safety. Ben grimaced from the tormenting pains but managed a slight smile as he yelled, "It's about time you saved my life."

Mochè pushed through the enemy ranks, determined to reach Solomon. He could see his wicked, scraggly face directing his troops. General Miriam and General Tamar had successfully executed their orders, joining forces behind the enemy. Meanwhile, General Luke and General Jeremiah attacked both flanks, while General Deborah supported Matthew, reinforcing the front. The combined armies of Helen's demon ghouls, mutants, and the malevolent followers of Solomon were completely encircled, caught in the grip of righteousness.

General Joseph obeyed Mochè's heart-wrenching orders and allowed the wicked armies to breach the stronghold's gate. A multitude of demons and other nefarious forces surged through the long, wide entrance, eager to rape the defenseless women, pillage the homes, and murder as many as possible in gruesome ways. However, the relentless horde halted at a roadblock that prevented their advance.

Then every combatant on that deadly battlefield heard the deafening explosion as the ground trembled and the stronghold entrance shattered, sending fragments of the gate soaring high and drifting like floating debris. The enormous boulders and rocks that had once provided a sheltered portal crumbled and tumbled upon all the wicked intruders. Mochè and all his followers glanced at the explosion, realizing that the shattered pieces of boulders and rocks, along with the remaining bits of the broken gate, blocked the path to their beloved homes and the cherished possessions they would no longer need.

God cast a great lightning bolt from the heavens to the

ground, where the wicked, evil hordes battled. It cracked the earth, fracturing it into a long, deep crevice.

Helen, the nude demon with a painted face and body for battle, fell off her white stallion from the tremendous vibrations. Having hurt her leg, she couldn't stand and struggled to crawl away from the hole while trying to avoid being trampled by the many horses galloping wildly from the thunderous sounds and the eroding earth.

Fires erupted from the enormous pit in front of the fortress, spewing high into the air as sparks flew and ignited other areas on the ground, where the battle climaxed and most of the evil beings lay vanquished. The ground split beneath the surviving wicked hordes of warriors, drawing them into the fiery blazes. Long, bony, clawed fingers from grotesque arms reached for the edges of the scorching deep crack as demons lifted themselves from the pits of hell. They walked among the remaining wicked souls as the followers made their way to the river.

Mochè ran swiftly, his strides matching Matthews's. He could see Zipporah's beautiful face beaming in the distance as Mochè sprinted toward her and his children. Then, the radiant brightness of an angel blocked his path. He stood, feeling the glow of the first Holy Being who had led him out of the great city of the East.

Mochè turned to see his brother's horrified face, scorched by the flames, yet managing to balance himself from falling into hell—a spear readied in his hand to hurl at Mochè. But Mochè quickly grabbed a sharpened lance and flung it with force as if empowered by God. The spear struck the center of his brother's chest, causing Solomon to stagger. A demon from hell kicked Solomon, and he fell backward, cursing Mochè as he succumbed to Satan's flames.

As Mochè stood gazing after his brother fell to his fate, he emerged from his momentary stupor to the howls of Helen. She fought to hold onto the edge of the crater of hell with her hands, slipping as her horrified eyes glanced back at the fiery pit she was sliding into.

Kicking away the little demon that tried to push her in, Mochè grasped Helen's forearm, her shrieks of fear echoing. Her arm began to slip away from his grip as another demon from hell pulled her in. Mochè punched the demon with the fist of his free arm, desperately trying to hold Helen's forearm with his other hand. Slipping from his grasp, Mochè struggled to keep hold of her arm. He watched her gradually slide away until only her wrist was in his grip. Mochè's arms were tired and numb, but he mustered all the strength he could. He reached down with both arms and finally locked firmly onto Helen's wrist, dragging her limp body out of the breaking crevice and onto a flat spot.

The long, deep crack splintered as the earth quavered around them, creating new rifts. On the shaking ground, Mochè quickly removed his large brown scapular, holy water, and sanctified oil from his belted pouch. Mochè knew he was facing a formidable battle against Lucifer that could destroy him in the exorcism he was about to perform. But as he began to bless Helen in the sacred rite, the luminous glow of the Holy Angel enveloped him, protecting and assisting him as he pronounced the sacred words and anointed Helen with the blessed oil and holy water. As the ground around them shook, Mochè consecrated her in the rite of exorcism, concluding it with the sign of the cross, and sprinkled holy water upon her painted face.

"Mochè, where are we?" Helen softly asked in a scratchy voice, emerging from the coma-like state that had entrapped her for so long and struggling to recall what had happened. "Did I fall in battle? Are we safe?"

"Thank God you're back," Mochè whispered, realizing that God had saved her soul. As the rumbling earth shook around them, more devils emerged from it, looking in various directions.

"Last I recall, I was battling demons..." she was thinking, "so you and Nikanyiso could escape..." Helen still seemed to be in a fog.

Mochè lifted Helen's body from near the edge and cradled

her in his arms. As her head tilted down, she asked, horrified, "Where is my uniform, my clothes? Why am I naked and painted like this?"

As Mochè ran while holding her, he told her, "Come, old friend; there's little time left." He sprinted faster toward the river. All of Mochè's followers assembled there. A few demons still roamed.

Matthew ran to his manhig with his sword in hand, determined to fend off some demonic stragglers from hell who were pursuing Mochè and the woman he carried in his arms. Zipporah, holding a blanket, followed him but could not keep up. Exhausted, Mochè laid Helen on a grassy spot while Zipporah covered her with a warm blanket.

"You show mercy and forgiveness, my love, just as God's greatest gift to us: his divine mercy," Mochè whispered to his wife, Zipporah.

Zipporah gazed into her husband's deep blue eyes and softly said, "You taught me about Jesus's love and forgiveness, my love." Smiling, her wide green eyes sparkling, she continued, "Just as you did for your people who had ears to listen, and for all the young children you instructed at Bible School, who have grown to be faithful followers of the Almighty as men and women. You succeeded; your mission is complete."

"Thank you, my love, but I have one last duty."

Mochè walked away with Helen, who hobbled from her wounded leg and covered her nudity with the blanket. Still wearing his holy scapular, he asked her, knowing she would face judgment, "Will you confess your sins to me as an ordained priest and renounce Satan, Helen?"

"Yes," she squeaked while sobbing, tears in her eyes, "the love of my life; please forgive me for that and all the wrongs I've committed against you." Then she knelt with Mochè and began the ritual of penance, confessing the lust she felt for him, seducing him with drugs, and the envy she had directed at Zipporah, along with other less serious offenses. Helen had no recollection of the many sins committed while under Satan's possession, but as a priest, Mochè absolved her of all her sins and offenses against God.

As Mochè blessed her and made the sign of the cross, Helen smiled radiantly at the sight of Sarah, her old friend and fellow warrior of God, who descended from a heavenly cloud nearby. Helen stood with Sarah while others from the heavens awaited judgment by God, accompanied by the followers.

Ben embraced Gabriela and his children, his long, sturdy arms spreading wide. Holding him tightly, Gabriela whispered, "I'm not afraid anymore, Benjamin. God gave me you, and I'll love you for all eternity."

After Matthew defeated the demons pursuing his manhig and fulfilled his final duty, he embraced Eliza and his children, and waited with Ben and Gabriela's family. "I love you, Eliza, as I always have," he said, expressing his last words on earth.

The Messiah emerged from the breaking, bright white clouds in the sky. Jesus Christ spread his arms wide, as if encompassing all his loyal followers. Zipporah sat, smiling beside her children. Feelings of serenity and happiness washed over most of the awaiting followers.

Mochè rose and began to trot to join them, trying as quickly as he could, but feeling exhausted and breathing rapidly from the last battle and everything that had ensued; he could no longer run, but staggered. Two arms extended to hold him on each side and carried him. Mochè hardly recognized his old friends, Andrew and David, as they appeared youthful. David had no beard, and Andrew was a handsome, tall, young man. As Mochè approached his wife, his two priestly friends released him. David and Andrew now stood beside the beautiful image of Sarah.

Mochè embraced a smiling Zipporah tightly while his children encircled and held onto him. Zipporah whispered, "You've returned to me, my love, as you always did."

As all the followers waited by the river with those from the heavens, an angel appeared to the manhig. Mochè arose and followed it to what became sanctified ground because he spoke directly to God for the first time. Mochè fell to his knees and bowed before the Lord Jesus Christ. He and all his followers received judgment based on the accounting of their deeds. Many of them He cast into the deep crevice that remained open and led to the pits of hell before it closed—many more than Mochè had expected were condemned.

Then Mochè rose and faced his many followers, who were now judged as the resurrected, yet remained in the splendid transformation taking place around him. Matthew, Benjamin, and Nikanyiso, their bodies renewed and no longer weary from battle, rested in the open meadow with their families, surrounded by the sweet scents of the gardens that had miraculously begun blooming around them. Gabriela clung tightly to Benjamin, just as Eliza did to Matthew. Helen's body also became renewed and no longer bore painted symbols. Birds chirped and hopped from the nearby trees that had sprouted. All remaining people closely embraced their families and friends as they prepared to listen to their manhig's words, much like all the faithful men and women who had always followed him had done for years. The purified bodies of the older individuals and many disabled from previous battles rejuvenated, becoming beautiful, youthful, and strong forms.

As Mochè stood, a magnificent rainbow appeared in the sky. Under its vibrant hues, he began speaking, "My loving followers, our battles against the wicked are over; they exist no more." He observed the bewildered expressions on the faces he cherished, knowing they were free from sin. "Satan and his wicked followers have been bound and imprisoned in the bottomless pit. He can no longer deceive the just." Mochè glanced at the crowd nearest him, where Zipporah sat faithfully, as she always had during his sermons since he met her, now with his family beside her. Locking his gaze with her piercing, deep green eyes, which shone even brighter under the pastel heavens, he proclaimed, "We can now live in this blessed, sin-free world," and as he spoke, the earth continued transforming into a paradise, "under the rule of Christ for a thousand years." Spreading his arms wide as if to encompass them all, Mochè declared, "Humanity has a chance to rebuild and repopulate the world our ancestors destroyed through their greed and lust, along with the many other sins they committed. However, we can now do this under the reign of Christ, with no more wicked demons or mutations to fight. We can live in peace and harmony as we have always dreamed." He looked at Zipporah once more, and she smiled at him before he added, "We can spread our love among this new world, and watch it grow with new blessed souls. Our Lord will return again, seated on the Great White Throne of Judgment, after a millennium, to read from the book of life for the last judgment—Ultimum Judicium."

—Finis

Coming in 2025

Augustine
The Warrior

The prequel & parallel novel for Ultimum Judicium

Using the same characters from Ultimum Judicium, this
novel tells the story of the early years of Damien Ignatius,
also known as Mochè—the Manhig, as named by God.
Based on a character introduced in Ultimum Judicium, it also
explores more details about life outside the strongholds—the
viciousness of that wilderness surrounding them.

Also Coming in 2025

My Dream Lover
The Sequel

Coralie and Robert Bryant's Children continue
their father's work and find themselves in
over their heads in this continuation of
the beloved, My Dream Lover: The Uncut Version.

Coming Soon

Articles of interest for writers and readers about publishing,
and other information on the blog at
DavidNavarria.com